RETURN TO WALKERS' MOUNTAIN

THE MADISON MCKENZIE FILES
(BOOK 3)

BEV FREEMAN

Jan-Carol
Publishing, Inc

"every story needs a book"

Return to Walkers' Mountain
Bev Freeman

Published October 2018
Little Creek Books
Imprint of Jan-Carol Publishing, Inc
All rights reserved
Copyright © 2018 by Bev Freeman
Front Cover Illustration: Bev Freeman

ISBN: 978-1-945619-81-6
Library of Congress Control Number: 2018962087

You may contact the publisher:
Jan-Carol Publishing, Inc
PO Box 701
Johnson City, TN 37605
publisher@jancarolpublishing.com
jancarolpublishing.com

Dedicated to the Walker Family,
who died in a brutal manner in the early 1950's,
and to their three children who survived by hiding under the bed.
Mary and Gracie were my friends in the 1960's,
and their story haunts me to this day.

DEAR READER

Thank you for following Madison McKenzie's path as she struggled from her sheltered youth into adulthood and independence. She's Appalachian Strong, overcoming life's obstacles and pitfalls. Madison has a positive love of nature and humanity. She'll be the first to lend you a hand, but cross the line between right and wrong and you will never outrun her dedication to justice. Although this is the third in my trilogy, *The Madison McKenzie Files*, she will by no means remain silent. In her young life, she's crossed paths with lots of interesting and memorable characters. Hopefully, you will find her future stories pleasurable as she and her friends bring you along for the ride in the Blue Ridge and Smoky Mountains of East Tennessee and Western North Carolina.

ACKNOWLEDGMENTS

I want to thank Janie Jessie, JCP, for seeing a value in my dreams and paving the way to fruition. Thanks to the best fans on earth! Without all my Florida friends and my family, I'd just have a huge stock of books on my hands.

1

The roadsides were a blaze of fall colors as Annmarie Morgan drove south into the Blue Ridge Mountains of East Tennessee. The few homes she passed on old SR 19 were landscaped with colorful dahlias, her favorite autumn bloom, and several varieties of mums and sunflowers, all with faces beautifully poised toward the sun. She continued on, noticing the many different shades of red, purple, yellow, and orange; like the leaves, they announced that winter was not far behind.

The tires screeched when she drove a little too fast moving into a curve. She jerked the steering wheel, returning to her side of the double yellow lines. *I'd better slow down! The last thing I need is a speeding ticket.*

She glanced in her rearview mirror, suddenly aware there was a car right on her bumper. When the road straightened for a sufficient distance to permit one car passing, she moved far to the right side of the broken white lines on the road. He remained close, but didn't pass.

"Don't expect me to speed. I gave you a chance to go around," she said aloud. The radio played nothing but static, so she switched it off. *There's never good reception in these mountains. Too bad I neglected to bring any CDs. Oh, well, silence of the golden fall. Say, that sounds like a good name for a book!* She laughed aloud.

The mountain crested, and she noticed a pullover with a view on the right. She pulled over, expecting the pesky car to go on without her. Annmarie stepped out of her older model Monte Carlo to snap a photo of the valley be-low. In the clear, crisp air, she thought she could see halfway to Knoxville to the west, or at least Asheville to the south. She gazed in silence at the breathtaking view. Returning to her car, she noticed the brown one had not gone on. In fact, it sat in the middle of the road. *What on earth?* She felt uneasy in the relative isolation, with the actions of the driver in that mysterious car.

The grade going down the mountain was steep; Annmarie slowed to pre-vent squealing the tires. The brown car ran right up on her bumper. She sped up, and the brown car continued to stay just behind her. *He's going to bump me,* she worried. She braced herself. He backed off a bit. Her car was going way too fast for the upcoming curve. Her heart pounded as she fought the steering wheel, hands sweaty; at this speed she might miss the curve or slide over. She glanced in her side mirror. The car rushed at her and she felt a jerk; his bumper had tapped hers. He allowed a small space between the cars, then rushed her once more. This time, it was a much harder hit; her car lunged at the curve. She slammed one foot on the brake pedal and stomped her emergency brake with the other, cutting the wheel as hard as she could to her left. Her tires screamed as her car spun around, now facing the brown car. She closed her eyes, ready for impact. Her head felt light as she waited—but there was no collision. She opened her eyes and watched smoke curl from his tires, then the brown sedan sailed into the air, plunging over the hillside.

She thought her heart had stopped for a second. Now it beat loudly in her ears. She'd avoided going over herself, but he hadn't hit her head on. Why? Was he trying to send her over, or scare her? Whatever, it had worked; she was scared half out of her wits.

Her engine dead, she sat in the middle of the curve. Quickly restarting the car, she drove to the pull off area. She had to wait a few minutes for her hands to stop shaking, then she called 911. The 911 operator connected her with Sheriff Madison McKenzie's office. "Sheriff McKenzie, how may I help you?"

"I'm at the top of the mountain on Route nineteen, at the pullover. A car tried to run me off the road, but he went over instead. I need someone up here right away. If the driver is even alive, I'm sure he's badly hurt," Annmarie gasped, then she began to sob.

"I'm on my way. Sit tight, I'll be about fifteen minutes. Will you stay on the line with me?" Madison asked.

"OK. I'm shaking like a leaf, and feel like I might be sick."

"Listen, tell me your name," Madison said.

"Ann... Um, Annmarie Morgan," she managed to say.

"I'm going to call you back on my cellphone. I have you on caller ID. OK?"

"OK," the shaky voice answered.

"Annmarie?" Madison asked when she heard the voice again. "Stay with me. I might lose connection for a minute, but I'll still be on the line—so don't hang up."

"OK."

Madison opened the door and Bud hopped in, settling into his seat on the passenger side. Maddy clicked the seat belt into his harness. "Hold on, boy; this might be a wild ride."

She talked to Annmarie all the way up the mountain. She could tell by her voice that the woman had calmed down. "You're parked at the pull off?"

"Yes, right at the entrance. I'm the only car around. Thank you for staying in touch with me. I don't know why the driver was acting so crazy. I don't even know who it is."

"I'm almost there. Stay on the line."

In a few moments, Madison saw the black Monte Carlo sitting at the edge of the parking area. She pulled in and turned around so that her Explorer was facing the same way. She got out of her cruiser and walked to the driver's door of Annmarie's car.

"Hi, I'm Sheriff McKenzie. Call me Madison, everyone does."

Annmarie stepped from her car, hands still shaking. She reached out with her right to greet Madison. "Thank you for coming so quickly."

"The ambulance and a wrecker might be a while. My office is in Cold Creek, not far down the old Asheville highway." She shook hands with the frightened woman, then asked her to tell her what happened.

Annmarie recalled her experience in detail, then leaned against her car. "I bet there will be a mark on my bumper where he hit me." Legs still shaking, she walked to the back of her car. "Yep; see?"

"These plastic bumpers are made to buckle and pop back. You should have it checked to be sure there's no damage underneath." Madison looked carefully at the bumper. "I see a scuff here; was it a brown car?"

Annamarie nodded. She kept looking back down the road, toward where the bumps happened.

"I suppose if you feel okay to drive, you can lead me to where the car went over," Madison said. "You're still shaking, though; let's wait just a short while. Take slow, deep breaths."

"Between my tire marks and his skids, you'll see plenty of rubber in that deep curve. But yeah, I want to go back. I'm OK now. Let's do this."

Annmarie led the way. She pulled her Monte Carlo over in the gravel where the pavement ended. Madison parked on the edge of the road with her emergency flashers on. She spoke on the radio to someone, then walked to the edge of the hill and looked over.

"That's a long way down. If that little patch of scrub hadn't caught the car, it could have gone out of sight." She waited there for a few minutes, because the ambulance had reported it was at the top of the mountain.

"There they are. I'll go down with an EMT, in case he's alive. You stay right here at your car, will you?"

Annmarie nodded again.

Brody, a robust EMT, emerged from the passenger side. "Need the lines? Looks to be pretty steep."

"It is. I haven't been down there; don't know if we have a deceased or an ambulatory. Here, let me give you a hand."

Brody was clearly a physically fit mountain climber, not just your ordinary EMT. He hooked up lines with pulleys and carabiners, strapped himself into a harness, and bounced down the shale and loose dirt over the edge, following the path of the car. He looked in the driver's side window and then went to the other side of the car. "Madison!" He shouted. "There's no driver!"

"Look underneath; he may have been thrown out," she called down to him.

Brody worked his way completely around the vehicle, then down to a pile of rocks below. "Nothing!"

Madison stood quietly for a while, and then said, "Did you look over after the car went down?"

"No, I just watched it go over, stunned. All I saw was a lot of dust. I didn't want to see where he went. He tried to kill me!" Annmarie burst into tears.

"It's all right, Ann. Brody says there's no one in the car or thrown out, as far as he can see. He must have not been hurt and climbed out." She asked Brody to look for anything that might identify the driver, like registration or insurance papers, whatever he could find, and bring it back up with him.

The wrecker arrived and backed to the edge of the road, the front end sticking out in the traffic lane. The driver went to the middle of the curve and placed one flare, and another around the curve to signal traffic. Not that there was much traffic, but it was just a precautionary measure.

One of the men from the wrecker joined Brody with a cable to hook onto the car. Brody pulled the man back up to the road with him on the lines. They winched the crumpled brown sedan up the hill and into the road.

Madison approached the car to look for herself. There was a small amount of blood on the front seat, and the windshield had been smashed from the outside. She noticed the seatbelt was cut but still fastened. She rifled through the floorboards, then checked the front and back seats. Next she went for the keys, intending to open the trunk. There were no keys in the switch, however. She studied the scene and then motioned for the wrecker driver to continue pulling it onto the rollback.

"Don't let anyone touch the car; drop it at the Erwin Police Department, and let me know if you need anything from me for your fee. I'll take care of it." After she made her orders clear, she returned to Ann.

"Where were you headed, Ann?"

"Nowhere, really; I just needed to get away. I thought I might go to Asheville, maybe stay overnight someplace."

"Where are you from?"

"Johnson City. I mean, I was. I've only recently moved into Unicoi County. I have a tiny home up on Spivey, on a three-acre tract of land."

"I know where those are. What is your address?" She pulled a notebook from her Explorer and made note of Ann's phone and address. "You said your last name is Morgan?"

"Yes," Annmarie answered. "Thanks for calling me Ann. I haven't heard that name for a while."

Madison stared at Ann for a couple of seconds. "Are you sure you don't know who might want to hurt you?"

"No, I have no idea. I don't know anybody in the area."

"I'd like you to contact me when you arrive where you plan to stay. I'll see what I can learn from the car. Keep in touch, OK?" She offered Ann her business card. "These are all the numbers you'll need to reach me. I want to hear from you tonight."

"I'll call. I promise." Ann scooted behind the wheel of her car. "Thank you, Madison."

"You be careful," Madison said.

"I will." Annmarie waved and drove down the mountain.

Madison returned to her office. She wrote up a report while it was all fresh in her mind. There was something just slightly off about this event; Annmarie was way too vague about her information. What was she getting away from? Or whom?

2

Madison fell asleep waiting to hear from the sheriff's department in Erwin. When her cell rang she jumped. "This is Madison," she said.

"This is Steve, with Erwin's impound. I got an answer for you, on the brown sedan you sent us this afternoon? It was stolen from Carter County's impound about a week ago. When it was abandoned last month, no one ever claimed it, and there was no information on where it came from. It was just sitting on their lot—until it wasn't," he laughed. "What do you want me to do with it?"

"Did you find any prints?" she asked.

"Clean as a whistle! Whoever took it this time wore gloves, because it was checked when it showed up here. Nothing was found; the black is still on the steering wheel. Strange, huh? I guess it'll be sold for scrap next week. So if you want anything from it, give me a call," Steve said.

"No, I trust your crew. This was no amateur. And he got away."

The call ended but her thoughts did not. She picked up her phone. "Henry, hey. Do you still have that bloodhound?"

"Yes, I do. You need me to track someone?" Henry was always ready to help out with Madison's investigations.

"I'll be out to pick you up; what time are you free?"

"I can drive into town in my truck. That'll save you a trip. Where we going?"

"Up Spivey, just past the top of the mountain. Had a car go over the hill there this morning, but didn't find the driver. I think he got away on foot." She readied a pack of items they might need as she spoke with Henry. "OK if I let Bud tag along?"

"Fine by me. I'll have Blu in a crate in the back. I'm sure they'll get along anyway. See you in about an hour?"

"Yeah, that's good." Madison gathered a few more items, then set the bag on the porch. "Bud... Here, Bud," she called.

Her black and tan Lab/heeler mix came running from behind Shirley's Restaurant.

"Aw, you've been visiting your lady friend. How's she doing? Not pregnant again, I hope."

Bud tilted his head as if to ask what she meant by that.

"Henry's coming to pick us up. You want to go tracking?"

She walked to her cottage, just a few steps from the Sheriff's Office. In her newly-built garage, she dug her hiking boots out of a trunk. The terrain was steep, and loose rocks could be a problem. She lifted her climbing equipment off the hook above the trunk. "These might come in handy getting back up that hill, Bud." She slung the canvas duffle bag over her shoulder.

Her phone rang; it was Rick, her fiancé. "Hey, Baby," she answered. They talked for a few minutes, then she put the phone in the thigh pocket of her camp shorts. This was a warm October; she had not brought out long pants for her uniform yet.

"Bud, Rick says to tell you hello. He'll see you this weekend. And he told me to get you an order of chicken livers from the restaurant, on him," she laughed. "As though you wouldn't know, a message from Rick will always pertain to food."

Henry drove up in front of her office. He parked next to her bag, which Madison had set on the sidewalk. She and Bud joined him. She slung the canvas bag into the back of his truck, then asked, "You sure you don't want me to drive?"

"No, that new interior doesn't need to get all dirty from Blu after he runs all over the mountain."

"I'm not really thrilled with this Explorer anyway. It isn't the vehicle I would have chosen, but since the mayor leased it for me to use, I should at least keep it clean. Don't you think?"

Madison's Blazer had been destroyed in a crash over the mountain—and then set on fire by a bad monster truck owner, back in the summer. She had not yet decided what would replace it. Rick wanted to help her, so she could get something she might not feel she could afford. But she assured him she could buy whatever she wanted without his assistance. Now she was rethinking that idea after finding out how much the Explorer cost—and she wasn't even satisfied with it. One day she'd make a decision, and that would be final. But in the meantime, she'd use whatever the county provided for her.

Henry drove to the spot, Madison guiding him. It was obvious from the tire marks that something had happened there. She studied the marks carefully.

"Ms. Morgan felt that the car was attempting to run her off the curve and over the hill. And if you look at these tire prints, it tells a different story."

Henry looked at the path of the skid marks. "This one spun around in the road and this one went over. I'm assuming Ms. Morgan was in this one. I can't help but notice that he deliberately avoided the head on collision by this swerve. If he truly wanted to wreck her, why not hit her and then push her over?"

"Exactly!" Madison photographed the prints on the faded blacktop.

"I can see where the car ended up. You want to start down there?" Henry opened the crate and released Blu.

The bloodhound was well trained, and he knew not to howl without a scent. He stood on the side of the road with Henry, waiting for instructions.

Madison attached a line to Henry's truck and cautiously worked her way down the slate hillside. Bud meandered back and forth seeking out strong footing, waiting for her when she reached the clump of saplings that had stopped the car from moving farther downhill.

Henry and his bloodhound followed Madison. As soon as they reached the site, Madison pulled a piece of fabric from her pocket. "I managed to snag this from the seat when the wrecker driver wasn't looking. Not that he would care; the seat was already torn."

She handed it to Henry who then placed the fabric under the dog's keen nose. "Find, Blu, find," was all Henry said. Blu put his nose to the ground, sniffing in a circle, then he took off around the hillside, over low brush, around rocks. When Blu reached a spot where there were lots of sizable trees, he cut uphill toward the road. Henry stayed close behind him. The dog stopped at the edge of the pavement and sat down.

"He's lost the scent. I bet a car picked him up. Otherwise, he'd have gone on across the road and up the other side." Henry walked Blu up and down the road. The scent was just not there. "He didn't fly into the air. Somebody stopped for him."

Madison bent slightly to catch her breath, then said, "That's what I think, too." She took a few more deep breaths before they walked back to Henry's truck with Blu. "Bud," she called. And then she whistled loudly. Bud finally came up the steep hillside, panting, with his tongue hanging out. "You and I are out of shape, fella," she patted his head. "We're going back to running in the morning."

When Madison returned to the Sheriff's Office, she put the camera on her desk and saw the flash of the answering machine. "Hello, Madison. This is Annmarie. I'm back home. I just could not relax, even in Asheville, so I decided to come back. Call me when you have any information, OK? Thanks."

Madison hit redial on her desk phone. After a few rings she heard Ann say, "Hello?"

"Hi, this is Madison McKenzie. I missed your call on my cell but I got your message on my landline. Thanks for calling."

"I just wanted you to know where I am," Annmarie said.

"Let me fill you in on what I have thus far," she said. "The brown car was stolen from the Carter County impound at the jail a week ago. There are no prints, no way of knowing who the car ever belonged to, and no new leads."

Ann was silent for a long pause. "What can we do?" Annmarie's voice sounded shaky. "I have the feeling he has been watching me."

"Do you mind if I come up for a quick visit?" Madison suggested.

"I'd love the company. I'm beginning to think I might need to adopt a dog. At least he'd bark if someone came poking around here."

"I'll bring my Bud and let him sniff around for a while. How about that?" Madison knew Ann was frightened—and rightfully so.

Following Ann's directions carefully, Madison and Bud drove up the mountain toward Coffee Ridge. She turned onto the gravel road by the old Ray store and continued on up the bumpy path until there was no more gravel.

"She's going to need some work done on this road if she plans to get in and out of here in winter," Madison said. Bud looked at her chuffed his agreement.

The woods dropped away to an open area at the crest of the hill. There on the other side of a natural bald, she saw Ann's Monte Carlo parked under a metal carport next to a tiny cottage. It was sky blue, with white trim and a silver metal roof. A covered porch surrounded the cottage, making it look welcoming. White fencing enclosed the porch. Flower boxes full of purple petunias and white daises adorned the windows.

"Oh, this is adorable!" Madison said as she approached the house.

Ann met her at the steps and welcomed her in. "Bud can come in too," she added.

Madison walked up the three steps, looking at every detail of the home. "I love this!"

"Thanks, so do I." Ann led her inside. "I sold my house in Johnson City. It was way too much house for me after my son moved out."

"This is beautiful, inside and out!" Madison looked around the room, her eyes flicking from one charming detail to the next. Western cedar walls and ceiling gave the space a warm feeling. The floors looked to be white pine, thinly cut boards laid close together in different lengths. Above the windows were yellow eyelet valances with white sheers, layered like an accordion. Some had been pulled up to allow all the light in; others across the front were lowered halfway. The kitchen lay along the far wall, smartly using every inch of space with shelves or cabinets all the way to the raised ceiling of the room's front half. The back came down to the top of the refrigerator, making a wall that divided the room in half. A drop-leaf table at the end of the wall formed a horseshoe. Two chairs sat at the table, one at each end, hardly taking any space at all.

Ann motioned to a futon in the corner next to the door. "Have a seat, Madison, I just made a fresh pitcher of tea. Sweet or unsweet for you?"

"Unsweet, please," she quickly answered.

Ann brought two glasses of ice and a short pitcher on a tray. She set it on a round table across from the futon, then she returned to the sink. She set a yellow bowl of water on a mat by the door for Bud. "Here you are, Bud. I'm sure you're thirsty too." She petted him as he took a drink.

Ann sat on another futon across from Madison. She poured the tea and handed one to her guest. "I know you have to be wondering what my story is, I could tell. You didn't want to ask, but you were clearly trying to figure me out," she sipped her tea and smiled. "Am I right?"

"Yes," Madison admitted. "I had so many questions, but you were shaken and I didn't want to make you feel any more uncomfortable than you already were. I hoped we could get together and I'd learn about your life. I'm trained to be suspicious, but I'm curious by nature."

"That's OK; I understand." she looked out the front window. "Do you want me to begin, or would you rather ask questions?" Ann rested her glass on her knee.

"You go ahead; tell me whatever you feel is necessary so that I can get to know you."

Ann took in a deep breath and blew it out. "I married Tom Morgan six and a half years ago. We lived in Johnson City on the south side of town, near ETSU. Tom was a carpenter, a builder. He learned to be a stone mason working with the Terranera brothers. He wanted his own company, so he took the contractor's licensing test and got his certification. His company had been in business for ten years."

"I worked part time for our dentist, but then after my first book was published, I quit to work from home. Tom was happy about that. He always came home for lunch, unless he was working too far out of town." She poured Madison a refill of tea and continued.

"I don't want to change the subject, but I want you to tell me about your book."

"I'd be happy to. And I can let you borrow one, if you have time to read it," Ann smiled. "Let me get one while I'm thinking of it. You just take it and read when you have time." She darted into the back and returned with a lovely *Blue Ridge Mountain Mystery* hardcover in her hand. "It makes sense that you'd like mysteries."

"Oh, I do! And that's a pretty cover." Maddy accepted the book. She looked on the back cover to see the selling price. She pulled some folded bills from her pocket and counted out $15.

"No, no, I didn't mean for you to pay—"

"Nonsense! I insist!" Maddy sat back down, placing the book on the futon beside her. "Please go on."

Ann sat down and took a sip of tea. "Tom loved me having supper ready when he came home. We often sat on our back deck and ate, looking into the old-growth trees at the back of our property. We saw all kinds of wildlife: deer, fox, squirrels, raccoons, rabbits... And the birds, we saw all kinds, even those pileated woodpeckers. We loved our back yard! Most evenings we'd have fifteen to twenty cardinals come in to the feeders, just at sunset. I loved our home and our life." She paused for a bit, sipping her tea.

Madison could tell that Ann was fighting back tears. "You were happy, but was Tom?"

Ann cleared her throat before she continued. "Yes, our feelings were mutual. The only thing that might have bothered Tom was some of his employees. He fired one just the week before he disappeared."

"What was his name?"

"Um, Frank—or maybe Francis? Something like that. I didn't really know all of them."

"Can you find out for me?" Madison asked.

"Maybe, if I can get in touch with Ricky." After a brief pause to think she went on. "One day, Tom left on his Harley for a quick ride. I was writing and just about to the end of my book, so I stayed home. I didn't like riding his Harley anyway, and I'd sold my Magna; I decided that my thrill was now the keyboard." She laughed to herself and swallowed hard.

Madison knew she was about to hear the sad part of Ann's story.

Ann stood and walked to the stove. She returned with a plate of cookies, setting them on the table. After she sat down, she plucked a tissue out of a box sitting next to her.

"Tom never came home," she batted away tears and wiped her eyes before continuing. "I called his friends, employees, everyone I knew who he might have gone to see. No one saw him that day or even heard from him. After twenty-four hours, I called the police."

"And when was this?" Madison asked.

"April fourteenth, two thousand sixteen," Ann said in a shaky voice.

"Listen, if you don't feel like saying anymore, I understand." Madison leaned forward and put her hand on Ann's arm.

"No, I'm OK. I appreciate having someone to talk to, Madison."

13

Madison asked the questions that her law enforcement training brought to mind. Finally she said, "Let me check into this and see if I can learn something as an officer of the law that they might not tell you. As for getting a dog, I think that is a good idea. You are up here in the middle of nowhere. Anything can happen, so at least have a well-trained companion. I'll keep an eye and ear out for anything I think might be a good fit. Do you want one to stay in the house with you, or outside?"

"I've never had an animal in the house. But a small dog wouldn't intimidate anyone. I thought of getting one for outside, so he can alert me if someone comes around. I also have a security system down the drive a ways."

"Bud has always stayed inside with me, but my cottage is a bit larger. And now that I added my addition, he still wants to stay in the cottage. You need to come and visit me."

"I'd like that. Are you at the sheriff's office?" Ann asked. "I can find that."

"Do you know where Shirley's Restaurant is?"

Ann shook her head.

"You've never been to Cold Creek, then."

"I've seen the sign on the interstate."

"Just follow the old road after you get off at the visitor's center. When the road forks, take the right and you'll head straight into our tiny town. Call me, so I'll know when you're coming through. Oh, and if you learn the name of that employee he fired, call me."

"Oh, I will. I promise." Ann stood, taking the empty glass from Madison. They walked out onto the porch, Bud on their heels.

"I'll call you tomorrow evening if I learn anything from JCPD," Madison said.

"Sounds good. Thanks for coming; and you too, Bud. You come and visit anytime!"

Madison and Bud drove away, Ann waving from the porch Bud put his paws up on the back of the seat, looking out the rear window at Ann.

"You liked her, I could tell. Maybe we can help find her a dog." She brushed the hair on his neck with her fingernails. "I'm lucky to have you. I realize that so much more when I see someone who doesn't have a dog in their life."

When they reached the paved road, she turned to head back to Cold Creek.

Bud settled down on the seat and closed his eyes.

A week passed; Madison was not able to find out any new information about Tom Morgan's case. She phoned Ann each day and apologized. Ann was coming to Cold Creek to have breakfast with Madison and spend some time meeting new friends. She thought Cold Creek might be just what Ann needed. It was only a fifteen- to twenty-minute drive, and there were plenty of folks for her to talk to.

Madison and Bud walked to the sheriff's office and sat on the porch waiting for Ann. After a brief time, she drove into the other end of town and slowly came toward them. She asked where to park, so Madison pointed to the driveway at the cottage and walked to join her.

"Welcome to the big metropolis of Cold Creek!" She smiled after saying it, truly feeling proud of her hometown.

"Oh, it's sweet! How could I have not seen this before?" Ann slid out of her car.

"That's my cottage, and my hideous addition. And that's the restaurant where I grew up. Shirley's is the only one in the area. My parents own it. They're traveling and a couple of friends run it for them."

"Well, I woke up hungry this morning, so a home-cooked breakfast sounds really good about now," Ann said.

"Then we shouldn't waste any more time." Madison held out her hand and took Ann's arm. "Everything they serve is delicious. Many are Jess and Shirley's recipes, but Margie is a great cook in her own right."

Betty brought a menu for Ann, knowing Madison didn't need one. She returned with two unsweet teas in tall glasses, took their orders, and went through the swinging doors into the kitchen.

Margie came to their table to greet the new face. "Welcome, I'm Margie," she smiled.

"Annmarie. Um, just drop the Marie; let's stick with Ann," she laughed.

"Not looking for a job, are you, Ann?" Margie asked. "We had another waitress quit."

"No, not just yet." Ann said.

"Who quit this time?" Madison asked.

"Sissy, bless her heart. She just couldn't pick up the pace during supper. I

15

moved her to breakfast and lunch, but she quit anyway." Margie walked back toward the counter, "Maddy, if you hear of someone, send 'em in."

"I will, Margie."

Their food arrived, waking up their senses and halting conversation for a while.

Eventually Madison told Ann about all the buildings on Main Street, including her own cottage and addition.

"Why did you call your addition hideous?" Ann asked.

"It was so cute before I had Henry build the three-car garage and master suite above it. When Rick and I get married, that's where we'll live. I just kind of wish I'd have made it a separate structure, farther back, closer to the creek." Madison stared at the structure for a while.

"But you designed it so nicely; it looks like an old barn...no, a livery stable," Ann said.

"Thanks, I'm glad you appreciate Henry's architecture. He did a good job of making the new structure fit in."

The remainder of the morning, they toured Cold Creek. In the afternoon, Holly invited them to come out and visit her. Henry took the twins with him on a call about acquiring a stand of trees down in Green County.

When Madison and Ann drove up, Holly was sitting on the porch rocking, her arms folded over her very pregnant belly. Madison made introductions and offered to go inside and get the pitcher of lemonade, knowing full well that Holly had made it fresh just for company. She returned with glasses and the pitcher, setting them on a low table.

"I haven't seen old-fashioned lemonade served this way in decades. I love the old-style pitcher, and the slices of lemons floating in it. Is that mint?"

"Yes, I learned from Grandma. She felt it aided in digestion." Holy smiled, thinking of the woman who raised her.

"I think she might have been right about that." She took a long sip. "Gives a nice crisp flavor too; I like it," Ann said.

"You know, it's hard to realize how warm it is for this time of year," Maddy said.

"No one feels these warm days more than me!" Holly laughed her signature laugh.

"When is your baby due?" Ann asked.

"Any time now." Holly sipped her lemonade. "Probably on a day like this, when Henry's out of town."

"You know I'm always close and will drop whatever I'm doing to get here," Madison said.

"Yes, and me too. I'll leave you my number in case the sheriff is busy. I have birthed plenty of animals, mostly puppies or kittens, but I helped deliver a colt one time. Now, that was one big baby!" Ann and Holly laughed together.

"Let's hope Holly's Maddie won't be so big!"

"So you know it's a girl, and you're naming her after Madison? How nice."

"I feel sorry for the poor kid, but I'm proud of my friends. That shows I'm loved!"

Madison listened as Ann and Holly talked about everything from plants to farming, with lots of laughter in between.

Madison told Holly to keep her seat while she showed Ann the quilting room upstairs. Ann said she was a fan of quilting. "When the group gets to-gether again, I'd like to participate."

Holly was happy to welcome a new member. "We hope to get together again after Christmas. I'll be sure to include you."

The afternoon went by quickly and Ann declared she needed to get home before dark. Upon arriving back in Cold Creek, she went straight to her Monte Carlo and waved bye to Madison. "Thanks for a lovely day. I really appreciate your time."

"Come back whenever you can. You still need to meet the rest of the town." As she watched Ann she couldn't help wonder about her husband. *Poor girl, she's really sweet. What could have happened to her husband? I really need to see if Rick can give me a hand with this.*

3

Madison walked to her office just after lunch on the last day of the month, anticipating getting through the stack of papers faxed to her the day before. She liked some of them, because they meant closure for cases and most ended happily. This batch was a different story.

The first she read was a letter from the TN Dept. of Corrections in Nashville, a notification about a prisoner about to be released from the Nashville State Penitentiary in November. After reading the entire sheet, Madison went to the computer and pulled up the file on the Walkers' Mountain murders.

As she read, the hairs on the back of her neck stood up. The story was about the murders of three people on the next mountain over from Eagle Ridge, her territory. She was the sheriff responsible for notifying the family members of the prisoner's release. But why was he being released?

She read further and learned that the man was charged with robbery and attempted murder of a store owner in central Tennessee. Murder charges were never brought against him due to the ages of the witnesses. *Witnesses?*

Madison realized she'd missed something. She read it again from the beginning, and noticed an asterisk at the beginning of one line. She scrolled to the bottom of the page and saw *the children's names are concealed to protect their identity.*

"All anybody has to do is check the census to find out the names of the children of the victims," Madison said aloud.

Bud raised his head as if to say, "You talking to me?"

"Yeah, I'm talking to you, Bud. We need to learn who these children are, and where they are now." She bookmarked the site for future use and pulled up the census for 2000. If the murders happened in 2003, she figured the place for answers would lie in the previous census.

Madison wasn't having any luck with what she wanted so she decided to take a ride up to Walkers' Mountain. She'd see if there was anyone who remembered the family. It was too late to start that today, so she'd have to put the trip off for tomorrow.

She tidied up her desk, putting the papers in a special drawer for her attention later. Bud stood, stretching his back legs one at a time, the way he always did after a long nap. Then he suddenly lunged toward the door, hair standing up on his back. Madison reached for the door knob. Before she could open it, the door was flung open and a short man in ragged clothes pushed his way in. His face was dirty. His back was bent, and she noticed hump on his right shoulder.

Bud lunged, catching the man by the arm. The man screamed—in a young boy's voice! Bud turned loose and slunk next to Madison. "Wow, Bud! Is my costume that convincing?" Nick pulled a mask off his face.

"Oh, my!" Madison knelt to calm Bud. "It scared me!"

Nick laughed, rubbing his arm. "I think I scared Bud, too. But he didn't break the skin. I'm sorry, Bud. I thought you'd smell me." The young boy dropped to the floor, his hands stroking Buds head. "We still buddies?"

Holly and a pair of small ghosts with big eyes and smiles painted on their white faces walked closely behind her. One even sported freckles across his cheeks.

"Gee, I've never seen real ghosts like you! Let's see, you look like Casper the friendly Ghost," she pointed to the freckles on the other ghost. "And you have to be Spooky, Casper's Cousin. Am I right?"

"But who is who?" One of the boys asked.

"I think Hugh is Casper, and Harry, you're the mischievous cousin," Madison guessed.

"No, guess again," Hugh said.

Everyone laughed.

"But one is missing. Where's Robbie?" Madison peeked out the door.

"Boo!" A bat with a three-foot wingspan swooped down at her from a chair on the sidewalk. "I gotcha!" Robbie giggled.

"You sure did! And I haven't eaten any garlic today!" Madison gave him a big hug.

Henry stepped out from behind the bat. "I'm going as a farmer, and Holly is barefoot and pregnant. How'd we do?"

Madison hugged Holly with a tight squeeze. "Holly wins my vote! Let me grab my phone. I want a group picture." She ran back inside.

The Jacob family lined up like stair steps. Madison told them to hold still while she snapped off two shots. "Where are you guys off to, anyway?"

"Erwin, to the Wrights' house first. We love the way the family all dresses up," Holly said.

"Yeah, and they give out real good chocolate bars, too." Henry laughed, "Want to go with us? You're already in costume, Sheriff!"

"Thanks, I'd love to, but I got candy to hand out at the Trunk or Treat over at the church. You should go by there first. I was just about to get my basket and head over there. I'm carrying it in this big Easter Basket, and I'll sit on the steps of the church with Doc. He's going as the Tooth Fairy and handing out brushes with small tubes of toothpaste. If the kids don't see candy, they'll skip him."

"Have a nice evening, Sheriff," Holly said.

"Everybody come inside to get your candy from me." She ran back inside to get her basket.

While the bat, ghosts, and hunchback of Notre Dame picked their favorite candies, the door swung open again and a man in a fairy costume fell into the room. With a red stain on the back of his shoulder and what appeared to be an arrow sticking through from the front, he lay motionless on the floor.

"OK, Doc, you look real enough to scare the twins. Now get up and stop bleeding your fake blood on my floor."

Doc didn't move. Henry knelt to touch the arrow and the blood. "Madison, this is real!"

"No, it's just a Halloween trick!" She set the candy basket down and stood over Chip. "Enough; get up. You're not only scaring the kids, you're scaring me."

Doc still didn't move. His eyes were shut. The red dripping off the tip of the arrowhead felt warm to her finger when she touched it. She smelled the blood. "Oh, my goodness, it *is* real! Holly, call nine-one-one, and get the kids out to the truck."

Henry rounded up the kids and herded them into their new Expedition. "You kids sit here and don't get out. I promise we will still go trick or treating, but it will be a little bit later. I need to help the sheriff until the ambulance comes for the doc. You understand?"

"Yes, Sir." Nicholas said, sounding older than his years.

"Good. You can eat some of the candy the sheriff gave you." He turned to go back inside.

Madison instructed him to get clean towels from the shelf in the closet. He held them to catch the blood while she grabbed wire cutters from the back room. One snip and the arrow's tip was separated from the shaft. Then she cut the other end of the arrow's shaft off close to Doc's collarbone. She held another towel on the front of Doc's shoulder.

At that moment, Mr. Olsen came through the door. "What happened? I saw him stumble just as he got to the sidewalk. Is that an arrow in his shoulder?" Mr. Olsen dropped into one of the wingback chairs.

"We don't know how it happened; he just passed out as soon as he came through the door." Madison tossed a towel to Mayor Olsen. "Wet that and bring it back to me."

Mr. Olsen hustled to the bathroom and came back dripping water. Madison placed the wet towel on Doc's face. The cold aroused him a little. He started to roll over onto his side.

"Lie still, Chip. The ambulance should be here in a minute," Madison said.

Holly came in from the Expedition and whispered to Henry, "I heard the siren. The ambulance is close."

"Good. We've got the bleeding stopped, but he's in a lot of pain. Are the boys OK?"

"Yes, they're very concerned about who is going to give out Doc's treats now."

"Holly, you tell them that Mrs. Olsen and I will make sure all the children get the doctor's toothbrushes," Mr. Olsen said in a jovial tone.

"I'll tell them," Holy said, and returned to the family's new vehicle.

Madison followed the ambulance in her leased vehicle so she could bring Chip home if the hospital did not admit him, or have a way home if he stayed overnight.

Henry and Holly took their children trick-or-treating in Erwin, and Madison promised to keep them posted about Doc's injury.

Madison paced in the hallway outside the Johnson City Med Center ER for what seemed like hours. Finally, a male nurse came out to update her on Chip's condition.

"He was lucky with the location of entry. The arrow missed all major muscles and main arteries. But just another inch toward center, he'd have been in some real trouble."

"Will he be staying overnight?" She asked.

"Oh, yes. They are taking him to a room on the third floor. You can go up in a few minutes. I imagine he'll want to talk; he's been asking for you."

"Thanks. I have questions, but he probably won't remember much. I won't try to question him now."

Sheriff Madison McKenzie had been on the job just under six months, but she'd been friends with the town doctor for most of her life. The entire town was an extension of her family. Was this injury a freak accident, or had someone tried to kill the doc? As a rule, Cold Creek didn't have real crime—at least, not since Madison was a young girl. She certainly hoped this was nothing more than an accident.

An hour later, she sat in a chair beside Dr. Chip McClellan's hospital bed. He had an IV drip attached to him, along with a heart and BP monitor. She placed her hand on his and he opened his eyes.

"What happened? I was coming to meet you, then I woke up in the ER," Dr. McClellan said softly.

"I don't have any answers now, but you were struck by an arrow." She waited a moment, letting the news sink in. "The arrow appeared to be homemade. It was a very nice homemade arrow, but nothing like what hunters buy or use—not even those used for target practice. We're hoping to get prints from the shaft or the metal arrowhead."

"I was right at your door. Maybe they were lined up on it and I happened to step in the way."

"That's possible. I'd rather think that way, than someone trying to kill you," Madison said as she stood. "You rest, I'll be back to check on you tomorrow. Get some sleep."

Just to be sure no one was trying to hurt Chip, Madison asked the JCPD to station an officer outside his hospital room for the night.

Bud woke Madison early the next morning to go outside. She dressed in running shorts and shoes and they took off for a refreshing jog. November 1st came in warm like late summer. Madison thought she'd better take advantage of this freak of nature. They could have snow within days. Bud always enjoyed running, no matter what the weather.

She had been a runner since her early teens after been led to believe her only living relative was Aunt Denny, a woman of robust build even though she had an active lifestyle. When Bud was a puppy and full of energy, Madison used him as an excuse to continue running. She'd learned running gave her a stress release that nothing else could. She enjoyed her freedom and her dog. Bud also loved their private time together; they are happiest on a trail in the woods.

This autumn day promised to be one of the prettiest she could remember in years. The mountain's hardwoods had vibrantly changed into their year-end showy colors. The hickory, some of the largest leaves, were a butternut gold. The maples ranged from lemon yellow, to pumpkin, to ruby red. Those were Madison's favorites.

This particular year, even the walnut leaves had joined the beauty of fall's rainbow with their foliage turning a pleasing lime-green before a freeze made them brown and drop to the earth along with the walnuts.

The various oaks ranged from gold to orange and yellow. On the sides growing among the grooves in the bark, a five-leafed brilliant red vine often winds up the trunks into the canopy. That red color comes from the Virginia creeper, vegetation frequently mistaken for poison ivy or poison oak. In the Appalachians children learn a rhyme as youngsters. It goes, "Leaves of three, let them be." That way they avoid the effects of the poison's allergic reaction, which can be extremely painful, if not fatal.

Madison had trained Bud to avoid the three leaves, thus reducing her chances of contacting the plant's oil from his hair. A very smart dog, Bud learned quickly when she pointed things out to him. The dog was not only her friend, he was also her safety companion. He'd saved her life more than once. She knew as long as he was with her, she could get through anything.

At the end of their run, she showered and dressed in her uniform of black short-sleeved shirt and tan khaki jeans. Holly had sewn a vest for Bud of matching fabrics, and embroidered *Deputy Bud* along the neckline. Madison was sure he took his vest as a sign of being her partner against crime.

Today Bud wore his vest as Madison loaded him into the back seat of the leased black Explorer. She had still not decided what type of automobile she wanted to replace her beloved Blazer, but she had more important decisions to make at the moment, as sheriff of Cold Creek.

After a long and tiresome ride up and down the mountain roads, she came to a fork. On the right was a store. She saw the lights were on, so she parked in front. Stepping up onto a small porch lined with wooden crates of empty drink bottles, she saw the bottles were glass—with names like Bubble Up, RC Cola, Orange Crush, Grapette, and the old green Coke bottles that she had not seen in her lifetime, other than in pictures. She opened an old screen door with a colorful loaf of Sunbeam Bread painted on the screen. This made her grin. She had not seen one of these since she was a young girl.

"No, it's not for sale," a voice from inside the store said.

Madison looked up, realizing she'd been lost in the memory of the old screen door. "Hello; I was just mesmerized. I haven't seen one of those in decades." She walked into the dimly lighted room, looking for the person speaking to her.

"Everybody that comes in here wants to buy it, but that screen has been on that door since I was a young whippersnapper," an older gentleman stepped into the light from behind a counter. "Name's Jennings; I own this old relic."

"Pleased to meet you, Mr. Jennings, I'm Sheriff Madison McKenzie, of Cold Creek."

"Not Mister; Jennings is my first name, Sanders is my last. Everybody calls me Jennings."

"Okay, Jennings. I'm looking for someone who might have been in this area when the family was murdered up on Walkers' Mountain. Did you know them?"

24

"Yeah, we're cousins, Zeb Walker and me. Zeb's wife Olivia was one of the victims. She lived with her son Zac, and his wife Belinda. They were also murdered." He looked up toward the mountain. "Lived at the top of that hill. There's the dirt road, goes up to the home place."

"I'm very sorry to bring up old memories. I'm supposed to notify the descendants that Snyder Watts will be released from the state pen next—err, *this* month."

"Released. Yeah, they should have electrocuted that monster. But no, Knoxville got their hands on him for attempted murder and robbery, before we even knew it was him. He should have gone away for life, at least."

"How do you know he was the one who killed the Walkers?" she asked.

"Macy described him to a T, but she was only seven so the law didn't believe her. She ain't been the same since."

"Does she live around here?"

"No, they were all sent off to Florida, Marion County, to Belinda's half-sister's house. But if Belinda had any say-so, she'd have never allowed it. They didn't get along."

"How many children did the Walkers have?" Madison asked.

"Three, two girls and a baby boy. They were hiding under their granny's bed. Only reason he didn't kill them."

"I'm really sorry to keep asking you questions that bring up painful memories, but I do need to notify the kids. Do you know how I can get in touch with them?"

"I get a letter from Marian, the younger girl, every now and then. I've got one here in the register. It's the latest." He opened the old-timey register and took out the cash tray, revealing a green envelope underneath. "This was a note telling me Happy Easter. She's such a sweet kid. Well, not really a kid anymore; she's twenty-one. She wanted to go to college, but they don't have the money."

"What about the property? Did they sell it?"

"No, it's still in the courts. Was waiting for her to turn twenty-one, because Macy is not really responsible and the boy, Zac, is only fifteen. Such a sad situation."

"Does Marian know that now that she's twenty-one, the farm is hers?" Madison's wheels began turning. "How can I get in touch with someone handling the case?"

"I'd have to get that information from my wife. Can you give me your number? She's in Asheville today."

"Sure." Madison pulled a business card from her back pocket. "Here, you can get me on all these numbers." She handed him the card, "I was twenty-one before I went to college. Maybe it's not too late for Marian." She copied the address from the green envelope and handed it back. "Thank you, Jennings. Can you give me your number? I'd like to keep in touch."

"Absolutely. Nothing I'd like better than to see the kids return to Walkers Mountain. My wife, too; she really took this whole thing hard."

Jennings waved as Madison got into her vehicle.

Bud whined to get out. "Sorry, I talked too long. You can get out for a minute."

Bud sniffed the weeds and found a nice spot to leave a message, then returned to his place on the back seat. She closed the door after hooking his seat belt. Walking back to the driver's side she looked up the rutted dirt road, wondering how far it was to the cabin.

"Go on up, if you want. The road's rough, but you're welcome to look," Jennings called from the steps of the store.

"Thanks, I believe I will take a look around," Madison said. "This is going to require four-wheel drive, Bud. Let's see how this new Explorer will pull up that steep climb."

Bud sat up, looking out the window.

"This is going to be bumpy ride."

On top of the mountain she found a clearing that looked to be a couple of acres, nicely mowed. Dahlias were blooming, and fruit trees laden with apples and pears. A lush garden had mustard greens, a row of pumpkins, and a few other root veggies that she didn't recognize. Madison parked the SUV, unbuckled Bud, and they walked toward the house.

The front door was locked. She looked in the window. The house looked as if folks currently lived in it. She noticed a rack by the door with coats, just as though the residents could grab one and go. She walked around the side following a pathway of flat rocks. There she tried the back door. It was unlocked; the path continued, leading to a large chopping block.

Madison felt a presence, as if she was being watched. Even though Mr. Sanders had given her permission to come on the property, she felt like she was intruding. Bud looked toward the house and his tail wagged. Did he see someone, or had he also sensed a presence?

She continued along the rock pathway right up to the chopping block. There was no ax. But if the murderer had used it to kill the family, the police would have removed it. She saw that there were three flat stones along the path, larger than the ones forming the walkway. One placed next to the chopping block, one at the corner of the house, and the last one just ten feet from the back door. Each had a small bouquet of dried flowers laying on them. The hair on the back of her neck stood up; she realized they marked where the three Walkers had died.

She returned to the kitchen door and went inside. Bud followed. She checked to be sure there was no mud or grass on his feet.

"OK, you can stay with me, and stay close!"

The table was set for five, and had a highchair at one end. There were clean dishes on the drainboard by the sink. Everything looked as if the family could walk in and sit down at any moment.

A movement out of the corner of her eye caused Madison to look back toward the door. At the same time, Bud waged his tail in a friendly manner. He walked outside and sat on the path. Madison didn't see anyone; Bud had obviously seen something.

"Good boy; on second thought, you stay there," Madison said. "Clean as this house is, I bet they didn't allow pets indoors. I'll be out in a minute, Bud." She didn't shut the door.

Madison's attention focused on an open living area. Kitchen and dining were in one end opposite a large living room. There was a rifle rack over the fireplace, but no rifle on it. She walked through the living room to the stairs over on the right wall.

Ascending the stairs, at the top and to the left, she saw a room with one full-sized bed and a crib. The bed was neatly made with a white chenille spread. The next room held twin beds, little girls' dolls, and stuffed animals. The last room had a high bolster bed with a beautiful handmade quilt covering it. Underneath the bed Madison saw boxes filled with fabric and sewing items. In between the boxes lay a blanket, and on it was a dust-covered baby bottle.

She studied the floor. It was original hardwood flooring, clean with a satiny shine, except under the bed. She found a layer of dust on the boards.

Is this where the children hid from Watts? How long did they lay here? What must they have been thinking? Only Marian can tell us now. She was five at the time; her older sister Macy, just seven, had hidden them after seeing their dad murdered. At least that's the story Jennings understood. Will Macy ever be rid of the image?

Madison stayed at the door, not wanting to disturb anything that might be left. She'd return with a kit and a CSI who could gather evidence and process it. "This room speaks to me. If we stand a chance of getting that guy, the secret lies here." As soon as she said it aloud, she felt the presence again. She turned slowly and looked toward the stairs. A ray of sunlight illuminated the steps, but there was no window close enough to let it in. She stepped toward the light and it faded.

"Mr. Sanders, is that you?" She returned to the living room. No one was there. Madison looked up the stairs and at the top, she saw a woman in a faded cotton house dress. Her hair was dark and piled atop her head in an old-fashioned style. The woman's face was porcelain-like and she had a warm smile. Her hand touched the railing as though she might step down... And then Bud barked, causing Madison to turn toward the kitchen. When she looked back up the stairs, the woman was gone.

Madison drove back down the bumpy road to the store, and Jennings came out the door as she got out of the SUV.

"You're taking care of the place?" she asked.

He nodded. "Planted the garden, too. That's some of the richest soil in these parts. I get a crop of potatoes off that spot worth near a fortune. I have it all set aside for the youngsters. I sell the fruit in my store. Locals buy it to make jelly and apple butter. They know the money all goes to the Walker kids. My wife cans as much as she's able. We sell the rest. She cleans the house once a month, without fail. She still sits up there and cries about the way they died. They were good folks; had so much happiness in that house. I want to tear that man to pieces with my bare hands. It wouldn't do for him to come back to these parts."

"I understand." Madison opened the car door and stepped out. "You wouldn't happen to have a photo of the family, would you?"

"Yes, actually I do. It's right here in the store. The funeral home used it at the service, because none of the coffins could be opened." They walked back inside the store.

There, on a shelf behind the counter, was a photo of three adults. Sanders picked it up and explained, "This was their wedding day. I've never seen two happier people."

Madison's eyes fell on the older woman: Granny Walker in her younger years, with dark hair piled atop her head in an old-fashioned style. Chills ran down Madison's spine. "You spend a lot of time at the house. Have you ever seen her up there?" She didn't explain.

"You mean Olivia? No, but my wife has. I think that's why she goes up there so often. She and Olivia Walker, Granny, were best of friends."

Jennings Sanders was a strong man and a farmer. He never even questioned Madison. He stated that his wife sees Olivia, like it was just normal for her to be there, like they were talking about a living person.

"You saw her too. That's why you wanted to see the picture," he said softly.

"Yeah, I did. And my dog, Bud, walked back out of the house as if he'd been told to stay outside. His tail waged all the while."

Madison settled onto a pile of feed bags stacked on one side wall. "I've felt things and known things, but this is my first full-body apparition. She was smiling, so she didn't scare me. She was beautiful. Her skin looked like..."

"Like a china doll? Yeah, that was her. My cousin Zeb use to refer to her as his porcelain baby doll. She was a lovely woman, inside and out, and had the softest blue eyes."

Madison saw a tear slip down the big man's cheek. She placed her hand on his. "You take care now, Mr. Sanders. I'll be in touch." Madison returned to her vehicle and drove away.

Those kids need help, as much now as ever. If Watts has learned they were home, he'll be looking for them. I have to find them first. Olivia wants me to find him. I know what I have to do. Marian, you and I need to talk.

4

Madison moved her clothing to the new wing of her cottage. Henry was still working on the finishing details outside, but the master bedroom was ready to move into. A new king-size Sleep Number bed was scheduled for delivery in the afternoon.

Her things scarcely noticeable in the walk-in closet designed just for her, Madison paused a moment to scan the unused space. *Rick and I could have shared this closet, but, oh no, he has to have his very own.*

She laughed to herself while bouncing downstairs, ending up in her small kitchen—where a totally different century glared at her. *Have I made a mistake? This little cottage was home for so many of my family members. It seems a waste, putting so much money into the addition, but it's already done. And I am looking forward to using the garage.*

"True, I needed a garage, but why such elaborate construction? What was I thinking?" Her attention was drawn toward the front door of the cottage.

Henry stood at the screen. "Is this a private conversation, or can I intrude?"

"Come on in, Henry. I'm just fussing at myself."

"Yes, I heard! Do you want me to tear it down?" He laughed as he opened the screen door and stepped inside. "I need to quit early today. Holly wants me home to entertain the twins while she takes our older boys shopping for school shoes." Henry shook his head and scoffed, "Our older boys; it's amazing that we have four boys now!"

"And a girl on the way!" Madison stepped close to Henry. "Is it too much on you?"

"Oh, no, not at all. I wanted a bunch of kids, and so did Holly. We're blessed with both adoptions going through. And that's your doing!"

"Not completely; I think The Lord wanted the brothers to have a good home, so he brought them into my life and eventually, yours. It is a blessing; they needed you, Henry. Those two are so happy being back together. You and Holly are the best possible future they could have."

Henry nodded, backed out the door, and turned to go down the steps. "Oh, I almost forgot," he said, turning around. "Holly asked if you'd ride in with her and help her decide on the shoes."

"I can't. Besides, those guys know what they want; they'll show her what to buy." She laughed. "I'd much rather be with her than what I have to do, but duty calls!"

Keeping up with her job as sheriff of Cold Creek is Madison's main desire. She'd left school at UT for the summer to do volunteer work. One thing led to another, and she found herself in the position of sheriff. She took the responsibility seriously.

Bud joined Madison as she walked next door to her office. The new sign read *Cold Creek's Original Sheriff's Office, Established in 1772*. She didn't care for the title of "old jail," so she and Henry had changed the wording and gave her office its historically accurate title.

Weathered boards from the roof of her old shack were saved and used to share the history of the buildings. In 1771 the shack was built as home for Madison's ancestors, who constructed the original Shirley's Café along the trading route over the mountain. The area was claimed by North Carolina at the time. Traveling settlers began camping near the old cafe as they passed through from Asheville to Jonesborough.

A miner staked a claim across the field for a silver and gold mine. No one paid the old miner much attention, until the day he struck a silver vein and built a cabin over the entrance to keep folks out. One dry autumn, lightning set a wild fire that destroyed the restaurant as well as the cabin covering the mine entrance.

Cold Creek runs through the edges of town, and was where the community got its name. The creek held just enough water that people were able to douse Madison's family's cabin long enough to keep it from burning. The miner rebuilt his shack closer to the creek and dug new tunnels; the original entrance had caved in during the fire. The next year the café was rebuilt, twice the size it had been. Additional residents gathered, claiming land and homesteading. Until a store owner determined a jail was needed to house greedy prospectors, there were daily disputes that led to fights—and finally, a death. In order to have a respectable town, they needed laws and a place to put the offenders.

Thus, the old jail was built in 1772. Its foundation continued collapsing until the basement was reinforced. The townspeople soon realized they'd encountered a tunnel to the silver mine. The same thing happened when the store owner built his general store next door. It was named Olsen's Mercantile, opened by Mr. Olsen's great-uncle. It eventually came to be known as Olsen's Hardware.

In time, Cold Creek attracted nearly one hundred year-round residents, and log cabins were built all around the outskirts of town. The saw mill was one of the oldest businesses. Settlers cleared the land, and the mill cut the logs into usable lumber. Cold Creek blossomed until the start of the Civil War. One by one, families abandoned cabins and moved west to escape the War Between the States. Shirley's restaurant and Madison's cottage, along with the old jail, the hardware store, and the museum, remain the oldest buildings, even older than many in Jonesborough and Flowerville.

Jonesborough holds title as the oldest town in Tennessee, simply because Flowerville lost its town charter for a while. Otherwise, Bean Cabin, Flowerville's store, and the mill would be known as the oldest buildings in the oldest town. Flowerville does hold claim to the birthplace of the first white European-American child born in what is now TN. His name was Russell Bean, son of William Bean, whose descendants later settled Bean Station, northwest toward the TN/KY border.

Madison always smiled as she thought about how her direct ancestors had settled her home town. Maybe that was why she felt doing the best job she could as the town's law was her duty. This was her way to contribute, and she was proud of the responsibility.

She sat at her desk shuffling through papers until she came to the letter reminding her of the prisoner, soon to be released from the state prison in Nashville. The sheet had the phone numbers she required to contact the families. She opened her laptop and checked the social networks for any updates. *The numbers on this sheet almost have to be outdated.* She typed in the names Macy Walker, Ella and Zachary Walker.

Bingo! She found an Ella Marian Walker and pulled up the information: *Graduated from North Marion High School. Presently living in McIntosh, FL.* She looked at posts and was shocked by Ella's picture; it was like looking into the face of Olivia Walker. The long dark hair fell across her shoulders in lose curls. Her eyes were the color of the ocean, turquoise blue. This had to be the young woman she was looking for. If you piled that hair on top of her head, she'd be the twin of the ghost Madison had seen on Walkers' Mountain. Madison sent a friend request, praying that Ella would accept.

After a few minutes, her laptop dinged that she had a message. It was not an acceptance; even better, it was a private message to Sheriff McKenzie. Madison opened the message and read, *I received your message a couple of weeks ago and thought it was a hoax. Today, I got notice from TN Bureau of Prisons saying that Snyder Watts is scheduled to be released the end of next month. What does this have to do with us?*

Madison quickly typed a short reply. *As Sheriff of Cold Creek, I, too was notified, and it's my duty to notify you, the survivors. Why don't you call me? Or send me your number so I can call you. I'd feel more secure speaking to you in person.* She typed her cellphone number.

Okay, you call me @ 352-555-1991. I'll be here all day. Thanks, Marian

No sooner had the number began ringing than Madison heard a jolly voice say, "Hello, Sheriff McKenzie."

"Hello, Marian. You can call me Madison. So, you're going by your middle name now; I like that," Madison said.

"Oh, wow—a woman sheriff! Gee, things have changed in Tennessee."

"Yes, they have. I have too, and I'm a native. Our sheriff was hurt, so after five years away at UT, I inherited this job. My ancestors first settled here in the late seventeen hundreds."

"Gee, that's a thing to be proud of. I hope I can meet you someday."

"I hope so too. So, you know Watts is going to be released. But I want to prevent that if we can." Madison paused. "That's why I wanted to talk to you. Mr. Sanders told me that your sister has had a rough life, between nightmares and the shock she must have been in. How is she now?"

"Macy is about the same. She never got over the shock, and she still has night terrors. I take care of her, now that our aunt passed away. Oh, but you might not know that story," Marian said.

"Yes, I know a lot about your situation. I make it my business to learn all I can when I'm involved. I'm very sorry to hear about Macy. Has she seen a doctor?"

"Dozens of them. The damage is done; she'll never be any better, or so they say. I wonder how much was already going on with her before the murders. I'm younger, as you know, but I don't even know if my older sister was ever any different."

"Well, Mr. Sanders says she was fine. She was very intelligent, according to him. He knew your family well."

"Yes, I kept in touch with him. Aunty got worried about Jennings calling so much, thought he wanted us to stay with him so he'd have the money. Since that's the only reason *she* wanted us, she didn't want us to talk anymore." Marian took a deep breath and let it out loudly. "She lied to us about everything. She never let us have the money. She used it for her kids, for new clothes, and we only got hand-me-downs."

"What about Zackary? Where is he?" Madison asked.

"She sent him to the military academy. He doesn't have anything to do with us now. He'll go directly into the armed forces when he graduates."

"What turned him against you?"

"Oh, it's such a long story! I wouldn't know where to begin, so I won't even try," Marian said. "Sheriff Madison, you haven't told me what's on your mind."

"I spent five years at UT studying for a career in forensic law. I only took this summer off to do some volunteer work, but ended up, like I told you, in this office after our elected sheriff got hurt. Point is, I know something about solving murders. Way more than the law knew even fifteen years ago. I want to connect Watts to the murders, if he's the guilty one. I'd like to talk to Macy as a witness. But if she's as bad as you say, what can we do?"

"Maybe there is something." Marian was quiet for a moment before she said, "Macy's story has never wavered. She screams the same sentences, almost like she's reciting a morbid poem. I know the words by heart, right down to the sounds she makes when she clenches her teeth and her eyes go wild and black. You ought to witness *that*! It's as though she's possessed with an evil spirit. She never remembers what she says, she just knows she's exhausted and feels sick for a couple of days afterwards. It breaks my heart to watch her and listen to her moaning. The pain she feels when she's remembering..."

"How long has it been since she's had the night terrors?" Madison asked.

"Just last week. Something on the TV or some sound she hears, I don't know what it is that sets her off, but she reacts to some outside influence, I'm sure of that. One of the doctors who spent time with her wanted to hypnotize her, but our aunty wouldn't let him."

"What about now that Macy is of age, she could consent to it herself. Maybe that will let us know what the trigger or triggers are. Have you asked her?"

"No."

"Have you ever recorded her having one of the night terrors?"

"No, although one of the doctors thought that might help," Macy said.

"Your aunt wouldn't let him, right?"

"Right."

"Marian, if I send you a recorder, will you tell Macy you're going to record it when it happens again? You can see how she feels about it. That might give us something to work with."

"Does it have to be a special type of recorder? I have one on my phone," Marian sounded as if she liked the idea.

"I don't know about a phone. You'll need light so that we can see her expressions and her eyes."

"Well, she can't be in the dark. There is always a light in her room, day or night. That would not be a problem," Marian said.

"Let me send you one anyway. I have one that's easy to operate; it's voice and motion activated. You can set it up in her room and tell her not to mess with it. Or not tell her about it, whichever you think is better. Let me have your mailing address."

Madison wrote down the address and they talked for a while longer. After she hung up, she heard a truck outside. *They're early. Good thing I'm here.*

She went outside to take the delivery of her new king-size bed. In less than an hour, she was putting her freshly laundered sheets on the only furniture in the new bedroom. Her old bedroom suit would remain in the cottage bedroom for guests. She planned to shop for additional new pieces to go with the headboard. The dresser and other items that matched the headboard were too large for her taste; besides she had all that built-in storage space in the closets. She didn't really even need a dresser.

The next morning, Madison found the box and all the information for the recorder she'd promised Marian. She wrapped it, addressed it, and walked to the post office to mail it. Per the postmaster, it would be delivered Thursday.

As she walked back home, her phone rang. She glanced at the screen. It was Marian Walker. She answered, "Hey, Marian. What's up?"

After listening for a long time while sitting in the swing on her front porch, she finally hung up. Macy had an episode the night before, and Marian had recorded it with her phone. She'd asked Marian if she had access to a computer to email the video; Marian was ready to send it, she just needed Madison's email address.

Madison went inside to get her laptop and opened the email. She watched the lengthy video over and over, listening to voice that did not resemble a little girl's. *She sounded like a demon, and looked the part as well. How could a little girl of seven turn into a monster like that?* Madison thought of her professor from UT, Dr. Welty.

She looked up his phone number and called. He answered immediately, saying, "Yes, what can I do for you?"

"Dr. Welty, this is Madison McKenzie. Have I caught you at a bad time?"

"Ms. McKenzie, as in the Sheriff Madison McKenzie?" he laughed.

"You've been talking to Dr. Baker. How disgusted is she at me?"

"Oh no, Ma'am. You are her hero! She hasn't missed a chance to tell her students about you. You're a real celebrity around campus now." The doctor laughed again.

"Okay, thanks for the heads up, I'll be sure to bring my autograph pen when I come back. Now, let me tell you why I've called." She went into the details of how the video came to be, and told him she needed his professional opinion of the individual.

"Hmm. Sounds kind of like a possession, but not really. You know?" The doctor paused for a while, tapping the phone with his finger, the way he did in class when he was thinking. Only in class, instead of his finger it was a pencil, or a piece of chalk, or his pipe. "Send it to my email and I'll check it out this evening. I'll call you if I think it's something I can diagnose."

"Thank you, I'm sending it now. I probably won't sleep tonight for thinking about it. I'll wait for your call."

"I'll let you know as soon as I can."

As soon as she hung up, her phone rang. It was Rick. They talked late into the night. After telling him of her conversation and the video from Marian, he told her he had some insight on the case. He'd be there in the morning to share it with her.

Madison opened the door, called Bud in, and went to take her shower. It was after 1:00 a.m. so she went to bed, not expecting to hear from Dr. Welty so late.

5

Bud paced the floor whining, wanting Madison to wake up and let him out. He finally jumped up on her bed, startling her. She jumped straight up in bed before she realized it had only been Bud.

"What are you doing?" She rubbed her eyes and dropped back onto the bed next to her best friend. "I guess you need to go out and I overslept, huh?"

Bud jumped to the floor and went down to the kitchen and into the laundry/mud room. Madison followed. "Aw, you've learned we have another outside door. That's so smart of you!" She opened the new door and Bud took off, nearly knocking her down as he passed.

"I guess we need a doggy door. Hmm, and it should be in this mud room. Yeah, that's a good place for a doggy door. I'll see what I can do about that, Bud."

She followed him outside and realized the temperature had dropped during the night. She left the outside door barely cracked, and also the door leading to the kitchen.

"Let's see if you're smart enough to figure that out." She went to her room to add some layers of clothing.

Bud's yapping signaled that Rick had arrived. She put coffee on and then went to the front door. It had been a couple of weeks since Rick was in Cold Creek, and she'd missed him. As soon as she opened the door, he grabbed her up and kissed her. Apparently, he'd missed her too.

Bud squeezed in past the bodies obstructing the doorway. He had breakfast on his mind.

Madison and Rick joined forces to fix breakfast. While they cooked, Madison filled him in on the idea for a doggy door going out the mud room, the video from Marian, and how she came up with a lead concerning the arrow that sent Dr. McClellan to the hospital.

Rick sat down and sipped his coffee. "In other words, you've been thinking so much that I haven't crossed your mind."

"Au contraire!" She picked up her mug of coffee and sat on his lap. "I'm letting you know how much I *have* missed you. I try to keep super busy, so I don't mope all day long."

Henry drove up and tooted his horn. In a few seconds he opened the front door and knocked on the frame. "Is it safe to come in?"

"Sure; come and have a cup of coffee, ol' buddy," Rick said.

"That sounds good. It's cool this morning!" Henry sat in the chair across the table from Rick and Madison.

"Holly sends her love."

"To me? Aw, that's sweet," Rick commented, knowing full well Henry meant Maddy.

"Yeah, to you, Rick." Henry laughed and stirred creamer and sugar into the steaming mug.

"How is Momma getting along?" Rick asked.

"Very well, thanks. She says she expected to gain more weight with a girl. But she's not even a pound over what she was at this point with the twins," Henry said.

"I'd bet it's because of the twins that she's keeping her weight down," Rick laughed.

"You're probably right," Madison said. "She keeps up with them herself when their brothers are in school."

"I think little girls tend to be smaller babies too," Henry refilled his coffee mug. "One more for the road."

"Say, you don't need to work outside today. Madison wants a doggie door in the mud room. I can give you a hand, too." Rick stood and carried his coffee cup and plate to the sink. "Don't you have to get one at Lowe's, or one of the other home improvement stores?"

"Yeah. I need refills for my nail gun anyway. You want to run into Johnson City with me?"

"Sure." Rick looked at Madison. "Honey, did you need me to do something here?"

"No, don't worry, I've got plenty to do here. You boys go on to the home improvement store. I know how exciting that is for you." She laughed and hugged Rick, giving him a reassuring kiss.

She waved bye to the men and looked around for Bud. He was nowhere to be seen. She whistled; still no sign of Bud. "I bet you're off with your female friend somewhere."

An hour later, when Bud had still not returned, she texted Rick to see if he'd gotten into the truck with them. Rick answered right away, *he's not with us.*

Madison felt a twinge in her gut. *Where are you, Bud?*

She walked to the sheriff's office, then next door to the hardware store. Mr. Olsen had not seen him. She went to the back of the restaurant, where the momma dog usually spent her time. They were not there,

Madison returned to her cottage and whistled again. This time Bud came running up from the creek. He was soaked to the skin. "What were you doing?" Madison yelled. She was scared but relieved at the same time. "You never get into the creek when it's this cold! Show me..."

Bud turned and ran back across the open field and into the creek, where some of the local kids had dammed it up. There, in the deeper water, Madison saw a tiny animal bobbing in the water.

"It's a deer!" She waded into the cold stream. Water reached above her knees, and she was still ten feet from the tiny animal. By the time she got to it, the water was to her upper thighs. She raised the fawn's head, hoping to see some sign of life. The animal was floating, his knobby little legs lifeless. She picked him up and carried him out of the creek, laying him on the soft short grass.

Mr. Olsen rushed toward her carrying a blanket. "Is it alive?" He called as he approached.

"I'm afraid not." She rubbed his cold body vigorously.

Mr. Olsen dropped the blanket on the fawn. "I saw Bud come out of the creek. When you followed him back to the water, I knew there was something in there. I hoped a warm blanket might help."

"Maybe it will. I feel a weak pulse." She shifted her position. "Let me see if I can pump his stomach, in case he swallowed some water." She straddled the lifeless form and began massaging his belly, pushing toward his neck. Miraculously, the fellow opened his mouth and puked out a large amount of water. She wrapped him tightly in the blanket and lifted him into her arms.

"He must be a newborn: barley weighs anything. I'm going to take him inside. Maybe he's just really cold." She looked back toward the creek. "Wonder where his momma is?"

Mr. Olsen shuffled along with her and opened the door to let her inside. They both sat next to the tiny fawn and watched as he moved slightly and began to look around. Bud licked him like he knew what to do.

In less than ten minutes, the little buck was up on spindly legs, trying to stand. His hooves slipped on the wood floors, so Madison slid him onto the braided rug. Then he stood very well, but shivered, still chilled from the cold, spring-fed water of Cold Creek.

The spring feeding the town's namesake was under the mountain behind the town, flowing from deep underground. The water used to be the main source of drinking water for Cold Creek's townspeople, but while the silver mine was worked, iron ore made the clear water yellowish: too much iron content in the tailings. Since those days, most residents have a well. Recently, Unicoi Water Company piped water in from their plant for anyone who wanted to pay. A lot of the wells are still good, but mostly used to water gardens and apple orchards.

Mr. Olsen returned to his hardware store, and Madison and Bud escorted the buck to her office so she could observe him while she made some business calls. Bud acted as caretaker, following Bucky's every move. After wincing as he fell numerous times, Madison put strips of duct tape on his tiny hooves so he could stand on the hardwood floors. This worked well, and the little guy explored all the rooms of the small office with Bud at his side.

The name Bucky just came naturally to Madison, so she assigned it as his official name. She knew she couldn't keep him for long, but he'd stay with her at least until the danger of drowning was no longer a factor. She put in a call to

Doctor Chip, in hopes he'd feel well enough to make a house call to check the little fellow over.

After about thirty minutes Chip entered the office, carrying a baby bottle filled with milk. "I'm looking for my patient." He laughed when he observed Bucky walking with the help of tape. "Gorilla tape, I presume?"

"No, actually just plain old ordinary duct tape," Madison answered. "Is that deer milk?"

"No, I was fresh out of doe milk. This is Karo Syrup and evaporated milk, close enough to mothers' milk. Let's see if the little guy is hungry."

"His name is Bucky." Madison put her arms around the neck of the tiny fawn and guided him to the doc, who sat in her swivel chair. "How's your shoulder?"

"Fine! You'd never know I was targeted, if it weren't for that ugly scar forming," he said with a chuckle.

"You were lucky it didn't hit something vital. I have a clue about what happened, and I'm going to check it out today," she said.

Bucky didn't take to the nipple easily, but when Bud licked it and the milk dripped, the fawn got the idea. In a matter of minutes, he'd emptied the entire eight ounces.

"Wow! He liked it," Madison said. "How much do you think he should eat?"

"I don't know. Maybe just enough to give him strength. We need to find his mom."

"And how do we do that?"

"I talked to Henry. Says he'll come by in a while; he's in Johnson City," Doc said.

"Yeah, I know. Rick is with him."

Madison's phone rang. "Sheriff McKenzie," she answered.

Doc checked Bucky as best he knew how, considering he was a human doctor and not a vet. He walked, letting the fawn follow him around the room. He listened to the stomach, the lungs, and heartbeat, then looked at the baby's eyes and ears.

Madison hung up the phone. "Well, according to that anonymous caller, Bucky's mom is laying out beside the highway. He said he hit her and stopped to see how badly she was hurt. He followed her into the woods and she dropped next to a male fawn. The little buck jumped up and ran away, and the momma couldn't get up. He said she was suffering, so the caller determined that she needed to be put down. He sent an arrow through her heart, and she died instantly." Madison propped her fists on her hips. "An arrow...he wanted me to know that he gutted the deer and took her for the meat, but he only shot her because she was too far gone to save. Hmm...an arrow," she repeated.

Chip stood quietly for a minute. "I'll go check out the carcass. Did he say where exactly he left her?"

"Just that she was running across the old road, where Rocky Fork runs under old highway twenty-three. Come on, I'll drive. Bud will look after Bucky." She led the fawn into the jail cell and placed the blanket from the bunk on the floor. "Bud, sit."

Bud sat on the blanket, and Bucky snuggled next to him.

"Well, Bud is a good caretaker," Chip laughed. "You going to lock the door?"

"No, just close it. The little fellow will probably sleep until we get back. Good boy, Bud. On guard," she said and petted his head. He recognized that signal.

Madison drove as Doc watched the sides of the road for any sign of a deer. She turned up Rocky Fork Creek and parked in the gravel. She walked south on the right side of the highway and Doc walked on the left. Not locating anything, they turned and walked down the other direction.

A dark blue pickup truck pulled in next to her vehicle. "Hey, Sheriff. You looking for that deer?"

"Yes, I had a call saying a truck hit one. Was it you?"

"No, Ma'am, but I saw who it was. He lives up on Edwards Branch Road. He's a young fellow, don't even think he's old enough to drive. But he drives his dad's old truck around here on the back roads. I've seen him a couple times lately."

"Did you see him hit the deer?" She asked.

"Yes, she darted right in front of him. I nearly hit her too, but she managed to get into the woods. I think he followed her, down that way, below the creek. I drove on by and then thought better of it and came back. By that time, he

43

was gone."

"I think I might know who that was. Thanks, I'll handle it from here. I appreciate you stopping," Madison waved as the truck drove off.

"So, you know who it might be?" Chip asked as they got back into her vehicle.

"Yeah, I thought I recognized his voice. I met him back in the summer. I'll check it out. If it was him, there should be some damage to the truck. He wouldn't lie to me. I'm sure it happened the way he said, I just don't know how we can prove it was Bucky's mom. And what will I do with him in the meantime?"

"Henry's raised little orphaned deer before. I'm sure he'll know what to do."

"Oh, yeah; Henry's a good caretaker, too," she said, smiling.

When Madison and Chip returned to her office, both Bud and Bucky were sleeping. They were snuggled closely together on the blanket. Bud's body nearly encircled the tiny fawn. Chip took out his phone and snapped a photo.

Bud opened his eyes, but didn't move. He was comfortable warming the baby, and said so by closing his eyes and not getting up.

"OK, that says 'leave us alone, we're sleeping,'" Chip laughed and walked outside.

Madison followed.

"That dog of yours is something, Madison. I think you and Bud are cut from the same bolt of cloth," Chip patted her shoulder gently.

"Thanks for coming to check on your patient. You do realize you were promoted to veterinarian when you took care of Bud's girlfriend and pups, right?"

"Why, absolutely; I agree, that *was* a promotion. Animals are more appreciative than most humans. But just between you and me, what happens in the animal world, stays in the animal world." He laughed and walked off, toward the other end of town.

Madison returned to her vehicle. She drove up Edwards Branch Road, to the house where she'd been called for a domestic dispute early in the summer. There in the drive was the old truck. Bobby Sullivan knelt by the front bumper. He straightened when she stopped in the drive and approached him.

"Hello, Bobby. Thanks for the call about the deer. I caught the fawn, and we'll care for him. He'll be alright. You did the right thing, calling me."

"Aw, um... Well, thanks. I'm glad you got her fawn. I cried when I hit her. I never shot a deer before. And I sure don't see no sport in it, either." He wiped his face on the sleeve of his shirt. "We could sure use the meat, though. I'd be obliged if you'd let me keep it. I put it in the fridge right away."

"Honey, I didn't come to take the meat from you. It's good you knew how to cut it up, and it looked to me like you did the most humane thing for her." She looked at the crumpled bumper. "I hope your dad won't punish you when he sees you were driving his truck. I know you're under age. I won't say anything about that either."

"I'll get it fixed 'afore he knows about it. He's gone away, you know?"

"No, I hadn't heard. Where did he go?" she asked.

"Got caught driving drunk in Knox County, and they put him in jail. Mom says he might get to come home around Christmas, but she's trying to talk him into going into some rehab center."

"That's nice to hear. Do you think he's going to listen to her?"

"I hope so. She told him not to come back here to live. He'd have to go somewhere else. So maybe he'll have a change of heart, after he's sober a while. They had to put him in the hospital the first week, 'cause he got so sick," Bobby explained.

"Yes, if he's truly an alcoholic, he would get sick. It's just like a drug to the body; once your body depends on a drug, even alcohol, it thinks it can't work without it. I hope he's feeling better. Maybe this will do him some good. Did he wreck?"

"Yes, but his was the only car involved. Nobody was hurt. He was lucky in that way."

"That was a good thing, Bobby. I hope your dad will come to his senses." She put her arm along Bobby's shoulders. "I need to ask you some questions. Is Kelly at home?"

"No, Ma'am, she ain't." Bobby glanced toward the house. "She's working late tonight."

"OK... Well, I just need to know where you were on Halloween night."

"I'm too old to trick or treat, so I just hung out with some of the guys. We didn't go nowhere in particular." Bobby's attention had returned to the crumpled bumper.

"You didn't come up to Cold Creek?"

"Oh, like I said, we are too old to get candy."

"I know what you said, but an arrow exactly like the one I pulled from the deer carcass was shot at my office. Are you telling me you did not shoot your arrow that night?"

Bobby starred at the ground. He wouldn't answer.

"Dr. McClellan was hit in the shoulder. He's fine now, the arrow didn't hit anything vital. But my friend Holly's four young children were in my office. The level it hit his shoulder, if it had hit one of the kids—"

"It was an accident, you know?! I'd never do nothing to hurt nobody! I can't even shoot an animal when I'm hunting. How could I shoot a person?" Bobby raised his voice fearfully. "I swear, it was an accident!" Tears streamed down his face. "Please don't arrest me. Please, Momma couldn't handle both Daddy and me being in jail."

"Oh no, Bobby, I would never take you to jail. I'm not going to say a word to Dr. Chip either. But you must promise me that one day, when you are big enough to admit you made a very dangerous mistake, you will tell him it was you, and that you learned a valuable lesson. I don't know how a bow can go off by accident, but you'd better come up with a good explanation when you tell Chip."

Bobby's hands shook as he swiped at his tears. His words wouldn't come out of his trembling lips. He just nodded his head, over and over. Madison felt so bad for making him face the truth that she wrapped her arms around him and pulled his shaking body against hers.

"Please don't cry now, Bobby. It's over. Chip is not going to hear it from me. No one will, I promise you! It was a stupid stunt, for sure. But that's the difference in you and me. I'm an adult. Adults have lived long enough to see the dangers in life. You shouldn't have, but you have and I know you are going to understand this next statement. Parents make mistakes growing up; that's how they recognize danger when their kids do something. That's why we fuss and tell you don't throw that rock, don't walk into the street, and don't aim your bow at something you don't intend to shoot. We don't always explain, but we recognize the danger because we've been there. Trust me, I'm not going to fuss at you or punish you in any way. But every time you pick up your bow, or a rock, or a gun, just remember to think it through. What will the result be? Will someone get hurt?" She pulled the small boy back to look into his face. "Do you understand?"

"Yes, Ma'am. I do. I really do." He buried his face in her chest. "I'm so sorry. If I could take it back, I would. But I want you to know I was scared so bad that I peed my pants that night! I had to tell Momma that I slipped down in the creek. She believed me, and I was relieved that I didn't have to tell her."

Madison just listened as he calmed down.

"I guess I knew you'd be smart enough to figure it out. You're good at what you do. I appreciate you, Miss Madison and I'll do anything for you. Just please don't tell Doc. I like him a lot, and I am so ashamed."

"Bobby, I won't tell, but one day you will. You'll man up, and you'll feel better for it."

"I'll think about it." He turned away and wiped his face one last time. "Thank you, Miss Madison."

"Come and see me next time you're close to Cold Creek. I'll buy you lunch and desert at Shirley's. Will you do that, Bobby?"

He nodded just a little, and smiled at the idea.

Back in her office, Madison completed her list of calls. After talking to Unicoi County Court house, Knox County, and even the Franklin Prison, she had no more answers. She found it difficult to believe that in just fifteen years no one was around that might have presided over the trial of Snyder Watts. But then she thought of a woman she'd met during mediation with the Jacobs' adoptions. Quickly, she Googled child services and found Diane Culp's extension.

Mrs. Culp's voicemail came on, so she left a brief message and her phone number.

Just at that moment, her cellphone rang. Looking at the CID, she saw that it was the professor from UT.

"Hello, got any good news for me?" she answered.

The professor began with, "Want the good news or bad news first?"

She simply answered with a sigh.

"Well...first, let me tell you, that gal is not possessed or anything supernatural. She's messed up, for sure, but I'd have to observe her to know what caused this. Can you bring her to my office downtown?" He tapped a pencil against the phone.

"Well, she's in Florida. Can't see bringing her to you happening anytime soon."

"Oh, yes; that does present a problem." More tapping on the phone. "Can you put me in touch with any of the doctors who treated her?"

"I can try that," Madison hesitated. "I'll get back with you. It might take a while."

"All right, then I'll wait to hear from you. You do what you can, Madison. This poor child certainly does need help. She's been terribly traumatized."

Madison tapped her finger on her desk rapidly, the same annoying way the professor did when he was thinking.

"I thought that drove you crazy, but now you're doing it," Rick spoke softly.

Madison jumped, causing her phone to fly across the desk. "I didn't hear you come in. You startled me," she laughed.

"What did these two do that was so bad you locked them up?" Henry's voice sounded from across the office, beside the prisoner cell.

"It isn't locked, and they were sleeping," Madison got up and walked to stand next to Henry, Rick at her side.

"This is Bucky," she said, opening the cell door.

Bud stood and stretched his back legs. Bucky opened his eyes, but didn't stand. Henry knelt next to him and stroked his tiny head.

"Boy, he is young."

"Yeah, and so unafraid," Madison said.

"Has Doc checked him?" Rick asked.

Madison nodded, "He brought some formula in a baby bottle. Bucky drank eight ounces."

"Evaporated milk and Karo Syrup," Henry commented. "Same thing I use whenever I have an orphan baby to nurse. I've never taken in a fawn this young. How'd you find him?"

"Bud found him in the creek. He almost drowned. I did CPR and he came around."

"You got to him just in time," Rick said.

"What are you planning to do with him?" Henry asked.

Madison shrugged her shoulders.

"I guess you should call the wildlife service. They'll call me. That's what they usually do."

"Well, Henry. What would you do?" Rick asked. The grin on his face said he already knew.

6

Rick got a call to return to Knoxville that evening. He was not happy about losing his weekend, especially after not seeing Madison for two weeks. But he repacked his car and drove out of Cold Creek just as the sun set.

Madison felt lonely because not only had Rick left, but Bud went home with Henry to help settle the new fawn into his stable at the barn. Henry had requested Bud's company, knowing he'd keep the little buck warm through the cool night. The new home he'd made for Bucky was completely enclosed and had six inches of clean straw on the floor.

Bud entered the small room ahead of Henry, who carried the fawn. The two animals lay down, settling into the warm bed. Bud instinctively knew what his role was in this relationship. Henry gave him a reassuring pat on the head and closed the door as he left.

All four boys met Henry at the kitchen door when he came onto the back porch.

"When can we see the deer?" the twins asked.

"Not tonight, he's sleeping. He had a tiring day." Henry swept his two younger boys into his arms.

"But he's *alone!*" Robbie cried out.

"No, he has a bodyguard keeping him company, and warm for the night. Can you guess who it is?"

Nicholas spoke up, "Bud found him, so I bet he's with him. Right?"

"Yes, you are correct!" Henry leaned down and kissed the top of Nicholas' head.

"Bath time, boys!" Holly called from the hallway.

"We're on our way, Mom." Nicholas rounded up Robbie and headed toward the stairs. "You bringing the little ones?" he asked Henry.

"I'll be right behind you!" One of the twins was now draped over Henry's shoulders, and the other was hanging on to his dad's waistline.

Holly watched the gaggle of feet and heads bobbing up the stairs. "And don't forget to brush your teeth."

"No problem, Mom. I'm going to inspect them. You can count on that," Henry said.

"I'll be up to tuck everyone in." Holly sounded tired.

"That's OK, Mommy. I'll tuck my brothers in. You shouldn't come up the stairs now that you're so fat," Robbie said innocently.

Holly laughed, "OK, Robbie, you give them all hugs for me, and I'll stay down here." She went into the kitchen and picked up her phone.

"Hey, Madison. I bet you're lonely. Henry told me Rick was called back to Knoxville."

"Oh, hi Holly, how are you feeling?" Madison asked.

"I'm feeling large—and Robbie just told me he'd do the tucking in of the boys, that I shouldn't climb the stairs now that I'm so fat."

"Oh, how funny!" Madison laughed. "Has the baby dropped?"

"I think so. I feel like I have a twenty-pound turkey in the oven, not a bun." Holly sighed.

"The moon will be full next week. Maybe you're about ready to deliver."

"My doctor says it won't be 'til after Thanksgiving." Holly sounded disappointed.

"Oh, what does he know? That little girl will come when she's ready, not when he's overstuffed on Thanksgiving dinner."

"Yea, I know. I do feel pretty miserable. I hope you're right."

Madison and Holly talked until Henry returned to the kitchen. Hearing his voice, Maddy said goodnight, and Holly agreed she was ready for bed.

As soon as Madison got into bed, she heard her phone ring in the living room. "Oh, I left my phone off the charger. Who's calling this late?" She stepped lightly onto the braided rug, as if to avoid Bud. Then she remembered he was at the Jacobs farm, with Bucky.

"Hello," Maddy answered.

"Hey, Madison. I'm sorry to call this late. I wanted to let you know, Macy's gone. She left the house to walk to church this morning, and I don't know where she went from there. She always walks to church by herself. I've talked to the preacher. He said he didn't see her. Maddy, I don't know what to do!"

"Marian, have you reported her missing?"

"Yes, but she's an adult. They don't understand how vulnerable she is," Marian sobbed softy.

"Tell me any changes that you've noticed in your sister. Anything, even if you don't think it's important. It might be something big to her."

The two talked into the night. Madison took down the names and phone numbers of all the local people she might need to talk to about Macy. But it was the wee hours of the morning, so she thought she'd do some research on the computer, waiting to make any calls until morning.

The night seemed long, and Madison already dreaded what results might come from this missing person report. She fell asleep in the rocker just as daylight peeked in her windows. It wasn't until her phone rang, waking her, that she realized it was the next day. She was groggy and couldn't think of where the phone sounds were coming from.

Eventually, she felt her pocket and stopped the ringing. She looked quizzically at the caller ID. *Marion County Hospital, Ocala, FL.* She blinked her eyes several times, then called the number back.

"This is Sheriff McKenzie; I just missed a call from this number," she said as the operator at the reception desk identified herself.

"Oh, Sheriff McKenzie, that must have been Dr. Bellows. Hold on just a sec."

"Dr. Jay Bellows," the next voice announced.

"This is Madison McKenzie, Sheriff of Cold Creek, Tennessee. Were you trying to contact my office?"

"Yes, Sheriff. We wanted to let you know that Ms. Macy Walker has been admitted to our psychiatric wing. She came in last night and signed herself in."

"And how did you know to call me?" Madison was confused.

"She told us your name and where you were, but we elected to wait until this morning and not disturb you late last night."

"What about her caretaker, her sister? Does Marian know Macy is there?" Madison asked.

"Yes, we alerted her just a while ago, too." The doctor was less than helpful with his answers.

"Is Macy hurt?"

"No, she wanted us to keep her here because she fears for her life. I cannot give you any more information, except that this poor woman is in a very delicate condition."

"Thank you for notifying me, Doctor. I'll continue this conversation with Marian."

"Very well. I suggest you do that." The doctor disconnected the call abruptly.

Maddy stared at her cellphone for a second before it rang again.

"Sheriff McKenzie," she answered.

"Hey, Sheriff, it's Marian, I wanted to tell you we found my sister."

"Yes, a Dr. Bellows just called me," Madison said. "Why did Macy go to the hospital?"

Marian took a deep breath. "I think she's been listening to my phone conversations, and formed her own opinion of how to fix her problem. Who knows what's been going on in her mind?"

"Did you tell her about Watts?" Madison asked.

"No, but she read the notice; I found it on her dresser. I'd left it in my room. I've never known of her to read my mail before this. Evidently, that letter was her trigger when she had the episode. I don't know of any other change in her days. I should have been more careful. She's not a child; she understands way more than I've given her credit for. I messed up."

"Now, don't take it so hard. Maybe she's as tired of her situation as you. Maybe she even realizes she needs a doctor's help. This could be the best solution. Are you going to see her today?"

"She requested no one, not even me, be allowed to visit. All I can do is call."

Madison could tell that Marian was crying. "Listen, Professor Welty wants to see Macy. I explained that she's in Florida. How 'bout I put him in touch with Dr. Bellows, and you come to Tennessee?"

"I thought about that. I'd love to see my home again. You know I own the farm, now that I'm twenty-one, don't you?"

"Yes. And I also think you could go to college up here. So, what do you say? Can you get a flight out and let me meet you at Tri-Cities Airport?"

"I've already checked into the flights. They have one from Gainesville to Charlotte and a connecting flight to Tri-Cities on Thursday. How about if I book it, then text you the time and flight number?"

"Sounds good, Marian. Or did you want to be called Ella?"

"It's OK. I don't mind. But I do like Ella better," she answered.

"That's it, then; from now on, you're Ella, to me." Madison was relieved that Macy wasn't hurt. "This is definitely for the best, right now anyway."

Before Madison could get into the shower, her phone rang again. She saw that it was Diane from child services.

"Good morning Diane, thanks for returning my call."

They talked for a while about the boys, and then Madison asked if she knew about the Walker children. Diane remembered them, all right, and in fact was instrumental in getting them relocated to Florida. She had been notified of Watts' upcoming release, and she knew the judge who had presided over his trial. However, he was deceased.

On Thursday, Madison waited at the baggage area for Ella's flight. She was ahead of schedule, as often happens with flights out of the South when a storm front was approaching. She noticed the baggage area beginning to fill with arriving passengers, and stood at the back of the room, out of the way.

One woman approached with a group. She stood a head above the rest of the passengers. Her hair fell across narrow shoulders in bouncy curls and she flashed a pleasant smile at Madison. Madison stepped forward to greet the face she recognized from the photo at Jennings' store. She'd known instantly that the woman was Olivia Walker's granddaughter.

"You look exactly like your grandmother! I knew that was you as soon as I saw you," Madison reached to take Ella's carry-on bag.

"Jennings told me you said that when you looked at the photo of my grandmother. He always said it too, so I guess it must be true. But I can't remember her face...just her eyes. They were aquamarine."

Madison nodded. "Did you have a good flight?"

"Yeah, I was really anxious to get here. And we had a tailwind." Ella stepped away to grab a larger suitcase matching the small one she'd handed off to the sheriff. "This one is mine."

"Very good. Let's go and get something to eat. I know you only got a snack on this flight."

"A glass of water and approximately ten peanuts, all but one in pieces. Quite filling, huh?"

The two women laughed as they walked out the door to Madison's waiting Explorer. She had parked in front, leaving her flashers on. That was a first for Maddy. She never took advantage of any privileges the title of sheriff could bring. But with the traffic jam leaving the parking area, this time she might even use her blue light to get ahead of the line. The toll gate was holding the other passengers, however, so she was able to turn left and get on TN-75 without any delay.

"What do you feel like eating?" Madison asked.

"What are our options?" Ella smiled. "Thank you for meeting me. I am happy you suggested this trip. I've wanted to come home for the longest!"

"So glad it was possible. As for restaurants, we have anything you could desire. That's one thing Johnson City is blessed with: lots of food choices!"

The women settled on Olive Garden due to the cool temperature. Ella said she loved their soups, bread sticks, and salad.

The lunch crowd was long gone and the evening rush had not yet begun, so they were seated immediately in a quiet corner. This pleased Madison, because she had so many questions for Ella.

As it turned out, Ella had her share of questions, too. Their meal extended into dinner and the room started filling with noisy diners.

"Good time for us to move on up the mountain. Are you OK with staying at my cottage?"

"Oh, I couldn't impose. Is there a cheap motel close by your home?"

"No, nor an expensive one. I'll be happy to put you up with me. I've just added on to my house. The master suite is ready, but I've not even slept in it yet. That leaves the guest room for you. You'll see when we get there. It's really no bother, and I welcome the company."

"What about Bud? I expected you to have your deputy with you."

"He's babysitting." Madison laughed. "I'll tell you all about it on the way." She signaled to the waitress for the check, paid with her office credit card, and they returned to the cruiser parked right in front of the restaurant.

The drive up the mountain on I-26 felt strange; Madison explained they were traveling south toward Asheville. The lack of experience in the East Tennessee mountains was enough to confuse Ella.

"Feels like we're going north, not south. I mean, we are going up..." Ella observed the terrain. "What's that town?" She pointed in the distance to Unicoi.

"That's Unicoi, and we are in Unicoi County. You lived in Unicoi County, but on the other side of this mountain," Maddy continued to point out areas of interest. "That's the county seat, Erwin. It used to be a big train hub. With the coal mines in Virginia and Kentucky shut down, there aren't many trains running through here anymore."

"I remember Daddy saying he had to go into Erwin to pay the taxes. I didn't have any idea what taxes were," her voice dropped to a soft whisper.

"You were young. You'll have a lot of memories, some good and some not. But you will get through this, Ella, and so will Macy. Professor... I mean, Dr. Welty has already been in touch with Dr. Bellows. He's excited about her case. I'm so glad you sent me that recording."

"Me too. And I think that's another reason Macy went to the hospital. She watched the video with me, and she cried. I think she remembered more about that day after hearing the things she'd said that she'd never remembered before." Ella stared out the window at the scenery going past.

Madison listened and made no comment. She drove up the mountain, passing the Welcome Center on I-26. The next exit led to Cold Creek. As she parked in front of the cottage, she saw Bud running off the porch to greet her.

"Hey, Deputy Bud! Welcome home. How's your friend?" Madison bent to stroke Bud's head. "Ella, meet Bud, my sidekick, my BFF, and my deputy."

Ella knelt next to the black and tan dog. "You are a pretty one. It's very nice meeting you, Bud." She accepted the raised paw and shook with him.

Madison carried Ella's suitcase inside and put it in the bedroom, on a small table. "This is your bathroom. I've moved everything out so you have plenty of room. Make yourself at home."

"I feel bad; this is your room, isn't it?"

"Come with me. You'll see what I meant about the master suite. See, Rick and I are planning to get married in the near future, and we wanted a garage. So Henry, Holly's husband, built this addition for me."

Madison led the way to the door between the living room and kitchen. They went up the newly built stairs to the second floor, over the three-car garage. They paused at the landing, where a tall window overlooked the creek and the rocky mountainside beyond. "That's my mountain. Not as impressive as Walkers' Mountain, but I own it."

She led the way up the remaining steps to the left and into a spacious sitting area, complete with fireplace, bookshelves, and a loveseat. Up two more steps and they looked into the master bedroom. Large walk-in closets stood on either side the entryway. "This is where I moved to. It's a slight change from the old cottage downstairs, which is over two hundred years old. But I think I can get used to it."

"I'll say! Gee, this is nice!" She walked to the window, looking down at the driveway. "Is that Henry?"

Madison looked down and waved to Henry. "Yep; he's still working on the garage. Rick had him build all kinds of storage. I doubt if we can ever fill it all up."

Ella laughed when Maddy showed her the separate closets. Rick's was filled with golfing paraphernalia: shoes, clubs, and lightweight clothes. "He hasn't moved his winter wardrobe in yet." She laughed too.

"And men say women use all the closet space."

"Let's go down and meet Henry. I want to ask about the little buck." Madison led the way.

Madison introduced Ella and Henry, and he explained that the fawn was doing well. Bear had taken over for Bud so he could return to duty as deputy. They all laughed about the thought that the dogs were communicating.

"I remember Walkers' Mountain had lots of deer. I hope they're still there. Daddy never let anyone hunt on our land; he didn't want any of the wildlife killed. It was a sanctuary for all of them. I think Jennings has tried to keep the hunters out, too."

"Let me know when you plan to drive over there, Maddy. I'd like to see

Walker's Mountain. I was there once as a young boy. My Grandpa must have been friends with your Grandpa Walker. I think he delivered an occasional jar of 'shine to him." Henry said with a sheepish grin.

"Grandma said he hid it out in the barn. She never let on to him that she'd discovered his hiding place. But when any of us kids got a sore throat, she'd give us a dose of strong medicine; I think it was moonshine from Grandpa's stash." Ella smiled at the fond memory. "With a necessary spoonful of Grandpa's honey from his stands of bees, of course. That was the sweetest honey ever!"

"We'll go whenever Ella wants to. I'll let you know," Madison answered. "Wouldn't it be nice if the beehives are still there?"

"Oh, I'm sure Jennings has cared for them. He loved that honey as much as we did. You know, I really need to call him to let him know I'm here."

"Sure you do, I agree. You can use the phone in my office. Talk to you later, Henry," Madison said, and the two women walked toward the jail.

After talking with Jennings, Ella was even more excited about heading to Walkers' Mountain.

"I think I'd like to go in the morning." Ella no longer had any hesitation in her voice. She was ready to return home.

7

During the drive to Walkers' Mountain, Henry told stories his dad had told him as a young boy, stories that could only have involved Grandpa Walker. Now it all made perfectly good sense to Henry. In those days, he could not have been less interested in what his dad had been involved in. He was almost a teenager, and had play on his mind. Taking a run across curvy country roads to visit someone he didn't know was not on his list of fun things to do. He knew better than to object, though; that was what Mr. Jacobs called disrespect. Henry and his brother learned at a young age to never disrespect the old man, or there would be hell to pay!

One story that stood out in his memory included a drive up to the barn of the man they were delivering quarts of 'shine to. In return, he remembered bushels of apples, and pears in the fall. But this was midsummer; the apples would not have ripened yet. Immediately after they stopped at the barn, Mr. Jacobs brought out two fishing poles.

"'You two can take these and go down to the pond. It's behind the barn. You'll need to snag a few grasshoppers as you go. I'll blow the truck horn when I'm ready.'" Henry repeated his dad's exact words. "That was one time I remember him smiling at us. It felt strange, like we'd earned something we weren't aware of. I never figured out why he sent us away. There were no fish in that pond."

"Did Grandpa Walker trade anything that you remember?" Ella asked.

"Yeah, we had green beans, potatoes, and corn. But he didn't have us help pick them. That's what was so strange." Henry removed his cap and scratched his head. "He didn't even ask if we caught any fish. Almost like he knew we wouldn't."

Madison glanced at him, but made no comment. She turned into the parking area in front of Jennings' store. Ella jumped out as soon as the wheels stopped rolling and ran into the arms of her lifelong friend, who had been waiting on the little porch.

Madison and Henry waited for a couple of minutes at the vehicle. Henry looked up toward the Walkers' property.

"That's the road up to the barn, isn't it?"

Madison nodded.

Jennings and Ella walked out to Madison.

"Thank you, Sheriff McKenzie. It's wonderful to see this young lady. I've wondered if I'd live long enough to ever hug her again."

"It was time, Mr. Sanders." Henry held out his hand, saying, "I remember you. I'm Henry Jacobs, Hiram Jacobs' son. I bet you remember my old man."

"Why, yes, Henry; I do! And I remember that he had two boys. You'd be the youngest. Am I right?"

"Yes, Sir. My older brother Russell lives in Arizonian."

"Good to see you've grown into such a fine man. You were a scrawny kid. You still farming the old place?"

"Yes, I am. And I have four boys to help me," Henry sounded proud of his children. "And a girl on the way, any day now."

"Congratulations. It's nice to have a big family," Jennings said.

"Is the missus home today?" Madison asked.

"No, she's over in Asheville again. Spends a lot of time there, with the grandchildren."

Ella spoke up, "Aw, I'd hoped I could see her too."

"She's been up there since the weekend; don't stay around here much these days. She knows winter's coming and she can't get across that mountain, so she goes whenever she can."

Ella looked toward the dirt road, realizing how close she was to home. "It's just up that road, three-quarters of a mile. I remember every inch of that mountain."

"Let me put a note on the door and I'll ride up there with you," Jennings said.

Madison drove slowly up the rutted drive, not much better than a wide path. "Looks like that last storm left its mark on this road. I don't remember the ruts being this deep."

"Never seen it rain any harder than it did last week. I tell you, this looked more like a river than a driveway. Worried me; I thought it was going to wash my store away!" Jennings recalled.

Madison turned at the end of the garden space and parked on a level spot where there was no grass. Ella stared at the house. Her eyes clouded and she swallowed hard. She put her hand on the door handle, then withdrew it.

"I thought I was ready. Now I'm not so sure." Ella's voice sounded shaky.

Madison stayed still, as did Henry. Jennings opened the driver's side back door and climbed out, walking around to Ella's side. He stood there patiently, waiting to see if she was actually going to get out.

"You don't have to go in the house, you know," Mr. Sanders offered.

"Yes, I do. Um, it will take me a minute," she said in a low voice.

"Take your time, Sweetie. No one's in a hurry." Jennings leaned against the SUV and folded his arms, whistling a soft tune.

"I remember that tune," Ella said. "Daddy learned it from you. He used to whistle all the time, when we were outside. Grandma didn't like him whistling indoors. Mom thought it was funny how he'd start a turn the minute he stepped outside. They laughed a lot, Mom and Dad did."

"They were one of the happiest couples I ever knew. No doubt, they were in love. It showed in their faces, and I never knew of them sharing a harsh word with each other—or anybody else. They were good people. All the Walkers were, and your mom fit into that family like she was special made for your dad," Jennings wiped his face with the sleeve of his shirt.

Ella opened her door and stepped out.

Madison felt as though she was glued to the seat. She could not move. She sat motionless, watching with Henry as Ella and Jennings walked hand in hand to the kitchen door. They didn't open the door at first; Jennings pointed to a hill behind the house, at a single oak tree in a fenced area on the rise.

"Must be where her folks are buried," Madison finally said. "I didn't notice it when I was here before." She still made no move to get out of the vehicle.

A cold chill ran down her back as Madison watched Ella's hand settle on the door knob. She turned it slowly and pushed the door inward. It seemed like an eternity before Ella moved her feet and stepped into the house, out of Madison's sight.

She and Henry sat in silence for a long time.

Finally, Henry said, "How about if I check out the barn? Maybe I'll even find an old bottle of 'shine my dad made."

"Yeah, sure. Whatever you want to do, Henry. I'm feeling odd, like I'd intrude if I go up to the house. You know?"

"Sure, Maddy. Just sit and wait, if you want. Or come to the barn with me. Maybe we can find that fishless pond." Henry laughed and opened his door.

"Think I'll just wait, but you go ahead," Madison's gaze stayed locked in the direction of the back door. "I might walk with her, if she goes up to the cemetery. Otherwise, I'll be right here."

Henry crossed the yard to the barn. Madison could not believe the feeling of loneliness she'd experienced since they arrived. It wasn't exactly loneliness; it was more of a dread. But why was she feeling this? She fully intended to help these kids, now adults, but how? *Maybe that's the dread.* She realized what they might need to go through in order to prove the case in court—if only she could find the evidence she suspected might still be in the house.

Her phone vibrated, startling Madison. She'd forgotten she turned the ringer off. "Hey, Rick," she answered.

"Hey. Where's my girl?"

"I'm up on Walkers' Mountain. Ella was ready to visit. Mr. Sanders is with her in the house. I'm still in the car," she said.

"I'm on my way up. Do I turn left in front of the store?" Rick sounded confused about which road to take.

"I didn't know you were coming. Why didn't you tell me?"

"I tried, but your phone went to voicemail. I guess now that you're up on the mountain, you get a signal."

"Maybe. OK, you see the rutted dirt road on the left?"

"I don't call that a road. Looks like a path for off-road vehicles. Is that the one you're talking about?" Rick chuckled.

"That's the one," Maddy realized her heart was beating quickly. "I'm so glad you're on the way. I really need some backup here."

"Is everything OK?"

"It will be, when you put your arms around me." She let out a sigh. "I don't know what has come over me. I feel weird today. Thank you for coming! Oh, how did you know I needed you?"

"That's what I'm supposed to do, right? Anticipate what you need and want." His voice was comforting.

"OK... I guess; I mean, if you say so." She looked behind her just in time to see a typical black SUV come out of the woods, which meant TBI Agent Rick Malone was on the scene.

He stopped the truck next to her and got out, stretched as though he'd had a long drive, then strolled over to her door. "My lady, are you going to get out, or do I hug you through the window?"

Her hand was already on the handle. Rick pulled the car door open, and she sprang into his arms, clinging like nothing could peel her away. "Am I ever glad you're here?"

"Wow; me too, when you greet me like that!" He kissed her neck, then pulled back to look into her eyes. "Honey, are you sure nothing happened?"

Maddy shook her head and tears flooded down her cheeks. "Nothing, really; I don't know if I have ever felt this mood before. It scared me, and I felt pure dread at the same time. I don't understand what it is."

Rick stared into her face for a while and then said, "You know why I'm here, don't you?"

"No."

"We need to process the house. I talked with the parole board today. If we can come up with his DNA inside, they won't release him yet. We've got to do it! That guy is still dangerous to the kids—well, the survivors. The story was all over the Nashville news this week. I'm sure if Watts didn't know before, he knows now that there were witnesses. We can't let him go free. He'd head straight for them." Rick slipped one arm along Maddy's shoulders. "We need to go in there to keep her from touching anything."

"Oh! Yes, we do. Did you bring a kit?" Then she laughed, "Of course you did, you were going in there even before you knew we were here."

He gave her that adoring smile she'd seen for the first time so many years ago, when they'd met in Shirley's Restaurant. It seemed like another lifetime ago. She'd come so far since that spring day, and she felt thankful he'd stayed in her life. Chills ran up her back just as they had when he'd touched her hand during their introduction. She was so in love with Rick at this very moment that she knew she'd never let him go. And she felt pretty darn sure he felt the same. That's what made the two of them so special.

"Shall we go, Partner?" Rick squeezed her close to his side and they walked together toward the house.

When they reached the kitchen door, Jennings and Ella were coming out.

"Look who I found," Madison said. "Ella, Jennings Sanders, this is TBI Agent Rick Malone, better known as my fiancé."

"I'm pleased to meet you, Agent Malone," Jennings offered his hand.

Rick gave him a brisk handshake. "It's my pleasure, Mr. Sanders. And please, call me Rick."

"And you can call me Jennings; Mr. Sanders was my grandpa." He laughed.

"Ella, I am both pleased and saddened to meet you, considering your plight. Please accept my sincerest sympathies for what you still have ahead of you. You should never have had this much pain in your young years."

Ella stuck out her hand like the strong woman she was. "It's so nice meeting you, Rick. I feel as though I already know you, and Madison. You're one lucky man."

"Yes, I am lucky to have this lady. Thanks. I hope to make your life a lot easier, I give you my heart-felt word." He shook her hand gently and held it for a moment. "Did your sister come with you?"

"No, she checked into a hospital. I'm afraid she remembers more than I ever dreamed she might," Ella wiped her cheek, where a single tear had left its trace.

"I hope you didn't touch anything in the bedroom, where you hid as a child. I'm here to process the scene. I pray I'm not too late to find something," Rick said.

"No, I couldn't bring myself to even climb the stairs. But I'm glad you're here to do your job. If anyone can find DNA, I know you will. Madison has worked hard thus far to solve this mess; I'm glad to have you both on our side." She turned to Maddy. "We're going to visit the graves. You take as long as you need."

"Henry went to look through the barn. If he doesn't come back soon, we'll just blow the car horn when we're done. Right?" She and Ella laughed, thinking Henry might get into the stash of her grandpa's moonshine.

Jennings and Rick just stared, not knowing the inside joke Henry had told them about.

Rick climbed the steps first. He stopped at the door and knelt. "Maybe a prayer would be appropriate while we're in this position." He pulled Maddy close, and she dropped to her knees.

"I agree, but I didn't know you'd suggest it," she said in a soft voice.

Maddy closed her eyes and lowered her head. Rick followed her lead, holding her hand tightly. Neither one looked around when they each felt a hand on their shoulder. They were sure Henry had joined them.

Madison whispered, "Dear merciful Lord, we know you witnessed the horror this family experienced. Your guidance can connect the monster to the scene, and you will deal with him on your terms. If it would be your will, let this family have peace to live their remaining years without fear. Rick is your humble servant. We have faith that you'll guide him. I ask this in your precious name, Amen."

She opened her eyes to look into tear-filled eyes of the man she loved. She smiled but did not speak. Rick looked over his shoulder, but remained silent. He wiped away the moisture on his face, then focused his attention under the bed.

Madison pointed to the pallet of blankets and baby bottle, surrounded by boxes of fabric remnants with threads jutting out their tops.

"Jennings' wife cleans the floors every month," she began in a reverent tone. "But she has not cleaned under the bed. Jennings told me that."

"Yeah, there's not a speck of dirt or dust on the floor. I'm hoping, after listening to that recording, that I can find blood in the cracks between the boards," Rick whispered.

"You heard that recording?"

"And I watched it. Your friend, that professor, brought it to me. He feels that the mud she spoke of might have been blood, not mud at all."

"Oh, I hope that's right."

"Me too," Rick said, withdrawing a sprayer from the evidence kit. He proceeded to spray along the edges, where the bed skirt hung straight down from the box springs. Madison held the skirt up to allow the luminal mist to drift underneath the bed and onto the dusty surface. Rick shined a light to see if there was any tell-tale glow, but he could see none. He glanced at Maddy, his eyes narrowed. He sprayed the entire room from the doorway. Then he stood and shined the light, stepping where there was nothing lighting up. He entered the room, moving slowly toward the head of the bed.

"Nothing has been moved or rearranged?" He asked.

"No; according to Jennings, it's all exactly the same. He said his wife cleaned the muddy footprints by hand. And from then on, she just damp mops or dust mops the surfaces."

"I'd hoped she wasn't this thorough," Rick voice cracked. "There has to be…" he fell to his knees again. There, in front of the nightstand, was a glowing blue dot.

Rick smiled. "You can't hide from GOD!" he exclaimed, then he swabbed the area. He sprayed more luminal in front of the dresser, then went back to the nightstand, and under the edge of the bed. The light made small segments of the lines between the boards glow. "I think we need to remove these boards to get a good supply of DNA," Rick sounded as if he was talking to himself.

"Well, I got here just in time, then," Henry said from the doorway.

Rick turned to him with a puzzled look, "Just now, what about earlier?"

"Just walked up as you said that," Henry crossed his arms and leaned into the door frame. "I saw some tools in the barn, I'll go and get them." He bounded back down the stairs.

"It wasn't Henry. So, you felt her too?" Madison looked knowingly at Rick. "I felt her hand on my shoulder before I prayed."

"Yeah, so did I, but I was sure it was Henry."

"Rick, you've been touched by an angel," Madison smiled, "She's here with us: Grandma Walker. I saw her the first time I came. I might have been dreading her presence in the beginning, but since you're with me, I'm OK."

"Let's not tell Henry that I mistook an angel for him." Rick grinned and winked at his love.

Henry returned with a crowbar and a couple of saws, Jennings right behind him.

"Ella wants you to come to the graves. She asked me to offer my help here," Jennings said.

Madison looked at Rick.

"Sure, Henry and I can handle this. You stay with her," Rick smiled as he answered.

Madison joined Ella on the hill, where she knelt at her mother's grave. She still felt as though she might be intruding, but Ella quickly put that fear to rest.

"Madison, you would have loved my folks. They were happy, always happy. We never heard a cross word in our home. Grandma Walker used to shake her head and joke that they were not normal, but they were normal to us. We had a wonderful life." She stood, walking to the head of her grandma's grave. "She understood what we kids couldn't. We waited for Grandma to come and find us, hiding under her bed. She never came. The baby was wet and started crying. I needed to go so badly I couldn't hold it. I cried after I wet my panties. Macy hugged me when we got out from under the bed. She told me to go to our room and change my clothes while she cleaned up the baby. She was in a fog: moved without effort, just floated along like a feather. She didn't cry, even though she knew why no one came to find us. I didn't know. And when we walked out the front door, I thought we were doing something special. We had on our Sunday clothes and shoes. I stepped around mud puddles to keep my shoes clean as we walked down the lane to the Sanders' store. Mrs. Sanders cried after Macy talked to her. Jennings grabbed his rifle and drove his truck back up to our house. It was a long time before he returned. We were in bed asleep, but I woke up because I heard Mrs. Sanders crying again. Jennings left with some men, and they all carried rifles. I thought it was an odd time to go hunting."

Ella stood quietly for a while. She knelt at her daddy's grave and put her hand on the headstone shared by his wife. "One big heart; that's fitting for them. They were still so in love. I'm happy they went on the same day. Otherwise, the one left would have been sad."

"I'm sure they're together, in Heaven. That's the most important thought." Madison put her hand on Ella's shoulder. "I saw their photo at the store. Your mom was beautiful, and your dad so handsome. Do you know how much you resemble Grandma Walker? She was a lovely woman. Her hair was naturally curly, a dark, soft brown, like yours."

"You saw her," Ella stated.

"She's in the photo, with your folks."

"Her hair was already gray in that picture. You saw her, just like Mrs. Sanders does. I hoped I'd see her. Why couldn't I see my grandma's ghost?"

"I don't know what I saw. She looked like your grandma would have as a younger woman. That's why I noticed how much you look like her." Madison stepped back, feeling a presence. "If she wants you to, you will see her."

"I felt her near me in the house, but I just could not go upstairs. Jennings says he's never seen her." She cleared her throat. "And I know why Rick is here; he's going to look for DNA, isn't he?" Ella stepped closer to Madison.

"Yes. From the sound of Macy's nightmares, that man was in your grandma's room. She spoke of mud, dripping... What if it was blood? His blood? You both said you heard the shotgun. Maybe your grandma hit him. If his blood is still in that room, we can charge him with their murders and he will not get out of prison."

"He took Grandma's jewelry. The lid to the box was already broken; when he picked it up, the earrings fell out with the lid. Macy said she pushed one earring out from under the bed skirt to keep him from looking under the bed." She took a shaky breath and added, "She kept him from finding our hiding place."

Rick and Henry walked outside followed by Jennings, who stopped to lock the door. Each man carried a small piece of hardwood flooring. Rick waved to Madison and she waved back.

"Are you ready to go yet?" she asked Ella.

Ella turned back toward the graves and whispered something Madison could not hear, then they joined the men at the vehicles.

Henry rode back to Cold Creek with Rick so the girls could be alone. Ella might be more likely to talk to Madison with neither of the men listening. However, Ella was completely silent after they said goodbye to Jennings. Madison asked if she was feeling all right, but Ella said only that she was happy he'd been with her on her first trip home.

Madison noticed a tone of satisfaction in Ella's voice when she said the word *home.*

Is she truly thinking of making Walkers' Mountain her home again? Would Macy be comfortable returning? And will Macy's testimony be accepted now?

8

Back at Madison's cottage, Ella excused herself to the bedroom, saying she wanted to take a nap. Madison went outside to talk with Rick. He planned to take the boards to the TBI Lab in Knoxville, and told her he'd call her later in the evening. Henry waved goodbye as he drove away.

Madison sat on her new deck and Bud joined her. She sat quietly, petting his head and thinking over what happened at the Walkers' farm. She felt hopeful that Rick understood, and was anxious to talk to him about their experience.

Rick had not ever professed to be religious, but he understand the connection Maddy felt with her maker. He respected Jess and Shirley for their devotion to their church. As far as his own thoughts, Maddy had never pushed for answers. Not that it would change their feelings for each other, but it might be time to dig a bit deeper into his spirituality.

At the house on Walker Mountain, he had sensed the same spirit Madison often encountered. It was a calming touch: a knowing strength and kindness. He was curious, wanting to learn more, and hoped they could talk privately soon. For the time being, he had to make the trip back to the TBI Lab to get results on the materials collected. Madison's entire case against Watts hinged on DNA. Any relief for Macy depended on the DNA evidence. The Walkers' entire future was at stake. The story had been run in all the papers and on TV, so a person would have to be comatose—or as sharp as a bowling ball—not to realize there were witnesses to the murders. He would seek them out when released, and that time was growing near.

Having spent a few romantic moments with his fiancé, Rick drove out of Cold Creek and headed toward Asheville taking I-40 to Knoxville. The northern route along I-26 and I-81 is shorter, but due to road construction on the west-bound lanes, traffic backs up for miles. *At least at this time of year forty hasn't had any rockslides to cause a shutdown—so far,* he thought.

Rick darted into a Taco Bell drive-through right before the ramp to I-40. He loaded up on tacos, burritos, and a large Mountain Dew to sustain him for the drive.

Maybe when I retire I can get serious about eating right, and running with Bud and Maddy will get me in shape. Until then, this will have to do.

He reached the TBI Laboratory just ahead of sunset. To his surprise, Dr. Gerre Baker waited in his office.

"Dr. Baker, great to see you. What's going on with you?"

"I heard you have some intriguing evidence. I came to witness the DNA extraction," she shrugged her shoulders, "just in case there are questions."

"Ah, good idea. Thank you!" Rick kept walking right into the lab. "We've got to get this right, Gerre! Those kids' lives are at stake here."

"So you've met them?" she asked.

"Just the one, Ella. The older one is in a hospital in Florida. She checked herself in; must have heard about Watts. I think she's scared."

"I heard from one of the professors at UT that she is one messed up young lady. I hope this DNA shows up. I agree with you. We've got to get this right, for the girls."

"And their brother," Rick added.

"I wasn't aware there was a brother. Oh, wait a minute; yes, he was the baby. Of course," she helped Rick ready the samples of the wood flooring. "Are you ready?"

Back in Cold Creek, Maddy tapped on the door of the guest bedroom. "Aren't you hungry yet?"

Ella opened the door and walked into the hallway. "I sure am. How long have I been sleeping?"

"It's been a couple of hours. I guess you really needed that nap. We can go to the restaurant and see what their special is tonight."

"That's very convenient."

"Yeah, it is—and the best part is, my parents own the business," Madison smiled. "Their friends have leased it now, but I still eat for free. And my guest, of course!"

After introductions, Madison and Ella both decided on the veggie burger and sweet potato fries. It was clear to both that their tastes were similar; eating would never be a problem with these two.

Maddy's phone rang with a happy tune. "Oh, that's Holly's ringtone." She answered it and immediately a cold chill ran down her back. "We'll be right there! Did you call for an ambulance?" She jumped up and motioned for Ella to follow her. When they were out on the sidewalk, she covered the phone and whispered, "Holly needs us. She's in labor. I have to locate Henry. I need you to run to the doc's office," she pointed toward his building. "Tell him to meet us at the Jacobs' farm."

"Bud!" Madison called loudly, and he ran to her from his newly built dog house, next to the garage. "Load up!" She opened the back driver's side door of her SUV. She pressed Henry's number a second time, and it went straight to voicemail. "Henry! Holy needs you home, *now*," was the message she left.

She jumped into the driver's seat and started the engine just as Doc and Ella ran up to get in.

"What's happened?" Doc asked, as he jumped into the back with Bud.

"Holly's in labor, and the pains are close. I can't get hold of Henry." Maddy backed out of the drive with a jolt and gunned the accelerator, aiming toward the Jacobs property. As she neared the old sawmill, she noticed Henry's truck was parked in front.

She slid to a stop and sounded her horn. Henry ran out from around back, his arm wrapped in a dirty-looking rag. He cried, "What's going on?!"

"Holly needs us, she's in labor. Why haven't you answered your phone?"

"I dropped it into the saw; it's in a couple pieces, and I got cut on the blade when I tried to get it," Henry supported his right arm with his left. Blood dripped from the rag.

"Here, Henry, let me see that cut." Doc was already out of the vehicle and pulled the rag away from the injury.

Madison jumped out too and supplied a white towel to replace the germ-filled greasy rag. "This has to be cleaner than that old thing."

"He needs stitches; might have nicked the ulnar artery. That's a lot of blood." Doc wrapped the towel around Henry's forearm tightly, holding pressure with both hands. "When did this happen?"

"I was running the saw and heard Madison's ringtone just as I powered it down. When I heard it a second time, I didn't wait for the saw to spool down, I tried to grab my phone. I knew if Maddy called twice it was urgent."

"That's been about seven minutes," Madison said, looking at her phone.

"Talk about timing! Henry, this is not good!" Doc pushed him toward his truck. "Key?"

Henry answered with a nod of his head toward the truck. Doc loaded the man in the passenger side. "You two go on to Holly. I'm taking this guy to my office before he bleeds out."

As Doc gunned the engine, Madison and Ella heard Henry's objection over the roar of the truck. They got in Madison's SUV and raced toward the Jacob's house.

Holly was in the living room, lying on the sofa. The twins were huddled around her head. Maddy told the boys to go with Ella into the kitchen, to get a glass of water for their mom. Ella grasped their small hands and led them away.

"They can have an ice cream sandwich if they want it, Ella," Holly called, glad she'd thought of a reason to keep them in the kitchen for a few minutes.

"How are you, Mommy?" Maddy knelt next to her friend.

"Too close for comfort. My water broke, so I came straight to the sofa. The boys brought me a sheet in case I was cold."

"Good idea. Well, Girl, it's just the two of us. Can you do this?" Maddy pushed Holly's feet up close to her hips and tented the sheet over her knees.

"Absolutely; I'm an Appalachian wo-o-ooo," she began, breathing quickly, and squeezed Maddy's hand.

"Remember your breathing from Lamaze."

Henry had not been able to attend the meetings in Erwin, so Madison was Holly's coach for the natural birth classes. "How long has it been since your last contraction?"

"Not long," Holly could barely speak between breaths. "We're close!"

"You'll be fine! I know we're strong Appalachian women. We've delivered babies at home for centuries!"

"Too bad I don't have vegetables to pick. I'd just go straight to the garden when we're done here," she declared, then let out her signature laugh.

"Yep, we'll be just fine delivering my namesake," Madison peeked under the tent to see how far her friend was dilated. "She's crowning! The next contraction, you can push."

"Get ready! Here it comes." Holly squealed with excitement, or pain. It was difficult to tell.

Ella rushed in with a hand full of clean dish towels. "The boys are on the porch feeding ice cream to Bud and Bear, hope that's okay."

"Sure, as long as it's not chocolate!" Madison grabbed one of the towels. "Great thinking, Ella. Have you done this before?"

"No, but I read a lot." She had brought one wet towel for Holly's head. "Want this?"

Holly smiled and went immediately into another contraction.

"Push," Ella said softly, and bent to place the cooling cloth on Holly's head.

Madison grabbed a second towel and said, "Oh, my goodness; she is a big baby!" She wrapped the towels tightly around little Maddie and carefully placed her on Holly's breast. "And she's beautiful, too!"

"Oh, she is!" Ella stepped back. "We need scissors."

"In the drawer of the end table…" Holly gasped, waving toward the table.

Madison pulled the small sewing scissors out, unwrapped them from their semi-sterile environment and clipped the cord, leaving it about six inches long. "Doc should be here in a few minutes; he can finish this." She laid a couple of the small towels between Holly's legs. "This will help save the sofa."

Holly admired her baby girl and checked all her fingers and toes. "She cried perfectly; I think her lungs are strong and clear. Should I try to nurse her?"

"Yes, if she will, that's good." Maddy sat on the floor. "When did you put this padding on the sofa? I just noticed it."

"I had a feeling I might need it. Like they said in those classes, you never know when the baby will come, so be ready." And she laughed again.

"This is amazing. I'm so happy we got here in time," Madison peeked under the sheet again. "Everything looks OK, but you might want to go to the hospital to be checked anyway."

Just then, Henry and Doc burst into the room. Henry had his arm in a sling, and a large white bandage encircled his forearm. "Is she all right?" He dropped to his knees next to his wife and baby.

"Doc, I cut the cord, everything else is your department," Madison stood up. "What was the verdict about his arm?"

"Deep, but no artery involved. Thank God." He looked around the room.

"I'll carry her to the bedroom," Henry said, then started to lift his wife.

"No! You'll bust those stitches! I'll carry Momma and baby!" Doc grabbed Henry's shoulder. "Move aside, Daddy."

"I'll take the baby," Madison spoke up, "She'll need washing."

"This way, Doc." Henry led them to the bedroom off the main hallway. "We've set up the nursery in here."

He opened the door, turned down the bed and laid an absorbent pad across the mattress where Doc was about to put his wife. "What else do we need?"

"Just give me a few minutes to check her, and then I'll bathe the baby," Dr. Chip announced. "Maddy, you fix the bath water. I'm sure Henry can show you where everything is."

"It's all set out and ready in this bathroom," Holly said, pointing. "I just knew, so I was prepared."

"You're amazing, Holly!" Ella peeked around the doorframe. "This is exciting!"

While the doctor took care of his new patient, Maddy and Henry made sure that Little Maddie's first bath was perfect. Holly had a special tub that fit into the sink, lined with a cushioning towel to set her tender bottom on. Everything looked straight out of *Parents* magazine.

"She's going to enjoy this little girl so much!" Madison said. She turned to look at Henry, who had perched on the bathtub. "How's your arm feeling?"

"Numb, weirdly numb. I dread the waking up part. He did a lot of sewing."

"You were really lucky it wasn't worse. Does that make you think about what could have happened? Because it should! You don't need to take unnecessary chances, Henry. There are so many people depending on you..."

"I know, Madison! And I realize this was stupid. The first thing I thought of was Holly!"

"I didn't mean to fuss. We all need you, Henry. You're our rock!" Madison bent to hug her best friend's husband. "And we all love you!"

Doc entered with Little Maddie, screaming at the top of her tiny lungs. "She's all clear, that's for certain! But just the same, I want you to make sure she sees her pediatrician as soon as you can get in with them."

"I'll call them first thing tomorrow," Henry said, then stood up. "Can I do anything?"

"I'm going to stay with Holly. The boys will be coming in any time now, after hearing that crying," Madison said. "Holly, where are the other two boys?" She realized Nicholas and Robbie weren't in the house.

"I'd better go and check on them," Henry said, as he came out of the bathroom. "They're supposed to be cleaning out the stables. Gosh, I forgot all about them!"

"Can I go with you, Henry?" Ella asked.

"Sure," he answered, as he went onto the back porch.

The twins were cleaning up the mess from the dogs' ice cream treat. "We cleaned it all up!" Hugh stopped, looking up at his daddy's arm. "What's that?"

"I got a little cut, and Doc had to patch me up. Thanks for taking good care of your mom and then feeding the dogs. Now, let's go and check the stables."

Ella, Henry, and the twins walked toward the barn.

Inside the stables sat the two newly adopted brothers, reunited after a couple of years of separation. They did everything together on the weekends, because they attended separate schools. Nicholas jumped to his feet when Henry walked into the stable.

"How's Mommy?" he asked and then looked at Henry's arm. "What happened?" He ran to Henry's side.

"Mommy is fine, and so is your baby sister, Maddie. As for this, it's just a scratch. Doc had to stitch me up after I tangled with the saw blade. Don't you worry about me. What's keeping you two up here?"

"Tipsy is having her puppies," Robbie said.

"No, not puppies; she's a cat. Cats have kittens, silly." Nicholas ruffed up his little brother's hair. "She has five now, but I think there are more. She's still got lumps in her belly," Nick knelt next to a box filled with straw. "What happens if she has more than six? There are only six teats."

"I hope she doesn't have more, but I'm sure she'll figure something out. Let's see what the kits look like," Henry bent to pick up a couple of the babies. "They all look healthy; these two are boys."

"Aw, they're so cute," Ella touched one of the newborn kittens gently. "I'll need one for the farm. I saw a couple of mouse signs when we were there. We always had cats in the barn and out buildings. Henry, can I have one of them?"

"You can have as many as you want!" he said, then added, "Here comes another."

The excitement of the new kittens had kept the boys entertained long enough to keep them out of the house while their new sister was born. But now it was time to get baths and into bed. Delivering kittens and a baby was a lot to take in for one day.

Madison and Ella were late returning to town, but it had been worth it. Henry convinced Ella that she needed two kittens, to keep each other company. Everyone was doing fine, and they'd all earned a good night's sleep.

"I'd better call Rick. You go ahead and shower—" Then Madison laughed. "I'm not used to having an extra bathroom. I'll be upstairs. Come on up if you like."

"Thanks, but I want to shower and get to bed. I'm really sleepy. I'll see you in the morning, Maddy," she walked down the hall before turning around, "You are such a dear friend, Maddy. I'm happy you and I met."

"Me too, Ella. And I'm looking forward to meeting your sister. If you talk to her, be sure to tell her I said hello."

Madison rang Rick's cell. It went to voice mail, so she left a short message. "If you call back before midnight I might still be up, but any later, just wait and call tomorrow. I'm getting out early to visit Holly and her new baby. We delivered her at home; she got out of there in a hurry." Madison laughed and hung up the phone. She stepped into the shower and enjoyed the double waterfall heads beating onto her tired body. Quickly washing and rinsing her hair, Madison stepped out onto the bath mat, thinking of how life was going to be when she and Rick were married. Besides the excitement of living with the man she loved, she worried. Would she feel comfortable with him?

Of course you will, silly; it's Rick, after all. He's the only man you'd ever feel comfortable with.

77

Just at that moment, her phone rang. She grabbed it and dropped onto her bed. "Hello."

"Hey, Babe. You weren't sleeping, were you?"

"No, just stepped out of the shower," she said with a deep breath. "I delivered my namesake this evening."

"I heard your message. How are they?" Rick asked.

"Fine. Both are going to see a doctor in Johnson City tomorrow. But Chip pronounced all of them well. He even put twenty-two sutures in Henry's arm, after he cut it on a saw. And Nicholas and Robbie delivered six kittens!" Madison took a breath.

"Gee, everything happened all at the same time, huh?" He paused for a moment and then said, "How are you?"

"I'm fine...excited, but tired now. It's been a busy day."

"We don't have any news yet. The lab has to do this by the book. We can't afford a slip up for Ella's sake, and Macy's. We're getting close to the parole hearing date," he let out a loud sigh. "How is Ella?"

"She's okay. She was with me today. I think she's already chosen one of the kittens to take to her house. I told her she ought to have two, because one will be lonely."

"Is she thinking of moving into the house?"

"Yes, but not right away. I'm sure she'll wait 'til her sister can be with her."

"She should. I don't think it's a good idea to make a rush decision," Rick said.

"I don't think she will. I let her know she's welcome to stay here as long as necessary."

"Not after we're married. At least I hope not," he laughed.

"No, of course not, but until we get back from our honeymoon, maybe?"

"We'll see." Rick yawned.

"Are you sleeping?" Madison sounded as if she expected his answer to be no.

"As well as I always do," he said.

"Meaning no. You never get enough restful sleep! What am I going to do with you?"

"Marry me?" he suggested sheepishly.

Madison glanced at the clock and saw it was after 1:00 a.m. when she put her cell phone down. She turned out the lights and fluffed her favorite pillow. After the events of the day, she hoped she could fall into a restful sleep right away.

Everything that had happened that day replayed in her mind. Questions continued running in and out of her thoughts. *Will the lab find DNA? Will it be enough to hold Watts over for a hearing? Will he confess when confronted with DNA evidence? When will Ella and Macy be safe? How long will this process hold up their lives? If only...*

9

Madison's phone rang, and she felt like she'd just fallen asleep. She looked at her phone to see that it was Professor Welty at UT.

"Good morning." She tried not to sound as though he'd wakened her.

"Sorry to wake you this early. I have a very busy day. Between students and our faculty meeting, this was my only chance. Can you spare a couple minutes?" Professor Welty asked.

"Sure!" She slid out of bed, carrying her phone to the bathroom. "I'm all ears, what's up?"

Dr. Welty delved into a conversation he'd had with Dr. Sharon Ott, a former colleague of his. She was a doctor of psychology at LMU, he explained.

Madison remembered Ms. Ott from her junior year at UT. Ott was famous all over the US for her research in brain trauma, and not always from an injury. It was her discovery that defined mental trauma in both physically and mentally abused patients. One young man who was a patient of hers had witnessed his parents' deaths at the hands of an intruder, much like the trauma Macy had gone through. The boy became mute immediately after witnessing the event. He had run out the back door and escaped the slaughter. His two sisters were not so fortunate.

It was days before a neighbor found the boy hiding in his tool shed. He had been living on apples from a tree just outside the building. Coming out only at night, he'd loaded up a half bushel of apples as a stockpile. When the sprinkler system came on at 3:00 a.m. he'd caught water in a bucket for drinking. Luckily for the boy, the neighbor had discovered a pile of apple cores outside the window and investigated to see what varmint was devouring so many of his apples. The small boy was asleep on a pile of tarpaulins. He didn't say a word when his neighbor asked him why he was hiding. Fear of getting caught by the intruder sealed the boy's lips.

Dr. Ott was able to break through the barrier of the brain's defense mechanism. Not only did the boy speak again, he also identified the intruder who committed the four murders of his family.

That was only one of the numerous cases Dr. Sharon Ott had succeeded in cracking. She and Dr. Welty felt there was a hidden trauma in Macy's case, like all the others, and Sharon wanted to meet with Macy to draw out the whole story.

Dr. Welty finished his explanation with, "I mean, yeah, she's been through a lot of trauma. That's for sure, but Sharon feels it is more personal. That's why she's flying down to Florida to see Macy. I thought we should let you know."

"I was impressed with Dr. Ott, and I'm happy she's interested in this case. Is it OK if I tell her sister?"

"You've been in touch with her recently?" Dr. Welty asked.

"Yes. She's here with me, in Cold Creek."

"Very good; then surely you should tell her. Let me know if she has any input in the matter." With that, Dr. Welty bid her good day and ended the call.

Madison came out of the bathroom just as Ella knocked on her bedroom door.

"You awake in there?"

Maddy opened the door. The aroma of coffee wafted to her nose. "I am now! That coffee smells amazing!"

Ella carried a tray with two mugs, a carafe of coffee, creamer, and sugar. She set it on a small table in the sitting area.

"I thought I heard you up and I didn't want to drink my coffee alone." Ella sat down and then filled the mugs. She put one sugar in hers and creamer. Then she passed the creamer to Maddy.

"Thank you for making coffee. That's so thoughtful." She sat and stirred creamer into her steaming mug. "I was on the phone with Dr. Welty, at UT. I told you about him, right?"

"Yes, I remember; you sent him a copy of the recording of Macy," she leaned back into the comfort of the bedroom chair.

"He's consulted with Dr. Sharon Ott, at LMU. She is famous for—"

"Yes, I've read about her. She's the one I tried to have Macy's doctor talk to. But he said she was just a charlatan, and in the practice for money only. I didn't think she was like that from the lectures I attended. I wanted to talk to her myself, but never could get close to her." She sipped her coffee quickly. "What did she say?"

"She's flying out to visit with Macy right away; in fact, she might already be on her way. Dr. Welty wanted me to tell you that he'll be in touch." Madison was relieved that Ella already knew Dr. Ott's name and was familiar with her work.

"I'm going to call Macy, right now," she glanced at her watch. "Or maybe I'd better wait a while. Macy sleeps late, if she can sleep at all."

"Do you call straight to her room?"

"No, I have the nurse on duty relay a message, and she calls me back when she's not in a session or eating her meals. That's what I'll do, just give them a message to have her call me when she awakens." Ella stood up and went to get her phone from downstairs.

Madison quickly dressed and looked to see where Bud was. She'd heard him slip out the door earlier while she was in the bathroom. Maybe Ella had let him out.

The early morning air had a sharp edge, even though it was sunny with clear blue skies. The patio was wet with dew or overnight rain. She called out his name and Bud came running from behind the restaurant.

"Hey Bud, how's your girlfriend?" She ruffled the hair on his neck and gave him a hug. "Is Shirley up yet?"

Shirley, the stray turned mascot for Shirley's restaurant was a late sleeper— unlike Bud, who woke at the crack of dawn.

Madison shivered, with her arms bare, and went back into the house. "I think winter is close. The temperature has dropped at least ten degrees from yesterday." Maddy pulled a long-sleeved black button-up over her T-shirt.

"I'm excited to feel some cold air. I hated the temperature in Florida: muggy year round, hot or hotter." Ella cracked an egg, dropping it into a sizzling skillet. "You want a fried egg or two? I cut up the leftover baked potatoes and have them in the other pan heating with some onions. Do you like them that way?"

"I sure do. I'll put some toast in. You want jelly?" She opened the fridge.

Ella cracked two more eggs and nodded as she glanced at Maddy.

It didn't take long to eat and clean up the dishes. Maddy walked to her office to check any messages on the sheriff's phone. Ella promised to come as soon as she heard from Macy.

Madison returned some calls and wrote out a check to Mr. Olsen's Hardware. She walked next door to deliver payment for the office account. Mr. Olsen greeted her with a big smile, showing her a photo of his grandbaby.

"We got this in yesterday's mail. She just had her seventh birthday. The missus is chomping at the bit for us to drive down to visit." He stared at the photo when Madison handed it back.

"I think you should, Mr. Olsen. Mrs. O always goes by herself. You haven't been down but one time to see that precious little girl."

"What about my business?" He looked at the photo again. "Folks need me here."

"Well, I have a thought about that. Let me talk to Ella. She might be willing to keep the store open a few hours a day. Once the townspeople know the new hours, they'll come at that time."

"You think she would be interested?" he asked.

"She might; can't hurt to ask."

Madison returned to her office just as Ella came out of the cottage.

"Did you talk with her?"

"Yes, and she was very excited to hear she's going to have company,"

"That's great. Have a seat, I have something to discuss with you," Madison sat at her desk.

Ella seated herself across from the sheriff. "What's up?"

"Mr. and Mrs. Olsen have a granddaughter, seven years old, and Mr. O has only been to visit her one time. Because of the store, Mrs. O always has to go by herself. I told him I think he needs to go see them for Thanksgiving, while their granddaughter is out of school for a few days. He never wants to leave the store closed up and inconvenience the townspeople. In past years, Holly used to come to town and open the store for him. She's really busy these days; with all the boys and now the new baby, it's out of the question." Madison stopped to get her breath.

"I used to manage a store, a Seven-Eleven. I worked the morning shift and had a helper for the late-night shift. I enjoyed it. I like talking to people, and helping them with what they need. I always thought it was a menial position, but in the case of Mr. Olsen's store, it's very important to the town. Do you think he might trust me to work for him?"

"Why don't you walk next door and talk to him?" Madison suggested.

"I'll do that. Right now, if you think it's a good time?"

Madison nodded and answered her cellphone. "Hello?"

Ella walked into Olsen's Hardware and introduced herself.

Mr. Olsen greeted her with a hug. "I know who you are. Honey, I am so terribly sorry to know your story. I hope Rick can find the necessary evidence to hang that S.O.B. high as the rafters."

"Me too, Mr. Olsen, me too." Ella walked past the counter and looked at the store shelves. "You sell just about everything in here, don't you?"

"Yes, I try to keep whatever the folks need to save them a trip into town."

"I managed a seven-Eleven in Florida. It's a convenience store, you know?"

"Yeah, like the Roadrunner Markets around here. I'm familiar with them," Mr. Olsen followed Ella around the store as she looked over the shelves.

"They sold out to some guy from India, and he didn't want me to work there anymore. I hated to leave, but I've never had trouble finding a job. I like to work. And I agree with Maddy; you should go to your daughter's for Thanksgiving. I'd be happy to keep your store open for you. That's a good way for me to get to know everyone in town. And I promise I'm honest."

"I know you are, Ella. I knew your grandpa, very well. It pained me when he died. He'd been here just the day before. Such a shame; he was a wonderful man." Mr. Olsen wiped his eyes with his handkerchief. "You must have been a baby."

"I was, just a few months old. But Grandma told us all about him. I miss her so much."

"I never met your grandma, but I know she was a good woman. It was a tragedy to lose her and your folks the way you did. I'm so sorry for the pain you've had."

"I'm a survivor, Mr. Olsen. I'm OK. I just want to help Sherriff McKenzie get the devil who did it. Maybe my sister could live in peace again, if he's punished."

"Why don't you spend the day with me and learn how I do things? If you're sure you have the spare time, I'll let our folks know that you'll be helping out. You tell me the hours you want to work." He smiled as though he really was pleased that she agreed to work for him. "I pay well too. I'm no cheapskate."

"It doesn't matter. I'll take whatever you offer. I should give it to Maddy for room and board."

"I doubt she'd take it." He scratched his head. "Say, I've got a room upstairs. Has a bed and a refrigerator in it. You might want to think of taking it for your time here in Cold Creek. Sometimes Rick sleeps up there when he's in town. But now, with their addition, I recon he's going to sleep in that new bedroom. Go up and take a look, if you'd like."

"I think I will. I feel so in the way at Madison's, especially when Rick is here. And I know they're getting married in January. If I haven't moved into my farm house, I'd need it for a while. Would that be OK?"

"Sure, no one needs it now. Our son used it when he came home from college. He's married now and living off on his own in Montana."

Ella climbed the stairs to check out the room overlooking the street. She examined the bed, a queen-size, with what looked to be a brand-new mattress. The refrigerator was an old style, maybe from the early days of the store. The room had plenty of space to add a chest of drawers and maybe a table and chairs. She noticed there was a wall AC unit, and it had a reverse cycle for heat as well. The door next to the entry turned out to be a small bathroom. A small shower stall, sink, and toilet were obviously from a camper. She liked the sink; shaped like a clam shell, it reminded her of the one she had at her place in FL.

She bounced back down the stairs. "I'll take it, Mr. Olsen. Do you mind if I add a chest of drawers?"

"Oh, don't go and buy one. I have a chest and a dresser at home. It used to be my daughter's. We turned her room into a den, but I never got rid of the furniture. I had it made for her out of cedar. She loved the smell of cedar. I'll bring it over, soon as I can get someone to give me a hand."

Ella stayed all day to watch everything Mr. Olsen did. She was a quick learner and he never had to show her a thing twice. They hit it off like family, making Ella feel she was needed. She met Mrs. O and loved her instantly. She reminded Ella so much of her own mother.

By the time she and Maddy talked that evening, Ella almost dreaded telling her that she was going to move into the room over Mr. Olsen's store.

Madison dreaded telling Ella the disappointing news Rick had given her earlier in the day. She would wait as long as she could, she decided.

The two women walked across the street to Shirley's restaurant for supper. Much to Madison's surprise, there sat Shirley and Jess at the counter. She rushed over to hug her parents.

"When did you get home?" Maddy squeezed her dad.

"Just a while ago. We caught an early flight, and didn't tell you because we wanted to surprise you." Jess stood up. The two embraced in a long hug. "We've missed you so much. It seems like coming home is the happiest part of our trips now."

"Are you sure it was just to surprise me? I mean, there's nothing wrong, is there?" Maddy threw her arms around Shirley. "You aren't feeling bad, are you?"

"No, Sweetie, we just had a chance to arrive early, that's all," Shirley kissed Maddy on the cheek. "No need to worry, just because we miss home and our little girl."

"Where are my manners?" Madison turned around and motioned to Ella, "Come here, meet my parents."

Ella moved slowly toward them. "Hi, I'm happy you're home. I'm Ella Walker." She extended her hand to Shirley first.

"You certainly are!" Jess boasted. "You look just like your grandmother. And she was a beautiful woman." Jess hugged Ella.

"You knew my family?" Ella looked up with wanting eyes and said, "You're the Jess my papa knew?"

"Yes, he and I were friends. You were a baby then."

"Yes, I was. My grandma talked about how everyone loved him, and she talked about you. She thought you were a good influence. I think Papa liked to drink 'shine."

"We all did. But your papa knew when to stop. He was a good man, and his passing a great loss to all who knew him." Jess turned to Maddy, "I'm grateful that you've taken a stand against Watts. There was a time that the Walkers' friends wanted to take matters into their own hands. We knew the law stopped short of justice."

"But that's about to change, isn't it Maddy?" Ella hooked arms with her friend, the Sherriff.

Madison dropped her head, "I need to tell you something about that. Rick called this morning." She turned and walked to a table as far across the room as possible. She waved for her folks and Ella to join her.

During a round of sweet and one unsweet tea, Maddy told the disappointing story of the DNA results. It was inconclusive, due to the mixture of Murphy's Oil Soap and years of mopping, and maybe even a dose of bleach water.

Ella propped her head in her hands. At first she didn't believe, but then she said, "We had such high hopes, and now we have nothing."

"Don't say that, Ella. You still have the evidence gathered at the time, and an eye witness the court can't deny this time. Don't give up now. Macy has suffered too much, for too long. Keep the faith, please. Never give up!" Jess placed his large hand on Ella's arm.

Ella nodded, but said nothing.

Madison began, "Do you remember the doctor at LMU who did the work on trauma therapy? Her name is Sharon Ott." She looked at Jess.

"I remember that name," he recalled.

"She's in Florida to talk with Macy. When Ella made the video, I sent it to Dr. Welty at UT, who then shared it with Ott. They both feel there is more to Macy's experience than we know. She plans on trying to learn what it is, if Macy responds."

"Oh, I haven't told you what Macy said when she called me back this morning," Ella raised her head. "She had read an article about Dr. Ott and was eager to talk with her. I think they're meeting in the morning."

"That sounds promising," Shirley encouraged. "Let's not rush to conclusions yet. This investigation has just begun."

Ella smiled at Shirley and nodded her head. "Thank you; someone needs to keep me on task." Then she added, "Oh, I have some news—good news, I believe." She wiped her eyes on the table napkin and continued, "Mr. and Mrs. Olsen are going to visit their daughter and her family for Thanksgiving."

"Oh good, so that's why you stayed over there all day. You learned the ropes." Madison felt a cloud lifting, "And you are the reason he can leave town."

"Yep, and there's more. I'm going to move into the room over the store. That way with them out of town, Mr. Olsen will feel more secure with me there. I like the privacy of that room, and it's cozy. Besides, I'll be out of your guest bedroom."

"I've made you feel uncomfortable?" Maddy felt hurt. "I'm sorry, I just wanted you to be close."

"And I will be. I know that when Rick is in town, you sleep in your own room. You said it yourself, the first night I arrived, that you'd never slept in the new bedroom. I'll still be close. And you are the one who said Mr. Olsen needed to get away, so now he can. I'll be doing what I can for Cold Creek, while I wait." Ella sat back in her chair.

Their meal arrived and the conversation changed to food. The spread on the table was family style, specially prepared for Shirley's family. After all, her restaurant, her namesake had been her life. And even though she and Jess had taken an indefinite vacation, it was still hers.

Mr. Olsen came in and Jess pulled another chair up to the table, insisting that he join them. There was obviously plenty of food. It wasn't long until Rick joined them also. He was worried that Madison would be depressed about the DNA, so he surprised her too.

Rick pulled up a chair, turning the back toward the table to sit straddling the seat.

"You don't pass a single Cracker Barrel on the way here; you have to be hungry!" Maddy put her hand on Rick's.

"I did pass two Cracker Barrels, but I didn't stop!" He tried to defend himself.

"Then turn that chair around and eat; you know you want to," Jess slapped Rick on the shoulder.

Once Rick joined the diners, he cleaned out all the bowls. Maddy and Ella began clearing the table and took their plates in the kitchen. Betty rushed over with a cart to help, but Maddy told her no, she could handle the dishes. Then she whispered something to Betty, who nodded with a big smile and returned through the swinging doors of the kitchen.

After supplying coffee cups and refilling tea glasses, Madison brought a fresh pot of special brew to the table. Betty showed up with an uncut carrot cake and dessert plates. She pulled a cake server from her apron pocket, handing it to Rick.

Rick's eyes widened, "That's carrot cake with cream cheese frosting! And it's all mine." He snickered, winking at Maddy.

"Here, Rick. Let me help you," Shirley reached for the serving tool.

"No, Mom, I got this!" He playfully pushed her hand away. "I'll give you the first piece."

Rick cut six slices, plopping each on a saucer, and passed them around the table. Carrot cake had always been his favorite, and Maddy never missed a chance to tempt him.

Ben and Margie joined the celebration but declined the cake offer. "No, Rick that is your gift for helping Ella. We all want justice for her family," Margie said.

"Yes, we do," Shirley added.

Jess stood and stretched his arms over his head. "Momma, you ready to walk home?"

"Yeah. I'm pretty tired, for sure. Now, with my belly full, it's time to turn in."

"It's closing time, anyway. I'm ready to get some shuteye," Jess said.

Shirley agreed, "I'm sure Ben and Margie are ready to lock up. We'll see you all for breakfast. Goodnight, all."

"Goodnight," the voices sounded in unison.

10

Ella met Mr. Olsen for breakfast at 7:15 the next morning. They were sitting at the counter, sipping coffee and laughing, when Jess and Shirley came in.

"Come and join us at a table," Jess suggested.

"We're going to the store early so I can show Ella the books." Mr. Olsen explained.

"Oh, yes; you have a really complicated system," Jess laughed.

Rick and Maddy came in and sat at the table with Shirley and Jess. Mr. O and Ella waved as they left the restaurant.

"I really didn't want Ella to overhear our conversation this morning anyway," Rick sat back in his chair when Betty came to take their order.

After being served coffee, Rick continued, "I don't want to give her false hopes with Dr. Ott's latest statement. Now that she's talked with Macy, she says the next step is to hypnotize her. The poor girl is so messed up with guilt, she doesn't even know why or what she's guilty of. Sharon is bringing her back to Knoxville. Macy asked that we not let Ella know yet."

"So, she's all for the idea of getting to the bottom of this nightmare," Jess leaned in closer.

"Yeah, she's carried this for nearly eighteen years. I'm surprised she didn't crack completely," Rick placed his hand on Maddy's. "There's a lot going on in that house. Maddy and I felt it."

"And I've seen it—her. The grandmother is still there," Madison wiped a tear from her cheek as she looked to Jess. "I didn't imagine it. You go there with me, and you'll see for yourself."

Jess stiffened and frowned at his daughter. "I don't want to go there."

Shirley said nothing, but the look on her face told Madison she'd said too much. Shirley didn't know about Jess's ability. After all, Jess was Madison's real father; that's how she had found peace with her gift. But to Jess, it was a curse; he hadn't told anyone but Maddy.

"Jess, I agree with Maddy. Just this once, you need to back her up," Rick put his arm around Maddy, kissing her on the forehead.

Shirley reached for her coffee, but her hand was shaking so badly she tipped it over, then hid her face in her hands. Jess consoled her while Betty quickly rushed in with a cloth to wipe up the spill.

"I'll get you another one, Shirley, don't worry about it," Betty said.

After Betty walked away, Jess whispered, "I'm sorry, Honey. I just could not bring myself to tell you. I have always tried to ignore the sense that I'm different. My own daughter embraces our ESP as a gift. I don't. It made me feel evil, and I wanted no part of it. But we don't choose to have the ability; it's just part of us for some reason."

"Dad, it's not a bad thing. I've helped many people with my foresight. Don't feel that way. I'm glad I am different." She reached out to touch Shirley's hand. "Please don't be upset. I'm the one who asked Jess not to tell anyone else." Maddy said.

"I'm not mad, Honey. I just feel like I've been shut out."

"We only wanted to keep you from having more to worry about," Jess added.

Shirley looked into his eyes, "I know; you've always tried to protect me, even when you realized you really were Maddy's father. I'm a big girl! I can handle the truth!"

"OK, Mom. From now on, you will be my sounding board on this kind of thing. I think your view will be better than Dad's most of the time, anyway," Maddy smiled across the table at Shirley.

"Promise?"

"Yes, we both do!" Madison looked to Jess, "Don't we?"

Jess nodded.

Betty returned with a big tray of food and the conversation lightened.

Meanwhile, in Knoxville at Tyson McGee Airport, Dr. Ott and Macy were met by Dr. Welty. The three drove to Dr. Welty's office, in the middle of UT's campus. Macy had begun to relax in the company of Dr. Ott, and since she was close friends or colleagues with Welty, Macy felt he was trustworthy too.

"Macy, this is your room. You are free to come and go as you wish. All I request is that you notify me or Sharon if you leave for any reason. Just settle in and make yourself at home. There are no cameras, no recording devices, and no two-way mirrors," Dr. Welty handed Macy a key on a key chain shaped like a glittery kitten. "The TV remote is on the table and there are several books in the cabinet, but the campus library is right there, across the courtyard," he pointed out the window.

"Show them your key and you can sign out any books you choose. We want you to feel at ease here. You have your phone?" He asked.

"Yes. Do you have my number?" Macy asked.

"Yes. I'll only call if I cannot find you, OK?" Dr. Welty smiled. "You have a small refrigerator. I've taken the liberty to put some bottled water in there, but you can add any drinks you prefer. Your meal ticket is on the table, and also an I.D. badge I want you to carry whenever you leave this room. You can get passage to any building with it. There is a small grocery section in the cafeteria, should you want to bring sandwiches or breakfast bars to the room. But you are here as my guest; you don't pay for anything. Do you understand?"

"Yes, thank you. Are you certain that no one else knows I'm here?"

"We've told no one, but you can be friends with the other residents and tell them as much as you feel comfortable letting them know. They are all medical students in some level of their education. No one else can get in the building. That's why you must use the I.D. badge at all times," Dr. Welty walked out the door. He turned to Dr. Ott, saying, "I'll be in my office."

"OK, I'll be in shortly," Sharon said.

Macy looked around, familiarizing herself with the room. She crossed the floor to the side with a small but full bathroom, peeking inside. She then opened a door next to the TV table and saw it was a closet, with plenty of clothes hangers. The white sheers across the window drifted with a slight gust of wind. She looked out, smiling at the sight of students below, milling around and heading in different directions. "Marian would feel happy here. She wanted to go to college. All her life, she's had to take care of me."

"Is there anything else you might need, Macy?" Sharon asked.

"Just my suitcase, I guess," she reached for the rolling case. "Should I take my usual medications?"

"Let me see what you have," Dr. Ott said.

After looking over the bottles Macy showed her, she said, "This is it? Nothing else to take at particularly anxious times?"

"No, this is all I've taken for the last few months. Dr. Bellows thought they were OK, but said as I need help, he'd add or take away some."

"Continue just as you've been instructed, for now," Dr. Ott smiled. "Macy, we hope that very soon you won't need any of these meds. Your body is not sick; your mind has closed down parts of itself to protect you from your memories. You will be fine, just you wait and see. Do you feel OK with this room? Are you afraid of being alone?"

"I noticed there are locking doors downstairs with a reception desk, and I know there is a lock on that door. Why should I be afraid?"

"There is nothing to be frightened of, except your own mind. You understand what I mean, right?"

"Yes. As far as I know, I've never let myself out of the house. And I don't plan to."

"The floor below you has a group of women, nurses and or physicians' assistants, who are still in training." Dr. Ott walked to the door. "No one knows anything about you except Pricilla, at the deck on the ground level. She's sworn to secrecy," she laughed.

"Anything you tell anyone is up to you. Like Alex said, they are all in medical classes and good students. If you need help, any one of them will come to your rescue. It's entirely your decision to meet them, or avoid people altogether," Sharon smiled.

"Alex?"

"Oh, I'm sorry. Dr. Alexander Welty, your friend! Our friend! And you know your way to his office down the hall. That's where I'll be most of the time. We want you to feel secure before we begin any therapy. You're on vacation for the next couple of days, at least. And you can call your sister, if you chose. She could even come to visit, if you want. I think that bed is a queen size, I'm sure you could share it with Marian. Or we can arrange for a cot," Sharon went to the door. "If she does come to see you, I want to meet her. OK?"

"OK. Thanks, I'd like to take a nap and later take a walk. I love the autumn leaves. It's been many years since I've seen them, and fall was always my favorite season." Macy took off her jacket, placing it on the back of a chair next to a small table in the corner. She noticed there were paper plates, cups, and plastic eating utensils. "Do I have access to a coffee maker?"

"I'll send one in for you. Do you have a favorite brand of coffee?" Dr. Ott asked.

"No, but I like creamer, no sugar."

"I'll send it over right away. Make a list if you think of something else. Pricilla will get it for you. Oh, and you can get her on your phone; her number is written on the map, there on the table."

"Sounds like you've thought of everything. Go on now, I want to rest. I promise, I'm fine, I really am. You will be the first to know if I feel a panic attack coming on," then to her surprise, Macy laughed, sounding like she was relieved.

"We're just down the hall, room six-twelve. And you're in six-oh-three." Dr. Ott stepped into the hall.

Macy crossed the room and closed the door. She noticed there was a dead bolt and secured it, but then thought better of it. The door locked automatically; she'd already seen that. And if she used the deadbolt, the doctors could not get in if she needed them.

Back in Cold Creek, Ella watched the store while Mr. Olsen went home for a nap. She walked up and down the aisles, noting where items were located.

"He has a good sense of location. This is very practical," she said aloud.

"Hello, Mr. Olsen? You in here?" A deep voice sounded from by the register.

"I'm here, but Mr. O is out for a moment. Can I help you?" Ella rounded the corner to find herself face to face with the most handsome state trooper she'd ever seen. Her heart jumped into her throat. She could not move or speak.

The Tennessee state trooper removed his hat and smiled at her. "Hello! I'm Bill Conway. And who might you be?"

"Mar...Ella. I mean, I'm Ella; Marian Ella is just too long a name. I go by

Ella." The flustered young woman extended her hand and stumbled over a box of groceries.

Conway jumped to catch her. Ella felt her face burn as he wrapped his strong arms around her torso, saving her from certain injury.

Ella was in a very awkward position, her feet behind her and this gorgeous man holding her up a couple feet off the floor. She managed to get one leg under her body and right herself.

"Gosh, that was totally embarrassing. I'm not normally so clumsy. Thanks for catching me," Ella brushed at the hair falling across her face.

"My pleasure, Ma'am, truly my pleasure. I'd hate to be the cause of you bruising those pretty legs," Conway grinned, enjoying the confusion he'd caused. "I was looking for Sheriff McKenzie, but I see Rick's vehicle. Not much use me looking for her now."

"Oh? Is something wrong?" Ella had caught a hint of something in his tone. "Are you here on business, or..."

"Yes, business for sure, but I don't think Agent Malone will be happy to see me. Maybe you can give Madison a message. If you see her, that is."

"I'd be happy to. And again, thanks for catching me. You startled me. I didn't expect to see an officer of the law in here. I was afraid something might have been wrong."

"Well, it's very nice meeting you, Ms. Ella." He removed his hat for the second time.

"Ella Walker; I'm sorry, I didn't properly introduce myself," she offered her hand for a shake.

"Ella Walker? Are you the lady Madison told me about, from Walker's Mountain?" Conway took her hand in his and held it tightly.

Ella looked at her hand in his, and then slipped it away gently. "I'm from Walkers' Mountain. What did she tell you?"

"I just know she's very concerned for your sister. Where is she?"

"She's in a care facility for now," she did not specify where.

"I'm very sorry for what you've been through, but if anyone can help you its Madison. She's the most compassionate human I've ever met. She's an amazing friend to have on your side." The trooper turned to walk back to his car. "Just tell her I have a lead on the monster truck. She'll know what you're talking about." He placed his hat on his head and climbed into his cruiser, waving good bye as he drove away slowly.

"Wow, and I though Rick was handsome! They really grow some good-looking men up here in these mountains." Ella turned around and nearly bumped into Mr. Olsen.

"And to think, Maddy had her choice of both those men. I suppose she chose the right one. Say, that leaves Conway up for grabs! Maybe you ought to go after him, Ella." Mr. Olsen laughed and walked into the store.

Later that evening, Rick and Maddy drove back into Cold Creek. Ella had packed her suitcase and was carrying it into the store as they pulled up to the sidewalk.

"Are you running away from home, little girl?" Rick called.

"Yes, I was, but you caught me! Hey Maddy, you want to come up and see what Mrs. O and I did with the room?"

"Sure!" Madison jumped out of the SUV, abandoning Rick and Bud. "You two can get cleaned up and we'll go eat in a while."

Rick parked the SUV in the new driveway, then he and Bud went inside.

Madison climbed the stairs, stopping in the doorway. "Oh gee, this looks nice! I can see Mrs. O's touch. She made that quilt, and I recognize those curtains. Where did the rug come from? It looks familiar."

"Shirley and Jess brought it by today. I love it!" Ella dropped to the rug, sitting in front of the window. "Look in the bathroom."

Madison saw a curved shower rod, pedestal sink, and a more modern toilet than she remembered. "When did Henry put that in?"

"I don't know, but Mrs. O brought the shower curtain. It matches this rug perfectly!"

Madison sat on the bed while Ella unpacked her things, hanging some in the closet and putting others in the chest of drawers Mr. Olsen had brought in. "I met Bill Conway today."

Madison smiled with a look that said she knew something about this subject. "He and Rick don't get on too well. Bill saved my life after I escaped from my kidnappers. And I'd bet he's the reason Rick finally got the nerve up to propose to me."

"He sure is handsome! But he's probably a real butt, isn't he? Usually the cutest ones are."

"No, he's actually a very nice guy! He's a great kisser too," there was that sheepish smile again.

"Come *on*, you've got to explain that!" Ella plopped on the bed next to Maddy. "I have to know the story behind that look on your face!"

A half hour later, the two walked down the steps giggling like teenagers. Mr. Olsen had already locked up, and Ella had her own key, so they went to find Rick and hunt something for supper.

Rick sat on the porch of the cottage with Bud on the floor next to his rocker. The girls waved and he joined them on the sidewalk at the door to Shirley's.

After the evening meal and an hour of conversation, Ella excused herself and said she wanted to retire early so she could place a call to Macy. Rick and Maddy walked her to the store, waited for her to relock the door, and watched until she flipped on the light upstairs.

Macy's phone rang and she looked at the caller I.D. "Hey, Sissy," she answered.

"Hi, Macy. How is everything in FL?" she asked.

"Same as always, I guess. I haven't heard any earth-shattering news. How are you?"

"I'm good. Got a temporary job in the little general store right next to Madison's house. I work for the sweetest old man, Mr. Olsen. He reminds me of Papa. You know, the stories you used to tell me about him," she said.

"Why did you have to go to work?"

"I didn't, but Mr. and Mrs. Olsen need a vacation, so I offered to watch the store for him. They have a pretty little granddaughter they want to visit. Oh, and Mr. O made me a bedroom up over the store, so I can sleep here too. It's a safety thing, you know, and he didn't have to close the store to go out of town. Gives me something to do while we wait."

"I wish this was all over with, don't you?" Macy said.

"It will be soon. I've met the investigators, and they are working very hard." Ella took a deep breath. "I wish you had come with me. You will love Madison and all her friends. You wait and see when you do meet them."

"It's time for me to go to bed, Ella, and I'm really tired tonight. I'll call you next, OK?"

"Well, all right. As long as you promise to call me in a few days. Take care of yourself, Macy. I love you, Sister."

"I love you too, Sissy. And I will call you soon. Good night."

Macy felt guilty for not telling Ella she was barely ninety minutes from her, right here in east Tennessee—but she wanted privacy. She thought Dr. Ott was onto a good idea about her treatment, and this was her own business, not Ella's. Not yet. There was something more in her mind than the recording revealed. She hoped she'd learn what that something was soon, and why it was so important that she'd crammed it way down in the banks of her memory.

As she slipped off to sleep, the only thought on her mind was, *what am I hiding from myself? And will I ever get it out in the open?*

11

Rick checked his phone early, before the sun rose. He had a text from his office notifying him of Watts' release date, which was less than a month away. With the DNA sample being inconclusive, he felt as if the Walker girls were being cheated. How could he prove that Watts was the man who killed their family?

Rick went down to the kitchen to make a pot of coffee. Madison was sleeping in her bedroom in the cottage. He didn't want to disturb her. It was still a couple of hours 'til sunrise. Bud's toenails tapped on the wood floor of the hallway, notifying Rick that he'd heard his second-string human was up and was joining him. Rick poured dry dog food into Bud's bowl and set it on the floor while he waited for the coffee to run through.

After Bud emptied the bowl and drank a large amount of water, he ducked through the doggie door in the laundry room. Rick poured the coffee into a carafe, setting it on the table. He took a mug from the cabinet, picked up the carafe and creamer, and walked back upstairs to the sitting area of the master suite. Almost immediately Bud appeared at the top of the stairs, but did not enter the room.

"Come on in, you might as well join me, Maddy will sleep for a while longer." Rick filled his mug and stirred in two heaping spoons full of creamer. He tested it and set the cup down to cool a bit. Opening his laptop, Rick scanned the transcript of the Watts trial. He'd done this at least a dozen times in the past few weeks. This time, one line stood out to him that he didn't remember reading before. The deputy stated, "Watts had a child's shirt wrapped around his wound. His right arm appeared to have been peppered by a scattergun." Rick sat straight up in the chair. He read it again, and followed to the next paragraph. "The wound was not life threatening, but the injury was infected. Dr. Smith removed the pellets and administered an antibiotic in the form of a shot."

Rick snatched up his phone. He texted a message to Stanley, in evidence. After a brief conversation, he tossed the phone onto the small table next to his laptop. Bud curled up beside Rick's chair on the new carpet. Rick continued reviewing the files. "Well no wonder!" he exclaimed loudly, causing Bud to jump up to see what was going on.

"Sorry, Fella. It's just that I had an amazing discovery. There are two different files here. One is from the hearing, and the other from the actual trial. And they are *not* the same! The evidence wasn't all entered for the trial. No dang wonder I missed that line about the child's shirt!"

Rick was so engrossed in reading this new transcript that he hadn't even noticed Madison standing at the door. Finally, she spoke. "Good morning. What's so interesting that you didn't notice the beautiful woman entering the scene?" she asked with a chuckle.

"Listen to this—oh, good morning, Sweetheart," he left his chair, greeting her with a hug. "You are certainly the most beautiful woman in this scene."

"You're very generous, Agent Malone..."

"Aw, come on. I made a breakthrough in this case. You've got to give me a break! Just this once?" He kissed her forehead, and then her neck, and then...

"OK, OK, I get it. Now that I'm in sheriff mode, what did you find?" She slipped on a pair of glasses and leaned in toward the laptop.

"What's with the glasses?"

"I realized I can read the computer screen easier with them, and these are over five years old," she laughed. "I've decided it's time to have my eyes checked again."

Rick had Madison read the paragraph aloud. She caught it right away, and like flipping a switch, she was in tune with Rick's train of thought.

They spent the next hour on FaceTime with Stanley, as he compared the list of evidence from the hearing transcript and the actual evidence that had been introduced in trial. There was no shirt mentioned in the trial transcript.

Later that day, Madison walked next door from her office to check on Ella at the hardware store.

"Good morning, Maddy. You're my first customer today," Ella said.

"Really? I wonder why?"

"Mr. Olsen said it might be this way. I think his friends will get used to me and come in more as the week goes on." Ella picked up a duster. "So, in the lull, I'm cleaning and straightening shelves, restocking, you know, the things Mr. Olsen doesn't do much when he can get out of it." She laughed.

"Aw, you've been paying attention. Sometimes he gets young boys to do that stuff for him and pays them in soft drinks or candy. He doesn't like the bending to reach lower shelves. I know he always gets Nicholas to help out when he can," Maddy looked up at a row of cereal boxes. "And like that shelf: he can't reach it anymore without a stool."

"I like busy work. You know, when you don't need to use your brain, just think about whatever you want and fill the space with matching items."

"That's a funny way to put it, but I guess you're right," Madison said. "All right, since I won't be interrupting your counting, let me ask you a few questions."

First she asked about the weather the day Ella's family was killed. "Do you remember what you were wearing?" Madison asked next.

"Yes, I do, because I wet my clothes. I was sad, because it wasn't a play dress, I was wearing my new Sunday dress so Grandma could mark the hem. It was too short, so she had to let out what hem was there and face the raw edge. I wanted to wear it for a while in the house to see if the hem looked OK. She was upset that the fabric didn't match my dress color perfectly. She didn't want it to show." Ella stared at the cans and boxes in front of her.

"And what color was the dress?" Madison asked.

"It was aqua, the prettiest color I'd ever seen."

Madison saw that Ella was entranced in the moment, so she said, "And what was Macy wearing?"

"A blue and yellow checkered shirt with a pair of boys' jeans. The shirt was unbuttoned; she wore a T-shirt under it. She liked to dress like Daddy..." Ella took a deep breath and let it out slowly.

"I'm sorry to make you think about the details of the day. We have to make sure we know everything. You do understand, don't you?"

"Of course. I'm all right, I just can't help worrying about Macy. I talked to her last night and she sounded good. I hate to say it, but I think she's improving, just being in the hospital atmosphere. But I don't want her to feel like she needs to stay there."

"And she won't. Maybe she feels safe there. That can make a huge difference in one's emotions. Feeling safe, I know… That's a big deal," said Madison, recalling a different time in her own life.

Meanwhile in Knoxville, Dr. Ott, Dr. Welty, and Macy spent the day in the office on the top floor of the building they were staying in on the UT Campus. The intravenous meds were working as Macy lay on the table, drifting in and out of consciousness. The sessions were recorded for the team's records, as well as Macy's security.

If she said anything under hypnosis, she wanted to be sure it was her thoughts that were recorded. She knew more than she could remember, but at the same time she felt anxious about learning the whole story. What could she be hiding from her own awareness, and why? If she recalled seeing her daddy's head split like a melon, what could be so bad that her memory shut it down? She might not want to know.

Stanley texted Rick's phone, requesting he call for an update.

"I need to talk to Stan," he said, kissing Maddy on the cheek and leaving the dinner table. Sitting in the seat of his SUV, laptop plugged in for charging, he dialed Stan's cellphone. "What did you find?"

"A goldmine, in my opinion." Notification of Stan's email dinged from the laptop.

Rick opened the email and looked through several photos. One shot caused his heart to race: a child's checkered shirt, scattered with dark brown patches that looked like dried blood.

"Stan, get that shirt to the lab ASAP!"

"Already there, just hoping the DNA isn't degraded too much. I left word for Jan to call you first! Oh, and I thought you should know; on the pocket of the shirt are the initials M.O.W. Any clue?"

"Yeah, Macy Olivia Walker. Thanks, man. Keep me posted." Rick returned to Madison with a smile. "Is Macy's middle name Olivia, like her Grandmother?"

"Yes, it is. Why?"

"The shirt had initials on the pocket. Ella said her mom had bought a new sewing machine, and everyone got their clothing monogrammed."

"Let's keep our fingers crossed that DNA matches Watts. There's blood stains on the shirt he wrapped around his arm after Grandma shot him with the shotgun."

Madison frowned. "That's the shirt Ella said Macy wore the day their parents were killed. How would he get her shirt?"

The two looked at each other, contemplating the situation.

"Are you thinking what I'm thinking?" Rick spoke first.

"Oh...oh, no, surely not..."

Rick read the look in Madison's eyes. "Let's don't jump to conclusions. We need to question Macy ourselves."

"Maybe you should call Dr. Ott and tell her what you've discovered," Maddy leaned into a hug, placing her head against Rick comforting shoulder.

"Let's wait for DNA results. No sense going there just yet." He wrapped his arms snugly around her thin body, pressing her against him, kissing the top of her head. "I hope this case doesn't drag out so long that our plans of a January wedding get pushed back. I miss you so much when I'm in Knoxville. I can't take this separation much longer."

She chuckled, "I know. It doesn't seem real that we've been close for so long, and still so far apart. I'm ready to be your wife!"

"We could elope."

"No, we can't. Nobody would ever forgive us." She pulled back to look into his jade eyes. "I've loved you since our eyes first met."

Rick tilted his head and kissed his fiancée. The cottage door burst open, and Bob Conway stepped in abruptly.

"Sorry kids, we've got an emergency!"

12

Trooper Bill Conway ran back out to the street, where his cruiser sat with lights flashing. He yelled to Rick, now hot on his heels, "Top of the mountain, the old road, got a couple of monster trucks going at it. One is the truck that shoved Maddy over the hill in her Blazer."

"We'll come up from the bottom. You head in from the Laurels' Road. I want that S.O.B. in the worst way!" Rick jumped into his Suburban.

Madison followed, buckling her gun belt. She jumped in with Rick, and they sped away toward the old Asheville Highway.

Bill Conway was a thorn in Rick's side, but if he'd found the driver who tried to kill Madison, Rick was there to back him up. They both cared for Sheriff McKenzie and had no pity for this homicidal redneck. As far as Rick was concerned, this was personal. He was sure Bill looked at it the same way. For this day, they were allies.

Rick drove up the winding old 23, or Asheville Highway, contemplating intercepting the monster trucks. Instead they met up with Conway, who looked as surprised as they were.

"There are only one or two roads they might have cut onto. We should check Rocky Fork and Rice Creek Road," Bill said.

"Wait; I'm calling the ranger at Rocky Fork," Madison waved her hand. "Hello, this is Sheriff McKenzie. We're looking for two monster trucks last seen on old twenty-three. Did they come your way?"

After a few moments, she said, "Thanks, Buford. I'll check with Murdock. Sounds like a good idea; we could use the back up," she disconnected and punched in another number. "Hey, Murdock. It's Madison McKenzie—so they're right there now? All right, we're heading that way from the old road at Simpsons. Be there in a few!"

"Devils Fork, at the top, where the Appalachian Trail crosses. You know where I mean?" she asked.

Bill nodded and took off ahead of Rick's vehicle. Rick and Madison followed as fast as safely possible. Rick did not have an outside light flashing, only a small one on his dash. But the Conway was lighting up the emergency blue, siren wailing.

Rick had not experienced this particular road before. He cast a quick glance at Maddy. She had a white-knuckle grip on the "oh, shit" handle. The curves on this road were sharp—and the creek was far below, with no guard rails. By the time they reached the lumberyard, Conway was two curves ahead of them. Rick shifted in his seat, a sure tell that he was nervous going that fast with Madison in the passenger seat.

The top of the mountain was just ahead when Conway pulled onto the side at a dirt road. Mr. Murdock stood there with a pitchfork in hand, a wad of tobacco pooching his left cheek out. He turned to spit before he spoke. "Those no-account scoundrels took off racing up the trail like it was a paved road! If I could get my hands on them, they'd be sorry!"

"They went up the Appalachian Trail in those monster trucks?" Madison stepped from the car to speak with Mr. Murdock. "Surely they can't get far through the woods."

Before Murdock could answer, a couple of young boys on 4-wheelers drove up, sliding to a stop. "Sheriff, you going to chase them guys?"

Madison recognized the Edwards boy from a domestic dispute call she'd answered back in the summer. "Hello, Trey. So you saw them?"

"We sure did! They ran us off the track, up there in the field. This is Mack Murdock; it's his four-wheeler track." Trey pointed up toward the A.T. to a point where the grass had been displaced by wide tire tracks torn into the ground.

"How far can they go with the trucks?" Conway asked.

"A fur piece," said Mack Murdock. "I've never been on the trail with my four-wheeler, but I've walked it all the way to Rocky Fork Creek."

"What will it cost us to rent your four-wheelers?" Rick pulled his wallet out.

The boys looked at each other, wide-eyed, then Mr. Murdock spoke up. "Nothing! You take off after them and if you catch them, let me at 'em!"

Rick took out two twenties, handing one to each boy. "That OK with you, Mr. Murdock?"

He shrugged and spit to his right once more.

Rick and Madison climbed on one four-wheeler, while Bill got the other. They took off north on the protected Appalachian Trail. Prominent signs clearly stated NO Motorized Vehicles on A.T.! Not only were they in pursuit of motorized vehicles, but the monster trucks were big enough to take out trees. The trail was easy to follow; small saplings had been run down and limbs ripped from larger trees in their wake.

Madison recalled there were some large rocks ahead, but she couldn't remember how far it was. She knew the rangers were heading toward them from the Rocky Fork side. She hoped the drivers of the trucks were not armed. She didn't think the rangers carried guns, but they might need them in this case.

The four-wheelers covered a lot of ground quickly. In less than thirty minutes, they were within earshot of the trucks. From the sounds, it was evident that one of the trucks had run aground, maybe on a rock or a tree stump. Either way, they were making a lot of noise, spinning the tires and trying to free themselves.

Bill and Rick slowed to approach undetected. They shut the engines off and all three moved in from different directions, guns pulled and ready to fire if need be. Madison scaled the high side of a big rock overlooking a gully, where the monster truck was stuck on a large hemlock stump. She looked for Rick and Bill, spotted them, and signaled that she had them covered. Bill moved in closer through some ground clutter. Rick approached from the blind side of the second truck. When all three guns were aimed at the drivers, Rick yelled out, "TBI, freeze! Hands in the air!"

The driver of the stalled truck raised his hands high. The second driver jumped up into his truck and took off up the trail, leaving his buddy to fend for himself.

Bill ran to the four-wheeler and took off after the escaping truck.

Rick told the driver to step down from the stranded truck, keeping his hands up. The man complied and was on the ground in no time. He continued holding his hands up. Madison saw that Rick had handcuffs out and moved down the rock face to assist him. She wanted to make the arrest. This was her territory.

As she approached the cuffed man, she realized it was Rain Toole, a boy she knew from the dental office when she'd worked for her Aunt Denny. "Rain? What in the world do you think you're doing?"

"Ms. McKenzie! I-I...it was...I'm... I mean, it was a dare! I didn't want to, but you know how mean Manny is. He wouldn't let me off the hook. We were drinking last night, and it seemed OK at the time. But when we got there to Old Man Murdock's, I didn't want to go. But Manny laughed at me and called me a sissy! I couldn't let him get away with that."

"You should have. Now you're in a lot of trouble! Were you with him when he ran my Blazer off the mountain back in the summer?"

"That was you?" He squirmed for a minute trying to get off his knees. "I mean, I didn't know he was going to run you off the mountain. I was in the passenger's seat, but I jumped out before he rammed you the second time. I didn't want no part of that."

"Yet you're still with him. Is he your hero?" Madison was angry, and she let it show. "You have strange taste in friends. This one is leading you straight to prison!"

"Please, Madison, don't..." he dropped his head and began sobbing. "My dad is going to kill me. You might as well shoot me and put me out of my misery," he sniffled loudly.

"Don't tempt me, kid!" Rick drew his pistol. "Who is the other driver? Tell me his name."

"Rick, don't. I've known this boy since he was six! You can't shoot him for no reason," Madison said, and pulled on Rick's arm.

"He and that other guy tried to kill you. Why can't I shoot him?" Rick pulled away from Madison's hold.

"Look, mister; his name is Pat, Pat Kennedy. He's not from here, he lives in Asheville! He's really bad. He said if I didn't show him around, he'd destroy my truck. I just built it this summer! I don't want to get in no more trouble, please, and I don't want to die! My dad is going to do that for you!"

The pitiful boy was shaking now, and Madison felt sorry for him. She placed her hand on his shoulder. "Rick wasn't going to shoot you. I'm the law here. You're safe."

"Aw, Sheriff you let my secret out," Rick said, and winked.

The boy's eyes narrowed, "You're a bully!"

"And you're a juvenile delinquent! But the more you cooperate, the easier the law will go on you." Rick holstered his weapon. "Come here," he directed, then pulled out another pair of cuffs, Rick used the second set to cuff the boy's feet together. "We're going after your friend. You will wait here."

Madison and Rick headed up the trail on the four-wheeler again. Soon they came across the other truck, tipped onto its side in a deep ravine.

"He's on foot. Conway is after him, still on the four-wheeler." Rick yelled, "Hold on, Honey!" and drove up the steep bank.

After topping the ridge, Rick shut off the motor. "We ought to be able to hear Conway's engine." They listened for a few seconds.

"I hear it," Madison called out, pointing "that way." Rick started the ATV up again, driving cautiously over rough terrain until they realized they were back on the beaten trail, the Appalachian. Rick cut the engine again, saying, "The sound is coming toward us now." Madison climbed off and Rick backed the four-wheeler into the thick underbrush. The two of them crouched, guns ready, in case Conway was driving Pat Kennedy their way.

But what they saw was the rangers' trail buggy from Rocky Fork State Park. Madison recognized the driver as Eric, one of the state rangers. The woman with him, also wearing the ranger uniform, was not familiar to her.

"Hey, Sheriff McKenzie. You must have stopped him; we didn't pass him from our direction," Eric shut off the motor.

"He's on foot. Ditched his truck back there, at the bottom of the ravine. State Trooper Bill Conway is on a four-wheeler chasing him, we presume," Madison said. "This is TBI Agent Rick Malone. Rick, Eric Whitson."

Eric spoke up, "This is Melanie, our newest ranger at Rock Fork. Nice meeting you, Rick. I've heard a lot about you from Sheriff McKenzie."

"Good meeting you, Sheriff, Agent Malone; call me Mel." She offered a brisk handshake. "Do you know what direction they went?"

"If I'm reading these mountains correctly, you came out of the north, and we came from the southeast. I'm betting on west," Rick looked at Maddy "We should split up?"

"Yeah. I doubt if Conway has a cell signal, so we probably can't get in touch with him."

"Actually, he might. I have a good signal up here," Erick looked at his phone. "What's the number?"

Madison looked at the contacts on her phone. She scrolled down and read off, "four two three, four eight three, five five five five.."

"I don't have a signal," Rick said.

"Me either," Maddy glanced sideways at him. "Bill has the same phone and service we have."

Erick tried the number. "Straight to voicemail."

"OK, this is what we need to do," Rick stood beside Maddy. "Can you drive this?" She nodded. "You two stick to the trail. He won't want to get lost so he might stay on the trail—or at least where he can see it. But these engines will alert him long before we see him, so I'm going on foot. He won't expect that," Rick said.

"Mel, you drive this and I'll take the other side of the trail on foot. If you come out at the paved road, stay there. We'll work toward you. Got it?" Eric asked.

"Sure." Mel slid into the driver's seat.

"Let's set up a time to meet there, where the trail crosses the road," Madison suggested.

Rick leaned in and kissed her. "See you in two hours, no more."

Madison nodded with a sweet smile, and they all headed in different directions.

Rick combed the ground looking for signs of footprints, broken branches, and uprooted ferns, anything that disturbed the lay of the land. But with the autumn leaves carpeting every surface, spotting signs was next to impossible.

He came to a low place with multiple rocks forming a small pool. Rick knelt down to see water seeping to the surface. "A natural spring;" he cupped his hand to catch a sip. "Maybe someone else found this," he leaned to one side and brushed a few leaves out of the way. There was a fresh track: a large, heavy boot print, sunken deep into the soft soil.

Rick looked for another, found one, and continued to the top of the ridge following disturbed leaves and an occasional print. He caught a slight movement up ahead and stood still for a minute, waiting for another movement. There he saw the white tail of a deer twitching in the underbrush. She moved suddenly, as though scared by something down the hill from her. She darted across the ridge and down the side Rick had just come up.

"OK, someone's coming this way. Thanks for the warning, Ms. Doe!" Rick sat quietly, watching for what had frightened the whitetail deer. He waited; nothing moved. Rick shifted his position slightly to see around a large poplar tree. There in the distance he noticed a black figure, low to the ground and dark as coal. It was unmistakably a black bear. He sat perfectly still, frozen in amazement at the way she moved through the brush with very little noise. What he did hear was the blows of her paw against downed trees as she searched for grubs. She moved methodically up the hillside, stopping at each rotting stump until she was within a few yards of her admirer.

The black form rose to a height of approximately six feet, in Rick's estimation. She'd spotted him, or smelled his scent. She stood tall on her back legs and reached high above her head, slapping the side of a broad tree trunk. This was her signal that she was bigger, and he'd better not mess with her space.

He sat waiting to see which way she went next. She wavered to the right, then the left, and she chose to walk up a path leading straight to the marked A.T. This was the same path the deer had taken. Rick was glad she hadn't decided to investigate him. He slid up next to the poplar, hugging the trunk closely. The bear waddled along in no hurry, pausing to dig up a root, which she devoured quickly, always watchful of the human lurking behind that tree.

Rick pulled out his cell and snapped a photo when she was about twenty-five feet away. He didn't feel threatened; there was a large pine knot branch laying on the ground next to him. If she moved toward him, he'd rap it against the tree to signal his territory. But it never came to that; the bear looked north and then back south on the trail. She turned and walked away from Rick, taking her time, and shortly disappeared down the wooded side of the trail.

Rick smiled, thinking of what such an encounter with nature meant to him. He was a city boy who had only seen wild animals in a zoo. This was priceless; he loved the mountains of East TN. He loved a woman who lived in the woods connected with nature. He was looking forward to his retirement. The idea of the simple life suited him just fine.

A loud scream squashed Rick's daydream. He listened for any other sounds. The scream could have come from any direction, bouncing off trees and rocks. Then a second scream set him running in the direction the bear had taken.

He realized it wasn't Madison; the sound was that of a higher-pitched voice, maybe a younger woman. Rick ran faster when he heard the scream for a third time. He broke through a thick patch of Mountain Laurel to see the driver of the monster truck holding the female ranger by her hair with a knife to her throat.

"Stop! Don't come any closer, or I'll do her in," the young man shouted.

"OK, I'm staying right here. What's your plan?" Rick studied his surroundings, taking in possible escape routes.

"Call off the other ranger and your friends, and I'll let her go when we get out to the road."

"Can't; I have no cell signal here. You let her go now, and we won't follow you," Rick said smoothly.

"I don't trust you. You'll follow and shoot me if I don't have a hostage."

"And if you hurt her, you'll be in double trouble. Let's end it here! Let her go. I'll help get your truck out, and you'll only be charged with trespassing today."

The man lost his grip on the ranger's hair, and she dove to the ground. Rick lunged forward, trying to reach him before he could grab her again. The blade found Rick's left arm, stabbing clear through it. Fighting excruciating pain, he landed one hard blow to the side of the man's head, knocking him off his feet. To Rick's surprise, the female ranger kicked him before he could get up. Her foot caught the man under his chin, and he didn't move after that.

Rick's arm was bleeding profusely. He tied the tail of his shirt around the wound with the ranger's help. She took his handcuffs and fastened the young man's wrists behind his back. He still did not move on his own.

Madison and Conway found their way to the site of the scuffle, having heard the screams as well. Madison used the rangers' vehicle to get Rick back to the road, then transferred him to his SUV. With Madison driving, they raced to the Erwin Hospital.

Rick's arm was numbed and stitched up quickly by the ER doctor, and he was released. There was no damage to any nerves. The doctor suggested he remain off from work for a minimum of ten days, at which time he was to return and have the sutures removed.

Back at Madison's home in Cold Creek, Rick relaxed on the bed upstairs. He heard a "Knock, knock," and looked up to see Conway standing at the top of the stairs.

"Hey Bill; come in." Rick threw his feet over the side of the bed. "Ouch," he said. "The numbness has worn off."

"That was quite a gash, Rick." Conway set a pot of white daises on the oval table between the two wingback chairs.

"Aw, you brought me flowers; that's so sweet," Rick said with a smirk. He winced and worked his way to one of the chairs. He dropped into it, supporting his arm just under the elbow.

"They're for Madison. She needs a consolation prize for putting up with you for ten days." Conway sat in the opposite chair. "Thought you'd have a sling on that arm," he said.

"Supposed to, but I left it downstairs. It didn't matter while I was lying down." No sooner had Rick gotten the words out than Conway stood and walked to the door. "Which room?"

"Living room, I think," he called out.

In just seconds, Conway returned and assisted Rick in placing the sling on his arm.

"Thanks, Bill. I appreciate that."

"No problem," he said, sitting down again. "That was some unusual chase! Is it always that exciting out here?" Bill asked.

"Seems that way—or maybe it's just Madison. She attracts extraordinary like a magnet," Rick chuckled.

"I believe it," Conway leaned forward, forearms on his knees. "Wonder what ever made that guy go after her to begin with?"

Rick shook his head, "I don't know, but thanks for tracking him down. It felt good today, you and me on the same side. I appreciate your efforts."

"We both want the same things, Rick. Safety for Madison, and to enforce

112

the law. I'm not trying to cause you any trouble. But understand, I care for her too. You marrying her won't change that. She's a lady, she decides, and you have nothing to worry about."

"I know that. I appreciate your honesty, Bill."

"Anybody up there?" a sweet voice called out.

"Yeah, come on up, Ella" Rick said.

Ella bounced up the stairs and froze at the door. "Oh, I didn't know you had company, Rick. Sorry to interrupt." Curls bounced along her slender face. She pushed one side away, tucking it behind her ear. "Trooper Conway, right?"

"So, you two have met?" Rick asked.

Bill stood up to offer her his chair. "She's already fallen for me, Rick," he teased, and reached out to her. "Take my seat, please."

She blushed as he took her hand, "I can't stay long. I was running an errand and thought I'd stop in to say hello."

Bill led her to the chair. "I'm glad you did."

"How's the arm?" Ella tried to focus on Rick's injury. "I bet that hurt really bad!" She winced.

"Kind of," Rick tried to sound tough. "Actually, it hurt way more than a bullet."

The three laughed.

"Where is Madison?" Ella asked.

"She ran back to Erwin to pick up my prescriptions and get something for supper. She wanted to cook instead of going to the restaurant this evening."

"Oh. Well, OK then; I'll catch her later, after I close the store. Be very careful with that arm, Rick. If you thought it hurt putting the sutures in, you ought to feel how bad it is when they have go back and re-stitch them after you break them loose." Ella rubbed her forearm. "Trust me, I know."

"You were stabbed?" Bill asked.

"No, I fell on a sling blade. Lucky to still have this arm attached." She rolled her eyes.

"Wow!" Rick and Bill said simultaneously.

Ella stood. Bill stepped to her side. "I'll walk you out. Rick needs to rest." He turned toward Rick and winked broadly. "See you later on, ol' buddy."

"Thanks for coming by, Bill. You too, Ella. I appreciate your sympathy."

"No, Rick, my sympathy is with Maddy," she laughed as they disappeared down the stairs.

"Thanks, Bill. It was good to see you again," Ella started walking away once they were outside.

He quickly caught up with her. "Got dinner plans?"

"Um, no," she answered.

"Good!" Bill slid closer, until their shoulders were touching. "Then I'll make some. What time are you closing up tonight?"

"Six."

He looked at his watch. "Fifteen minutes; OK, what time can I call for you?"

"How about six thirty?" she suggested.

"I'll be back then." Bill watched her walk into the store, then returned to the cottage as Madison pulled into the driveway.

Madison noticed Ella going into the store.

Wonder what she and Bill have cooked up? Surely they weren't visiting with Rick? Wouldn't it be a nice match if the two of them got together?

13

Madison slid out of the Explorer. "Hey, Bill. Did you stop in to see Rick?"

"I did, but I got lucky: Ella came by too. I asked her out to dinner, and she accepted."

"Well, that's nice. Where are you taking her?" Madison reached into the back seat and pulled out a small bag from the pharmacy.

"Let me get those grocery bags for you." Bill retrieved two heavy bags from the floor of the back seat. "What would you suggest? I haven't had a chance to think about it. I just left her." He looked back toward the store.

"Hmm, you and Ella... I like that idea! Good for you, my friend. Just promise me you won't hurt that woman. She's been through a lot, and I happen to know she has not had time for boyfriends. Go slowly, please; promise me you'll be as patient with her as you were with me."

"Maddy, when I walked out of your life, I knew there would never be a more perfect lady for me in the world. But then you brought Ella onto the scene. Trust me, I still believe things happen for a reason. I'd never hurt her; she is a precious flower too." Bill followed Madison into the house.

"Thank you. I believe you. I hope the two of you can find a good place together, and that neither of you get hurt." Her smile said she also cared for his feelings.

"I was going to ask Rick if I might borrow his shower. I have clothes to change into, but I don't have time to run to the hotel in Erwin and get back here by six," he said.

"You're welcome to use the bedroom and bath of the main cottage. You don't need to ask Rick; I'm in charge in this part of the house," she laughed.

"Yes, Ma'am. Thank you. I'll get my bag."

"Make yourself at home. I think you'll find anything you need. The sheets are clean, and there are fresh towels in the bath. Just consider this your home away from home—as long as you behave yourself." She laughed and went up the stairs to Rick's room.

"Hey, Honey. How are you feeling?" she sat on the opposite side of the bed. "Here are your prescriptions. You need something for pain by now, I'm guessing. I'm sure the numbness is wearing off."

"Please. I can't believe how bad this is hurting." He sat up. "Bill Conway came in to see me. He brought you those daises, as a consolation prize. And he went downstairs to find my sling. I've got to keep it on. I think that's why I'm hurting so bad."

"Let me see." She slipped the sling up above the bandage. "It's bleeding badly. Maybe they didn't get everything sewed up. I'm calling the doctor."

"Why don't you just ask Chip to take a look at it?" Rick asked.

"OK, but he'll say go back to the ER, I'll bet you!" She pulled up Doc's number and in just seconds, the local town doctor answered. "Hi, it's Madison. Ricks arm is still bleeding a lot, and hurting terribly. Can you come and take a look at him? Or should I run him back to the ER?"

"I'll be right there," Doc said.

"He's coming right over. Bill is downstairs showering. He has a date with Ella. I told him he can use the guest bedroom. So that means I'll be sleeping with you, my dear."

"Fine with me, as long as you promise to let me sleep, and that you won't take advantage of my weakened condition." Rick smiled.

"I promise I'll control myself," she said, then leaned over and kissed him. "I'm so sorry you were hurt. I love you, Rick."

"I'm not hurt, I'm hurting. There is a difference. And I love you too, Maddy, more than anything."

"OK! You have company, so lighten up, you two!" Chip walked briskly into the room, set his black doctor's bag on the foot of the bed, and stood next to Rick.

He examined the bandages for a second, then reached for the scissors in his bag. "That's not good. What did you do to break the stitches?"

"Nothing, really; I've babied it! When the numbness wore off, it started hurting real bad," Rick said.

Chip slit the bandage, exposing the wound and all the stitchery. He supported Rick's arm with a clean white disposable pad, examining the wound carefully. "Something is not closed up; the vasoconstrictor in the numbing agent held off the bleeding for a short time while they sutured. But as the meds wore off, the bleeding returned to normal. This means they missed something. You've got to go back. I'm afraid you're going under for surgery, Rick."

"Can't you do it? I don't want to go back to the ER."

"No, they need to fix what they did wrong. They are liable. I'd do it if this wasn't such a tricky area. I'll go with you and scrub up with the doctor. I have surgical privileges there." Chip quickly rewrapped the wound, then rolled the disposable padding around it as well. He helped Madison replace the sling, and said, "Let's get going. I'll call them on the way down the mountain."

Bill walked out of the guest bedroom, dressed and smelling nice. "What's wrong?"

"We have to take Rick back to the ER. Doc discovered they missed a bleeder. Don't tell Ella; you two go and have a good time. I'll text you later," Madison said as she hurried out the door.

The ER orderly waited with a stretcher when Madison pulled up to the emergency room entrance. Chip rushed in with the patient and explained to Dr. Jones that he intended to accompany him during the surgery, letting the ER doctor know he had current surgical privileges with the OR.

They disappeared through the double doors, leaving Madison alone and scared. She stood silently, watching the doors swing together as if they were in slow motion. Her heart beat high in her throat, her hands shook, and her legs felt like she could not move them.

Suddenly aware of hands on her arms, Madison turned and saw Ella and Bill, one on either side of her. She was going down and fading out, sparkles and blackness...

When Madison came to, she was on a gurney in a room in the ER. A nurse in blue scrubs stood over her. "How's your blood sugar doing Maddy?" The voice was familiar; it was Tammy, a friend from high school.

"I'm OK. I just got light-headed when I saw Rick go out of my sight. I'm fine," she sounded weak.

"Yes, I'm sure you are fine, but you haven't eaten. That's why you passed out. Here, drink this," Tammy helped Madison raise her head, and she tasted some kind of sweet liquid in the small medicine cup.

She sipped it cautiously, then drank the rest of it. "What's that?"

"Energy for your internal battery. You know better than letting yourself get so low. What was your excuse today?" Tammy squinted, looking sternly into Madison's face.

"Rick's injury distracted me."

"That's what I figured you'd say. Blame it on Rick. Don't you carry peanut butter crackers or orange juice in your vehicle anymore?"

"We were in his Suburban, on a case—I mean a chase."

"Have you ever had a CBC?" Tammy asked.

"Yes," she said.

"OK;, just try not to keep letting yourself go for so long. You were driving just a few minutes ago. What if this had happened then? You don't want to hurt yourself or someone else, do you?"

"Of course not." Madison sat up. "Thank you for the pep talk; I will try to do better. I was really worried about my fiancé. They took him to surgery. Can you check on him?"

"I can, and I will. You just stay here, we don't need this room. There are several people in the waiting room asking about him. I'll go get your friends."

Madison sat alone for a few minutes. She considered her circumstances. Rick getting stabbed kept returning to the front of her thoughts. Her memory was fuzzy; she shook her head trying to clear the fog. The love of her life was in surgery, and she was letting him down by letting her own health go. It wasn't a deliberate action; it just hadn't seemed so important that she maintain regular eating habits lately. Today, that decision had been a dangerous one.

Her friends followed Tammy into the ER treatment room. "Feeling any better, Madison?"

Tammy put her hand on Madison's shoulder. "Don't try standing for a while. I'll check with OR to see how Rick is. You stay right here," she said firmly. "Please keep her here, will you?" she asked Ella.

"Absolutely," Ella smiled, stepping closer to Madison. "We'll take care of her."

After Tammy left the room, Madison slid off the table.

"Oh, no you don't," Bill caught her with both hands around her slim waistline, lifted her back onto the table, and said, "Now, *stay*."

"Why are you two here? You're supposed to enjoy your first date, a lovely evening out to dinner. Why are you even here?" Madison sounded irritated. She dropped her head. "I'm sorry, that didn't come out right."

"It doesn't matter, Madison. We're your friends first. There is no us at this time, we're just friends, and your friends and Rick's. Are you telling us we don't deserve to be here to pray for his wellbeing?" Ella folded her arms across her chest.

"Oh, no... I didn't mean it that way!" She looked to Bill for help. "You know what I mean, don't you?"

"I know, and the answer is still no. We're here for the duration." He winked at Maddy.

In the OR, Tammy observed through the glass in the closed door. She saw that Dr. McClellan and the ER doctor were struggling to stop the bleeding. They both had arterial spray on their scrubs. Obviously they had found the bleeder, but clamping it off had been difficult. She watched the two men work together to save the Agent's life. What had earlier appeared as a clean through and through wound involving no major veins or arteries was in fact a hematoma that had blown out like a cheap tire, causing all the pain Rick had experienced and the additional bleeding.

Thirty minutes passed. Tammy moved out of the way as a lab tech came through with three liters of blood for the patient. She moved to the window on the other door, where she could observe his vitals. Rick's heart rate was up, and his BP was falling fast. They were losing him.

Tammy felt compelled to return to Madison, but didn't know what she would say. *Maybe I'll talk with the gentleman, Madison's friend, first.* She waited a few more minutes, then went to speak with Bill. She called him out into the hallway.

"They're having a rough time with him. He's losing a lot of blood. Apparently, he had an aneurism develop after the stabbing. Both doctors are fighting to get him patched up, and they're going to give him some blood. Should we tell Madison? I don't know if he's going to make it. They're engaged, aren't they?"

"Yes, Rick and Maddy are getting married in January. Oh. my God; how can this happen?" Bill paced back and forth. "We have to let her know," he stopped suddenly and returned to the ER treatment room, where Madison waited.

"What's wrong, Bill?" Madison leaned forward on the table. "Tell me!"

"Rick developed an aneurism, apparently. He's losing a lot of blood. Do you know his blood type?" Conway asked.

"He's O-positive. Does he need us to donate?" Madison slid off the table again. She stood straight and tall.

"Not you, but I'm going down to the lab right now. You wait here. Ella, will you stay with her and keep her out of trouble?" He winked at Ella, turned so Madison could not see him.

Tammy led him to the OR, and they watched the monitors through the window. Steadily the BP was going up. "That's a good sign," Tammy whispered.

About ten minutes passed, and it began dropping again. "That's not!" Conway said. "Where's the lab?"

Tammy showed him, and stayed to assist in getting him set up. Then she told him she was going back to check the monitor.

An hour passed; Madison was a wreck. She couldn't wait any longer. "Ella, why haven't they come back?"

"Let's pray, Madison. That's all we can do for him," Ella led the way out to the reception area. She found a sign pointing to the chapel. "This way, Madison."

The two women entered the tiny chapel. The warmth of candles burning gave them a feeling of comfort in the dimly-lit room. Ella knelt next to the candles. She said a silent prayer, then made the sign of the cross and lit a candle. Madison bowed her head and took a seat on the bench.

Ella joined her. "I'm not Catholic, but my aunt tried to convert us. I believe in all prayers, so I figured it can't hurt."

Madison smiled but said nothing. She bowed her head again, praying in her own frantic silence. Tears slipped from her eyes and dropped onto her knee.

Ella reached for Maddy's hand, holding it in both of her own. They had only known each other a few weeks but at this point, time didn't matter. They knew Rick's life was at stake.

When Bill returned to the room where Madison had been, one of the ER nurses guided him to the chapel.

He entered and sat behind the women. He placed both hands on Madison's shoulders, and whispered, "They are taking him to a room for tonight. His BP is holding; that means they stopped the bleeding. He should be OK now. He's very weak, but Chip will let us know when we can see him. Then, the three of us are going to eat!"

Madison turned around. "OK."

"What, no argument?"

She shook her head, but said nothing more. An hour passed—or maybe just minutes. Madison couldn't tell anymore. She was still feeling very down.

"You may go in for a few minutes, Madison, but Rick needs to rest tonight. Understand?"

It was Tammy from the ER.

"Yes, I promise. I just have to see him!" She stood, slowly following Tammy.

Rick looked as pale as the sheets he lay on. He was covered all the way up to his chin with a thin, tan blanket. She observed his two-day old beard growth, noticing how it stood out so dark against his pasty coloring. His eyes were closed. She touched his cheek softly with her trembling lips. "Rick?"

His eyes opened and tried to focus. "Maddy..."

"Don't try to talk. You were in surgery for a long time. Chip and the ER doctor finally patched a bleeder that was missed the first time. You'll be fine, but you need to rest. I'm going to go eat with Ella and Bill. I'll be back by sunup. You just lay here and sleep, OK?"

His normally green eyes even looked pale; they were more of a hazel, which she'd never seen before. *How can this happen? You're always so healthy...* "I'll see you in the morning. I love you, Rick."

"Love you, Maddy." Rick's eyes closed before his words drifted to her ears.

She kissed him on the forehead and walked away, then turned back for one more look. The thought occurred to her that he looked more dead than alive.

She felt tears trickling down her cheeks and dripping onto her chest. Her eyes blurred and she stumbled against the wall in the hallway.

Trooper Bill Conway came to the rescue, as always. "He's going to make it. Chip will stay by him tonight to monitor his every move. You need to eat and get some rest yourself."

His voice was little comfort to Madison, but she knew what her responsibility was at this time. She didn't like it, but she had to follow the lead of her friends. Her phone rang, making her jump. It vibrated in her pocket until she pulled it out. She could not make out the name of the caller through her teary eyes.

Ella took it from her hand. "Hello?"

She took a deep breath, then said, "He'll be fine now, Holly. We're taking Maddy to supper." She chuckled and said, "Yeah, I'll tell her. We sure will. Chip is going to stay with him tonight."

Maddy nodded and took the phone from Ella when she hung up, stuffing it back in her pocket.

Ella stayed with Madison in the new upstairs suite, while Bill slept in the guest room.

Daylight streamed through the open blinds, awaking Ella. She let Maddy sleep while she took a shower and got dressed. The smell of coffee led her downstairs to the kitchen. Bill sat at the small table, but stood as soon as she walked in.

Ella thought he looked very handsome, considering he'd only gotten a few hours' sleep. "Good morning," she said.

"Sleep well?" Bill pulled the pot of steaming coffee from the warmer, poured a mug, and slid it toward Ella. "What do you take in it?"

"This is fine, thank you." She sipped slowly. "Ah; I needed that."

"Yeah, me too." He sat back down after she dropped into the opposite chair.

"Did you hear anything from Doc?"

"No," Bill replied. "And I'm taking that as a good sign."

"Maddy was still sleeping when I came down. She had a rough night, talking in her sleep and turning over and over. I tried to comfort her, but it didn't really help."

"She's had a rough life at times; misery finds her too easily. But I think she'll be OK when Rick gets out of the hospital. She's worried; he's been her rock for so long." Bill refilled his cup. "I owe you an evening out. What are we going to do about that?"

"What do you mean? We had an evening out."

"An *uneventful* evening," he stressed.

Ella's phone rang, interrupting a potentially tender moment. "Hello?" She didn't recognize the caller's number. "This is she," she replied.

Bill sat quietly as she carried on a conversation with someone who seemed to have a lot to say. He looked sideways at her, obviously curious.

She put her phone on speaker. "So, Macy is here with us in Knoxville, and you can come for a visit if you'd like. She's doing great! We've made good progress with her memory. I wanted her to call you, but she asked me to—I suppose so I can answer any questions you might have."

"I see, Dr. Ott." She paused, looking at Bill. "Tell me how to find you."

Dr. Ott gave her directions, and Bill nodded as though he knew where it was. He gestured, letting her know with hand signals that he'd take her to Knoxville.

Ella thanked Dr. Ott and ended the call. She stared at her coffee, nearly in disbelief, and finally said, "Why didn't Macy tell me? She's been there all week! No wonder she didn't return my calls."

Madison came down the steps at that moment. "Have you heard anything from the hospital? I overslept!" She reached for a coffee mug.

"Sit down, catch a breath," Bill poured a mug for her, handing it across the table, followed by the creamer. "No, we haven't. I was just about to call there. Ella got a call of considerable interest, though."

Maddy stirred white powder into the black coffee. "What do you mean?"

"Dr. Sharon Ott called. Macy is in Knoxville, at the University of Tennessee. She's been there for a week." Ella sounded confused.

"Well, that's a good thing, right?" Madison commented.

"We don't exactly know what it means, but I'm taking her over there today to find out," Bill spoke up before Ella could answer.

"Good; I don't think I want to leave Rick alone. I mean, Bud will be by his side, that's for sure— but I intend to be with him as well. You don't know how scared I was last night. He looked like death itself!" She shuddered. "I never want to see him look like that again."

Bill and Ella headed to Knoxville, and Madison drove to the hospital in Erwin.

She parked in the ER lot and walked in the ER main entrance. Tammy was not on duty, but the staff had been expecting her. "Glad to see you, Sheriff McKenzie. That TBI bigshot is raising a ruckus." A large man in blue scrubs motioned for her to join him as he walked toward the patient rooms.

"What kind of ruckus?" she asked.

"We couldn't get enough breakfast to him! He was threatening to walk out and hitchhike to a Cracker Barrel."

"What kind of meds do they have him on?" Madison sounded concerned. Rick was usually a very calm person.

"I don't know, but I hope he isn't like this with you." The man laughed.

"I can handle Agent Malone!" She laughed.

They stopped in front of room 103. Rick was laughing loudly with someone, and the door was closed tightly.

He knocked first, then the man in blue scrubs opened the door and went inside. "You've got company, Agent Malone."

Rick sat straight up in bed, with the hospital gown nearly hanging off one shoulder. He was also wearing scrub pants, and had the legs rolled up. "Madison, my baby girl. Come here and give me a hug!" His left arm was wrapped tightly, and a sling hung loosely around his neck.

"What is he taking?" Madison snatched his chart from the foot of the bed. She looked over the meds, declaring, "He's obviously having a reaction to whatever it is." She stepped back toward the door, intent on finding the doctor.

Dr. McClellan came in before she could storm down the hall. "I've got the problem covered, Maddy," Chip said, as he brushed past her. He pulled a syringe from his lab coat pocket, and popped a shot into Rick's right arm before he knew what hit him.

"Ouch! Why'd you do that, Chipper?" Almost immediately, he lay back on the pillow and quickly calmed down.

"Rick, we had no idea you were sensitive to morphine. You'll be all right now. This is a sedative. After you wake up, if you're still OK, we'll let you go home with Madison."

"OK," Rick said sleepily, as his eyes closed.

By the time Madison sat on the side of his bed and leaned over to kiss him, he was sound asleep.

Madison walked into the hallway with Chip. He explained that the procedure the night before was a new technique. "In fact, I'd only read about it. Luckily, Fernando had seen it done in a hospital in San Francisco. We are not FDA approved to use this experimental substance, but we felt it was Rick's only chance. That artery blew out and we came close to losing him. So naturally, we're writing this up as a normal bleeder closure. Otherwise, there could be problems for the hospital. We don't want that, and I wouldn't let Rick die because of a technicality. You agree with me, I'm sure."

"I have no idea what you're talking about. But whatever you say, I'll go with. Thank you for saving his life." She stood silently for a moment, looking at the floor. "He looked dead when I left for the night. I didn't know if he would make it. When Bill told me you were staying with him, it gave me hope."

"It's my job to save lives, even if it is the man who's marrying the love of my life." Chip blushed. "You're the best, and he better take care to appreciate that, Madison."

"We're like brother and sister, Chip. I couldn't be in love with my brother, now could I?"

"Suppose not; that would give our town a bad rap." He leaned over to kiss her cheek. "Well, Sis, I'll be home if you need me."

"Thanks. I do love you, Doc."

Her smile was heartfelt, but that was not enough to soothe the rejection she'd handed to Chip over the years. She knew he was fond of her, but she was already in love with a tall, green-eyed TBI agent from Washington, D.C. Still, she whispered a silent prayer that he'd meet someone. Chip was a very intelligent man, and would need an understanding woman to care for him. Not that he was needy; in fact, he was the most self-sufficient male she'd ever met. Maybe that was why he didn't have a girlfriend. His independence would intimidate the average woman. But she held tightly to the hope that there was someone out there. *After all, don't they say, there's someone for everyone?*

14

Bill Conway and Ella Walker entered the correct building on the UT campus and found Dr. Welty's office. There inside the waiting area sat Macy, all by herself, reading a magazine.

"Macy!" Ella cried. "I'm so glad to find you!" She rushed to her sister, who jumped to her feet in surprise.

"Ella, how did you—I mean, oh, it's good to see you!"

The two hugged for a long time, talking over each other. Finally, Ella turned to Bill.

"Macy, this is Bill Conway, my friend. He brought me here from Cold Creek. Bill, this is my sister, Macy."

Bill stepped closer and offered his hand, "Pleased to meet you, Macy."

"It's my pleasure, Bill." She shook hands, then looked at Ella. "Wow! You picked a handsome one." They both laughed.

"Actually, he picked me," she said, blushing.

"Now, tell the truth, Ella. You fell for me the minute you saw me," he teased, recalling how she'd tripped over a box and fallen into his arms in the hardware store.

"Yeah, I did, didn't I?"

"So, how did you know I was here?" asked Macy.

"I called your sister, Macy." Dr. Sharon Ott entered the room.

"Oh." Macy turned around to face the doctor. "I was going to call her as soon as I knew how this experiment is going."

Dr. Ott placed one arm around Macy and held the other out to shake hands with Ella. "I told you, we are very encouraged by where we are in your therapy. This is not an experiment, Sweetie. And you are doing extremely well."

"No matter; I'm here now, and I want to know all that has transpired," Ella said.

Bill's phone rang. "I'll step outside to take this. Excuse me, ladies." He walked into the hallway, pulling the door shut behind him.

"Wow! He's a looker, Ella! I hope there is something between you and that guy!" Macy watched him through the window in the door. "What does he do?"

"He's a Tennessee state trooper, a friend of Madison's and Rick's, and now mine. He's very nice. I was pleased that he offered to bring me here to see you," Ella took her sister by the arm and led her to a sofa. "Talk! Or you, Dr. Ott. Somebody tell me something."

"I'm going to let you two talk for a while. We can all go to lunch together later, and you can ask me any questions you have." Sharon turned and went through the door into the back area of the office.

Ella and Macy sat on the sofa talking for some time before Bill returned.

"That was Rick. He's at Madison's in Cold Creek, and feeling pretty good. He has to come to Knoxville to see the doctors on his government insurance, you know, because of the TBI. They will be here after two. Madison is driving him."

"So, he's up to the trip?" Ella asked.

"Well, she's driving, and the passenger seat reclines, so he should be comfortable enough," Bill said.

"What happened to Rick?" Macy asked.

"He was stabbed while trying to apprehend a criminal. The guy got him in the arm and it was stitched up in the ER, but after a while a bleeder burst open. They nearly lost him!" Ella explained.

"Since he's with the TBI, he has to see their doctors here," Bill repeated.

"Can we get out of here and walk around campus?" Macy suggested.

"If you're allowed, sure," Ella sounded like she was questioning how much freedom Macy was allowed.

"I'm completely free to come and go as I please," she smiled. "Let's go outside. These autumn leaves are captivating!"

"OK then, let's go," Bill said, and opened the door for the ladies.

Madison drove into Knoxville and took the exit toward the zoo. "Rick, you need to guide me. I'm not sure I can find your apartment from this direction," she said, waking him up.

"Which exit did you take?" He put the seat up and looked around. "Oh, I see; you did right." After yawning, he said, "Take the next left."

She soon drove into the parking area of his condo complex. "Does Bill know how to find us?"

"I gave him the address. We'll see how well he can follow his GPS," Rick snickered.

"You're mean!" She unlocked the upstairs unit's door and opened held it open for Rick. "I'll be right back," she said, and went back downstairs to get the rest of their bags.

Rick sat in his recliner, looking out the sliding glass door at sunbeams filtering through the screened room of the balcony. "We need to be ready for the thought that the agency doctors might make me retire. From what Doc told me, I can't be on active duty right now with this arm, and maybe never again. Because if I get another injury there, I could bleed to death."

"I know, Honey. He told me too." She wrapped her arms around his neck, leaning over the back of the chair. "I'd feel a lot safer if they do."

"And then you support me, and I'm on disability for the rest of my life?"

"It isn't like you're confined to a wheelchair. Look how well Drew Perry has done." She tried to encourage Rick, but it wasn't working.

"That's different!"

"OK, maybe it is. But please don't worry before they even talk to you." She kissed his cheek and pulled her phone from her pocket. "I'm calling Ella to let her know we're here."

Rick didn't reply.

"Hey, Ella. We're here at Rick's condo. How's Macy?" She listened for a while, then said, "See you then."

She put her phone on the table next to her purse and the keys to Rick's SUV. "They're bringing Macy with them. She said they'll be here in about thirty minutes."

"What do I have in the fridge to drink?" Rick asked.

"Oh, let's see: three beers, a bottle of club soda, two bottles of water, and a bottle of lemon juice. Hey, I can make some lemonade, if you have sugar."

"In the cabinet, above the stove," Rick said. "You might want to dump the ice and get a new bucket down the hall; it's just around the corner."

"Good! I'll put it in...do you have a pitcher?"

"Don't have one. There is a gallon jar, though, under the sink. That ought to work," Rick sounded tired.

Madison clattered around in the kitchen for a few minutes, then went out the door with the ice bin from the freezer. When she returned, he was sound asleep. She snooped in the crisper at the bottom of the refrigerator and found some fresh lemons. She located the cutting board and a sharp knife, then thinly sliced one for floating in the lemonade.

"Ah, that looks pretty," she said softly.

The only glasses that matched were beer mugs, so she put them in the freezer to chill. In the other refrigerator drawer, she found several varieties of cheese, which she sliced and placed on a plate. Next, she rifled through the pantry coming up with Ritz Crackers, saltines, and pretzels. As she placed them on the bar, the doorbell sounded, waking Rick.

He started to get up, but sat back down as soon as the weight of the sling and his left arm hung heavy on his neck.

"Come in; glad you found the place." Madison stepped aside, allowing the three people to enter.

The short woman who looked thin as a pencil stopped in front of her. "I'm Macy Walker. You have to be Madison!"

"Yes. Macy, its great meeting you."

They hugged and Maddy led her by the hand to Rick's chair. "This is my fiancé, Rick Malone. Rick, say hello to Macy," she said.

Rick looked up into a tired, stress-filled face. "I'm glad you're here, Macy. We've been anxious to meet you." He held her free hand for a moment.

For a few seconds, the three were connected. Macy, as a transmitter between them, seemed to be sending thoughts to Madison and Rick. When they broke the chain, each one knew there was an energy at work between them.

"We will get him, Macy. I promise you, we will put him away." Rick didn't say any more about the case all afternoon.

Bill insisted on escorting Rick to his bed for a nap. Reluctantly, Rick conceded. "What's this about, Bill?" Rick shut the bedroom door.

"I got a message from your office. Guess they knew I'd be with you. Anyway, while you were in the hospital, they couldn't get the latest news to you. The shirt had not only Watts' blood, but also Macy's. That proves he was there. And that's not all. There was semen, too."

Rick dropped to the bed. "*No... He didn't, did he?*"

"Don't know yet. But it makes sense when you hear what Welty and Ott have learned through hypnosis, from Macy. And she doesn't know yet herself." Bill leaned against the dresser.

"I've gotta talk to the lab. Tell them I'm napping," Rick said, nodding toward the living room.

"Will do," Bill said. He walked out the door and closed it behind him.

The three women were sitting on the screened balcony eating cheese and crackers and drinking lemonade when Bill returned.

"He's going to take a nap." Bill helped himself to one of the chilled mugs of lemonade. He walked to the balcony, then back to the kitchen, then around the small living room and back to the balcony, repeating this pattern until Madison noticed he was pacing. She followed him to the kitchen and asked, "What's bothering you?"

He just shook his head and walked back onto the balcony. This time he sat down. Madison followed, and kept her eye on Bill.

"Say, Rick doesn't want to go out tonight, so I was planning to get takeout from Calhoun's on the River. I can get enough for all of us," Madison offered.

Macy stood up quickly, spilling her lemonade. The mug shattered on the tile floor. She stood with both hands on her cheeks and screamed.

"It's OK, Macy. Don't worry. It's just an old beer mug. It doesn't matter." Madison grabbed a roll of paper towels from the kitchen.

Ella was on her knees, picking up the bits of glass. Bill led Macy to the sofa and sat with her. "They don't need us. I think they've got it handled."

"I'm so sorry!" Macy sobbed. "I have to get back to my room on campus."

"And we'll take you, don't be upset. I bet Rick breaks them all the time." He laughed, trying to lighten her mood.

It wasn't working. She played with a cloth napkin she still held to. She folded it and refolded it, again and again.

Ella and Maddy soon had the mess cleared away and came to Macy's side. She continued folding the napkin.

"Don't think about that accident again, Macy. They happen to me all the time. Rick will never even miss one of those mugs. His cabinet is full of them." Madison reached for Macy's hand.

Macy jerked it away, and held napkin tightly. "I'm sorry; I've gotta get back to my room! I'm very sorry, Madison. Please tell Rick I'll get him another." She turned and stood at the door, with her back to them.

"We'd better take her back," Ella whispered in Bill's ear. "I'll call you later, Maddy."

Madison nodded, watching them go down the steps.

Rick was awake when Madison entered his bedroom. He held his phone as though waiting for someone on the other end.

"They left," she said in a low voice.

"I heard." Rick put the phone on speaker. "Rick, the DNA is a definite match to Watts and the older Walker girl. No doubt he was there, but we can't say *when* he was there."

"Keep me in the loop. I'll stop by tomorrow after the doctor's appointment," Rick said. He hung up and laid the phone on the nightstand.

"Are you hungry?" Maddy asked. "I thought I'd get us something from Calhoun's."

"That would be nice. Get me the rib dinner, with baked potato," Rick said.

"I'm going to call it in and go pick it up; see you in a few minutes." She went to the living room to call in their order, then went out to the SUV. On the way to the restaurant, she noticed a package store. *Wine would be nice with dinner,* she thought, then gave her signal and turned into the parking lot.

Inside, she quickly located her favorite red wine and took it to the counter.

"I haven't tried this yet. You seemed to go right to it. Do you recommend it?" the cashier asked.

"Yeah, I like it with lots of things. It's a semi-sweet, very light," she smiled. "Even my fiancé likes it, and he's not a huge wine lover."

"Oh, that's encouraging. I'll take one home this evening. Thanks." The cashier rang up her purchase, then added. "I'm new to wine and liquor sales. I'm a student at UT; it's the only job I could find close to my apartment."

"It's a nice area. Good luck with your wine education," Madison replied.

As she passed the package store on the way back from picking up dinner, she noticed several police cars and an ambulance in the parking lot. She pulled in and got out, then walked up to one of the police officers, identified herself, and asked what had happened.

"I'm sorry, Sheriff; I don't see how this is any business of yours," the young man was not rude, just short with his answer.

"I was just here, not fifteen minutes ago. I bought a bottle of wine," she said.

"Come with me," the officer led her to a man in a dark suit. "Captain, this lady was here just fifteen minutes ago, she might have seen something."

"Thanks, Coats. I'll take it from here." The captain opened the door and walked into the store. "Was anyone else in here?" he asked.

"No one that I saw. The young lady at the counter was friendly. We talked for a moment about the wine I chose. Is she all right?" Madison looked beyond the captain and noticed blood on the floor. "Tell me what happened."

"Did you look around at all? I mean, before you chose the wine?"

"No, I found what I wanted right away. I just went to the counter right after. But as we talked, I glanced into the mirror behind her. There was no one else, that I saw. I might have been in the store a total of five minutes; no one came in or went out while I was here."

"And the parking lot?"

"No, there were no other cars; I wondered if they were even open. The woman working said she took this job because it was close to her apartment. I guess she walks to work."

The captain nodded, "Yeah, that's what I figured, too." He looked Madison up and down. "You live near here?"

"No, I'm Sheriff Madison McKenzie, of Cold Creek. My fiancé lives a short drive away. After buying the wine, I drove to Calhoun's for our take-out dinner, then headed back to his condo. I stopped when I saw all the cars and the ambulance. Please, tell me—is the young girl hurt?"

He nodded and said, "She's alive, but it's not looking good for her. She lost a lot of blood. GSW, straight to the heart. I don't expect she'll make it to the hospital."

Madison sighed. "Oh, and she was so sweet. What is her name?"

"Stacy Spencer, from Nashville. She's a student at UT," he said.

"She told me," Madison bowed her head. "I'll pray for her." She started out the door. "Oh, you might want me in the future; here are my numbers." She handed over her business card. "Thanks, Captain."

Madison walked back to Rick's SUV. She saw a man across the street watching her. She thought she'd seen him there as she left the parking lot earlier. Instead of driving away, she crossed the street and pulled up to where the man had been standing. He'd ducked inside the gas station and went behind the counter.

"Hello," she said, entering the convenience store.

"You with the cops?" he asked.

"No, I was a customer right before— Did you see anyone going in the liquor store after me?" she asked.

"No!" He answered too quickly.

"But you saw me leave, and I saw you. Did another car pull in after I left?" She leaned on the counter.

"I thought you weren't with the cops."

"I'm not. But you saw something; please, tell me what you saw. Stacy was a really sweet girl. Did you know her?"

"I've seen her, going to and from work," he said.

"Don't you think if you were robbed, she'd tell the police what she saw? I mean, if it were you dying, instead of her?"

"She's dying? Oh my God! I didn't know, I thought she was just robbed."

"What did you see?" Madison grabbed the man by his shirt collar. "Tell me!"

"It was a white pickup truck, an older, classic model, you know? It has blue ghost flames on the hood and the doors. I've seen it in here a time or two. There's a couple different guys that drive it. Maybe they're brothers? One went inside, and when he ran back out, they drove away fast. I thought they might have stolen a bottle or something. Don't tell them I said nothing!"

"Oh, I wouldn't dare," Madison turned and stopped at the door. "Don't leave; the police are going to need your statement."

She drove back across the street, spoke to the policeman outside, then drove away.

By the time she reached Rick's condo, her cellphone was ringing.

"Sheriff McKenzie, what did you do?"

She recognized the captain's voice. "Hello, Captain. I remembered seeing a man as I was leaving the first time, outside at the gas station across the street. He was out there a while ago after I talked to you, so I went to talk with him. You ought to get his statement. He saw something." She waited, expecting the captain to yell at her.

"So you broke the case by interviewing him. Hmm. Why not just tell me what he told you?"

"That would be interfering with your investigation. No, I'll let you talk to him."

She walked upstairs, and Rick met her at the door. "What took you so long? I heard sirens, and I was worried."

"I stopped for a bottle of wine." She brushed past him and into the condo.

"Did you see a wreck or anything?" Rick followed her.

"No, just stopped for wine." She fumbled through a drawer. "Where is your wine opener?"

"Here," he said, taking the bottle. "Are we sitting outside?"

"Yeah, it's really nice out." She got two wine glasses from the cabinet. "Did the doctor say anything about you drinking alcohol?"

"No hard stuff, but wine is OK." He poured two glasses.

Madison brought the bag of take-out to the outdoor table setting. "It might not be real hot. You want me to heat yours up?"

"Nah, it's fine. Thanks for doing this. I was getting pretty hungry."

"Me, too." She sipped her wine. "Do you know a Captain Driggers, with the Knoxville Police?"

"I've heard the name,"

"He'll probably come by here in a little while. I think I might have upset him." Madison picked up a rib.

"I knew you got into something! How do you always do that?" Rick dropped his fork.

"I just thought he needed help. There was a robbery right after I left the liquor store. If he pulled the tapes, he'd have seen your SUV. I only saw one person, the guy across the street at the BP Station, so I stopped to talk to him. That's all."

"And I guess you are going out looking for a vehicle that the guy said he saw, right?"

"No, I already know where it is. All the captain has to do is go pick the brothers up at the truck show, in the park. It's on the tape too, if he looked."

"Maddy, are you ever going to stay out from trouble?" Rick asked.

"Not when I liked the victim, and she might be dead now," Madison emptied her glass and reached for the bottle. "Maybe I should have gotten two of these."

"She was a sweet girl, that new one. I met her just last week—a student from UT?"

Maddy nodded. "Stacy," she said.

When Maddy cleared away the containers and put the rib bones in a baggy in the refrigerator for Bud, there was a knock at the door.

"Got it," Rick said.

"Evening, I'm Captain Driggers. Is Sheriff McKenzie in?"

"Sure, Captain, come in." Rick stepped backwards and showed the captain into his condo.

"I should charge you with impeding arrest," the captain snarled at Madison.

"But you won't, because you need to get to the park and pick up those two before the Truck show is over." She folded her arms across her chest. "Heard any news about Stacy?"

"She's going to be all right. The bullet narrowly missed the heart," he said.

"Happy to hear that. Which hospital is she in?" Madison asked.

"UT Med," he said, "but you don't have any business going up there."

"Well, yeah, I do," she stated. "Don't worry, Captain. I'm not looking for a position here in Knoxville. Your job is safe," she laughed.

The captain stomped down the stairs and didn't look back.

15

Rick's doctor appointment was at 8:30 a.m., and he grumbled about Madison driving him the entire trip. She didn't listen to him. She did, however, remain in the SUV until he returned two hours later. She was on the phone with Holly.

"Holly, Rick is coming back. I'll hang up now and see what the doctor told him."

"Do you know how to get to the lab from here?" he asked.

"Not exactly; you can direct me." She started the engine and backed out of her parking space. "What's at the lab?"

"DNA puzzles," he said. "Carnes thinks he's figured out what happened, but he can't prove a timeline." He went on, explaining what he'd been told the night before.

Madison gasped. "Oh, no! Is that why Macy is so messed up?"

"Possibly." Rick shifted uncomfortably in the passenger seat. "You will be my chauffeur for some time into the future," he didn't turn to face her.

"Can I get a uniform and one of those cute little caps?" She snickered.

Rick didn't laugh. She knew this was going to be extremely hard on him. He wasn't the kind of guy who sits back and lets folks do for him.

They arrived at the lab, and he invited her in. "I want you to meet everyone. Now is as good a time as any."

Madison walked close to his side, and he held her hand. When they stopped at the door, Rick didn't raise his left arm. She pulled it open and stepped inside, holding the heavy door for him. She noticed he glanced around the room to see if anyone had noticed that she'd opened the door, instead of the reverse.

Introductions were passed around in each room they entered. "I won't remember everyone's names. You all have me at a disadvantage." Madison laughed.

"That's all right, Maddy; we've known who you were for years!" one of the men said.

The lab smelled like the one at UT, where she'd taken so many hours of training. She felt right at home. Carnes showed Rick the testing results he'd been working with.

"It's a good step. Unfortunately, we need a timeline to go with it." Rick scratched his head.

"What about pollens? Can you determine the season?" Madison suggested.

"Sure; that's a good idea," Carnes said. "And if I can get the specifics, we can determine the month, hopefully."

"The murders were in early autumn. What can we learn from that?" Madison asked.

"Plenty! Why didn't I think of that?" Carnes busied himself getting out testing materials. "You two scoot, and I'll contact you when I get something. This will take a while."

"Rick, we should go," Madison agreed.

They drove back to the condo and Rick sat in his favorite chair, facing the balcony. Madison slid open the doors. She pulled a wingback chair up beside Rick and waited for him to tell her what the doctor said.

"I'm finished. They recommended retirement. The job Chip did to save my life, changed my life. Even Dr. Ford admitted I probably would not be here, had he not done the procedure. But that doesn't change the bottom line; I'm a walking experiment."

"How long does he say you have for down time?" Madison slid her chair closer.

"Too long."

"You were thinking of retiring anyway. Why is it bothering you now?" she asked.

"Because I feel inadequate, unacceptable; I can't even take the job of small-town sheriff."

"Ah. Now I see." She sat quietly for a while. "I can always use help in the office. It's better having you there when I go into the field; at least you can keep up with where I am and what I'm doing. Who else can I trust so much?"

"No, I won't be your keeper, or your pet; you have Bud for that." Rick was throwing a full-blown pity-party.

"Bud doesn't stay; he's my deputy dawg!"

"Don't patronize me. I feel diminished. What good am I now?"

"I bet Drew can help you with your state of mind, if you'd listen to him." She got up and walked to the kitchen. "Want some lemonade?"

"No thanks," he said.

Madison returned and sat without talking for a long time.

Rick got up and went into his bedroom, slammed the door, and she heard a loud groan. They'd never had a real argument, except over Trooper Bill Conway. This felt like a wedge between them. How could she help the man she loved without him knowing that she was interfering?

Madison called Holly. They talked until she heard the baby crying, and Holly had to hang up. Then she thought of calling Doc. Surely he'd have some advice for Rick.

Carnes called Rick's phone, waking him from a disturbed slumber. "What?" He swung his feet over the side of the bed, listening. "How is that possible?" he asked. "I'll be right there!"

Madison and Rick drove back to the lab. Carnes explained that once he had the pollen narrowed down to the season, he then compared it to history of the weather and the seasons. The results were a match to the year the Walkers were murdered. Further tests of the blood on the inside of the shirt matched that of Mr. Walker.

"That can only mean the blood spatters on his shirt were there when his arm was injured. The mixture of all these DNA fragments can only lead to one conclusion. The S.O.B. is guilty of murder!" Carnes slammed the paperwork of the results down on his desk. "We've got him!"

Madison didn't know what to say. They had the answer they wanted, but how would they introduce the evidence without tearing Macy apart again? She was already so fragile.

"We have to speak to Drs. Ott and Welty," Madison said.

"Yeah, that's our next step. Let's get going," Rick agreed.

Dr. Welty welcomed Madison and Rick into his office, "How can I help you?" he asked.

"Can you tell us anything about your progress with Macy?" Madison began. "We have a real dilemma with the DNA evidence."

"I'm sure you do. Maybe you need to tell me what you've proven or disproved..."

Rick spoke up. "This is very sensitive, and we can't divulge information that might mess up our case against a criminal. I guess that puts us equally in a standoff position."

"I see. In that case, I have to consult my patient." He reached for the phone on his desk. "Hello Macy, can you come up to my office for a few minutes? I have some friends of yours here."

In just minutes, Macy walked into the doctor's office. "Hello, Madison, Agent Malone. What are you doing here?"

Madison greeted her with a hug. "Macy, we need to know about what Dr. Welty and Dr. Ott have learned from you. We have some DNA results, and need your permission to compare notes for our investigation."

"Tell me; what have you learned?" Macy sat in a chair next to Dr. Welty.

"I can't allow that, Macy," Dr. Welty said. "We are making real progress. If they tell you something you haven't remembered, or in a different way than you remembered, it could delay your progress."

"Oh, kind of like the power of suggestion. I get it," Macy said.

"What we need is for you to allow me to compare our work with their results. Without you hearing it from them. Do you understand?" Dr. Welty asked.

"Oh, like patient confidentiality. You need my permission, but I can't know the whole story," Macy pondered the idea for a while. "OK. I'll sign something giving them—and only them—permission to know my results. Not my sister, not any lawyers, just Madison and Rick."

"Thank you, Macy. We only want to help. There will be no breach of confidentiality, I promise you," Madison said with a sweet smile. "And so will Rick."

"Rick?" Macy stood up as she demanded his word.

"Of course, Macy. I'll sign a confidential agreement with you and Dr. Welty. But you have to think about the fact that whatever we discover could convict a criminal, or let him go free to strike again. Promise me you'll think about it?" Rick asked.

Macy nodded, then signed the paper Dr. Welty provided and left his office.

Dr. Welty opened his laptop and turned it to face Madison and Agent Malone. He pushed play to start the video of the session he'd recorded. He handed Madison a tablet and said, "You'll want to take notes." Then he left the room.

An hour went by before Dr. Welty and Dr. Sharon Ott came back into the office. They sat on a sofa across Madison and Rick, watching the end of the recorded session.

Madison leaned back in the chair, tears running from her eyes. Rick comforted her with his hand on hers.

"What's going to happen if she remembers what she told you?" Rick asked.

"She might accept it as her answer to continue moving her life forward, or she might draw deeper inside herself and become impossible to reach," Dr. Ott told them.

"Our test results confirm your worst fears. Watts was there at the time of the murders, and he was with Macy, presumably in the barn. We have semen that's a match to him, but we don't have a sample from her. Is it possible he didn't physically molest her? Maybe he was only fixated on the thought of her when this occurred. Without an examination, we have no way of knowing," Rick spoke softly, knowing Madison was shocked and feared for the worst of what might have happened that day.

"We have other recorded sessions, but this is the only one with the compelling, unmistakable evidence, where she's speaking directly to him. In her mind, he's there and she's talking about what he's done—"

"Wait! Rewind that to the part where he's talking about his little girl." Madison instructed. "There; now watch her, and listen to her voice. She turned her head, as though she's looking at someone else. She's not talking to him, someone else is there. She's talking to..." Madison stopped, "It wasn't herself she's talking about! It's...his *daughter*. She's telling him what he had done to his own little girl!"

Dr. Welty sat straight forward. "Madison, what are you saying? She's talking about the spirit of his little girl?"

"Yes!"

Dr. Ott jumped up and rifled through a desk drawer. She pushed a small flash drive into the laptop. "Remember, I told you; it wasn't her voice? This is that recording. I didn't think they were connected, but listen,"

The four played and replayed all the recordings from Macy's sessions. Madison was sure she had the right idea, and Dr. Ott agreed with her. They played the recordings in order and in reverse order. Either way, it was clear to the women there was something more going on than the men were picking up on.

"I think it's time to bring Macy in to help decipher them," Dr. Ott suggested.

"Absolutely not!" Dr. Welty objected. "You don't know what damage might come from that."

"It's late; we should stop for now and resume tomorrow. Let's sleep on the idea. Things might be clearer in the morning," Rick said.

"You're right. Let's meet for breakfast and start again," Dr. Welty collected the recorded information and locked in his desk. "How about nine o'clock? Come to campus for breakfast. We can discuss our feelings and take it from there."

Madison drove the SUV to Rick's condo. It was a quiet drive. She knew Rick was worried, but she kept her fears to herself. "You sleep in your bed; I'm taking the couch. And I won't take no for an answer."

Rick let her shower first. He made the convertible couch into a bed, then went to the kitchen for a glass of milk. Twenty-two seconds in the microwave was perfect. He placed a sleeve of graham crackers next to the milk and retired to his bed.

"Thanks, Rick," she called through the closed door. "Goodnight!"

"I love you," he answered.

"I love you, too."

Madison dipped the graham crackers into the warmed milk and ate several of the sweet treats. This was what she did at home when she couldn't sleep. Rick had prepared in advance, because he knew she wouldn't sleep for a while. She had too much to process.

The next morning, Madison awoke to the sound of the shower. She dressed and stepped onto the balcony. The temperature had dropped considerably since they'd come in late the night before. There were dark clouds on the horizon to the west. She hated to see winter coming on, but considering that she and Rick had planned a winter wedding, the idea of cold weather didn't seem so bad. She smiled as she thought of a white world around them, her in a white gown, Rick in a white tux with red tie, and her bouquet of red roses with white candytuft...I It was all she'd ever wanted.

"You awake?" Rick startled her from her daydream of their wedding.

"Yeah. It's very cool today; I'm not sure I brought a warm jacket."

"You can wear one of mine." He opened the closet next to the front door. "Here you go," he said, and handed her a bright orange UT jacket. "I've never even worn it."

"Oh; then I'll take very good care of it!" She snatched it and put it on hurriedly. "Ah, I'm going to be warm today."

Rick started to get into the driver's side. "Not yet!" Madison exclaimed, and took the keys from his hand. "You told me the doctor said not to drive for at least a month."

"You listen too well." He walked to the passenger side and climbed in. "And you're getting awfully bossy, too."

"The better to love you, my dear."

Madison got lots of attention while wearing the UT jacket as they walked across campus. Rick acted a little jealous when the entire cafeteria clapped as she walked in. "I would have worn it if I'd known you'd get such a reception."

"Why is this jacket getting such a reaction?" she asked.

"Did you see the back? It says coach, and has a basketball underneath."

"Oh, it's in memory of Pat Summit. How sweet."

Dr. Welty stood up and waved from across the room. They joined him and Dr. Ott, sharing coffee and an assortment of sweet rolls.

After eating too many carbs and sugars, Rick and Madison suggested they get back to the doctor's office.

Doctor Welty stopped to knock on Macy's door. She opened it and welcomed them in.

"No, my dear, I want you to come up to my office in about thirty minutes.

Will you do that?" Dr. Welty asked.

"Sure," she said.

Inside his office with the door closed, Madison asked, "Are you seriously going to tell her? Is that what you two have decided?"

"Not exactly," Sharon Ott assured her.

"We're going to let Agent Malone tell her that Watts is going on trial for the murder of her family. Rick, you can divulge as much information as you wish, or as little as you'd like. We only need her to prepare for the possibility that she might have to face him in a court of law. We will make our assessment at that point, depending how she reacts," Dr. Welty explained.

"Makes sense to me. Yes, I can handle that." Rick nodded with approval.

They heard a light knock at the door, then Macy walked in. "I'm here."

"Yes, you are. Please take a seat, Macy. Agent Malone has something to tell you," Sharon said. "Feel free to stop him if he upsets you in any way with his choice of wording."

"Sharon, that is uncalled for. I'm sure Agent Malone will be sensitive to our patient. He's a very intelligent young man," Dr. Welty scolded his co-conspirator.

"I'm not worried about what Rick will say. I understand his objective is to bring a monster to justice." Macy crossed the room and sat in a chair next to Madison. "It's about time, isn't it?"

Rick stood up and smiled at Macy. "We only want what's possible, with your tolerance. OK?"

"I'm not as cracked as I used to be. I'm a hardboiled egg now. I believe the inner me has become thicker-skinned. Don't worry, I can handle whatever you throw at me." Macy sounded confident.

Madison prayed silently that she was indeed ready.

16

Madison and Rick hosted Thanksgiving dinner at the Jacobs farm. They invited family, of course. Jess and Shirley came, and Mrs. Jacobs (Harriet) and her son Russell also flew home for the holiday. Ella and Bill brought pumpkin and pecan pies, along with a huge coconut cake.

Dr. Welty drove to Cold Creek accompanied by Macy. Dr. Chip McClellan arrived carrying Madison's favorite: cranberry gelatin salad in a lovely mold shaped like a rose, the center filled with whipped cream. Ben and Marjorie brought a spiral ham and sweet potato casserole. The rest of the food was prepared by Rick and Madison, while Holly, Henry, and the children churned homemade ice cream in three flavors: chocolate, strawberry, and vanilla.

Mr. and Mrs. Olson surprised them all with apple, cherry, and mincemeat pies. And finally, Drew and Nell arrived at the last moment, carrying green bean casserole and five dozen homemade yeast rolls. The entire room filled with the aroma of homemade bread instantly.

"Well, if we weren't already hungry, those rolls would give us an appetite!" Rick clasped his hands together. "Let's eat!"

"One second, Rick," Jess said, then bowed his head. The guests all followed his lead. Jess said a great blessing, ending in "Now, let's eat!"

Dishes clanked as the food was served, and little talking went on for the first few minutes. Finally, Harriet shared their plans to move back to Tennessee in the spring. Henry was happy beyond belief. He had wanted his mother to come home so her grandchildren could get to know her.

"Holly needs help with the children. You just don't know how much that would mean to us. Russell always wanted to raise crops. There are acres filled with timber, good level acreage, and perfect for gardening. I can't do it all by myself, but with the two of us, we can make this into a productive farm. We can harvest the timber for his house. This is amazing; thank you." He got up from his seat and hugged Harriet and Russell. "Let me know when, and I'll fly out and help you move back east."

Henry was excited that his Mother, brother, and nephew were planning to move back to Tennessee. The Friday after Thanksgiving used to be a big event in the Jacobs' household. Santa visits the Johnson City Mall, so the children have photos taken with Santa and tell him what they want for Christmas. This year felt like the perfect time to revive that tradition.

Holly packed a picnic lunch for the kids and her mother-in-law. They'd stop at one of the city's parks and eat, since it was more like summer than fall.

Nicholas and the men left the house before daylight to go hunting. Nicholas advised them that he planned to get a turkey. That way, they wouldn't have to buy one for Christmas Dinner. Henry promised to dress it and freeze the bird. However, in his heart Nicholas knew he'd probably never be able to actually kill anything. It was the thrill of the hunt for him. Henry would go along with his decision, either way.

Madison walked to her office to check for messages and any faxes that might have come in over the holiday. The day was warm and humid, uncommon for late November. She thought of what such warm weather could bring; storms often brewed under conditions like these in the mountains. She hated the thought of another flood or tornado.

Her office fax machine was printing out a bulletin as she walked in. She caught it fresh off the printer. It was a weather alert for a front moving through west Tennessee, heading quickly to the east in a direct line toward her mountains. She sat down and pulled out a list of the town's residents' phone numbers, and started calling to pass along the warning. Then those folks had a list of numbers to call, and those also had a list, and so on, until everyone in the area was alerted to the approaching storm.

Just as she made the last call, another fax printed out. Carter County had discovered a body in Watauga Lake. They had determined the man's identity, and it was up to Madison to notify next of kin. He was a Johnson City resident whose next of kin was now living in her county.

Madison dropped into her chair, reading the name a second time. *Tom Morgan. Notification to be made to Annmarie Morgan.*

Madison could not believe her eyes. She'd just recently met Ann, and gone to her tiny house up on Coffee Ridge. *Now I have to notify her that Tom, who has been missing for just over a year and a half, was found dead in the lake!* Madison called the number on the fax and asked to speak with the sheriff. She was told he was working a case out at the lake, and couldn't be contacted. She asked for more information.

"I'm sorry, Sheriff McKenzie, we don't have any more details. The body was identified by the sheriff himself as Tom Morgan."

"How does he expect me to notify the widow and not be able to tell her what happened?"

"I'm sorry, Ma'am. I don't know what to tell you," the voice on the line said.

"Then I'm going out there, so give me directions. I'll talk to him one way or another."

"There are no roads to the area where the corpse was found."

"No roads, yet your fax says his motorcycle was found too, and the body chained to it. Surely you don't expect me to tell the widow that." Madison didn't get angry very often, but considering it was her place to break this woman's heart, she meant to have details of how it happened.

Madison got directions to Carter County's Midway Marina, where the sheriff's department boat was to meet the coroner's van, and headed out. It took over an hour to reach Midway, and she saw that the boat was already docked. She approached a group of uniformed officers, asked for the sheriff, and paced until he came toward her.

She'd never met Carl Click, but she knew his face from the news. He was always doing interviews on local arrests, or something to do with the always crowded Carter County Jail. He stuck out his hand, turning his head to spit out a wad of chewing tobacco. After shaking her hand, he wiped his mouth with the back of the same hand.

She stared for a moment and then shook her head, looking away. "What can you tell me about the victim?"

"Not much, except that it weren't no accident." He smiled, showing brown teeth. "You just tell the widow to go to the Quillen College of Medicine to see the coroner and make a positive ID."

"No. That is not happening. Ann is a friend of mine. She's a strong woman, but no one deserves to hear this kind of news in that haphazard manner. I'll meet the coroner myself and learn what I can before I meet with Annmarie Morgan." She turned and stalked to the coroner's van.

After what seemed like an eternity, Madison left, dreading the drive back to Unicoi County, and then up to see Ann. *I guess it's better this way; at least she knows she can trust me to tell her the truth.*

The evening brought a strong north wind. Madison stopped at her office long enough to grab her uniform jacket. All the way to Ann's, she tried to think of the best way to relay the news.

She soon turned onto the steep gravel drive leading to Ann's tiny home.

Madison stopped the SUV behind Ann's car. Ann met her at the door.

"What's wrong, Madison?" Ann stepped back, allowing Madison to come inside.

"There's no easy way to tell you this."

Ann motioned for her to take a seat. They both sat down, and Madison unzipped her jacket.

"Ann, some boaters found a man's body in Watauga Lake. They have identified him as Tom. I'm so sorry."

"My Tom? What happened?! Did he run his bike off in the lake?" Ann was shocked, naturally.

"No, there were no roads where he was found. Someone had to have dropped him and his bike from a boat. He was chained to the Harley, and dead when they put him in the water. Ann, he was shot, execution style."

Ann stared at Madison. Her mouth opened, but she could not speak. She stood up and walked to the window. "All this time, he's been in that lake?"

"They aren't sure how long just yet. The coroner needs to complete an autopsy before he can determine that. They requested you make a positive identification."

"I can't do that!" She wheeled around. "He's been under water for *how* long? No; I can't see him. I don't *want* to. I want to remember him as the handsome man I loved, not some...freak that will cause me nightmares! No, I won't do it."

"I understand. And you don't have to. We can get his dentist to ID him by the dental records."

"Johns, Dr. Johns will do that."

"Dr. Johns on Walnut Street?" Madison asked.

"Yeah. He's—he *was*—Tom's dentist."

"I know Dr. Johns. I'll call him and ask that he do this for you." Madison stepped close to Ann, "I'm so sorry. I wish it hadn't been my job to tell you."

"No, I'm glad it was you. I believe people come into our lives for a reason, and this was the reason you came into mine. I know you wouldn't tell me anything wrong. You will find out what happened to my Tom. I know you will, Maddy."

"I will. I promise, I'll do everything I can to figure this out." She wrapped her arms around Ann, who had started crying as the news finally settled in her mind.

After a while, Madison talked Ann into going home with her so she didn't have to be alone. "Just ride with me, so if anyone comes around they'll think you're home. I'll go with you tomorrow to make arrangements, if you want."

Ann was understandably quiet all the way to Madison's cottage. Rick had ridden with Doc to the Erwin Hospital to x-ray his arm. Madison hoped to have Ann settled and resting before they made it back.

The next day, Dr. Johns and his wife Tonya went to the Quillen College of Medicine. They met with the coroner to view the body believed to be Tom Morgan.

When the sheet was pulled down, Tonya gasped, "It *is* Tom!"

Dr. Johns asked, "If he's been in the lake for all this time, why is there no more decomposition?"

"The temperature of the water, is what I first thought," the coroner said. "The water level is lower than it has been in at least a couple of years. The weather has been warmer, otherwise they might not have found him. But then, as I got into the internal organs, I realized the inner tissues were frozen. He hasn't been in that lake but a few days, at most. This man's body was frozen. And he was dead only a few hours when he was put into a big subzero unit."

"Not much point in us doing a charting. I know this is Tom," Dr. Johns said.

"Well, then... If the widow doesn't want to see him, I'll zip him up."

"It's been more than eighteen months. I think it's best if Annmarie doesn't view the body. Especially with that hole in the middle of his forehead. I know I wouldn't want to have that as the last memory of my loved one," Tonya said.

"I agree." Dr. Johns nodded.

By the first week of December, Tennessee and many surrounding states received record snowfall. Life slowed to a crawl, especially in Cold Creek. The elevation of their small town and the surrounding community made them vulnerable to icy roads, because they had plenty of steep inclines. The county highway department salted the roads in advance of winter weather and used snow plows to scrape the loose snow away. However, the more traveled routes of the lower valley roads took priority over the mountain communities.

School buses don't run under such icy conditions, which results in snow days throughout the county. The children don't complain. First snowfalls bring out the sleighs and any form of sliding discs for bundled bodies to enjoy a fun day away from their studies.

However, snow and ice don't last more than a day or two at most in the area. The sun warms the earth quickly, melting away the wonderland playground. Then it's back to school, and plotting for the next snow day.

Ann feared that whoever killed Tom might have been her stalker. But she had no idea what he was involved in, or why he'd been killed. She didn't know why the man was watching her. Ann traded cars to be safe. She got a four-wheel drive truck, even older than her Monte Carlo. But it was low mileage and ran well on the snowy roads.

She'd inquired about having a gate put up across her drive. Madison recommended Smitty, the man who had bought Denny's ranch. He had done some work for her before, and was the older brother of a good friend. She trusted him to know about Ann's unique circumstances.

Smitty had lost his wife a year ago, to cancer. He kept to himself since and worked all the time. He was available the day Ann called him. He met her at the road to help decide where best to place the gate. With thick underbrush and old hardwoods, Smitty advised the gate be set a quarter of a mile from the clearing and her tiny home.

The former owner had left the wild blackberry vines and mountain laurels. This made for a rough patch to walk through, and would deter all but the most determined trespassers. With a gate, Ann would feel more secure. She let Smitty use his best judgement on what to put in. He suggested a camera too, so she'd see whoever approached the gate. With a remote entry, she could control who it opened for. In less than a week, Smitty had the gate and camera installed. Ann called Madison to let her know how pleased she was with her recommendation.

"Yeah, I've known Smitty and his family since I was in second grade. They're good people," Madison said. She thanked Ann for calling, and asked how she was doing otherwise. She had no new information to offer about Tom's murder, making Madison feel she needed to work harder for Ann's sake.

The coroner's office called the next morning to tell Madison they had completed all the tests and collected the clues, though not many, from Tom's body. She would need to relay the message to the widow and funeral home.

Maddy called Ann first. "Good morning, Ann. I got the call from the coroner's office. Do you want me to call the funeral home for you?"

"If you don't mind—and ask them to choose the soonest date available. They can call me, or tell you. Whatever works; I don't have a preference," Ann's voice sounded weak.

"I'll take care of things, then I'll call you back," Maddy said.

The funeral arrangements were set for Tuesday, at Dillon-Taylor in Jonesborough. Tom had been friends with one of the undertakers there. Madison recognized that Ann was comfortable talking with them, as opposed to the places in Johnson City.

A line of mourners streamed out the door by 2:00 p.m. on Tuesday. Services were to be held at 5:00. Madison and Rick recognized many businessmen and ladies Tom had known from his construction company, people from area banks, and city and county police department employees. It was obvious that Tom was well known and respected.

Madison stayed by Ann's side through it all. She and Rick accompanied her to the graveside the next morning, too. By the time everyone left, it was noon.

Ann appeared to be tired and washed out. Madison suggested they go to her tiny house; Rick was to stop and pick up meals for the three of them. Ann was too exhausted to object.

Rick arrived shortly with three large paper bags from Olive Garden.

Ann's face lit up, "How'd you know that's my favorite restaurant?"

"Well, most women are fans of soup and salad. I figured that was always safe. We have three different kinds of soup, salad, the dressing, and then the main course, chicken fettuccini Alfredo. And breadsticks, of course," Rick explained.

But Ann corrected his commentary. "And chicken fettuccini Alfredo for *you*, Rick!"

It was the first time they'd seen her smile in weeks. Rick was pleased the food had brought out a smile.

After an uneventful afternoon while Rick explored the woods around Ann's property, he and Madison said goodbye and headed home. On the way out the half-mile drive, they saw Smitty on his way in.

"Hey, how's the gate holding up?" he asked.

"I think it's exactly what Ann needed for some peace of mind," Madison answered.

"What are you two doing up here?" Smitty had somehow not heard the news of Tom's discovery and funeral.

"Ann just buried her husband," Rick said.

"Oh, no! He wasn't the one they found in Watauga Lake, was he?"

"Yeah, I'm afraid so," Rick said. "But she seems to be on the upswing now. Do you have business with her?"

"No, I was just coming up here to check the gate. After being in use for a while, I like to check to see that everything is tight and working smoothly. I won't need to bother her."

"I don't think she'd mind, Smitty. If she doesn't want to be bothered, she'll tell you," Madison assured him.

"OK, I'll check on her."

Madison drove off, waving as they left. When they reached the road, Rick noticed a panel truck parked on an old abandoned bridge across the creek from Ann's property.

"Keep driving, but look at that old truck. What's he doing there, on that old bridge? I'm not even sure it's safe to drive on." Madison looked as they passed. "No tag on the front. But there can't be that many, what—maybe a 1957?—Chevy trucks, licensed and still running, in this part of the country."

She called Erwin PD, asking the deputy on duty to check for blue '57 Chevy panel trucks with Tennessee or North Carolina tags. He said he'd call her back.

In a few minutes, she got a call from Unicoi County. "No blue '57s, Sheriff, but there is a black '56 Chevy truck, registered to Paul Hensley in Washington County. However, I called and he says it's not running. The motor was pulled for some repairs. There are none within three states."

"OK, thanks, Stan. I'll keep an eye on it for a while to see where it goes." She hung up, then pulled into the driveway of a house down the road. There was a Century 21 Real Estate sign in the yard, so that would be a good cover if the truck drove past. But it didn't.

Ann noticed Smitty's truck and spoke to him over the speaker at the camera, "Hey, is there anything wrong, Smitty?"

"No. Ma'am, I didn't intend to bother you. I always check connections and tighten any loose bolts after a gate's been used awhile, in case something isn't quite up to snuff."

"Well, is it up to snuff?" She laughed.

"Looks great, Ann. I'll be going now."

"Why not come on up for a visit? I'm pretty lonely today. I guess you heard they found Tom."

"Actually, I didn't know until I spoke to Rick and Maddy a few minutes ago. Are you sure you feel like being bothered?"

The gate swung open. "It's no bother. Come on up."

Smitty parked behind her car and walked to the porch. Ann met him at the door. "Have you had lunch this afternoon?"

"No, actually, I was on my way to Cold Creek to the restaurant." Smitty stepped up to the door.

"This might not be as good as Margie's cooking, but it isn't bad." Ann seemed to be happy to share with her visitor, relaxed and smiling.

"I'd like some soup. Olive Garden knows how to do soup!" Smitty said.

"Sit down, I'll heat it up." She opened the refrigerator and brought out the salad. "Salad?" She asked.

"Oh, no thanks, I'm good with just the soup. Is it the pasta and bean?"

"Yeah, there's some of that left; my favorite is the chicken gnocchi. There's plenty of both. Rick brought it."

"Rick seems to be an all-round good guy. I'm glad he and Maddy are getting married."

The conversation was interrupted by a strange vehicle at Ann's gate. She looked at the camera monitor. "Do you recognize this truck?"

"No, I've never seen it before," Smitty stepped closer. "No markings... Let's see if they push the buzzer."

They watched it for a few seconds, then the blue truck backed out and drove away. "Hmmm. Why would it come up this far and not buzz?"

"A few weeks ago, I had an encounter on the mountain above Spivey. That car ran over the cliff, but authorities didn't find the driver." Ann sat down in the chair opposite of where she had seated Smitty.

He turned off the gas to the soup and poured some into the bowl she'd set down for him. "Ann, tell me about Tom. Maybe this is connected to him somehow."

Smitty and Ann talked into the night, and Ann asked if he'd care to stay. She was afraid to be alone after the suspicious truck. "I guess I'm more of a scaredy-cat than I knew. But if you're worried about your home or your reputation, I understand."

Smitty laughed. "I wouldn't worry about my own reputation; this might be a feather in my hat if word got around. But what about your reputation?"

"Nobody knows me here, and I really don't care what people might think. I know what I am capable of and how I feel. Right now, I feel scared. I understand if you don't want to stay; I can call Maddy and ask her to come back."

"No need for that. I'll be happy to stay. I have a gun in my truck. I'll get it, and if you don't mind, I'll stay on the porch."

When he returned to the tiny house, Ann said, "No, these are futon sofas. You'll sleep in here, and I'm up there," she said, pointing to the balcony. "I really appreciate this, Smitty."

17

Unusually warm temperatures arrived while the children were out of school for Christmas break. The Jacobs household received two small four-wheelers from Santa Claus, bringing new opportunities for fun for the older boys and the twins.

They built an obstacle course and carefully retraced the route over and over to wear it down to a round, semi-level track. Henry approved and followed on his adult-sized ATV, observing until he was sure they had a safe area.

Then he and Holly sat back and watched the display of dirt tracking, enjoying the laughter of their four boys.

"How is Rick doing with his arm? Any idea how long he'll be off?" Henry sipped a cold glass of water. "I think I'll call him and invite him out here. Watching the boys might cheer him up some."

"Good idea. Madison says he's driving her crazy, but the doctor says he might not go back to active duty for months, if at all. That was a really experimental surgery, and they don't know how it will hold up. Worst case, she says they might retire him on disability. That'll kill Rick!" Holly shook her head slowly. "He's not the type to just sit at home and enjoy life."

"He told me that he's thinking of postponing the wedding. I'm afraid Madison will be hurt by that," Henry said.

"No, actually, she agrees. They talked about waiting until after the case against Watts is finalized." Holly shifted little Maddie to her other arm. Her baby girl was enjoying her first dose of sunshine.

"Well, good. I was worried." Henry sighed in relief. "I'm going to call him."

"Tell him to bring Madison, if she's not busy. Little Maddie wants to see her."

An hour later, Rick and Madison—as well as Bud, of course—unloaded in front of the bright yellow farmhouse. Madison carried a large pan of lasagna, which she'd gotten from Shirley's Restaurant. She had put together a colorful salad in her own kitchen. She recognized that Holly had six mouths to feed, plus taking care of laundry for them all, and doing everything for the new baby. "Thought you might enjoy someone else cooking for a change."

"God bless you, my friend!" Holly met her with a hug and traded the baby for the lasagna. "And we all love Margie's lasagna; how on earth could you think of a better gift?"

Madison gladly accepted the bundle in the pink blanket. "She's grown since just two days ago! What are you feeding her?" They both laughed. Madison knew Holly was a perfect mother, and had the two best natural bottles any hungry baby could want. "As if I didn't know! You have the best mothers' milk! Your twins proved that."

The two women stayed in the kitchen as Rick went out back to join Henry.

"Hey, buddy. How's it going?" Henry stuck out his hand.

Rick accepted a brisk handshake, "Okay, I guess. Madison's year-end reports have kept me busy for a day or two. At least the warm weather lets me get outdoors. I'm going stir crazy on the snowy days." Rick sat in the lawn chair next to Henry. "Looks like the four-wheelers are a big hit."

"Oh, yeah. And amazingly, they are all taking turns, sharing time on them voluntarily. I'm proud of all my boys!"

"That's great!" Rick sat quietly, watching the boys going in circles on the dirt track. "I hope the weatherman is right. He says this warm front will hold out right on through New Year's Day."

"So does the *Farmers' Almanac*, so maybe they're right," Henry said. "How's the arm?"

"It's doing well. I forgot and tried to do a pull up in the door facing at the bottom of the stairs. That caused some sharp pain. But I don't think there was any lingering damage. It's not even sore today," Rick flexed his bicep, "But I'm going to tell Doc and see what he thinks."

"Man, I sure hope that surgery is holding up. I'd rather read about you in the pages of a medical journal as a successful guinea pig, instead of 'Mad TBI Agent on the Loose!' in the paper." Henry laughed.

"Yeah, me too," Rick laughed along with his friend.

"Are you planning on taking Madison someplace special for New Year's Eve?"

"Shush, don't let Holly hear about it, or you'll have to find a baby sitter." Rick glanced toward the house. "I've made reservations at the Grove Park Inn. Do you think she'll like it?"

"Who wouldn't? And you're right, don't let Holly know!"

"We'll go early for brunch, and she'll spend a comfortable afternoon in the Spa. Then we have a dinner reservation for seven," he explained. "From dinner we'll go into the ballroom for cocktails and dancing 'til midnight, then back to our room. I wanted a suite, with two beds, but there were none available."

"I'm sure she's comfortable enough to stay in the same room with you by now," Henry glanced at Rick. "You two have such a special relationship. I wouldn't worry, whatever happens."

Rick smiled, but said nothing. He so wanted to keep it a secret, but how could he get her to pack what she needed? "Why don't you and Holly go with us? I believe I can still get you a room. You could ask Nell and Drew to stay with the children."

Henry looked at Rick like he'd suddenly grown antennae and had three eyes. "Seriously?"

"Yeah, why not? Have you two ever been out for New Year's celebration?"

"Well..." he paused. "No, not really. I think she'd enjoy it, since you and Maddy are going to be there. I'll have to feel her out, but I promise we won't tell Maddy. I suppose of all people, she'd trust Nell with our little Maddie. She has plenty of milk pumped and frozen already. By golly, you're right! My wife deserves a night out in the city! I'll do it!"

Rick pulled out his phone and pressed one button. "Yes, good afternoon. This is Agent Rick Malone, TBI. I need a second room for New Year's Eve, as close as possible to mine, please. Absolutely! I believe you have my credit card on file? And add an additional reservation for the Spa. Yes...yes, thank you very much. And you too."

"You really carry clout. That's amazing, Rick." Henry shook his head. "I don't know if I have any clothes suitable for the evening. And Holly will need something new. Her clothes are all tight in...spots, with her breast feeding... Well, you know."

"Are you blushing?!" Rick laughed uproariously and slapped Henry on the back.

"Then you'll have to buy her a new dress—and you better get it right! Maybe Nell can give you a hand with that."

"I need to call Nell and see if she and Drew have plans first," Henry lowered his head, looking at his phone.

Rick walked away and took a call from his office. "Oh, really? Fantastic! Thanks for letting me know."

When he returned, Henry had a big smile on his face. "Did you ever notice that Drew and I are the same size?" He laughed. "Well, I didn't either, but apparently Nell has. She suggested I try on Drew's suit coat and pants."

"Well, that's good. So, can I assume she agreed to stay with your family?"

"Oh, yeah; she even asked if she can throw them a ball-dropping party. That Nell is so crazy about kids. I hope she and Drew have one of their own soon."

"I need to discuss something with Madison about that call. Where are the girls, anyway?"

"Where else? They're either in the kitchen or the quilting room, as usual. Yeah, we ought to get them away, for sure!"

"Yep!" Rick agreed with enthusiasm.

The men's noses led them to the kitchen. They were greeted with cold beers and big kisses.

"What do you want?" Henry asked, winking at Rick.

"Nothing!" two voices protested simultaneously.

"You ready to eat?" Holly asked.

"Yeah, I'll get the boys in to wash up," Henry said, then walked out of the kitchen.

"Madison, we need to talk a minute. I just got a phone call from the lab," Rick said.

"OK. Um, Holly, need me to do anything else?"

"No, you two scoot on out of here, and let the heard of wild boys get settled. Then the adults can eat."

"I like the sound of that: feed the kids first. When my folks were little, the men were fed first, then the women, and lastly the children. That was just what they thought was right." Rick stated.

"Oh, maybe your grandparents, but you're too young for your folks to have been raised that way," Holly laughed.

"OK, fine; I read it somewhere," Rick admitted.

Madison pulled him by the hand to the front porch.

Rick and Henry managed to whisk their women away for New Year's Eve without giving away the destination. The Grove Park Inn New Year's Celebration in Asheville was the furthest thing from both Madison's and Holly's imaginations. They stepped out of Rick's SUV in shock, stunned by the lights. Especially Holly, who had never even visited the landmark hotel.

Christmas decorations held Holly's attention like a child's dreams. She rushed over to the enormous fireplace, accented with a full-size sleigh and winter scene. On the opposite wall smoldered a fire built of nine-foot tree trunks. It warmed the stone room, providing the feeling of a winter wonderland in a magical setting. Brightly decorated evergreen trees encircled the room filled with rocking chairs and benches. When she squealed with jubilation, Henry caught her arm and tried to quiet her.

"Hey, don't worry, Henry. She's reacting the way I feel! We should have brought her and the kids here before now. Isn't this an amazing experience?" Madison hugged her life-long friend. "I can't wait to show you around!"

A handsome but elderly man in a red uniform introduced himself as Laird, and guided them to the elevator built into the rocks behind the fireplace. Two young boys wearing green uniforms followed, pushing a cart with all their bags. Laird smiled and welcomed Holly to Grove Park. "Where have I heard that laugh before?" He looked closely at the giggly blond.

"No relation, but I know who you mean," she said.

"Ah, do you now?" Laird tapped the tip of her nose with his white gloved hand, "I'll show you who I mean. One of the perks of this job is that I get to provide guests a guided tour of the premises—a historical tour, that is. Do any of you know the history of the Grove Park Inn?"

Madison nodded and said, "I've only been here a few times, but I've read all about it."

"I think you will find there is way more to this place than what you read online. Enjoy your stay with us." He winked. "Just give me a ring when you're ready for the tour."

He handed Holly a business card and unlocked the door to the first of two quaint little rooms. Both were furnished identically with simple hand-crafted furnishings, reminiscent of the early period when the hotel was first built. The only difference was that Rick and Maddy's room had two double beds, while Holly and Henry's room had a king-size. Neither room had a lot of excess floor space.

The rooms were adjoining, and Rick suspected the women would take advantage of that access to go back and forth many times. They hurriedly put away their things, hanging up dresses and suits. In Holly's case, there was a complete surprise: a new black dress and shoes.

"How? Oh, I don't even care! Thank you, Henry. Thank you so much! I can't believe that I'm here, that it isn't a dream!'

"You deserve everything here and more! Besides, Rick wouldn't come without us," Henry laughed. "I love you, Holly."

They embraced in a long hug, followed by an endearing kiss until Rick intruded. "Come on, I'm hungry! Let's get down to brunch."

"Rick, maybe the adjoining rooms wasn't such a good idea!" Madison pulled him away from the door. "From now on, you knock before you enter!"

"Well, I *am* hungry," he grouched.

"We'll meet you two downstairs," Madison called out as they left their room.

As Madison and Rick were walking slowly toward the elevator, Holly and Henry soon caught up with them. Holly was laughing, as usual.

They strolled to the Blue Ridge Restaurant for Sunday brunch. After being seated beside the large windows overlooking the golf course, the four of them marveled at the way the mid-morning sun lit the majestic Blue Ridge Mountains to the west.

"I see why they named this the Blue Ridge Restaurant," Henry commented. "I bet there's one heck of a view at sunset."

"There is." Rick reached for Madison's hand and continued. "Especially after a rain storm in mid-summer, huh?"

Madison's gaze met his, and the memory of the night they became engaged caused a stir in her gut. "And to think, I was afraid the rain would subdue the view."

A waiter greeted them then, dissolving the memory for the moment. "Welcome, I'm Tyler. I'll bring your drinks while you help yourself to the first tier. Now, what can I get for the ladies?"

"Coffee, please," Holly and Madison answered simultaneously.

"Unsweet tea for me," Rick said, then looked at Henry.

"I'll have coffee too, and a glass of water, please," Henry said.

"This way to the excitement," Tyler urged.

"Thanks," said Rick. He stood, then stepped behind Maddy's chair as she slid out of her seat to join him.

They all made their way over to the food. Rick realized Henry had never been to such a fancy brunch, so he made it seem easy by leading the way. "See anything you don't recognize, just ask me, I've tried it all, and I've never found anything I didn't like. The food here is unmatched anywhere!"

"Thanks, Rick. I think I'll follow your lead."

Holly and Madison landed at the Belgian waffle bar. They loaded up their fresh-off the iron pastries with fresh fruits and yogurt and returned to the table. The guys returned with plates heaping with steak, country ham, bacon, and link sausage surrounding cheesy omelets.

Rick had a second plate, pumpkin pancakes with cream cheese syrup and warm chocolate pecan brownies with whipped cream.

"Rick!" Madison stared, wide-eyed, as he sat down. "Oh, my...what do you plan to do with all that food?"

"Eat it! I'll need the energy to hold out for the tour of the facilities." He laughed.

Henry shrugged and said, "He's got a point."

Conversation lagged, replaced by the sound of forks on china plates. Madison and Holly ate all their fruit and yogurt, leaving most of the waffles. They returned to the tier where eggs of all description sat in steamy serving dishes. Madison chose eggs Benedict and turkey bacon, while Holly went for poached eggs on an English muffin with cream cheese. She added a small side of spin-ach, following Madison's suggestion. They laughed when they returned to the table. Both men had slowed to a snail's pace, and looked as if they were about to burst at the seams. Rick pushed back from the table, took a deep breath, and said, "Henry, while the gals are at the Spa, let's check out the beds for comfort."

"Second best idea I've heard all day." Henry pushed his plates away and sipped some coffee. He reached over and snagged one of Rick's bite size pas-tries, lemon with cream cheese and almond slivers. "Holly, eat one of these, so you can figure out how to make them. They're delicious."

"OK... Or, I could ask the chef what they're called." She laughed and patted her husband's tummy. "You better just call Laird, and let him walk this food off you."

"I will, after a brief nap," Henry assured her.

The women spent the rest of the afternoon in the comfort of the Spa. When they finally decided they'd had enough—the full treatment, being bathed in luxury—they returned to their rooms. There on the beds lay Rick and Henry, knocked out.

"Wake up, you lazy bums!" Holly stood in the doorway between the rooms and called out.

"What? I'm up!" Rick snorted, mumbled, and rolled over to see who had caught him off guard. "Oh, it's just you, Holly. You sounded a lot bigger!"

"Well, let me assure you, I'm bigger!" Madison jumped onto the bed next to her fiancé. "So get up from there, and let's do the tour together."

"We did the tour, just lying down to rest a few minutes—really," Henry stood, looking at Rick and Maddy on the same bed. "Listen kids, we'll have none of that! Madison, that's your bed. Now, if you don't want to be grounded, you'd better remember that," he laughed.

"Are you practicing for when little Maddie is a teenager?" Maddy got up and walked to the window. "What a beautiful view! This is such an awesome place."

"I'm glad we got to spend this time here. In little more than a week, we have to be in court. I'm sorry we had to delay our wedding." Rick reached out to hold Maddy's hand.

"We didn't really have a choice. It's all right. Maybe it will be over by Valen-tine's Day," Maddy squeezed his hand. "This weekend is beautiful. I couldn't have asked for a better honeymoon, except that we're sleeping in separate beds." She felt her cheeks burning. "You know what I mean."

"Yes, and I agree. Our day is coming. Time only makes it sweeter for us," Rick whispered.

Madison accepted Rick's hug, wondering: *Will we ever make it to the altar, Rick?*

Meanwhile, back in Knoxville, Macy found she had time on her hands, and a thought occurred to her. If she "borrowed" Ms. Trammell's identification, she could get into the Jonesville facility, and maybe even talk to a prisoner.

June Trammell was a medical student who worked the front desk of the building Macy was staying in. *She's still away for Christmas break and if her badge is in her desk...*

Macy left her room and took the stairs to the lower level. June's desk was right inside the front door. No one was covering for her, because most of the students were also gone due to the holidays.

She walked to the desk and picked up the phone, pretending to be using it should anyone walk in. The top drawer indeed held the identification she needed. June was a psychology major; that fit right in with Macy's plan.

If she had some big, dark-rimmed glasses and piled her hair on top of her head in a loose bun, she could easily pass as June. Macy took the ID and returned to her room. She dressed as conservatively as possible while she awaited a call back from the Jonesville Center.

Her cellphone rang, making her jump. She was very nervous, but she had to go through with this plan. She could not face Watts in court without this interview. She had to make sure he did not recognize her.

The drive to Jonesville took her through some beautiful scenery. She listened to the radio, enjoying the warmth of the air blowing through the windows and her hair blowing across her face. She'd brought the things she'd need to put her hair up in a bun, like the photo on the ID.

Macy stopped just a mile from the facility. She stepped outside the car and turned her head upside down, brushing all her hair to the top of her head. The elastic held the long strands in place as she twirled them into a messy, roughly-circular bun. Small hairpins secured the sides in place. She sprayed it with hairspray to smooth down any loose ends, then she put on the cheap pair of oversized reading glasses she'd purchased at Walmart.

Macy looked the part of a UT medical student. Now all she had to do to pull this off was act the part.

"June" parked Macy's car in the guest area. She followed the signs leading her through the proper entrance to visit the trustees. Her heart pounded as soon as she passed through the doorway. A man behind a counter surrounded by bars spoke to her immediately. "Please register here, if you have an appointment."

June smiled at the guard and made her legs move in the direction of the guest registry. She almost signed in as Macy Walker, but caught her error in time to change the M in Macy to Medical Staff UT, Dr. June Trammell. Under the column asking the inmate's name, she looked toward the guard. "I'm not sure. I requested the warden choose one for me."

"Oh, you're that shrink, huh?"

Macy said, "I am a *doctor*, specializing in psychology. Criminal minds specifically."

"Yeah, they set you up with a trustee who's about to be released. Watts, I think is his name. He's new here."

"Thank you. That will be just fine," she said, dropping the pen.

The guard spoke into a microphone, then a door slid open and she was allowed to pass. The feeling came over her that this was the point of no return. She had to get through this and back outside without anyone hearing her teeth chattering.

A clang of steel doors shook Macy back into Dr. June mode. She went in the interview room as directed, reminding herself that she had an important job to do. The prisoner was brought in moments later. *No chains?! Oh, my, how do they expect... Well, I'll just have to be very watchful.*

The man who'd given her nightmares all of her life stood in front of her, just a couple of feet away. Only a heavy table stood between them. Macy was relieved that she was already seated; her legs had turned to rubber. Her knees knocked together under the table anyway. She glanced at the guard, a pleading look for security.

The guard stood at attention and stepped back against the door. Macy swallowed hard, searching for the bravery of Dr. June Trammell's character.

Watts spoke first. "Looks like you've seen a ghost," he laughed. "How would you react if they'd brought a hardened criminal?"

"I would have smiled," June smirked. "This is serous research for me. I'm specializing in deeply criminal minds. What can you offer? They say you continue to claim your innocence."

"Of robbery and attempted murder, I *am* innocent. I never stole anything from that store, except I used some peroxide to clean up my arm and wrapped a bandage around it. Then I left. That man lied." Watts sat back in his chair. "That sound to you like I'm the villain?"

"Why was your arm bleeding?" Dr. June asked.

"Now, that's where I'm guilty. But they never asked."

"I'm asking." June leaned forward on the table, feeling like she might vomit.

Watts leaned forward, elbows on the table, and began his story.

Inwardly, Macy cringed while listening as he described the horrible scene that had played out in her mind all these years—but "Dr. June" took notes. She'd never expected him to tell her what she wanted to hear, but he did.

When he finished speaking, he sat back again and waited for her to catch up with her notetaking. "Well, Doc, am I criminally insane enough for you?"

She scribbled a couple more words, then stood up. "No, you are not insane. You are just a cold-blooded predator, with no feelings whatsoever. You deserve to spend the rest of your miserable life behind bars." June calmly closed her notebook and turned to leave.

"I was pulling your chain, Doc! I made it all up. Or maybe I heard another inmate tell that story. Don't get all high and mighty, you got what you wanted. You heard the gory details; isn't that what you were after?"

"You're right, you gave me exactly what I wanted." Macy continued to the door leading to freedom. The door opened, and she passed through it gratefully.

Back in Asheville, Henry and Rick led the women on a tour of the historical Grove Park Inn. Madison and Holly appeared shocked that the overstuffed men had actually joined Laird and listened to his stories. Henry stopped in front of an 11 x 14 sepia photo of a group of guests.

"See that woman in the big floppy hat?" Henry put his hand on Holly's shoulder. "She's the lady he says laughed like you. He was a young boy, but he remembers her."

"Why, that photo's got to be nearly a hundred years old! How'd he remember that?" Holly clearly did not believe her husband. "Next you're going to tell me that's Dolly," she laughed.

Rick came to Henry's rescue. "He really did say that, Holly."

"There's the date: July, nineteen forty-one. Laird is eighty-seven, so, yeah; he could remember her," Henry said.

"His mother worked here in those days, and he got to come to work with her. She dressed him in a little uniform and let him carry bags for tips. The hotel approved it, and he became a bell hop," Rick explained.

"Wow, he's worked here all his life," Madison said. "No wonder he's so comfortable in his job."

They continued looking at the many pictures, a photographic history. Rick pointed to his watch and reminded Madison their dinner reservation was for 7:00.

"How much time do you girls need?" Henry asked. "We fellows are going to get ready and go up to the lounge for a beer while you ladies get ready. I know Holly wants to do your hair and makeup, so we're going to get out of the action," Henry said.

"That's a relief. I thought I was going to need to dress and do all that stuff in that small bathroom," Holly laughed.

At ten minutes 'til six, Rick and Henry left the room. The girls had showered at the Spa, so Holly began working on her makeup while Madison did hers. Then she quickly did a fancy braid on her own hair. Madison had requested she go with a French twist, so Holly got to work.

The guys returned an hour later and were met at their doors by two gorgeous women they pretended not to recognize.

"If my wife catches me with you, I'm dead!" Henry laughed, and gingerly gave Holly a hug.

"She'll allow it, just this one time," Holly said, and then they all heard her signature laugh.

"If Madison gets any prettier, I'm not going to be able to keep my hands off her until Valentine's Day." Rick reached for his fiancée's hand and kissed it. "My love, will you reserve all the dances for me this evening?"

"We'll see." Maddy gave him the sexiest look she could imagine, batting her eyelashes, which were layered with three coats of volume boosting mascara. Her black dress fit like a glove, the perfect background for her white pearls. Matching black two-inch heels were embellished with white faux pearls, and she carried a small black clutch evening bag.

Madison felt truly elegant on the arm of Agent Rick Malone. Clean shaven, sporting a black suit, light gray shirt, and black silk tie, he was looking even more handsome than the day she first met him.

Holly looked like a movie star in a black off-the-shoulder, knee-length dress, form fitting in all the right places. She hooked arms with Henry, looking tall and slender dressed in Drew's dark gray suit and a light blue shirt with a black silk tie.

Madison smiled at her amazing friends. "We've got to take photos. I've never seen you two look so beautiful." She pulled her iPhone from her bag and posed them for the shot. Henry took her phone to freeze the moment for Madison and Rick as well. At the elevator, Rick snapped a selfie of all four of them.

The foursome emerged from the elevator and joined dozens of handsomely-dressed couples heading toward the Blue Ridge Restaurant to begin the evening of celebration welcoming the New Year.

The couples lingered over dinner, desert, and coffee, knowing the night would be long. It had already been a lot of fun. They were seated next to a table of folks from Charlotte. They were about Rick's age, and all of them talkative and funny. Henry noted that as the bubbly flowed and hours passed, their antics might become very comical. Sometimes it's worthwhile to sit and watch others.

When the couples strolled to the ballroom, Rick asked the ladies if the other group was offending them in any way. If not, he suggested they sit at a table close by, to observe and listen to the conversations but not necessarily have to take part.

As the orchestra began playing, Rick pulled Maddy onto the dance floor. He knew she'd need a lot of persuading. The song was a slow one, and several other couples joined in. Madison bumped elbows with a tall lady wearing an emerald green dress. When she spoke to excuse herself, she was surprised to see it was Ella, and that Bill Conway held her close.

"Hey, you two. How nice to see you! I had no idea where Rick and Henry were taking us. Did you know?" Madison asked.

Ella answered, "No, I had idea either. Bill asked me to accompany him to Asheville for dinner, and we drove up here. Isn't this a wonderful coincidence?"

Rick looked disappointed to see his former rival. He nodded to the man. "Conway," he said coolly. "Ella, you look magnificent! I barely recognized you."

Madison insisted they move to the table occupied by her friends. Bill balked at first, reacting to Rick, but Ella and Madison were so excited that he gave in. After a couple more dances, Holly suggested they go powder their noses. All three women stood up and disappeared in the crowd.

"Rick, listen, I didn't plan this because I knew you and Henry were bringing your ladies here. I had no idea. I've been here for New Year's many times, and I wanted to share something beautiful with Ella. She's special to me. I was as shocked as you were when she and Madison bumped into each other."

"Madison and Holly didn't know, either. So...how could you?" Rick admitted, grudgingly. He slid back in his chair, as if to pull as far from Conway as possible.

"Let's give our women the night of their lives. They obviously love Ella, and she loves them. Whatever grudge you hold against me, let it slide; let this night be about them," Bill said.

"He's right, Rick. This is all for the women we love," Henry declared, then picked up his beer and chugged it. "As for you, Conway, I trust your intensions are honorable where Miss Ella is concerned?"

"Nothing but honorable. She's amazing! I really care for her." Bill stared straight at Rick.

"Good, then let's enjoy ourselves." Rick raised his frosty mug.

Bill and Henry toasted with him when he exclaimed, "To the three most beautiful women in the world!"

Some time passed before the girls returned. When they did, their arrival was heralded by Holly's laughter.

"Rick! This is my favorite song," Maddy pulled him to his feet. "Hold me, baby!" she cried. Then the two whisked across the dance floor, out of sight.

"Rick Malone, you'd better behave tonight. Ella is on cloud nine. She's falling for Bill, and I know he's really fond of her too. Please be tolerant, for Ella's happiness," Maddy pleaded.

"I am, I promise. We guys already signed a treaty." Then Rick laughed and pulled Maddy against his body, swaying to the music and singing in her ear. "Every song we dance to is my favorite, my love."

The orchestra took a break, and Holly mentioned the photo upstairs. Bill explained that he had a friend who owned property and a house close to the Inn. He told them he spent a lot of time here when Wheezy was in Europe. One week, when he happened to be in town while she was here, she told him some of the old stories about the Inn.

"You know this was a prisoner of war camp at the beginning of World War Two, didn't you?" Bill whispered to Holly. "There are all kinds of stories I can tell you about this place."

"I read on one of the photos that there were German officers here. Is that what you are referring to?"

"Oh, yeah, and Wheeze's grandfather had a notebook with names and addresses of local residents, many of them women, who were invited to the Inn on occasions to 'entertain' those officers. High-dollar call girls, you know."

"The ones in the *photos*?!" Holly shrieked.

"Possibly, and there were a number of babies born from those encounters. It was all very hush hush, but some of the women were very young, and single. Some of their babies were adopted out to rich people, in secrecy. Those who did not want to give up their babies were run out of town."

"Oh, that's just awful!" Holly's eyes welled up.

"Now, Holly, don't get your tears flowing, or we'll have to redo your make-up," Madison said. "I'm sure Bill is exaggerating."

"No, I'm not. I'm telling you what Wheeze's grandpa told her. He was a chef here at the Inn. He saw a lot of things, and because he was a trusted employee, he kept the notebook. He only gave it to Wheezy because he was dying. He swore her to secrecy while she was young. She's going on eighty-something now; she'd never lie about this. This Inn is like family; every one of her relatives worked here in some way, at some time or another. She inherited the house, and she's the only one left. That's why she adopted me. She thought I was trustworthy, I guess."

"Have you seen the book?" Rick asked.

"I have. There were descriptions of women the officers liked. The women thought it was honorable to be included. One family in particular had a son who was a high-ranking United States Army officer. He learned that his younger sister was one of the women, and he convinced her she was a traitor. She ended up going to Germany to visit the families of the prisoners. When she returned, she was arrested and charged with espionage."

"Where is the book now?" Henry asked.

"At Wheeze's house, but I don't know where," Bill said. "Wheezy knows, but she's very protective of it. I'm only telling you because I know you won't say anything."

The orchestra returned, and the music seemed louder than before. The scandalous conversation was over.

18

January 12 was Snyder Watts's hearing. The courtroom was full of buzzing reporters and spectators because someone had leaked the story to the news that he was going to be charged with murder. The prisoner was brought into the room in cuffs, but no shackles. Seated across the room from the judge, in a box large enough to hold several prisoners, Watts sat alone. Two sheriff's department deputies stood guard.

The charges were read: murder in the first degree, three counts. Watts jumped to his feet, "No way! What are you talking about?"

"Silence!" the judge yelled, followed by pounding his gavel three times. "You will not address this court unless spoken to." Old Hardnose, as he was called behind his back, had spoken.

Judge Hargrove was the best the district attorney could hope for. He was known as the hang 'um judge. The closer he got to retirement age, the harder he got on criminals. Rick felt grateful for his selection in the case against Watts. He wanted the maximum penalty, and Hargrove was the judge most likely to hand that sentencing down.

Rick winked at Madison as she came in and sat next to Macy and Ella. Tennessee State Trooper Bill Conway, now a regular figure at Ella's side, sat on her left. The prosecutor called Rick to explain the charges. The court-appointed attorney objected, and the judge reminded the attorney that this was not a trial, only a hearing.

Rick took the stand as representative of the State of Tennessee Bureau of Investigation against Watts. He explained how the state came to the charges of murder.

Watts jumped to his feet, yelling out, "No way!" once again.

"I will not warn you again! One more outburst, and you will be gaged or removed from these proceedings." The judge remained somewhat calm this time.

The assistant district attorney excused Rick, then he turned to Macy. "I understand you are the material witness. Do you have anything to say at this time?"

"You bet I do." Macy stood and made her way through the swinging door to the witness chair.

"This is highly unusual, Your Honor!" the defense attorney exclaimed, standing.

"Not in my courtroom! Sit *down*!" he barked, and slammed the gavel three times again.

Macy sat down, looking straight at Watts. She took a deep breath and blew it out slowly.

"Take your time, Ms. Walker," the ADA said.

Macy began with, "You thought you got off easy, seventeen years ago, when you were not arrested for murder. You just got a brief reprieve." She looked toward Ella, swallowed hard, and leaned toward the prisoner. "I watched you slaughter my father with his own ax. You did the same to Momma, when she ran out to help Daddy. And then my grandma took down the shotgun, and ordered me to take my siblings and hide. She too was murdered, but she got a shot off at you, hitting your left arm."

"We were under the bed when you came upstairs and went into each bedroom, picking up whatever you could find to steal. One of Grandma's earrings fell to the floor and rolled under the edge of the bedspread. I was afraid you'd bend down to look for it. You were facing the mirror, looking at your arm, so I slid it out from under the bed. You bent to pick it up and nearly saw my hand. I knew you would kill us too, if you did."

Macy left her seat, doing the unthinkable; she approached the man she accused. It was as if the judge was entranced by her story, allowing her to walk closer. One of the deputies held out his hand, stopping her just short of Watt's reach. Macy didn't blink. She stood where he'd stopped her, but never looked away from the monster she'd held inside her mind for all these years.

"I was afraid you'd come back, so I followed you. My little sister was asleep, and so was the baby. They didn't know I'd left them. You saw me on the stairs, from the kitchen door. I followed you to the barn, where I knew I could find a bottle of Granddad's hidden moonshine. You wanted more than the drink, but I begged you not to hurt me. The shine was good, and it was powerful. You began telling me I was about the size of your little girl. You told me all about her, and how she died from running into the road in front of a truck.

"Hannah was there in the barn with us that day. She told me what you did to her, how you made her sit on your lap. She didn't want to play house, but you made her. The more you drank the meaner you got. She didn't run in front of the truck accidentally. She ran to get away from you! She turned and laughed at you when the truck hit her.

"You cried and blamed Daddy, but Hannah said it was *your* fault she died, not my daddy's. You came after him anyway. You killed them, all three. You thought you took my childhood innocence from me that day. But you didn't; Hannah stopped you. You saw her. She scared you out of the barn and away from our property. Your Hannah saved me, but she won't save you. No one can save you now."

There was not a sound in the courtroom. No one moved, except Watts. He threw his arms over the deputy's head, pulling the chain between the cuffs tight against his throat. The second deputy pulled his gun and fired, hitting Watts. He pulled harder, and the officer fell to his knees.

Watts was bleeding but not down. He jumped over the railing with the deputy's pistol in his right hand. He grabbed Macy in a flash, and warned the other deputy to stay back. Rick leaned forward but with the gun pointed at Macy's head, he didn't dare try anything that might get her hurt.

Watts pulled her backwards with him to the door he'd been led into the courtroom through. No one moved. The handle wouldn't turn; the door was locked. Watts tried again, desperate. His arm was bleeding badly down the front of Macy's clothes. He cried out in anger.

When he suddenly released his hold on Macy, she ducked from under his arm and fell to the floor. Watts put his hand out in midair, as though reaching for someone, but no one was there. His hand turned, as if cupping a child's face.

Macy slid away and stood up, then walked backwards to Rick. He pulled her against him.

"You did great!" he whispered. "Are you OK?"

Macy nodded slowly, gaze locked on something most of them couldn't see. "It's Hannah," she said quietly.

Watts dropped the gun, then dropped to his knees. "I'm sorry, Hannah! I'm so sorry!" he wailed.

The deputy approached, kicking the gun away. He pulled Watts roughly to his feet, then both deputies led him to the door. One turned the handle, and it opened freely. The prisoner was taken away, and additional charges added.

The judge stood, then everyone else stood slowly. "This court is adjourned," he said. He carried his gavel out of the courtroom with him. Ella and Madison sat perfectly still, not knowing which way to turn. Bill Conway put his arms around Ella and held her close to his chest.

"Are you all right?"

"Yes, and Macy is OK. What will happen now?"

"He'll be charged with three counts of murder, in addition to the attempted escape," Bill said.

Madison got up and went to where Rick and Macy stood, talking with her doctors.

"That was some idea of yours, Dr. Ott. I'm glad it worked."

Rick wrapped Madison in his arms and held on to her.

"Are you all right?" he asked.

"Yes. What just happened, Macy?"

"What do you mean?" Macy had a wicked smile on her face.

"How did you know about Hannah?" Madison asked.

Then Dr. Sharon Ott explained that there was one session when Macy remembered seeing Hannah. After digging into the files, they located the story of a little girl hit by a truck. It happened that Macy's dad was the driver of the truck; that was why Watts came to kill him. Sharon recited, "Zachary Walker's truck kills young girl identified as Hannah Watts. Witnesses reported the girl ran into the road and froze. No charges were brought against Mr. Walker."

"Oh, gosh! How did we not know this before? That's the connection between Watts and the Walkers."

Ella and Bill joined the group.

"Why do I feel like you, Rick Malone, had something to do with this? What did you put my sister up to?" Ella asked.

"No, you've got this all wrong," Rick protested. "It was Sharon's idea, and Macy's."

"I'm expecting a full explanation!" Ella stood with her arms crossed.

"I know how you must feel to be in the dark, but it all happened over the New Year's weekend. I didn't get time to talk to you." Macy hugged Ella. "It was the only thing to do. He was about to be released."

Rick allowed Macy to leave with her doctors. "They want to keep her under observation a bit longer to make sure she's really OK with this."

They said their goodbyes, then Rick, Madison, and Ella returned to Cold Creek. Bill had to be back on duty in Knoxville for the next five days.

Bill shook Rick's hand. "You still want me to stand up with you?"

"Sure do," Rick said.

"What? You want Bill in our wedding?" Madison sounded shocked.

"Henry will be my best man, and Bill an usher," Rick explained. "Ella and Nell are your bridesmaids, with Holly as your matron of honor. I'm still short one man."

"No, you have Drew, remember? But it's okay with me. Does make more sense than having Jess up there with you."

"I've never been in a wedding," Bill said, then looked at Ella with an arched eyebrow. "I need the practice."

Ella blushed, and they kissed goodbye.

* * *

Every day that passed, Holly thought about the weekend stay at the GP Inn. She knew nothing about her family history. Her grandmother had raised her, and she was told that her mother ran off when she was just a little girl. She suspected that her mother had not been married, because she got into her mom's things one day and found no photos of a wedding or of her father. In fact, a father figure was never even mentioned. She hadn't thought to ask until it was too late. Her grandma had lost her memory and went down quickly.

Holly was a teenager then, left to fend for herself. Shirley took her in because she and Madison were together all the time anyway. Before Holly could go through her grandma's things to find some answers, the house was hit by lightning and burned to the ground. There was no one left to ask. Holly had never even known what happened to her grandfather. She knew there had to have been a man in her grandmother's life at some point, or there wouldn't have been a mother to give birth to the granddaughter.

Holly felt so alone at times when she thought about where she came from. How could she find out? Her grandma didn't have any friends. She stayed home and made apple butter and jelly, as well as canning wild honey, potatoes, green beans, and other vegetables she grew in her own garden. She had lots of fruit trees and berry plants, too. She'd always had a neighbor plow her garden next to the road. As long as Holly could remember, she'd helped her grandma in the garden. There was a barn up the holler, a cellar against the hill above the creek, a woodshed out back, and a vegetable stand next to the house.

Cars passing through the area often stopped to buy the preserves and honey. Sometimes they even bought potatoes and beans. From the time she was five, Holly sat at the veggie stand and took money for the items her grandma put up. She knew how to count change back; sometimes people in nice big cars gave her money and told her to keep that for herself. She liked those days, but she always gave her grandma the coins. She had nowhere to go to spend them.

Holly's grandma worked in the garden from sunup to sundown in summer. She and Holly picked berries every day while they were in season. On rainy days, Holly helped her grandma make the preserves or can the beans and potatoes.

Holly was disturbed by the mystery women from the Grove Park so much so that she began looking up anything she could find to read about who had stayed at the Inn. One day it distracted her so much she almost let little Maddie fall off the bed while she read an article online. It scared her bad enough that she stopped worrying about the history of the Inn. Little Maddie was rolling over very early. She'd require closer watching than the twins ever had.

However, in a day or so she found herself thinking about Laird and the stories he knew, so she called the Grove Park Inn and asked to speak to him. To her amazement, he came to the phone.

"Hi, this is Holly Jacobs. We met over New Year's. Um, I'm wondering about the lady that you said laughed like me. Do you know who she was?"

"Yes, I do. She always interested me as a child, because she was so much fun to listen to. I still remember her voice; it's so much like yours. Why are you asking, Holly?" Laird asked.

"Because I think she might have been my grandmother," Holly said, her voice shaking.

Laird was quiet for a few minutes, and then he said, "Where do you live?"

"In Cold Creek, Tennessee. It's just across the state line."

"Yes, I know where it is," he said. "Can we meet someplace and talk? I don't think this is appropriate on the phone."

"I suppose we can, but where?"

"How about at the Visitors' Center? Is that near your home?" He asked.

"The one on the Tennessee side, or the North Carolina side?

"Tennessee is easier to get to for both of us. Tell me a good day and time and I'll be there, Holly."

They agreed on a time the next day, and Holly set into motion a plan to have someone watch the children for a couple of hours.

By 10:30 the next morning, she had Maddie down for her nap. The twins were playing in the fenced-in back yard, in their sandbox. Bear was lying next to them protectively when Nell drove up.

"Good morning, Nell. Thank you so much for coming. How is Drew?"

"He sends his love. He'd have come with me, but he's working from home now. You know, on the computer?"

"Yeah, Henry told me about that. Something about taxes, was it?" Holly asked.

"Yes, he's filing tax returns for people. Some days he has more than he can handle. I even helped him out last week, he had so many," Nell said.

"I'm glad he has something to keep him busy. He's such a wonderful man. I know he'll be able to walk completely without that walker one of these days. I pray for him every night." Holly hugged Nell and said, "And for you too, Nell."

She pulled Nell into the house by the hand. "Maddie is asleep in our room; she should sleep a couple of hours. The twins are out back, playing in the fenced playground. I have a pitcher of tea and one of Kool-Aid sitting on the table on the back porch. You help yourself to tea, and if the boys are thirsty they can have Kool-Aid."

Nell stepped onto the back porch, settled onto the swing, and pulled a book from her purse. "Go on now; you scoot, and take your time! We'll be just fine. Don't you worry."

"There are sandwiches already made in the fridge, and there's one for you too. If Maddie does wake before I return, you'll find her bottle in the door of the 'fridge." Holly backed into the house and closed the door quietly. She went to the garage Henry had built for their SUV and quickly drove away.

In just ten minutes, she circled the parking area of the Tennessee Visitors' Center until she spotted a white Caddy parked near a picnic table. She recognized Laird standing next to the table. She waved, and then parked her car beside his.

Laird met her at her vehicle, greeting her with a big smile. "I'm so happy you called me, Holly. I've always worried about what happened to those babies."

"Those babies...you say that like they were a special breed." Holly said slowly.

"They were. They came from the most beautiful of all the ladies in Asheville. And those prisoners were the elite, the best of the best: blond-haired, blue-eyed, super intelligent. They were the most outstanding men Germany had to offer. It only made sense that the babies were exceptional!"

"You say that like it was a plan; like that was the purpose of the parties. Is that what it was? A baby-making affair?" Holly's eyes fogged over.

"No, no, my dear. Not at all. The officers were gentlemen, but most had never married. They longed for love. They wanted to take the women with them back to their home country, but the government would not allow it." Laird sounded angry.

"The German government? Not our government?"

"The US didn't really know all there was to know. The people of Asheville kept secrets: the babies." He placed his hand on her shoulder and walked her to the table.

Holly saw that he'd put down a tablecloth and placed a couple of glasses and a bottle of wine on the table. There was also a picnic basket, which he opened to pull out a loaf of bread that smelled freshly baked and was wrapped in cloth. He opened a plastic container of cheeses, some grapes, and apple slices to go with it.

"Have you eaten lunch?" he asked.

"No, but I don't..."

"Well, I'm hungry. Eat with me while we talk. We don't look suspicious that way," he laughed.

He and Holly sat down on soft cushions he had provided. Laird poured two glasses of wine, then handed her a paper plate and napkin.

"I love picnics!" he exclaimed. "And I rarely get to share one with such beautiful company. Go on, help yourself." He reached back into the basket and brought out another container. "I nearly forgot the chicken salad. Chef Devon made it up for me, first thing this morning. He makes the best I've ever eaten."

Holly watched as Laird sliced off a chunk of bread, spooned some chicken salad into a hole he dug out in the middle, then topped it with a dab of cheese. He offered it to her. She accepted it and waited until he made another. They toasted their wine, then she tried the chicken salad.

"Oh, my goodness!" She took another bite. "That's the best I've ever tasted, too."

The conversation was light during the meal. As soon as they finished eating, he asked her to walk in the sunshine with him. They strolled across the grassy field and Laird told her everything he knew about the woman in the photo.

When he had been quiet for a while, she pulled a photo from her pocket. "This is my grandma who raised me. I never knew my mother, father, or grandfather. I didn't ask questions when I was growing up; I was happy, and just never thought to ask. I suppose it was foolish of me, but I trusted that I knew all she meant for me to know. She worked so hard to care for me. As I look back on it, I believe she worked herself to death. She had a big garden every year. We collected berries, fruit, and vegetables—and when she could find some, she brought honey home from on the mountain. She preserved it all, and we ate what we didn't sell. We had a hog one year, and I remember she cried the day she butchered it. But we had pork all winter. It was the best eating we ever had in the winter. Sometimes our neighbors traded beef for honey and jelly, and we had plenty of chickens. But that was the best tasting pork I ever put in my mouth."

"This looks like Gretchen. She looks much older, but that's only natural; she *was* older. What about your mother?" Laird handed her back the photo.

"All I know is that Grandma said one day she was sitting in the veggie stand talking to folks that passed through, and the next she was gone. I was just about a year old, maybe a bit younger. Grandma had a rough time that year, because she had to keep working with me at her side."

"Did she have any idea where your mother went?"

"Nope. She told the sheriff of Cold Creek, but he claimed she must have just run off. I don't think he ever even looked for her."

"What about your grandmother's house? Do you still have the place?"

"No, it was hit by lightning and burned to the ground, not long after we buried Grandma."

"Hmmm. How interesting." Laird stopped and turned to walk back toward the table. "So you have nothing left that belonged to her?"

"Nothing."

"What was the name she went by?" Laid asked.

"Louise Grover, and my momma was named Sonya. And that made me Holly Grover."

"Same name as your grandma. So that means your mom wasn't married." He rubbed his chin. "It's a shame that you don't know who your daddy is."

"Do you think that was Grandma in that photo?" Holly stopped and faced Laird.

"Yeah, I do, Holly. Because her full name was Gretchen Louise Hollister, not Louise Grover. Think about it: *Grove* Park Inn, Grover. She wouldn't use her family name, Hollister, because they might find her. The Hollisters are a big family in Asheville; they came from old money. See, your grandma was well endowed, but she was only fifteen. I knew her because we had gone to school together. I was just seven or eight, but I remembered seeing her. After she started going to the Inn, she ran away from home. Mr. Hollister looked for her for years! He spent a fortune looking for her, when all along, she was just across the mountain in Tennessee."

"Thank you for talking to me, Laird. I wish I had asked more questions before, I really do."

"Are you sure there's no one who might know anything about where she came from?"

"No one I can think of." She shook her head. "She worked all the time. I mean, she was friendly, with the neighbors and all, but she hardly even slept. She was up when I got up and still up when I went to bed."

"What about neighbors?"

"We had a few, but they were old and most have passed. There are a few of their kids still around, but I doubt if they knew anything."

Laird promised to keep their secret quiet, and he wished her good luck. "If you ever want to know for sure, I bet you can get your DNA tested against the Hollister Family."

Holly nodded as she put the SUV in reverse and backed away. She waved at Laird who stood outside his car.

She drove slowly past the old home place on the old Asheville Highway. She and Henry had sold it a years ago, but no one was living on the property or even using it. She turned suddenly into the drive beside the foundation of the old house and stopped. The barn looked to be in pretty good shape. She walked up to it and climbed the ladder leading to the loft.

She remembered playing in it as a little girl. There was an old black snake living under the hay. She saw him every year, but her grandma had told her that they'd never have a poisonous snake as long as that old black snake lived there.

She noticed a wooden box sitting in the corner of the loft. It had been her safe keeping spot for things she drew and notes she wrote. She approached the box slowly and lifted the lid. A puff of dust made her sneeze cough for a moment. When it cleared, she got on her knees to look at the papers, still in the bottom where she'd put them long ago. She laughed at the figures she'd drawn.

Then she noticed a notebook under the next stack of papers. She pulled it out and sat on the floor to look through it. She didn't remember this notebook. It was very old, and more of a scrapbook than a notebook. Its pages were crumbling on the edges as she turned them.

The notebook wasn't hers. *Did Grandma put it in here for safekeeping?* Did she know that one day Holly would find it and look at it? She closed the book carefully and took it with her.

When Holly returned home, Henry wasn't back yet from his trip to Johnson City. She was relived; that meant she didn't have to explain herself right then.

Making a quick check in her bedroom, she found Maddie still sleeping. Nell was on the porch reading her book, and the twins were sitting with her on the porch swing.

"Hey, have you brought the sandbox to the porch?" She wrapped an arm around each boy. "Were they good?" She looked at Nell.

"Perfect little gentlemen! What more could I ask for?"

Holly thanked Nell and tried to pay her for the time she'd spent, but Nell would have none of it. "Will you at least come back for supper one night this week? I know Drew won't turn down my spaghetti, or chicken and dumplings. Let me know which he wants and what night he can come, OK?"

"All right, that I will do. Besides, I have to bring back a book for the twins. I bought it for them in Asheville and forgot to bring it. I think they'll like it. I met the author, and she's fun to listen to. I figured her books should be good to read."

Holly and Nell walked to the front door just as Maddie woke up. "I guess its feeding time," said Holly. She hugged Nell, who left to go home.

By the time Henry came home, supper was over. The twins were in bed, and Nicholas and Robby were finishing up with their baths. Holly and Maddie sat at the kitchen table, looking through the old scrapbook Holly's grandmother had left for her. She handed a letter to Henry that she'd found tucked into the back of the book.

"Read this. I found it in this scrapbook in Grandma's old barn today." Holly set Maddie in her baby swing next to the table. "You hungry?"

"No, I grabbed a sandwich at McDonald's in Jonesborough." He kissed his wife and sat down at the table. "I'd love some lemonade, though, if you have any."

"Sure." She got a glass and put ice in it. "I thought you went to Johnson City."

"I did, and Jonesborough, and Limestone, and almost to Greenville. Since word got out that I'm opening up the saw mill again, everybody wants me to saw lumber for them."

"That's a good thing. Isn't it?" she asked, setting a tall glass of lemonade down in front of him.

"Absolutely! But I decided to see them all and get the estimates out of the way in one day. I'm beat! I'd forgotten how hard we worked when we ran that mill."

Henry read the letter and looked quickly at Holly. "Why were you at the barn in the first place? It could have been dangerous."

"No, it's very sound. I was surprised. I remembered that old wooden box I kept my treasures in. Something just kept nagging at me to go up into the loft and see if it was still there. This was in the bottom, under all my scribbling that I did when I was very young. I hadn't been near that box since I became a teenager. I guess that's why Grandma knew it would be safe."

"She says you have family in Asheville, the Hollisters. I've heard of them. Does that mean your grandma was a Hollister?" Henry asked.

"Yes. And she was one of the women at the Grove Park Inn. Remember the pictures we saw?"

Holly explained that she had met Laird at the Visitors' Center, and he'd told her all about the women who were invited to entertain the prisoners. Henry looked at all the clippings in the scrapbook. When he got to the end, he found another letter from Holly's grandmother. This one explained how she acquired the farm. She'd written:

> I was not a Trollip, Holly. I was in love with Fredrik Von Sayers. I was only 15, but I passed for much older. When he learned I was "with child," he only wanted to take the baby from me when it was born. I would not let that happen. Even my family was eager to give up my bastard child, just to keep it quiet.
>
> I stole from Fredrick. He was a clever gambler. It probably wasn't his money anyway, so I fled under cover of darkness in the back of a farm wagon. It brought vegetables to the Inn every day or two. I knew they would go far from the Inn, and I could get away. The wagon stopped in Flag Pond; I stayed in the wagon, which had been loaded with apples, and when the sun came up I slipped away. I followed the road but stayed out of sight when I heard a car passing. Shortly, I came to a farm that had a FOR SALE sign out in front.
>
> As I was looking it over, a man came up and asked if my husband was interested in buying it. I explained that my husband had been killed in a battle over seas and that I had the cash to buy the place. He was surprised, but he showed it to me and told me the price. I had no idea how much money I had. I counted out $17,000 and he stopped me, saying, "No ma'am, I am not going to take your money. You can lease the house

and land for $1200, cash now and in five years, if you still want to buy it. We can settle on a price then." I asked him to put it in writing; not that I didn't trust him, but I wanted to have something to show it was mine.

After four years, he got real sick and had a lawyer in Erwin draw up a deed. He signed that it was paid in full, and had the lawyer bring it up here to me. I signed it and he took it back to the courthouse to record the deed.

So that means this is your farm. Do whatever you want to with it. Your mother ran off with her real daddy. I know she did, because she asked me all kinds of questions about him, and the next week she was gone. Far as I know, she never looked back at you. I'm sorry; I know I wasn't the best mother, but neither was she. You were cursed from the beginning, just like your mother was.

I won't be around much longer. Doctors say my heart is wore out. I hope you have a good life. If you need anything, go to Asheville and look up my family. They will help you, child. They wouldn't help me, but they are old now and I know they've softened up. I named you Holly, after them. Your mother named you Vonda. I never did care for that name.

Your Loving Grandma,
Gretchen Louise Hollister, (That's my real name.)

Henry folded the letter and held his wife in his arms. "Holly, at least now you know. You were loved, and she did the best she could by you and your mother. I guess your mother was not as grateful as you."

"Aw, Henry, why didn't she tell me this while she was *alive?*" Holly wailed, and buried her face in his neck. "I loved her so much; none of that would have mattered."

"I know that, and she knew that, but maybe she was afraid you might have been tempted to leave like your mother did. Maybe she couldn't handle losing you. What does it matter now, anyway?"

"Because I'm the child of one of 'Those Babies!'"

19

Madison spent every waking hour of her day looking for the panel truck and any clue she could dig up related to Tom. She'd heard there was a marina on the lake that was undergoing some major remodeling. She thought of what the coroner told her, "Tom's body was stored in ice soon after he was shot."

She drove to Butler, out on Watauga Lake. Butler was the little town that had been relocated when TVA built the dam making the lake. They had moved the buildings that were movable, and relocated he cemetery. Old Butler was visible when the lake level was very low, like it had been when Tom's body was found. She'd never seen the old town, so she drove to where it had been. All that was left were some rocks outlining foundations of old home sites.

Maddy returned to new Butler location. She asked directions to the marina and followed a curvy road around the lake's edge. There, she saw lots of large houseboats moored nearly in the middle of the lake. She drove through a new iron gate and followed a newly-paved road to a construction site.

A man stopped her and explained there might be nails on this section of the road, so she shouldn't go any further. She thanked him and pulled into a parking space, then walked to where the construction crew was rebuilding a small structure.

"Hello, Sheriff. Aren't you out of your county?" A rough looking man wearing a yellow hardhat spoke as she passed by him.

"That's right. I'm curious about what you're building here. Who owns this marina?"

"I do, Ma'am. Chuck Buckner." He extended his hand.

"Sheriff Madison McKenzie, Mr. Buckner. Where is your icehouse?"

"You mean the old one? This is the new one." He pointed to where the crew worked.

"The old one," she said.

"Oh, it's over there, that pile of useless boards. We were just about to have a bonfire." Buckner laughed.

Madison ignored his humor and headed to the pile of lumber. She poked around, looking to see if there was any sign of a floor. After pulling down the entire stack of busted and rotted debris, she located the original concrete floor. She saw a dark stain that looked like it could be blood.

At that moment, the Carter County sheriff drove up and parked next to her SUV. He walked briskly toward her, scowling.

"Madison, you are out of your jurisdiction. What do you think you're doing here?"

"I'm investigating a murder, Clyde. Maybe I am in your neck of the woods, but if you were on the ball, I wouldn't have to be here."

"Now wait just a minute!" Clyde Nutley objected.

"Come look at this," she demanded. "Tell me what you call this."

Clyde looked closely at the dark stain. "Looks like blood, but it's a marina; could be fish blood or from a side of beef, for all I know."

"Or a man who was shot in the head might have been stored there until word got out that the marina was undergoing remodeling. How else could he be so well preserved, after eighteen months?"

Clyde scratched his head. "Don't talk so loud. I might have been suspicious of this already. But you don't need to let the entire countryside hear what you found." He took hold of Madison's arm.

She snatched her arm away, causing the construction crew to turn and look. "Keep your hands off me, Clyde!"

"Well, aren't we touchy? Just because you're about to marry that TBI Agent, that don't make you any better than just a local gal from Unicoi County to me!"

"Let's not be disrespectful, Sheriff." A voice from behind her spoke up. It was Rick.

"You were supposed to be in Knoxville. What are you doing here?" Madison puffed up when she realized what he'd done. "You pinged my phone."

"Yes, my dear sheriff, I did. And I have apparently arrived just in time. This country bumpkin just assaulted you." Rick said in a low voice.

"That's ridiculous! I never touched her," Clyde said.

"I *saw you*. Now, do you want me to pursue this, or give you a hand testing that blood?"

"Get your kit," Madison said. She walked closer to the concrete floor. She moved another board and there she saw a piece of maroon cloth. She pulled a pair of gloves from her pocket, picked it up, and dropped it into a small plastic baggie.

While Rick chipped away a segment of the floor, she removed all the other boards from the concrete pad. She reached into a crack and pulled out a man's ring, dropping it into another plastic bag. Madison looked around to see if Clyde was watching her. He was not. *Good; if he saw that, he'd take it from me. And Rick would have no say.*

Rick finished up, putting the small portion of concrete in a plastic baggie he had. "Let's go; we got what we came for."

"Yes, we certainly have!" Madison winked at Rick. "See you later, Clyde."

"Not if I have any say about it." He smirked.

"Oh, you won't," she said, not stopping to explain.

Rick followed Madison back to Cold Creek. When they got home, she revealed the ring she'd found in the crack in the floor. Inside the wide gold band was the inscription *TRM & AMSM Love Eternal.*

She looked at Rick. "What do you want to bet this is Tom's wedding ring?"

"No doubt it is, but you need to confirm that with Ann."

"I'll drive up there this evening. What are you going to do?"

"I need to get this to the lab, but if that is his ring, there's no hurry. We'll have our answer. He was in that icehouse."

"Go with me?" She smiled sweetly.

"Need you ask?" He swept her into his arms. "I can't wait for Valentines' Day to get here!" And then he kissed her.

Madison drove to the gate and Ann buzzed them in. They were surprised to see that Smitty was there again.

"Smitty, you're not having trouble with that gate, are you?" Rick teased.

"No, just a suspicious truck hanging around. You and Maddy find out who he is?"

"No, haven't seen it anywhere. Has it been here again since Tuesday?" Madison asked.

"No. But I like the company I keep here," Smitty answered.

"Can't blame you for that," Rick said.

Ann came outside, asking, "Hey, what brings you two all the way up here this evening?"

"Ann, I need to speak to you in private a moment," Madison said.

"Anything you have to ask me, you can say in front of Smitty. He's my bodyguard," she said. She slid her arm around his waist, giving him a little squeeze.

"OK, if you're comfortable with talking about Tom in his presence, that's fine with me. I couldn't approve more," Madison said. She pulled the small plastic baggie from her pocket and held it toward Ann. "Can you identify this?"

Ann reached out to take the bag. Her hand began shaking and her voice dropped to a whisper when she confirmed their theory. "It's Tom's."

"Are you sure? You didn't look inside." Rick suggested.

"I don't need to. You see that cut in the side here?" She pointed with her fingernail at a small dent. "That came from his drill. If you look at it closely under magnification, it's a tiny spiral pattern." She smiled as she remembered when it happened. "I offered to have it melted down and recast, but he said, 'No, that just might identify me someday.'"

Smitty wrapped his arm around her shoulders. "Where'd you get it? The coroner?"

"No. We found it in the old icehouse at Midway Marina," Madison said.

"I'm convinced; the coroner was right, and with that evidence, now we know where," Rick said.

Back in Knoxville, Watts' attorney made a guilty plea on his behalf. There would be no trial, only the sentencing for three counts of murder. No one in the courtroom knew what had caused the change of heart, but Macy and Madison knew. They had both seen Hannah's apparition.

Drs. Welty and Ott finished up their observation of Macy soon after. She had all her memories in place, and she was urged to stay in touch to report if things got out of hand in the future. Macy told them she was going to settle in East Tennessee on her family farm; even with its cruel past, she had hopes of a bright future there.

Madison, Rick, and Ella drove to Knoxville to pick up Macy and bring her back to Unicoi County. Ella worried that being where all their problems began might not be good for her sister. There was no talking her out of it, though; she'd set her mind on returning to Walkers' Mountain.

The four drove to the Walkers' family home with a picnic lunch. Macy stated that she wanted to go in the house alone, but Ella wouldn't allow that.

"We left together, we'll return together," Ella said in a calm voice.

"All right," Macy agreed.

The two sisters walked to the back of the house and disappeared through the kitchen door. Rick moved closer to Maddy, putting his arm around her shoulders.

"They'll be OK. The spirits should be settled now, after Watts has been locked up for the rest of his miserable life," he whispered, his lips tickling her ear.

Madison rolled her head onto his shoulder. "Ella doesn't want to stay here. She told me so."

"Maybe she'll feel differently after today. I'll get the table out of the truck. Let's set up our picnic." He kissed her forehead and walked away.

Madison followed and got the box of goodies. Rick brought four chairs and set them around the folding table. Just as they sat down, a truck rumbled up the steep drive. It was Bill Conway.

"How did Bill know we were here?" Rick asked.

"I guess Ella told him. Don't you have a lawn chair in your truck?"

"Yeah, I always carry one. Good idea." Rick walked to his SUV and retrieved the blue canvas lounge chair for the fifth person.

Bill parked his truck next to Rick's. "Did they go into the house alone?" he asked.

"Yeah," Rick answered. "They've been in there a while."

The three waited nervously and eventually, the sisters returned. Ella was crying, but Macy seemed just fine. Ella walked straight into Bill's arms.

"I'm glad you came," she said in a low voice.

"You all right?" he asked.

She nodded. "I will be. It's all behind us now."

Macy was excited when she saw the picnic. "What a great idea!" She sat in one of the chairs. "What's on the menu?"

"We've got just about everything you can imagine," Madison said. She began opening containers and foil packets.

"Come on, you two lovebirds. Let's eat. I'm starving!" Rick exclaimed, then handed Bill and Ella paper plates.

As they each filled their plates, Rick surprised everyone, including himself. He stood and asked them to all hold hands. And for the first time in his life, Rick Malone said a prayer aloud. He said, "Lord bless this food, bless these precious sisters, and bless this land. Bring them peace and happiness as they return to their home. Thank you, Lord for putting that monster away. I ask these favors for the love this farm holds and needs restored. Amen"

"Rick, that was awesome!" Macy said. "I had no idea you were religious."

"Neither did I." He looked into Maddy's eyes. "Was it OK for me to say the prayer?"

"More than all right, Rick. Prayer sounds good coming from you." Maddy leaned over and kissed his cheek.

Bill stretched across the table to pat Rick's shoulder. "Cool, man. Very cool."

As they were about to eat, another truck came up the drive and parked facing the barn. It was Jennings and Mrs. Sanders. They carried chairs and a covered dish.

"Welcome, neighbors!" Macy said. She jumped up and ran to hug the couple. "I'm so happy to see you!"

"We hope we're not intruding," Jennings said. "I told the wife that we ought to bring a dish and welcome you home."

"And I'm so glad you did." Ella got up to hug them, too. "Can you believe we have this lovely warm day in February?"

Mrs. Sanders hugged her and said, "Your grandma knew you were coming."

"And I'm staying," Macy said.

"Are you sure?" Mrs. Sanders asked.

"I am." Macy folded her arms and looked around. "I'm home."

The afternoon was filled with laughter and stories of long ago. No one said a sad word. They brought life back to Walkers' Mountain, and the girls made plans: what to plant in the garden, updates for the house, including a garage... Ella claimed it was too far to walk from the barn to the house through the snow or rain. She and Jennings walked around the left side of the house, discussing tearing down the smokehouse to make room for the garage. Bill joined them.

Macy, Mrs. Sanders, and Madison went into the house. Mrs. Sanders brought clean sheets for the beds. Rick carried in an armload of wood, stacked it by the fireplace, and then went looking for kindling. As soon as the sun goes down, the temperature drops in East Tennessee—even after a 65-degree day filled with sunshine, it could get cold at night.

By sundown, the place looked as if it had never been empty, and felt full of life. Bill and Rick had built a fire shortly before the Sanders left for their home in the valley. Mrs. Sanders requested they come down for breakfast in the morning.

Rick pulled Bill to the side. "You planning on staying here tonight?"

"Yeah, Ella made up a bed in the room with twin beds for me. She's taking their parents' bed, and Macy chose their grandma's room. I don't want them here alone tonight."

"I agree. And I'm happy to see you and Ella hitting it off this way. Is there a secret in your future?" Rick teased.

"It wouldn't be a secret if I told you, now would it?" Bill popped a quick, light punch into Rick's left shoulder.

Rick winced and let out a grunt.

"Oh! I am so sorry! That's your injured arm. I completely forgot."

"So had I," Rick said ruefully. "Thanks for the reminder!" He laughed and rubbed his bicep. "Guess this thing is never going to heal."

"I'm really sorry, Rick." Bill hung his head.

Ella had borrowed Henry's dad's old truck, so the sisters had transportation. She'd begged Henry to sell it to her almost immediately. She planned to fix anything on it she could to keep it running. Reluctantly, he'd agreed. After all, he had a new truck and the family SUV. As long as Ella planned to keep the old truck to use on the farm, he thought that was a better life for the antique pickup than sitting idle in his outbuilding. Ella promised he could come and drive it anytime he felt the urge.

Rick and Madison's wedding was just a week away, and Rick had another doctor's appointment. Madison planned to pick up a couple last-minute items in Knoxville, so she went with him.

Rick was unusually quiet as they drove the nearly two hours to the medical center used by government employees in the area. Madison figured he was just a little nervous because of the wedding—or worried about what the doctor might tell him.

She made notes on her list, trying not to let Rick know she was worried about him. Finally, he looked over at her and pulled the pen from her hand.

"You can't still need that many things! Why are you so distracted?"

"Me? Oh, no, I'm just thinking." She neglected to mention what she was thinking.

"What are you thinking about?" He was persistent.

"You know I've totally neglected my sheriff duties lately. I'm thinking about who should be our sheriff. I don't plan to continue; I didn't plan to do it this long."

"What about me?" Rick stared straight forward.

"You? Does that mean you aren't staying with the TBI?"

"I can retire now. I have enough time in. Besides, I can't stay on sick leave forever."

"Would you be content with just sitting around Cold Creek?"

"I won't just sit around. You never have. I'd solve the unsolved cases and chase down all the bad guys, just like you do," Rick said.

"There are no unsolved cases," Madison argued.

"We still don't know who shot the Doc with that arrow. We could have an Amazon warrior lose in the area," he said with a smirk.

"I know who shot Doc. I just chose not to do anything. I know it was an accident."

"An accident? That was carelessness! What if they'd hit one of the kids? It would have killed them!"

"But he didn't. Besides, Doc doesn't want to press charges," she said. "And that's the end of that case!"

"Maddy, I'm afraid my doctor is going to retire me. My arm is still not healed."

"I'm confused. Do you want to retire or not?" she asked.

"I do, but on my terms. Not due to a medical condition," he said.

The conversation went back and forth until they arrived at the medical center. Rick asked Madison to come in with him.

The doctors did all kinds of tests and scans. Finally, after about two hours, a male nurse led them into a room with a desk, not another examining table. Madison felt this was a positive development, but by the look on his face, she didn't think Rick saw it that way.

A doctor he hadn't yet seen came in, introduced himself, and sat down. He showed Rick all the test results, then hit him with a devastating blow.

"Agent Malone, I'm afraid you need to consider retiring if you want to keep that arm."

The room was quiet for several seconds too long as Rick comprehended what the doctor had said.

"Your prognosis?" he asked.

"If you continue using the arm in your present position, you're almost certain to lose the use of it completely. It will just hang at your side. The muscle is not repairing itself. However, if you wear a sling and follow a therapy regimen, say for a year, you might have limited use of it."

"How many of your peers agree with this diagnosis?"

"All of them." He named five other doctors who had been involved with Rick's treatment. "The immediate repair your hometown doctor made is the only reason you kept the arm in the first place. Had you come straight here to us, we would have most likely removed it that night."

Rick swallowed, then glanced at Madison. She wore her poker face; he could not read her emotions. But he felt sure she would not want a handicapped husband. "I need to talk this over with my team, and my..." he paused, looking back at Madison, "and my soon-to-be bride. This is a life-changing decision."

"Not really, Rick." She turned to face him and put her hands out to grasp his. "If Drew can come back from his prognosis with such dedication, you can too."

"That was a different type if injury," he said.

"It was a spinal injury, and he was told he'd never walk again. Now he's married and walking with the help of the walker. Who knows what the mind can overcome?" Madison argued.

"She's right, Rick. As doctors, we have only the stats to go on. Your mind can change your outcome. Your attitude can make all the difference. Be positive, have faith, let me know what you decide."

Rick and Madison returned to his SUV. Rick wasn't saying anything, so Maddy kept quiet too. They drove to the strip mall where Monique's shop was. Madison went in to pick up the personalized napkins, plates, and cups she'd ordered. Monique met her halfway to the door with a big hug.

"Claudia, look who's here! It's Madison!" she called loudly.

Claudia came from the back room with a couple of boxes in her arms. She set them down on the counter and reached out to hug Madison herself. "So nice seeing you, Maddy. How's Rick?"

"He's in the parking lot. We just came from seeing the doctors. They weren't very encouraging. I'm afraid he's upset and doesn't want to talk."

"They want to retire him with a disability, right?" Claudia asked.

"Something like that," Madison said.

The women looked at the personalized items. Madison was very pleased. She gave Monique a list of items she'd forgotten. While Monique gathered them up, Claudia and Madison talked. Claudia reminded her that time makes things better, and not to worry.

They said goodbye and promised that they'd be there for the wedding on the 14th. Maddy put the items in the back of the SUV, noting that Rick had moved to the passenger's side to let her drive.

"I'm not going to be so stubborn from now on. You're my official driver again." Rick's face looked pouty; Madison knew he felt he'd been wronged.

"The first time you saw Drew at the hospital, did you even think he'd live?" Madison looked Rick straight in the eyes.

"Not really," he turned away.

"That's because you are mostly pessimistic. I, on the other hand, was hopeful, I felt sure he'd live, and knew he'd be determined enough to walk again—*because he loves Nell that much.*" She stared out the windshield. "How much do you love me, Rick?"

Madison drove home; the time passed with very little conversation. Passing one Cracker Barrel after another, she realized he was in a trance. *Not thinking about his stomach? Unheard of! Rick always wants to eat when he can go to a Cracker Barrel.*

Finally, when they came to the exit with a Cracker Barrel in Boone's Creek, she said, "If you aren't hungry, let's at least stop for a pee break."

"Are you hungry?" he asked, but didn't take his eyes off the road.

"We ate breakfast at nine thirty, after they drew blood at the hospital. It's nearly eight p.m. now. I don't think we have anything at home to eat, and the restaurant will be closed by the time we get there."

"I'm sorry. I've been inconsiderate. Sure, let's stop."

Back on the road, he was in a better mood. His tummy was full. "What if I take the position as sheriff of Cold Creek? You think I can do all the duties with my arm in a sling?"

"Yes. If something comes up, I can handle it. But I want you to talk to Chip before you decide. Will you do that for me?"

"Yes; I even brought a copy of all the test results and the scans."

"How did you get the scans? They don't normally turn those lose."

"I know," he grinned that mischievous smile of his.

Madison couldn't help but smile with him. "You stole them."

"No, they're mine; I *borrowed* them," he said.

"No, they're the property of the medical team. Your insurance pays for them, but they never belong to you." Madison sounded firm.

"OK, fine. I stole them," he snickered.

Rick said he was going to walk over and give the test results and scans to Chip. So Maddy told him she'd drive out to Holly's and get Bud. "He spends more time with them than with us these days. I want him home."

"I'll be back in a little while." Rick waved with his right arm over his head.

Madison had noticed that he never lifted his left arm very high. She feared he'd been in a lot of pain, and kept it from her. They postponed their wedding once already; she wondered if she should suggest they postpone it until he decided about his arm.

There's that nagging question again: *Will we ever be married? How can I help Rick see that he's the same amazing man I fell in love with over five years ago? Maybe if I talk to Mr. Olsen, he'll have a thought on this subject.*

20

Ann phoned Madison to say the panel truck had been back to the gate. Smitty and Ann had followed it, heading toward Cold Creek on the old road. Madison jumped in her Explorer and sped away to intercept the truck.

She stopped at the intersection of Spivey Road and old 19/23. Ann was still on the phone with her. "He's almost there," Ann said. "I think he must realize we're following him. He's speeding now, and taking the curves really fast."

"I see him, Ann. I'll call you back." Madison tossed her phone on the passenger seat. The truck was rounding the sweeping curve underneath the interstate overpass. She pulled onto the old road, facing oncoming traffic. Madison stopped in the middle, straddling the center line, and turned on her blue lights.

She braced for impact, seeing the truck was not slowing down. At the last second, he swerved and lost control, running off the road onto the left shoulder. As soon as the wheels slid into the grass, the truck flipped; it landed on its top in the creek.

Madison pulled to the shoulder of the road, blue lights still flashing, and ran to the water's edge. The creek was not deep, but the top of the truck had been crushed by the impact and the weight. She could tell the doors were jammed. The doors to the back of the panel bed were partially opened. She called out, "You in the truck, come out the back with your hands where I can see them."

There was no response. Smitty and Ann arrived then, running down the hillside and into the creek beside her. Smitty grabbed a long tree branch that had been washed down during the last heavy rain. He slid it under the driver's side and leaned all his weight on it, lifting the truck enough for Ann and Madison to pull the man from the front seat.

From the amount of blood, Madison feared he might be dead. She felt a faint pulse and asked Ann to grab a blanket and some towels from the back of her SUV. Smitty had already called 911 to request an ambulance and backup. Sirens soon wailed in the distance, and in moments the fire department's crash truck was on the scene, followed by an ambulance. The Erwin PD also showed up, just as the EMTs brought the victim up to the ambulance. They rushed off toward the hospital.

Madison and the Erwin officer waited for the wrecker to remove the truck from the creek bed. Unfortunately, she could find nothing in the cab to identify who the driver was.

"This is so frustrating!" She slammed her hand against the side of the wrecked truck.

An additional Unicoi County PD unit stopped on the scene. "Sheriff McKenzie, I just passed that ambulance, sitting on the roadside not two miles down the road, no EMTs or patient to be found. What the heck is going on?"

Madison jumped into her SUV and spun around in the road heading toward Erwin. When she reached the ambulance, she saw the rear door was hanging open, and there was no one around. *Where did they go?*

She looked in all directions at the scene, then she spotted a stethoscope in the ditch. On closer inspection, she noticed tracks in the muddy bank leading toward a culvert.

Smitty and Ann, followed by the Erwin PD car, pulled up on the scene. Madison waved, signaling for them to come to her. She knelt and looked into the four-foot pipe.

"We've got two DBs, the EMTs," she said. "I'm going to the other side." She climbed up the bank and ran across the road to the other end of the culvert. In seconds, she ran up the ditch into the woods. "I've got footprints leading away, and a blood trail," she yelled. The officer and Smitty followed. Ann stayed with the cars.

Madison moved cautiously up the hillside, listening as though she were tracking a wild animal—which in her mind, she was. Her pistol drawn and finger on the trigger, she stepped lightly over branches and deadfalls, trying to move quietly in the damp underbrush.

Thirty minutes later, she lost the blood trail. She radioed Erwin PD, advising them of her situation. She was informed there were ten deputies and PD officers in the woods searching, as well. She phoned Henry.

"I need your bloodhound again," she said. She gave Henry specific directions to where she was waiting, and he and Blu joined her in no time.

Madison had a piece of bloody bandage she'd taken from the ambulance. Blu sniffed it and headed up the hill, with Henry and Madison close behind. They followed Blu up and down mountainsides through thick underbrush and open fields. As night closed in, Blu lost the trail in a mountain stream. Henry walked him up and down on both banks without another trace of the scent. Madison recognized the area as part of Rocky Fork State Park. She also knew there was a dry cave somewhere in the rock face. She radioed for one of the state forest rangers to meet her at Slab Trail. Henry sat on the creek bank to let Blu rest. They had been going strong for nearly six hours b that time.

When two rangers showed up, Madison shared her suspicions. The older ranger doubted any man would go into that cave in the darkness, but said he'd lead Madison and a group of officers to it. Before they reached the entrance, they heard gunshots. One deputy called out, "I've got him." But as they closed in on the sound, they only found a dead Unicoi County deputy lying across a downed tree. His throat was cut, just like the EMTs' had been.

"That's three deaths today. We can't face this man alone. Everyone, partner up. Stay together, and let's get this bas—"She cut off the epithet with obvious effort.

She phoned Rick and it went to voicemail for the third time. Was he out looking for her and his signal not working? She hadn't seen him all day. He had slept upstairs in their new bedroom, and she had stayed in the smaller bedroom of the original cottage. *Was he even there when I left?* She didn't know. *He might have gone out during the night.* She didn't look in the garage for his SUV; hers was parked outside. Madison admitted she couldn't worry about Rick's whereabouts at the moment. *Rick's a grown man; he can take care of himself, and I need to do the same.*

The deputy who paired off with Madison was known by the nickname

Moose. She asked him what they meant by it, and he told her he'd wrestled a moose in Alaska to free it from a vine she'd been tangled in. Her calf was weak from hunger, and the cow would have died. He said that he left the wilds of Alaska because of the terrible, cold winters. So far, he liked what he faced in Tennessee. Madison found Moose really funny, enjoying his stories. However, she advised he talk less and be more watchful.

The ranger signaled to Madison that the cave entrance was just ahead, but he wasn't going any closer. She stepped up and made her way to the opening. The Maglite she carried was getting dim, so she borrowed one from Moose.

There were footprints in the limestone dust. She shined the light slowly around the walls of the cave. There was a passageway in the back, just large enough for a man to slither through. Madison approached but Moose caught her arm. He shook his head. She frowned; his body was obviously too big to fit. He pointed up at the overhead. Without a sound he scaled the side of the boulder wall, ending up on top and looking down the other side. Then he motioned for her to move through.

Madison began feeling the tightness as she neared the end of the opening. She saw a stain on the wall; it was wet, and it appeared to be blood. She could only hope any rattlesnakes or copperheads had been scared away by the wounded man. She aimed the light beam on the floor as the passage opened up into another room. She panned the light all the way around the walls until she came to a heap on the floor, almost directly opposite where she was standing. It looked like a body, motionless and slumped over a rock. She took a step closer, then gravel fell from above. It was Moose, shaking his head at her. She tossed a piece of the gravel, hitting the form. It did not move, but if he was playing possum to trick her into moving closer, he would remain motionless.

"Show me your hands," she ordered.

He didn't move.

She took one step closer. "Show me your hands, or I'll shoot!" she commanded. "You've already killed three people today, so I have no problem putting you down. You can believe that!"

The form moved slightly. One hand raised into the air.

"*Both hands!*" she shouted. "Both hands, or you're dead."

The sound of a knife dropping to the floor echoed in the room. Then a bloody hand went into the air.

"Turn toward me," she said.

He turned halfway around and got to his knees, placing his hands together behind his back. Moose dropped to the floor and grabbed him, snapping handcuffs on the man in one swift move.

He turned him around to face them and Madison gasped, "*Clyde?!*"

It was difficult to recognize him with all the blood on his face, but she knew he was the Carter County sheriff.

"*You,*" she spat in disgust. "I should have shot you in the truck, or maybe let you lie in the creek and bleed to death. You are a worthless piece of sh—"

"Careful, Ms. McKenzie," Moose said. "I've been told you don't curse. Don't spoil my image of you now."

Moose shoved Clyde into the crevasse, then heaved himself up and over the rock he'd slid down. Madison pushed from behind until Moose got hold of the prisoner on the other side. As they hauled him out into the open, deputies and police officers cursed the murderous sheriff when they saw who they'd been chasing.

Several of the deputies roughed him up as he was taken down the mountain to the trail by the creek. On the trail, he was loaded onto a four-wheeler and driven down the mountain to a waiting patrol car. Madison and Henry had started walking back out the trail when another four-wheeler, driven by a park ranger, met them and gave them a ride.

The ranger handed them water bottles and gave Madison a pack of peanut butter crackers. "I know your history, Ma'am. You don't stop to eat until you get your man. I don't want you passing out on my watch," he said.

"Oh, thanks; I really need this." She ripped the package open and consumed the crackers quickly, then killed the bottle of water.

Back in Cold Creek, Madison found Rick in the sheriff's office, waiting by the radio. When she walked in, he beat Bud to her side.

"Maddy, why would you go without me? You could have been killed! Don't ever do a dumb thing like that again." And he hugged her so tight she thought she'd break.

"I tried calling you off and on all day, but it went straight to voicemail. I didn't even know if you were here. You could have gone back to Knoxville, for all I knew."

"No, I won't be going back to Knoxville to the TBI anymore. My retirement papers are in place, and Mr. Olsen plans to swear me in as soon as we get back from our honeymoon," he smiled. Madison remembered that amazing smile from day one, when he first showed up in the restaurant.

She fell in love all over again. "Rick Malone, I love you."

"That's *Sheriff* Rick Malone, my dear," he whispered, his lips barely touching hers.

"Not yet!" she reminded him.

Madison marched to the upstairs shower and then fell into the king-sized bed. Rick lay beside her on top of the covers.

"I suppose this means I'm sleeping downstairs with Deputy Dawg."

"That's exactly what it means. But before you go to bed, please bring me a bowl of soup. All I had today was a pack of peanut butter crackers, and I'm too exhausted to walk back downstairs."

Rick kissed her on the cheek and got up from the bed. "Come on Bud; you're with me."

By the time he returned, Madison was sound asleep and snoring. Rick set the bowl of soup down on the night stand beside a glass of milk, and turned out the light. He and Bud retired to the bedroom in the cottage for the night.

* * *

Three funerals were held the next week in Erwin at the funeral home on Main Street, all on the same day. Three caskets filled the front of the chapel, with flowers lining the walls and spilling out into the entryway. Many more lined the sidewalk out in front, as did the people. They filed past the honor guard and into the chapel for hours, hundreds showing their respect for fallen heroes.

Families of the deceased filled the pews; everyone else stood during the eulogies and ceremony. Three different preachers said their piece, and three separate soloists sang requested songs, different for each soul being honored.

Madison and Rick stood with the Erwin Police Department, Mayor Lynch, and various city officials and judges. All of Washington County, Green County, and Sullivan County police departments were there. Carter County officers expressed their respect through a hand-written letter to the families, and remained absent from the services.

The procession drove the short distance to Evergreen Cemetery, where the mourners split up into three lines. Each of the fallen were interred in a different section of the gardens.

A reception was held at the courthouse, catered by all the local restaurants. Rick asked Madison if they could made an appearance, since he would be the new sheriff of Cold Creek. She agreed, and they joined the crowd of hundreds.

When the investigation wrapped up, it turned out that Tom's undercover work with the Washington County and Johnson City Police Departments had been his undoing. Clyde learned about Tom through a drug dealer out of Chicago. Interstate 26 was routed through the length of Unicoi County, making it the perfect connection for drug traffic. Over a ten-year period, Clyde had woven his small-time racket into the big leagues.

Tom had to be eliminated because he was so close to pointing the finger straight in Clyde's direction. Although Tom was not fully aware of Clyde's role at the time, he was on the trail of the main player from Chicago. Clyde's position had to be earned, so he was elected to take out the threat: Tom Morgan.

After concealing Tom's body in the icehouse, he believed he was in the clear. But as news of the marina changing hands and being scheduled for an update came out, Clyde saw the need to move the body and dump the bike. He hadn't counted on the lake level dropping to an all-time low, or the temperature being high enough to thaw the body. By the time these issues dawned on him, it was too late to relocate Tom a second time.

Why he was after Ann was anybody's guess, unless he feared she knew something. She was totally in the dark, and never knew Tom had a secret life with the police. Ann felt blessed to have spent ten happy years with him. Now that she knew what had happened, she could move on to a new phase of her life.

Smitty certainly had nothing to hide. He had lost his wife to cancer, and that put them in similar circumstances. They became close friends quickly out of need. Ann trusted her new friend to protect her, but she was still in the market for a dog. Especially when she visited Smitty's ranch, and found those amazing dog kennels and barn.

Ann visualized what she could do with all that space and the dream in her heart—a dream that Smitty had also entertained, when buying Dr. Denson's property. But that was before his wife learned about her breast cancer. He had felt that his life crumbled along with hers. Was he given a second chance with Ann? Time would tell...

21

February 14th fell on a Wednesday. Cold Creek had never seen so many people. The wedding of the decade was held next to the creek, under a huge white tent. Cars parked all over town; they filled the parking lot of Shirley's Restaurant, all the side streets, and even at the parking area for Cold Creek Caverns.

Shuttles ran all morning, delivering out of town guests to the tent. Henry had decorated his washed and waxed four-wheelers to drive the wedding party in. He, Drew, and Bill Conway drove so the lovely ladies didn't have to walk in heels on the grass to get to the tent.

Rick and Drew stood up front, with the mountain as backdrop and the creek providing the natural music until time for the family to walk down the aisle. Then Mr. Olsen played a solo on the violin as Nell walked gracefully to the front in a burgundy satin off-the-shoulder gown, with long sleeves and a mermaid style sweeping train.

Next came Ella in the identical dress, and Holly followed wearing the same style gown in a shimmering gold fabric. As Madison appeared walking with Jess, Mr. Olsen played the most beautiful rendition of the bridal march. It brought tears to Madison's eyes.

She wore a long white gown, similar to the others, form-fitting to silhouette her lean figure. She wore flats, not wanting to be taller than her groom. Besides, with her luck she figured she'd stumble in heels.

Her chocolate, silky hair had been intertwined with tiny white flowers, lily of the valley, and pearls at the back of her head in a soft puffy braid. The veil gathered in the back, shadowing bare shoulders. No veil concealed her smiling face.

Rick held his breath as she walked closer, until Drew nudged him to make him breathe. He'd never seen Madison in glamor make-up, and she was gorgeous.

Shirley blotted her eyes with a hankie, then handed it to Jess when he sat next to her after giving the bride away. The ceremony was sweet and simple in the rare February sunshine, shaded by the tent.

Sheila Carlton, Maddy's friend from UT, sang a solo, "The Rose." The music came from small Bose speakers placed at the front and back of the tent. As Sheila finished the song, Maddy turned and winked at Rick. She expected that to be the only song, but additional music played.

Madison was completely surprised. Rick had arranged for Sheila to sing "Wind Beneath My Wings" as well, another of his bride's favorite songs. Madison stood spellbound, looking at Rick with tears streaming down her cheeks. They spent the few minutes looking into each other's eyes while Sheila sang, and Rick mouthed the words to Maddy.

But Sheila wasn't finished yet. She stayed there in front of the congregation, and the music of a third song began. It was another Gary Morris song, "The Love She Found in Me."

Maddy was overcome with adoration for her groom. She couldn't resist hugging him.

After the vows were said, rings exchanged, and the introduction made of Mr. and Mrs. Richard Austin Malone, the couple led the procession to Shirley's Restaurant. Ben and Margie had decorated in a theme of Alaska to surprise Madison. The wedding party looked lovely against a wall of snowy mountains, painted especially for this occasion.

Margie had created a triple-tiered cake with a tiny real waterfall streaming from a glacier on the top layer, pooling into a half-frozen lake at the bottom layer. All along the sides tiny lily of the valley blooms outlined the stream, which Maddy later learned was aquamarine-colored pineapple-blueberry punch. She squealed when Margie dipped into it with a ladle to fill the crystal glasses.

The ambience of the rooms had been transformed into a wonderland, just for Maddy and Rick. Shirley, even though she knew what they were trying for, was amazed by how beautifully the interior of her restaurant had turned out.

"Margie, this is remarkable! How on earth did you do all this?" Shirley studied the scenes.

"Who cares how? Ben and I wanted to make her wedding and reception the best anyone in this town ever witnessed."

"Well, you've outdone yourselves! It's so lovely!"

"Thank you, Shirley. And we are considering keeping it this way. You know, as a tribute to our hometown girl. Do you think she'd mind?" Margie asked.

"No, she would be honored," Madison said. "Oh, my, you are amazing. You should enter the gingerbread contest at the Grove Park Inn next Christmas."

"That's what I told her," Ben agreed. "Isn't this monumental?!"

"It sure is," Madison couldn't look away from the cake. "Rick, we can't cut this! It's too gorgeous!"

"Oh, yes we will! And I bet it's carrot cake?" Rick looked anxiously toward Margie.

"Well, Rick, you know I wouldn't leave you out!" She smacked a bright red lipstick kiss on his cheek. "Each layer is different. If you can guess the correct one, we'll separate the carrot cake to freeze for your first anniversary."

"Hmm... I'd have to say the top: the iceberg, of course!"

"That's right!" Margie laughed, then lifted the layer away, exposing the punch bowl. "I'll freeze this for y'all." She disappeared through the swinging doors of the kitchen.

Gerad, their photographer and DJ, had taken all the photos he needed, so he asked if Madison wanted one of anyone specifically. She replied that while he ran the DJ music whatever he wanted to take was fine. She knew he was a professional and knew what to do.

"Thank you, Mrs. Malone." He moved through the sea of people to where his DJ equipment was set up. The first song was a slow dance for the bride and groom. Gerad chose "My Love," by Little Texas.

Rick led Maddy to the dance floor in the second room, which was also decorated in the new Alaskan wilderness motif. Folks gathered around, watching the couple swaying to the music. This time Maddy sang to Rick. He never took his eyes off the woman in his arms.

Then next song was lady's choice. Maddy caught Jess's hand, leading him to the music of Vince Gill's "Look at Us." Immediately, Shirley tapped her daughter's shoulder and took Jess away. Rick and Maddy clapped their hands. Henry and Holly joined them on the dance floor, as did Mr. & Mrs. Olsen.

The room was crowded until the buffet bell rang and Margie announced, "Let's eat!"

The three couples on the dance floor stayed to finish their dance. Rick filled a plate and made Maddy sit down for a few bites. He knew she wouldn't think about eating, and he didn't want her to pass out the way she had at Drew and Nell's wedding.

Nell and Drew sat next to the new couple. Drew had been on his feet for a couple of hours. "Time to get off these feet. Don't want to wear them out." Drew laughed.

"That was a beautiful wedding—and Rick, what a surprise! You big old romantic, you!" Nell shoved at his shoulder. "How'd you know to ask Sheila to do those songs?"

"I'm observant," he said. "I know who keeps my lady company when I'm not here: Gary Morris and Vince Gill. Do I feel threatened? Absolutely not. I've grown to like them too. I even enjoy The Gatlin Brothers!"

"Well, who doesn't?" Sheila said, joining them at their table.

"Who are The Gatlin Brothers?" Drew asked.

They all laughed. Everyone knew that Drew was not a country music fan.

"Sheila, I want you to meet Ella Walker and Bill Conway. You remember, I told you about the state trooper who saved my life?" Madison got up, motioning for Sheila to follow her.

"I'm so happy Ella came into Bill's life!" Rick's comment was not sarcastic at all. Nell smiled as if she completely understood.

"Who knows, there might be another wedding here by autumn," Drew said.

The time came to cut the cake. Jess brought in a pick ax. "You might need this on the snowbanks."

Gerad caught every funny moment in a photo. He fit into this group like he belonged there. Everyone liked him, too.

"I can't wait to see your photos, Gerad." Shirley said.

"I'll have them as soon as the honeymooners return. How long will they be gone?" he asked.

"We don't know. Don't even know where they're going," Shirley whispered. "I'll have Madison call you."

The sun was setting quickly by the time the guests left. Holly and Henry carried all the gifts to Madison's cottage, while she and Rick went upstairs to change clothes. Rick carried the two suitcases down to Madison's Explorer. He had been required to surrender his when he retired from the TBI. His suitcase was already in the SUV.

The couple said their goodbyes and drove out of Cold Creek. When Rick turned right to get on southbound I-26, Madison said, "Ah-ha! We're going to the Grove Park Inn."

"Nope," was all Rick said.

"The airport?" she asked.

"In the morning."

"Oh, we're going to sleep in the vehicle tonight. How quaint." Madison laughed.

Rick thought she sounded nervous. "Maddy, please don't be nervous. I'll never push you. I've waited all these years for your love, I can wait a little longer." He pulled her hand to his lips and kissed it.

She dropped her head, her face burning. She was glad it was dark inside the SUV. "You didn't try to slip Bud in here, did you? I should have checked in the back."

"No, but I did think about it," Rick said.

Conversation lagged as they crossed the state line into North Carolina. Rick held on to her hand. A few minutes passed, then he asked, "Need to stop at the Welcome Center?"

"No, I'm good," Madison said. "Rick Malone, where are you taking me?"

"Mrs. Malone, it's a surprise. You'll find out in the morning."

Madison pulled her hand away, crossing her arms over her chest as though she was pouting.

Rick reached for her in a playful manner. Suddenly, he looked over his shoulder and yelled, "Get down! Cover your head!"

"Rick, what..." She ducked. Then she felt the vehicle spinning and heard metal crunching, glass breaking, and tires squalling. Then nothing.

Madison woke up in a hospital, with doctors and nurses all around her. She didn't understand what was happening. She didn't hurt anywhere, but she couldn't focus on one thing or one person for more than a second at a time. She felt as though she was in an isolation chamber of some sort. The voices she heard sounded muffled and far away. She couldn't understand a word they said. She closed her eyes; the room was spinning.

The next time she opened her eyes, things were calm. The room was still and dimly lighted. She was no longer in the middle of bright lights with masks and scrubs fluttering frantically around her. She still didn't feel pain...*Oh, wait; yes, I do.* Her head felt as if a woodpecker worked inside her skull each time she tried to move it.

A nurse walked in at that moment. "Oh good, you're awake," she said in a soft voice. "How's your head, Madison?"

To Madison, it sounded almost like the nurse spoke in a whisper. But even that low voice made her head throb. "What happened?" She scrunched her eyes up as though to clear a screen.

"You were in a bad automobile accident. You and a dozen others. Best we can tell, your car was smashed by a tanker truck as it turned over. You were lucky; you only got a hard knock to your head." She smiled and listened to Madison's heart, her chest, and finally her lower intestinal area.

"Where's Rick? Where's my husband?"

"Oh... Honey, you were in the car by yourself. Your seatbelt broke. Otherwise, you might have gotten hurt much worse."

"No! Where is Rick? Where is my husband? He was driving, not me! We just got married. We're on our honeymoon. Was Rick hurt?" She tried to raise up.

"Woo! Hold it right there. You can't move around. You have a really severe concussion. You must be hallucinating. Now, lie still."

"Look at my hand! Do you see my wedding band? I just got married! I'm not crazy. My husband, Rick Malone, was driving my SUV."

"OK, I'll check to see the names of the others patients, but I don't recall seeing a Rick." She hung her stethoscope around her neck. "You have to promise me you will not move! Or else I will not go and check for you!"

"All right, I'm sorry, but you have to find out where Rick is, if he's hurt, or—" she squeezed her eyes shut.

"I'll be right back. Don't you dare move!"

The nurse left the room, leaving Madison thinking the worst. *No patient named Rick? Is he—oh God—in the morgue?*

Madison lay there for what seemed like hours, but her head hurt so badly when she moved, she decided she'd obey the nurse and stay still.

Eventually the door opened and in walked a doctor and the same nurse.

"Good evening, Madison. I'm Dr. Allison. You've had a bad head injury, and you can be having all kinds of crazy thoughts. The EMT said you were alone in the car, and we have admitted no one named Rick. I want you to calm down. Tell me how to contact your family. All your personal items burned up in the vehicle when the tanker exploded. Luckily, one of the onlookers pulled you to safety before that happened."

"I'm the sheriff of Cold Creek, Tennessee—or I was. I resigned the day Rick and I married. I'm *not* imagining this. You have to believe me. You can call my mom and dad, Jess and Shirley McKenzie. They can clear this up." She rolled her head toward the window and felt tears run from her eyes. "Please, Rick is real. He must still be out there. Maybe if they use bright lights they can find him."

"The wreck happened two days ago. The vehicles have all been removed. There were five cars besides that tanker truck. We have a total of seventeen injured admitted to this hospital, and one sent to Chapel Hill to the burn center. But he's the truck driver. His brakes failed, causing the truck to hit all the other cars. Then it tipped on its side, sliding into yours and crushing it."

Madison said nothing more. She knew Shirley and Jess would be there as soon as they could. She closed her eyes and pretended to fall asleep. There was no use trying to talk to these people.

22

Shirley and Jess rushed down the hall toward the room they had been told was their daughter's. The head nurse stopped them to update them on Madison's condition.

"I'm afraid Madison has a very bad concussion. We can't allow her to be upset, or we'll have to isolate her. She's been asking for Rick somebody, but we have had no patient admitted by that name. I'm afraid she's out of her head, understandably so."

"No, she isn't. Madison was married on Valentine's Day. Rick is her husband. Now find out where her husband is!" Jess demanded, in no uncertain terms.

"Yes, Sir. I'm sorry, we really didn't have a patient that was unaccounted for. I mean, the man they flew to UNC Jaycee Burn Center didn't have any ID, but he was found under the edge of the truck. He must have been the truck driver. There were no other bodies or patients."

"Well, somebody goofed! My daughter is not out of her mind, she's missing her husband!" Jess and Shirley pushed past the nurse and continued on to room 411. Madison began crying as soon as she saw her parents. A different nurse walked in behind them. She said nothing, just listened as Madison told them that Rick had not been found.

"I'll go to Chapel Hill and check on that patient. It has to be Rick. There is no one else, according to the nurse." Jess turned to Shirley. "Will you stay with our girl?"

"You know I will. Be careful, Jess." Shirley hugged her husband.

"Wait, don't leave yet: I think we have a Med Flight helicopter going in that direction. Maybe we can get you on it. Save you a long drive." The nurse smiled. "Looks like we've got a real mess up somehow. Let me see what I can find out." She left the room.

An hour later, Jess was on the helicopter and headed for Chapel Hill. He had not been told anything about the condition of the patient believed to be the truck driver. He had no idea what he would find when he arrived at the burn center. He could only pray that if it was Rick, he wasn't hurt too badly. But if it wasn't Rick, how would he tell Maddy?

When the chopper touched down, Jess was escorted to a room in the wing of the building to the right of the ER. He held his breath as he walked into the room. The patient was wrapped in bandages from head to waist. Both his arms were hooked to pulleys, extending above his head. The openings around his eyes were wide, and Jess thought they looked OK, not burned at all.

He walked closer as a male nurse came into the room. "He's in an induced coma. Are you family?"

"Maybe. We're trying to find my son-in-law. He disappeared the night this man was injured. What can you tell me about him?"

"The worst of his injuries are isolated to his hands and arms. He has a few burns on his chest, neck, and top of his head. The injuries are odd, actually. They're more consistent with someone trying to pull a body out, than for someone trapped in the cab." He crossed his arms over his chest. "Want to see his face?"

"Yes, if I could," Jess answered hesitantly, but also knew it might be the only way.

The nurse snipped the bandage in one spot and then unwound it across the man's face. As soon as his eyes and nose were uncovered, Jess dropped into the chair next to the bed.

"That's Rick Malone, my daughter's husband. Thank you, Lord!"

"That means there's still a body missing. I need to let someone know this is no longer a John Doe," the nurse said, then walked out of the room.

Jess knelt next to the bed and said a prayer for Rick. When he sat back in the chair, Rick's eyes opened. He looked toward Jess, but then looked away.

"Rick, it's Jess. We've found you! I need to let Madison know you're alive. Can you understand me?"

But Rick's eyes closed, and he didn't appear to be aware Jess was even there.

Jess phoned Shirley and told her to let Madison know Rick was there, in the burn center at Chapel Hill. "He's not bad, except for his hands and arms, from what the nurse told me. I hope to speak with his doctor soon."

"That's the best news Maddy could hear. I have you on speaker phone." Shirley sounded as if she was crying.

"Let Maddy know I'm staying here with Rick until he wakes up. They have him in an induced coma, for some reason. I'll talk to the doctor as soon as I can find him. Madison, his face is as pretty as ever, no need to worry about that. They have his hands and arms all wrapped up. The injuries seem to be the worst in those areas. I think he might have tried to pull the truck driver out. But if he was, I don't know where that body ended up. I intend to speak to the police also."

"Thanks, Daddy. Tell him I love him and will see him soon!" Madison said, with tears streaming down her face. She turned her head toward the window and sobbed.

"Those better be tears of joy," Shirley said. "Now we know he's alive and where he is; that's all we needed. Now you have to concentrate on your own injury. You have to get better, because he needs you to help care for him."

"OK; I'm OK now." Madison smiled at Shirley, but turned back to the window.

Meanwhile in Chapel Hill, Jess paced the hallway waiting for the doctor to examine Rick. Finally, Dr. Burns, as his nametag read, stepped up to the desk area outside Rick's room. He wrote a few entries on the patient's chart, then he smiled at Jess.

"Your boy is going to be all right, in time. He has some nasty burns on both hands, but I don't expect any long-term damage," Dr. Burns paused for a moment and then he changed his demeanor. "I noticed from his MRI that he's had some type of surgery to the left arm. Looks experimental, but that's one heck of a job. There are signs of young nerves growing. What kind of injury was that?"

"He was stabbed in his bicep back in the fall. Our hometown doctor did emergency surgery to seal the blood vessels. It saved his life; at the time he was bleeding out. The specialists at UT Medical told him they would have wanted to remove the arm immediately, if he'd been brought to them, " Jess explained as best he could.

"Well, damn good thing he wasn't; that arm looks amazing to me. I would like to meet this hometown physician. Can you arrange that? Perhaps get him to come here, and share the details of his procedure?"

"I can." Jess pulled up Chip's number on his cell. "Tell me what time works best for you, Dr. Burns."

"I'm here five days and off three, beginning today, from five a.m. to nine p.m." He handed Jess a business card. "Give him my private number. I'm very anxious to talk with him."

"Yes, Sir." Jess put the card into his wallet. "Can you tell me when I'll be able to talk to Rick?"

"Go on in, he's awake now. He might be a bit loopy from the pain meds, but he's on his own now. I'm sure I'll be seeing you later today, Mr. McKenzie."

"Jess, please; just Jess," he replied, then went into Rick's room.

Rick looked surprised to see his father-in-law. "Man, am I glad to see you, Jess. Where is my bride? Is she all right?"

"She's in Asheville. Has a concussion, but otherwise she's fine. Worried about you, of course."

"She's in Asheville? Well, where am I?" Rick was confused.

"Chapel Hill, at the UNC Jaycees Burn Center. For some reason, they thought you were the truck driver. Apparently, he hasn't been found."

"What? I remember pulling him out of the burning truck, right after I pulled Maddy out of her SUV. That's the last thing I can remember."

"The truck exploded, catching the SUV on fire. So it's lucky for Madison you pulled her out. I guess the truck fell on her side of the vehicle? Anyway, the driver hasn't been found. They didn't have any record of you, but I followed up on this lead. I just had a hunch this John Doe they thought was the truck driver was you. I'm sure glad I did."

"I don't even know if the man was alive. My hands were burned, but he was out. I know I didn't imagine that," Rick said.

"We aren't concerned about him; *you* are our interest. You need to get rest and let your burns heal. Madison said tell you that she loves you and will see you soon."

"Can I talk to her?" Rick asked.

"I suppose, as long as you both stay calm. Shirley's watching over her while I'm here with you." Jess pulled out his phone once again. "Hey, Honey. Rick is awake and wants to speak to Maddy." Shirley gave Madison the phone.

"Rick?" Crying, Madison asked, "Are you in pain?"

"No; Baby, they have me *all* shot up with goodies! I wish we were together. I love you so much. You're all I could think about, even in my sleep. Are you in pain?"

"My head hurts some, but mostly just when I move it. They say that will pass in a few days. I just have to lay still. You know that's hard for me to do."

"Yeah, I sure do."

They talked for a few minutes, then Jess spoke. "Maddy, he's dozing from the meds. You should get some sleep, and let Rick rest too. I'll call you again later. I love you, my little girl."

"I love you too, Daddy. Thanks. Will you stay with Rick, since I can't be there?"

Jess promised that he would be there until Rick could come back to Asheville, or go home. The next time Rick opened his eyes, he asked Jess to make another call for him. Jess got Rick's phone, which miraculously was protected in his back pocket. He pulled up the contact Rick instructed and pressed *Call.*

A man's voice answered, and Jess told him he was calling for Rick Malone. He explained that Rick and his bride had been involved in a car crash on their honeymoon, then told the man that today was the first day Rick was awake. Then he put the phone on speaker so Rick could hear.

"Gosh, I hate to hear that! I was afraid something was wrong. Rick is an upstanding guy; he'd never stand anyone up. I'm sure happy to hear they're alive, and hopefully getting well fast. Does he have any idea when he'll need the place again?"

"Hey, Danny, it's me. I don't know when I'll be able to leave the hospital. I got some pretty bad burns. I just appreciate your understanding."

"No worries, Rick. This is my wedding present to you and Madison. You just let me know when you're up to it. Nobody's living there. It's yours when you're well."

"Thanks, Dan, I'll call you. I imagine I'll have a long convalescence. And Maddy has a bad concussion. She'll need time to recover as well."

"Bring a nurse and come on down, anytime. No better place to spend this time of the year. Of course, I guess it will be a while before you can hold the rod to catch those bonefish. Just call me."

Jess thanked Danny, and the call ended. "A friend of yours, obviously."

"Yeah, we grew up together in DC. Danny Moss—*Captain* Moss, that is. He owns a fishing fleet in the Keys. But please don't let Maddy know that you know where we're honeymooning. She begged me to tell her, but I didn't want to. We were going to fly in to Fort Lauderdale, rent a car, and drive on down to the Lost Key, just off Islamorada. Dan owns one of the Islamorada Keys, the entire island, and there is only one house on it. It's accessible only by boat. Sounds like paradise, doesn't it? That's why he calls it Paradise Island."

"It sure does. Why doesn't he live there?" Jess asked.

"He invested in it for his retirement, but he loves his job, so why retire? When he heard I was retired from the TBI, he offered the place for our honeymoon. I couldn't pass it up."

"And you will have that honeymoon, Rick. If I have to drive you two down there myself!"

"I'll rent the motorhome, and you and Shirley can go on down to Key West," Rick said. "I believe I've heard you say that you wanted to visit Key West."

"Yes, I did. Well, we'll talk about it when you feel better." Jess scratched his head, "You know, that does sound like a good idea, but instead of you renting a motorhome, why don't I trade mine in for a bigger model? We like the little pull trailer, but frankly, I'd love to have a class A. And Shirley would enjoy it more, with the conveniences of an upgraded kitchen, bath, and larger beds."

The two discussed motorhome units until Rick fell asleep again. Jess pulled up RV dealers on his phone and located the one closest to the hospital. He wrote a note for Rick and taped it to his IV bag, then he went for a long walk.

The next morning, Madison's head felt like a new one had grown in place of her old one. Shirley came in just as Maddy began moving around. Her mom had gone home at Madison's request, so she could shower and get a good night's sleep. Nell had followed Shirley to the hospital so that she could stay with Madison that night.

By lunch time, Maddy was begging to get out of bed and go for a walk. The duty nurse helped her to her feet and observed how well she walked.

"I guess you have a pretty hard head, Madison. You're coming along very nicely. I'll let you walk up and down the hall, as long as one or both of these ladies accompany you. Deal?"

"Deal!" Madison promised.

Nell and Shirley walked with her, one on each side of the patient. They walked until the nurse ordered Madison back to bed. She didn't object; it felt good to know she could get up on her own to go to the bathroom and take a shower, but she decided to rest for the moment. *Maybe after supper I'll do the shower*, she thought.

Jess spent several hours at the RV dealership, checking out the different units available. When he found one he liked that they had taken in on trade, he felt sure he could persuade Shirley to give up the trailer. He asked for a test drive, and the salesmen who had talked to him all day flipped a coin to see who'd move forward with the deal, if there was one.

The test went very well, and Jess asked if Jeff—the winner of the coin toss—would drop him off at UNC. Jeff agreed and thanked him for the business. "I'll have the service department go over it to make sure everything is in good working order. I knew this unit wouldn't sit on the lot very long. It's a good one!"

"I'll get my trailer down here for your examination, and we'll talk money. Thanks for your patience with me today, Jeff. I appreciate you."

Jess showed Rick photos of the prospect on his phone. Rick couldn't believe how gung-ho Jess was on the idea. When supper was served, the attendant brought a tray for Jess too. He helped Rick eat first, then he ate his food.

Rick thought he could hold the spoon to eat his Jell-O, but the doctor had given specific instructions for him to not use his hands for anything until the next bandage change. Rick was impatient; he was not used to being waited on, and liked it even less coming from his father-in-law.

Jess's phone rang while they were arguing over the Jell-O, so Madison told Rick to stop giving her dad a hard time. She also announced that she'd see him the next day.

"Nell is driving me to Chapel Hill to visit you!" Madison was excited, and she could not disguise her emotions.

"That's wonderful, Maddy. I might have my hands free tomorrow, and be able to actually hug you."

Jess laughed and put the phone to his ear. "Whatever you told him sure put a smile on his face."

They talked for a while, then Jess asked to speak with Shirley. For that conversation, he walked out into the hall.

Madison and Nell joked quietly while Shirley talked to Jess about the class A motorhome.

"Daddy and Rick have cooked up something. That's what he and Mom are discussing. But they won't tell me anything!"

"Don't be so nosy, Madison. Let Rick have his surprises. One day he might stop surprising you, and you'll miss these little special times. You two have an entire life ahead of you. It's going to be great. Give him time."

"I know. I also know how impatient Rick can be. This has to be rough on him. Look at the photo Jess texted to me. Poor thing, his hands are all tied up and elevated. He's a prisoner."

"Have you heard anything about the truck driver?" Nell asked.

"No, I was hoping you might have some news."

"Nothing. Drew can't understand where that man got off to. If Rick was burned that badly, you know he was too. Yet he got away, somehow. They had dozens of volunteers combing that area yesterday on foot, and they still came up with no sign of him. It's like he vaporized!" Nell flung her hands into the air, making a whooshing sound.

"I know. It doesn't make a bit of sense. I just wish Rick and I could join the search."

The next morning, Nell drove Madison to Chapel Hill to see Rick. They had been married four days, and spent all of that time apart. Going up in the elevator, Madison became dizzy and had to sit down as soon as the doors opened. There was a long bench just outside the elevator. A doctor walked up to see if there was something he could do.

"No, thanks, I have a concussion from a car wreck, and the elevator made me dizzy, that's all," Madison said.

"Are you here to see Rick Malone?" he asked, on a hunch.

"Yes, I'm Madison McKenzie-Malone."

"I'm Dr. Burns, Rick's physician. I'm pleased to meet you, Madison. Are you feeling better yet?"

"I'm glad to meet you too, Dr. Burns. Thank you, I'm feeling fine now." She stood up slowly, "This is Nell, one of our very best friends. She brought me here to see my husband."

"Let me walk with you to his room."

The doctor offered his arm. Madison took it and allowed him to assist her. As they neared Rick's room, Jess came out.

"I thought it might be time for you two. Oh, I see you've met Dr. Burns, Rick's buddy." Jess hugged his daughter gingerly. "Thank you, Nell, for bringing her."

"No problem, Jess," Nell said with a wide smile, and he hugged her too.

Rick was sitting up in bed. His hands were free of the hangers, but still wrapped in bandages. Madison rushed to his side, but was afraid to touch him. He pulled her into his arms and winced with pain, but didn't let her go. "I'm so glad to see you!" He kissed her.

"I'll come back in a while, Rick. Don't overdo it! You hear me?" Dr. Burns said as he backed out the door.

Rick ignored him, so Maddy answered, "I won't let him, I promise! I'm just so happy to see him."

Nell and Jess walked with the doctor into the hallway. "Any idea how long he'll be hospitalized?" Nell asked.

Dr. Burns took a deep breath. As he let it out he scrunched up his face. "That's hard to say, with burn victims. They can get infections so easily."

"Yes, I understand that. So, what about him seeing our family doctor at home in Cold Creek?" Jess asked.

"Oh, Chip. Awesome doctor, that one! I don't know when I've engaged in conversation with one so smart. I'm scheduled to meet him in person tomorrow. I'll see what he can tell me about Rick's condition. Then I can make that call."

"Dr. Burns, I just have to ask, did your name help you chose your specialty?" Nell asked.

"Yes, in a way. I come from a long line of doctors, from both sides of our family. When it came time to choose, I had a friend who was burned badly. So badly that he didn't make it. I decided that with my name, I had to work in a burn center. It just made perfect sense to me. And as much as you'd think the opposite, burn patients don't feel as much pain as a lot of other injuries."

"Thank you; I was wondering, but didn't want to ask. I'm sorry you lost your friend." Jess patted the doctor on the shoulder. "I'm glad you're here for Rick."

The doctor continued his rounds, and Nell and Jess returned to Rick's side. Madison had found a seat next to him on the bed. She held his right hand in hers and didn't take her eyes off him.

"Rick, you look good. I was worried. But you're pretty as ever!" Nell laughed.

"Well thanks, Nell. I'm glad to hear that. No one told me why I had bandages on my face."

"It's because of your neck and the top of your head, that male nurse Buster told me," Jess said.

"Am I going to be bald?" he asked with a chuckle in his voice.

"I don't know; he didn't mention that part," Jess teased. "No, he says your hair will grow back in—but it just might be curly."

"No! I'll shave it!" Rick winced again. "I thought I wasn't supposed to have pain. Why is my neck hurting when I move?"

Buster walked into the room at that moment, and said, "Because you're a redneck!"

Madison declared that she was not leaving Rick's side. Buster rolled a recliner into the room for her, so she'd at least be somewhat comfortable. Jess rode home with Nell. He'd return the next day with his truck and the camper trailer. Madison laughed, suggesting he just get a motel room. She had a real surprise waiting for her.

Just after breakfast was served the next morning, a tray for Rick and another for his bride, Jess and Shirley strolled into the room.

"You're here early," Madison said. "Did you bring me a change of clothes?"

"I sure did. And you can shower right down the hall. A nurse showed me the family bath," Shirley said. She moved closer to Rick and kissed his cheek.

"Is that area painful?"

"No, but maybe you should try the other side, too," Rick had his full sense of humor back already. "Did you bring me a change of clothes?"

"Honey, I don't think you have any. I couldn't find anything at the house, and I know your suitcase was burned along with Maddy's. I planned to go shopping for you today. I hear there's a nice mall a short distance down the road," Shirley said.

"Oh, I hadn't even considered that we lost every single thing we packed. Aw, man!" Rick said.

"Don't worry, our insurance will replace it all. This might be fun, choosing a new wardrobe; we can get matching outfits," Madison laughed and squeezed Rick's arm, forgetting his arm was also burned until she felt the squish of the lose skin under the dressings.

Jess recognized what happened and caught her as she fainted. He placed her on the recliner and Shirley put a cold wet cloth on her head. Nell pulled the foot rest up to lower her head. She was out for a short while.

When she came to, she cried out, "Oh, I forgot! I'm so sorry, Rick!" Ten she threw up on the floor.

A team of nurses came in, and wheeled Rick's bed and IV out into the hallway. Another nurse stripped his bed. Jess rolled Madison's chair out, and a cleaning crew came in to sanitize the room.

Dr. Burns walked up at that moment, accompanied by Dr. Chip McClellan. "What happened?"

"Don't ask," Madison said, knowing her face was red with embarrassment. She tried to stand, but Chip advised she stay reclined.

"You have one hell of a concussion, Madison. Any excitement or quick movement can cause you to be sick. You need to be in bed as much as Rick," Chip consoled her.

"Hey, I'll go along with that!" Rick laughed.

Back in Cold Creek, word was getting around about Rick and Madison's wreck and hospitalization. Holly and Henry had known from the day Jess was called. But with Bill Conway's schedule and Ella's seclusion out at Walkers' Mountain, those two were unaware of their friends' disaster and the delay of their honeymoon.

Bill had stopped at the store to say hello to Jennings and Mrs. Sanders when a neighbor came in. "You all heard about that sheriff from over in Cold Creek? She's in the Burn Center at Chapel Hill. Says she's real bad off. Weren't she friends with them Walker gals?" Webster asked.

"What? Madison McKenzie? Uh, Malone? What happened?" Bill asked quickly.

"Ya heard about that tanker truck that blowed up over in North Carolina other night? Well, they was in one of the cars that got involved, and I heard she was burned real bad."

"Web, are you sure? We've not heard anything from Cold Creek," Mr. Sanders said.

"Well, I can sure find out," Bill said, pulling his phone out of his pocket. "Miller? Hey, it's Conway. You know any of the names of the people involved in that tanker explosion on the mountain below Sam's Gap Wednesday night?"

He listened for a while, then said, "Call me back, soon as you find out."

"I'm sure Jess and Shirley would have told us if it was true. I mean, unless they're in Chapel Hill," Mrs. Sanders said. "Oh my, that is just awful!"

"Well, I did hear that the truck driver was burned pretty badly and they had to medevac him to the burn center at UNC. Maybe this is just a mixed-up story," Bill hoped he was right.

His phone rang. "Hey, Miller, what'd you learn?" He listened, and then said, "Oh my God! Oh, no. This just can't be. Are you sure? OK... Well, thanks. Call if you hear any more. They're friends of mine."

"So it's true?" Mrs. Sanders put her hand over her mouth. "That will kill Macy and Ella. How bad is she?"

"Madison was released from Asheville hospital today. It's Rick Malone that's burned. He's at UNC's burn center." Bill put his phone away. "I better break the news to the ladies before they hear it the wrong way, like we just did."

Ella was in the front yard when Bill drove up. She knew him well enough to know something was wrong as soon as she saw his face.

"What's wrong, Bill?" She grabbed his shirt.

"Madison and Rick were involved in an accident on their way across the mountain. She was released from the hospital today, and Rick is in the North Carolina Jaycee Burn Center, at UNC in Chapel Hill. There was a tanker truck that overturned and blew up. Five cars were involved. Madison and Rick got the worst of it, sounds like."

Ella beat against his chest and cried. "No, that can't be true! Why are you just now telling me?"

"Ella, honey, I just learned about it myself. I work in Tennessee, remember? I called a pal in North Carolina to get the story straight. Some guy just came in Jennings' store and said it was Madison that was burned. I had to find out. The mix up was probably because she's the sheriff, and he assumed the sheriff was a man."

Ella dropped to her knees. Bill lifted her up and carried her to the porch of the family home. When Macy saw them, she came running out.

"What's the matter with my sister?"

Bill told Macy the highlights of the story. She sat next to Ella.

"Marian Ella, don't be so upset. Bill said Maddy was released from the hospital. I'm sure Shirley and Jess are there with her. I bet they went to Chapel Hill to be with Rick. Don't worry, they'll let us know when the time is right. She'll be OK. Don't worry, Sissy."

Bill was taken aback. He expected Macy to fall apart. Instead here she is consoling Ella. *Does Macy fully realize how bad a burn patient can be? Maybe she's not realistic about delicate subjects? Was she hardened by the murders she witnessed?*

After supper, Bill and Ella walked up to lay some flowers on her parents' and grandmother's graves. Bill gave Ella space and didn't try to interfere. This was a ritual she did every week. She bought the flowers at the Food City, down the mountain.

She walked into the woods and he followed. Ella led him to a creek with a long cascading waterfall. There were dozens of fresh green ferns all along its banks. Crystal-studded rocks shaped the direction the creek flowed and the depth. A canopy of hemlocks shaded the beauty of this spot.

"I loved coming here when I was little. It was cool in summer. Grandma always came with me, because she was afraid I'd slip and fall. That pool at the bottom is actually pretty deep—or it seemed that way then. I don't know now; I haven't been down there in so long. I like it up here.

"On the other side, over there, among the rocks the loveliest flowers bloom in spring. I think they're called lady slipper orchids. Only they're white; I have only found yellow and pink in books. These have little petals of purple on each side."

"Are you serious?" Bill couldn't believe his ears.

"Well, yeah; I didn't dream it. Grandma would never let me pick them."

"My grandmother told me about finding white lady slippers where she lived in Virginia," Bill said excitedly. "She told me she hoped I'd find them someday. I want to come here when they bloom, to see them for myself."

"It's always right around Mothers' Day, in mid-May. You do believe me, don't you?" she asked.

"Of course I believe you. But you know what? I've already found my lady slipper, and her name is Marian Ella Walker."

Ella stood silently, and then she said, "Did I hear you right?"

"Ella, I'm of the opinion that we can't be sure we'll be here tomorrow, or mid-May. I don't want to miss a moment with you. Look at all that's happened to Maddy and Rick. How many times have we heard her say, 'If we ever make it to the alter.' I mean, think about it."

"Yeah, I noticed that, too. It's almost like she doubted she'd ever be with Rick."

"Ella, will you be my lady?" Bill stood with both hands on her shoulders.

"Bill Conway, I'd be honored to be your lady." Ella smiled with all the sweetness she felt.

"You realize I mean as my wife, don't you?" he asked anxiously.

"Yes, I do. And yes, I want to marry you. I knew it the day I fell for you in the store. You were the best-looking man I'd even seen, and the more I learn about you, the more I like what I know. But I didn't think I stood a chance with you; I'm so plain and common."

"No, Ella, you're a natural beauty. You're the woman I want to spend the rest of my life with. And don't you ever doubt yourself, you are my beautiful lady."

"But you wanted Madison in the beginning. You told me so yourself."

"That was before I met you. Besides, wanting to be with someone and wanting to marry someone are two different things. I eventually realized Maddy was the 'like a sister' type. Now, you, oh, wow; I had trouble being alone with you in the beginning. I hate to admit this to you, but... Honey, you've caused me some sleepless nights, and a lot of cold showers."

Ella felt her face burn. She was glad the sun was setting, dimming the light. He might not see her blush. If he only knew he was her first crush, first kiss, first dance, and first love. She wondered how she'd won over this gorgeous man.

They returned to the house, and Macy met them at the kitchen door. "Madison called. She says that Rick will be released from the burn center tomorrow, and they'll return to Cold Creek. Jess bought a big motorhome to drive Rick home."

"What? Jess has a trailer camper," Bill said.

"Not anymore! He drove his truck down there this morning, and traded truck and camper in on a class A motorhome."

"Wow; Rick must be in bad shape," Ella concluded. "Maybe he's dying!"

"Honey, don't jump to conclusions. Jess is just bringing him home." Bill wrapped her in the warmth of his arms. "Do you want to tell Macy our news?"

"Well, if you didn't ask her to marry you, you're a real dummy. The girl is so in love with you, Bill Conway. And I know you feel the same for her. So, what's the news?" Macy crossed her arms over her chest.

"You guessed it, Sister. We're engaged." Ella held out her hand to show Macy the lovely half-carat diamond on her finger. "I thought I'd never be this happy."

"You deserve happiness, Ella. You have put up with me all your life, pushing your own needs away just to keep me going. I hope the two of you will have a long, very happy, kid-filled life together." Macy hugged them both.

"Thank you, Macy. I'm glad we have your approval. That's important to both of us."

That night, as Bill lay in the small bed once slept in by the Walker girls, he sensed a presence. The air felt cold, but the room was warm with a light breeze blowing through the curtains. Bill sat up, then walked to the window and closed it. The cold air hovered around the bed. "I don't fear you. I know you must be family. Are you here to give me your approval? I'm going to marry Ella. But I'm sure you know that."

He lay back down on the bed and said, "Goodnight." Shortly after, the room was warm again. He smiled, feeling that he'd earned another Walker family member's approval.

23

The motorhome topped the mountain at Sam's Gap just as the sun set. Rick raised up to look down into the valley. "Ah, home, beautiful home." Then he settled back down on the bed Shirley had made for him behind the driver, a table/bed.

Madison snuggled up beside him. "*Our* home, my dear. Our home sweet home."

They drove into Cold Creek, stopping in front of the restaurant, and were met by dozens of clapping friends. Dr. Chip was in the motorhome with them. He and Jess, along with Ben, helped Rick to the new bedroom suite upstairs. Margie brought them chicken Parmesan with pasta and a bottle of sweet red wine.

Holly had baked them cupcakes, and she let the children take them upstairs so they could see Rick. They wanted to be sure he was all right, and reported that he was still injured, but "will make it," as the twins said. That was important to them. They had feared that Rick might be in Heaven.

Drew and Henry were conspicuously absent from the reception party. Jess singled Nell out to ask where they were. She claimed she didn't know, but it involved Blu, the bloodhound. Jess nodded in a knowing manner, but he kept quiet.

Eventually, everyone was gone except Chip and the newlyweds. He was going to sleep downstairs in the cottage, in case Maddy or Rick needed him. They assured him he was welcome to sleep with them, there would be no hanky-panky tonight. But he declined.

The next morning, everyone gathered at Shirley's to talk about the strange threesome in the cottage across the street.

Mr. Olsen was the first to make a bet, "I'll say Chip slept sitting up in the chairs in the suite, not downstairs in the cottage."

Jess accepted his bet, and stated his own theory. "Madison ran him off so she could take her bra off. She won't sleep in it, and she would never let Chip see her without it."

"Jess, don't talk like that about our daughter! I'm surprised at you," Shirley scolded.

Mrs. Olsen declared that she was not taking any bets; she didn't want to question the couple.

Betty and one of the other waitresses challenged Ben. "What do you say, Boss?"

"I say it's none of our business. I'm sorry they had to postpone the honeymoon. Those two are cursed, and of that I'm sure. But Madison can overcome anything. She's already proved that to us by tracking down Denny in the wilds of Alaska, to avenge her mother's name. She can do this too. Madison is the strongest woman I know. She'll pull Rick through and make him the best wife the man could ever imagine. Why, if she hadn't already been hooked on that boy, I'd have traded Margie off for her."

"Oh, is that right?" Margie rubbed her knuckles along Ben's nearly bald head. "We'll see who trades whom!"

Betty giggled, "Margie, you don't have a tradable product there." They all laughed uproariously at that.

Jack Kelly came into the restaurant then. He rarely showed up at town functions, so they were surprised to see him this morning.

"I was down at the forks of the river, and you'll never guess what Henry's hound, old Blu, tracked down." Before anyone could guess, he added, "That truck driver they've been looking for! He dragged his half-burned body up that mountain and down the other side to the river. Henry was all by himself. Drew talked to him all the time on a radio. When Henry saw the feller, he called for backup. Unicoi county deputies got him, but not without Henry. He figured out what to do. That's one smart boy."

"Why did the guy run? Or crawl, I guess?" Mr. Olsen asked.

"That tanker truck was stolen! It was filled with jet fuel. I guess that's why it exploded. So far, they ain't saying who he is, but his body is a *mess*. He's got infection in those burns."

Chip walked in just in time to hear only that last statement. "No, Rick doesn't have any infection."

"Not Rick. Henry tracked down that truck driver. Well, Henry and Blu, that is," Jess said.

"Wow, that's good to hear. Except for the infection part. Where'd they take him?"

"Don't rightly know. Didn't ask. His actions could have killed our Madison and her hubby," Mr. Kelly said.

"Well, it's good to hear he's been found. I've come to get some breakfast for the patients." Chip walked to the counter where Margie stood. "Maddy wrote it down. She was very specific."

"Yeah. She always is, when it comes to Rick's food. He has a rough road ahead. She's going to change his eating habits." She laughed. "I wish her luck; that boy loves to eat!"

Chip returned with the special-order breakfast of poached eggs on English muffin, fresh fruit, turkey bacon, and two sides of oatmeal. Madison lifted the spoon with oatmeal first. Rick tasted it and made an awful face.

"There's no sugar in it!" He reached toward his coffee mug, but with the thick bandages, he could not get a grip on it.

"You don't need sugar; there are raisins and walnuts, and a bit of honey. It's delicious. Open up." Madison waited, with a spoonful aimed at his tightly closed lips.

"Let's try the eggs on English muffins. How can you ruin those?" Rick looked past the thick goop on the spoon.

Madison set the spoon down and raised the muffin to his lips. "Doc, I think we need a highchair for our baby."

"Oh, you moved straight to baby. Hmmm, I'll see what I can do about that chair," Chip laughed as he exited down the stairs.

Breakfast was over, as far as Rick was concerned, and Madison closed the door and stepped into the shower. She washed her hair and discovered she had a very large knot on her head. She hurriedly rinsed it well and wrapped up in two towels.

"I'll be right back," she called to Rick as she ran down the stairs. *I think I have a pair of jeans in my old bedroom down here.* She slipped into them and grabbed a flannel shirt and some socks, and slipped on a pair of shoes. She raced across the street to Shirley's.

Dr. Chip was sitting next to Mr. Olson at the counter.

"Doc, feel this knot. It was not there last night." She pushed his hand into her wet hair.

"Let me see that." Chip stood, guiding Maddy to the stool. "Oh, this is not good. What does your head feel like?"

"Pressure," she gasped, then slumped into the doctor's arms. Mr. Olsen caught her shoulders. Ben noticed what was going on and emerged from the kitchen. He helped Doc carry her to a table, kicked the chairs out of the way, and swiped the salt and pepper shakers and napkin holder to the floor. Mr. Olsen slid over a second table to hold her feet.

"Call nine-one-one and request an ambulance ASAP, Margie!" Chip barked.

"Mr. Olsen, you need to go and stay with Rick. Call Nell to come help you. She knows what to do about the dressings. I'm going with Maddy to the hospital."

Jess and Shirley ran through the front door. Margie called them after she instructed the 911 operator where to send the ambulance.

Mr. Olsen tried to hide the truth from Rick, but he could tell there was something badly wrong. He slid out of the bed, stepping into a pair of slippers. He caught himself on the door frame just as Mr. Olsen grabbed him around the waist.

"I'll help you to the door, if you will promise me you don't touch anything," Mr. Olsen held Rick tightly. Nell ran up the stairs.

"Rick, stop! You can't help her. You need to stay here!" She stood blocking the doorway.

"Nell, I'm going to Maddy," he declared. Rick pushed his bodyweight against her, but he was weak from his injuries. Nell stood firm, and Drew joined her on the stairs.

"Back to your bed, buddy!" Drew's voice was unyielding.

Rick stepped backwards, grudgingly allowing Mr. Olsen to guide him. From the chair next to the window, Rick watched his wife being loaded into the back of the ambulance. Dr. McClellan stepped in behind her. The driver slammed the doors and sounded the siren as he drove away.

"Please find out which hospital they are taking her to. Will you, Nell?" Rick blinked away tears.

"I'm sure they told Margie, I'll be right back."

"What happened?" Rick looked up at Mr. Olsen.

"She ran in and asked Doc to look at a knot on her head that she said wasn't there last night. He stood to get a better look, and she sat down. But in a space of two, maybe three, seconds, she slumped into his arms and was out like a light," Mr. Olsen explained.

"Was it bleeding?" Rick asked.

"Not that I saw. Her hair was wet, but I didn't see the knot."

"I didn't hear any noise; I don't believe she fell. Could this be from the head injury in the crash?" Rick looked at Drew for an answer.

"I don't know, Rick. She might have some bleeding going on under her skull. Didn't they do an MRI? Or do you know?"

"I don't know. I was at a different hospital. She seemed to be fine; made me eat no-sugar oatmeal for breakfast, with runny eggs and turkey bacon. I'll eat anything she gives me, just come back, Maddy." Rick dropped his face into bandaged hands.

Doc called Nell's cell phone to check in. He'd requested the ambulance drive them to Asheville instead of Johnson City. "I think there's a skull fracture that didn't show up. She's got bleeding on the brain, and it found a way out. Let Rick know I'll be with her every minute, and I will call him as soon as they get the CT scan. She's stable. Make sure he understands that!"

Nell explained Madison's condition exactly as Chip told her. She watched Rick's reaction and said, "You think I don't know how you feel, but I do, Rick. Don't forget what we went through, Drew and me. You have some healing to do, and you have to take care of yourself. And you have to promise you will listen to me!"

He looked at Nell, but said nothing. She felt that he was sizing up the situation with an eye toward escape. "I don't trust your look, Rick. I know you think you're bulletproof and indestructible. But humor me, please, and let me help you stay out of trouble. You know Maddy needs you—but not there with her. She needs you right here, healing and getting well for her!"

Rick held his words, but his look softened. He allowed Mr. Olsen and Nell to assist him back to the bed. He stayed there, and quickly fell asleep.

"One of us will have to stay with him all the time. I don't trust him. He'll get away and try to go to her if we don't watch him," Nell said. Drew and Mr. Olsen agreed.

Drew took first watch, and he asked Henry to bring Bud to sit with him. He realized that Rick loved Bud and might feel the need to care for Madison's dog while she was away. Henry agreed and brought Bud immediately.

The rest of the day, Rick stayed in bed and rested. He asked every fifteen minutes, "Anybody called? What about Shirley and Jess? Are they there at the hospital?"

Drew assured him Maddy had plenty of support, and she would talk to him when she woke.

The day was long and the night longer. Henry had given Bud a bath immediately upon bringing him into the cottage, carefully drying him as well. Normally the dog was not allowed in the bed, but this was an entirely different situation. Bud lay on the bed with Rick, serving as the alarm if he tried to get up.

Nell took the night watch, sleeping in one of the reclining chairs at the foot of Rick's bed. Bud whined, needing to go out, so Nell walked him and used sanitizing wipes on his feet before he returned to Rick's bed.

The next day, Chip called on Rick's phone. Nell put the cell on speaker and they both listened to the diagnosis. The CT scan showed a swelling in Madison's brain, thus the bleeding and the knot. She had undergone surgery overnight to place a stent that would relieve the pressure as fluids built up. Chip advised Rick that he and Dr. Allison were working together to form a patch to place on the brain injury. They would not know if it worked until the bleeding stopped and the injury heald. Maddy was going to be in the hospital for at least a week or two.

Rick had an appointment in Chapel Hill with Dr. Burns. Instead of Rick coming to him, Dr. Burns met Rick in Asheville where he and Dr. Chip McClellan, with the help of Dr. Allison, returned Madison to surgery to place the patch they had devised and remove the stent. Within twenty-four hours, they'd know if the dressing patch had worked. Rick was allowed to stay in the room with her after the surgery.

Rick's dressings on his hands and arms were removed the same day. His arms felt tingly and appeared red, but the skin was nearly healed. His left hand was almost healed, but the right was still missing layers of skin and tender to touch. The doctor told him he would heal better with the bandages off, and emphasized that he must keep his hands scrupulously clean.

Rick nodded, but Dr. Burns knew he wasn't listening to anything other than news of Maddy's condition. "She's strong, Rick. Your Maddy will be fine, I promise you!"

"You can't promise anything!" Rick's eyes looked dark and hollow from lack of sleep. His normally good temperament had been stretched beyond its limits. He'd waited nearly six years to have the woman he loved; so many obstacles had been thrown in their way. *So much evil, why is our love continuously tested? What is keeping us apart? Could it be the evil of Denny, somehow?* Rick had felt the touch of a good angel; was there also a bad presence? Was the woman trying to control Madison's destiny from the grave? He'd seen her headless body, and the ashes they spread on the winds of Alaska.

Could such evil have a hold on the living? At this point, he didn't dismiss any possibility. Madison had a gift, an insight, a way of knowing and feeling things others might not. He'd been with her when Mrs. Walker touched them as they prayed. Was it only the nearness of his Maddy? Could he have seen her and felt her if he was alone? No, he thought not. Her faith was strong; his, not so much. He doubted everything and everyone. But since the day on Walkers' Mountain, Rick trusted his connection, his link to a higher power, more and more. He'd prayed as he pulled Maddy from under the SUV. She was alive, but in what capacity? And his own burns—Rick shuddered as he remembered how he'd felt the pain as he pulled that man out of his own torment. *And for what? He was not a good soul.*

Rick stared at the skeleton on the hook beside the table he sat on. He thought of his own inner man. Was he good enough for Madison? Was he the problem? Was something trying to show him? Should he forget his feelings for her and walk out of her life? Would she be better off without him? Rick concentrated on the options. He didn't notice when the door opened and Dr. Chip entered the room. He was lost in his thoughts. There was only one that made sense to him; he needed to get away, give her room to breathe. He needed to remove himself from the equation.

"Rick!" Chip repeated. "Where are you, man?"

"What do you mean? I'm right here. What's going on? How is Maddy?"

"She's awake and asking for you." Chip looked sideways at Rick. "Are you OK? Rick, I swear you were off somewhere else, not in this room. What's wrong?"

Rick slipped off the table. "Where is she? Take me to her."

A team of nurses and technicians and a couple of doctors stood at the door of her room. They all looked at the chart one of the doctors held. They hushed as soon as they saw Rick.

"Can we go in?" Chip asked, but didn't wait for an answer.

"Maddy, you have company."

She blinked, but didn't move her head. Chip motioned Rick to step closer. "She can hear you."

"Maddy? Are you in pain?" Rick picked up her free hand. The other had lines, straps, IVs and anything else you could imagine. She blinked her eyes.

"I'm going to leave you two for a minute and see if I can make any sense from the crowd out there." Chip touched Rick's shoulder. "Keep talking to her, she's hearing everything, but she won't move or speak."

Rick waited for the door to close behind him. "Maddy, what's happening? I can't face this world without you. You can't go anywhere. I need you. I love you." He listened for a moment, hoping for some sign, a word, a squeeze of his hand, something, anything!

She blinked again and this time a tear trickled from her right eye. Rick touched it with his lips. He kissed her forehead. He lifted her hand, kissing it. "As long as I know you can hear me, I trust your eyes. I will pray for you, for me, for us. Do you think anybody will listen?"

Her eyes blinked three times. Rick felt her smile, but her lips had not moved. He looked at her head, a mass of bandages and a tube. The fluid ran clear: no blood. Was it going in or out? He couldn't tell. He wasn't sure he wanted to know. He closed his eyes and put his head on her breast, listening to the sound of her heart, her breathing. He smelled the medicine running through her. This was not the first concussion she'd had. Her head had taken some serious injuries before, and like the football players, he wondered how much damage she'd really had. Was she going to regrow a strong skull, or always have a soft spot, like a baby?

She made a gurgling sound in her throat. He raised his head to look into her all-telling eyes. She blinked again. "Are you trying to tell me something?" He leaned closer. Her eyelids closed and he was drawn to her lips. When he pulled away, she managed a smile, this time her cheeks raised up slightly and her eyes narrowed.

"You wanted to be kissed. You hussy, you're trying to seduce me." He whispered low so no one outside the room could hear. "You get well, and I'll kiss you *all* over, like that old song!" Then he winked.

Then it hit him; leaving was not an option. He couldn't walk away from her, she had too much of a hold on him—and he liked that hold! "I'm going to hold on to you forever, my love."

Chip cleared his throat. Rick turned to see Dr. Allison and their hometown doctor standing there, just behind him. "She's going to be fine, Doc. She told me she is." Rick kissed her hand and stepped back.

"Yes, Rick, I believe she could. Those eyes tell all. She's very anxious to get out of here and get on with that long-awaited honeymoon. Where are you taking her, anyway?"

"Oh, no... I'm not telling! She has a real surprise waiting. I'll let her tell you someday." Rick stood at the foot of her bed.

"Still keeping it a secret, huh?" Chip asked.

"Just say the word, and we're out of here!" Rick winked at his wife again. "Aren't we, babe?"

24

Madison listened to Rick's voice with her eyes closed. He talked with Dr. Burns and Chip about non-medical subjects, mostly sports. She became drowsy and let go of her conscious attention. Even in sleep, she heard the strength in Rick's words. A deep sleep fell upon her. She was aware of conversations, but the people in her head were a long ways off. She crossed a meadow moving toward them, but they remained far away. She walked faster but they drifted away even quicker, still in the group formation. She couldn't close the distance. She stepped up, pausing on a downed tree stump, looking at the far-off people. As long as she was still, they were too. But when she jumped off the stump, they moved, becoming a tiny blur in the distance.

She turned around, looking back at the stump; it also moved away from her. A bird landed in a blueberry bush, and Madison reached out to touch it. The cedar waxwing stayed where it landed. The blueberries were an oddly bright purple. The waxwing ate one, then another. She pulled her hand away as not to scare him. As she watched, he too faded into the distance until she could only see the smudge of color on the branch. He was a beautiful bird. Usually they were quick to fly, but he'd let her touch him.

Madison heard a sound behind her. She turned to see a fox sitting three feet away. The fox turned its head, watching her but not afraid. She knelt down, and the fox leaned his nose in toward her outstretched hand. She gently felt the coarse hair on his neck. He reminded her of a dog—but with those markings and that long pointy nose, he was clearly a fox. A beautiful and wondrous critter. Almost as soon as she touched his coat, he too faded away without moving. She stepped in his direction, wanting to follow. But his shape grew smaller and further from her reach.

Why were all these wonderful visions fading away from her? It made no sense to Madison that she'd touched a waxwing or a red fox, yet she had. Was this a way of seeing that what was in her reach could be removed as quickly as it appeared? In recent years, life had escaped her the same way. Her wedding, her honeymoon, her husband, and now... Was she drifting away? What was the meaning of this dream?

She tried to wake, but her eyes would not open. The field, which had been sunny and warm, dimmed until she was in complete darkness. Madison heard sounds all around her, but could see nothing.. She took a step, slowly, anticipating something close: the stump. She felt for it with her hand; yes, it was there. She kept one hand firmly planted on it and turned in the direction where the group of people had been. Their voices drifted on the breeze, but she had no recognition of their words. The air felt colder; she shivered. She sat on the stump, waiting for... What? She had no idea, but she knew the darkness could hold danger so she stayed on the stump, solid, and not moving.

Madison eventually felt warmth, but there was still no light. The stump felt less rigid, and stretched out to the point she could lie down and snuggle into its softness. Then she smelled a familiar odor, and felt a blanket under her chin. She forced her eyes open, seeing Rick's medicated hands tucking the covers up around her.

"You shivered. I added a blanket to warm you up." His breath tickled her ear. "I didn't mean to wake you."

Maddy was fully awake. She'd lost her dream-state and couldn't think of what she'd seen. But somehow, she knew it was a message—if she could only remember

The next time she opened her eyes, Rick was gone. The blinds were open and sunlight spilled through the slits, draping across the beige blanket. She felt the warmth on her legs. The smell of food wafted to her nose. *Coffee! Oh, what I'd give for a cup of coffee this morning!*

Almost as if on command, Rick entered her room carrying two cups of coffee from Starbucks. Madison breathed deeply, pulling the aroma inside. She felt her head move just slightly. The movement had given her no pain. She turned her head to face Rick. It moved freely. The day before, she could only move her eyes. The pressure was gone, the force constricting her neck was gone... She opened her mouth, and one word came out: "Coffee!"

Rick set his cup on the windowsill. He slipped his hand to the base of her neck for support. Maddy sipped slowly, testing the temperature, then she took a longer sip. "So good!" She smiled with such ease, and that gave her as much joy as the coffee.

Dr. Allison entered the room, pleased by her movement. He waited until Rick took the coffee and set it on the bedside table. "You're much improved, I can tell already," he said, walking to the foot of the bed. "How do you feel?"

"No pressure or restrictions on movement, as far as I can tell." She raised her hand to Rick's. "How are your hands? The heat of the cups didn't hurt?"

"No, I'm good!" He leaned over and kissed her forehead, just under where the bandages stopped.

"Let me switch places with you, Rick. I want to remove her bandages." Dr. Allison moved around out of Rick's path.

After a few satisfying minutes of examination, he said, "I need to text Chip. Looks like his patch is working. How does it feel to be an inner tube?" He laughed.

"Is that what I am now?" She chuckled softly.

"Kind of," Dr. Allison smiled. "That hometown doctor of yours is onto something. I believe he'll be in the medical journals very soon!"

"Then that makes Maddy and I his guinea pigs?"

"Oh yeah. Well, at least one guinea pig married the other, keeping the secrets in the family," he teased. The doctor walked to the door. "Madison, when you can move around under your own power, I'd be willing to release you. But please, don't rush it. Rick will assist you, I'll bet."

By the end of that day, Madison could get up by herself, walk a short distance, and even go to the bathroom by herself. Dr. Allison was satisfied; the swelling was gone because the fluid and pressure were gone. The surgical patch held, and she was going to be just fine. He asked that she return in two weeks for another scan, and he released her the next morning.

Jess and Shirley picked them up in Holly's SUV to drive them back to Cold Creek. By the time they arrived at the cottage, Madison had made a long list of things she needed, beginning with a new suitcase. *Filling it up will be fun*, she thought. The next day, Holly and Shirley took her to the Johnson City Mall. Everything she needed she found in Belk's, except shoes. They stopped at Academy Sports for sandals and tennis shoes.

Henry drove Rick to his apartment in Knoxville to gather what clothing he had there, and they visited an outlet mall in Sevierville as well. Rick was outfitted with new clothes and two pairs of casual shoes. He removed the tags and stuffed them into his new suitcase right away.

By the end of the week the newlyweds, Jess and Shirley, and Dr. Chip were settled into the motorhome and rolling south on I-26. Holly and Henry had Bud for the week.

Madison wondered about the possible destinations, ruling out the Outer Banks when Jess failed to turn east on I-40. *Well, that could leave the way open for Charleston or the islands off South Carolina*, she mused. But Rick was not leaking any hints. She knew he'd observed her map checking. He grinned each time they passed the turns to any particular direction.

"Tell me one thing, Rick Malone. Will we travel all night, or reach our destination before dark?"

"Jess, whenever you get tired of driving, just give me a yell." Rick said. But he just smiled at Madison.

"That's my answer?" She went to the back of the motorhome. A few minutes passed, and then she said, "I know where we're going! I figured it out! Rick, you talked to Danny. Was it Danny Moss? Your friend from high school?" She didn't wait for him to answer, she went on with her theory. "Danny is a fisherman, captain of his own boat. He's in the Keys; I remember you talking about how much you'd like to go deep sea fishing. We're going to the Keys! That's why Jess and Shirley are along, and Doc. We're all going fishing."

"Aw, you figured it out," Rick sighed.

Little did she know how far off her idea was. Even though she'd guessed the location, Madison still had a big surprise in store that Rick was not letting on about, and neither was Jess. Shirley wasn't asking questions; she wanted to be as surprised as Maddy.

They cruised down the east coast of Florida along I-95, through West Palm Beach, Boca Raton, Fort Lauderdale, and Miami Beach. At Miami, they cut west onto US Route 1, toward Homestead. Madison felt her excitement welling up inside. She watched as they skirted the Everglades and crossed to Key Largo. Darkness soon filled the eastern sky, and they witnessed a beautiful sunset over Florida Bay.

Rick suggested they eat at a hole-in-the-wall mom & pop restaurant on Tavernier. Danny had told him all about the best local seafood. They spotted The Crab Trap, and Chip steered the motorhome into the empty parking lot.

"Are you sure, Rick? There's nobody here."

"Yep. The locals eat early, and the tourists don't know how good it is. This is the place!" Rick stood, straightening his shirt and looking out the front windshield. "Come on, get parked. I'm hungry!"

As they went through the door, the smell of fried fish overwhelmed the hungry travelers. Rick pointed to a long table at the back, facing the water. They seated themselves, picking up a menu along the way.

The bell on the door jingled. Rick covered the distance from the table to the entry in three quick strides. He greeted the short man who had just walked in with a hearty hug. The man had dark skin and white hair. He was dressed like a well-to-do tournament fisherman in an aqua collared shirt of quick-dry fabric with short sleeves that had *Captain* embroidered across the left breast pocket. Velcro pockets on camp shorts carried the logo of a dealership; Madison could not read it from her vantage point. She knew from the greetings the men were exchanging that this was Captain Danny Moss.

Rick and the neatly dressed man stood looking down at all those seated. "This is my family," Rick said. "My lovely wife, Madison, her parents, Jess and Shirley, and our friend and hometown doctor, Chip. This is my long-time friend Danny," Rick said, and draped his arm along the captain's broad shoulders.

Everyone exchanged handshakes as Danny walked around the table, settling beside Madison. Rick sat in a chair across from them.

Rick let Danny order since he was familiar with the menu, so he requested the family dinner. Before they could even finish their tea or lemonade, the food began arriving. First came a terrine of New England clam chowder and another of seafood gumbo, then three baskets of crusty breads and crackers were set on the table. When the soup or chowder was finished, the servers brought trays of mahi-mahi, fried shrimp, scallops, crab, and lobster tails, as well as a large bowl of steamed veggies. The serving dishes were lined up in the middle of the table, just like a family dinner at home.

Just when they thought they couldn't eat another bite, a sample tray of deserts appeared. Rick spotted the key lime pie, and Maddy chose one as well. Doc chose the mile-high coconut meringue, but Shirley and Jess both declined, protesting that they were too full. "Then you must choose yours to go," Danny said, "as well as taking all the leftovers. I trust you can find room in your refrigerator?"

"You bet we can," Jess spoke up. "This is amazing! Don't think I've ever eaten such good seafood!"

"Well, Jess, welcome to the Keys," Danny said, then smiled.

Rick rode with Danny as they continued to their destination, Islamorada. He said he and Dan had some negotiations to discuss. Madison didn't care; she was so full and sleepy she'd try to catch a nap, if possible.

As it turned out, the drive was only twenty minutes. Danny showed Jess where to park at his marina so he could hook up to water and electricity. They could stay the night and decide whether to fish in the morning, or go on to Key West.

In the meantime, Rick and his bride were whisked off by boat to a different destination. Jess explained it to Shirley when they left the dock. "Rick and Maddy are staying on an island with only one house, completely private. We won't see them until the end of next week. That's why the three of us are going on down to Key West. I made reservations at Boyd's Key West Campground. We'll take the Conk Train for tours. There's lots of things to see. If we need to, we can rent a car at the airport. I've checked and they have plenty available." Jess had done a lot of research.

Madison was nervous getting on the boat in the dark. "Lopez will shuttle you to your honeymoon cabin," Danny informed them. "I'm sorry, Maddy, that you didn't arrive in the daylight, but the moon will be up soon." He cast the line off and they motored slowly into the channel. Just as Dan had said, in minutes a brilliant full moon rose, reflecting sparkles from the water and silhouetting a small island in the distance.

Rick pulled her against him, wrapping his arms tightly around her body. "I hope you won't be disappointed. This is paradise, according to Danny. If you don't want to stay, he'll come back and get us."

"We're going to be alone on that island?" A lighted dock came into view. Beyond, darkness loomed over the entire land area. "Is it safe?"

Lopez heard her hesitation. "Ms. Maddy, you're going to love it on Paradise Island. Just wait 'til the morning. You will see." His confident words comforted her.

"Thanks, Lopez. I hope you're right."

"If you're not satisfied, you call and I'll run back out for you."

"Oh, I'm sure we'll be just fine, Lopez. Don't worry." Rick defended his capability to take care of his bride. "But thanks for the offer."

Lopez docked and tied up the boat, then he carried their suitcases up a path lit by solar powered ground lights. They walked through a flower garden full of tropical blooms and coconut palms, with just enough solar lights to create a romantic atmosphere. Just ahead, Maddy spotted a modern house, high off the ground and dimly-lit inside. Behind glass doors and windows, she saw the beauty of *Southern Living* magazine at its best. They walked up a staircase entwined with blooms of pink and white Mandevilla, yellow jessamine, and lilac Chinese wisteria. Madison knew them all from an art class she'd taken at UT. "This is beautiful!" She stopped to smell the blooms.

Inside, Lopez walked straight to the master suite. He turned on small lamps to light the room. "What do you say, Mrs. Malone?"

"I say this is paradise! Thank you so much for coming in with us."

Rick walked out with Lopez, but he refused Rick's tip. "No Sir; Captain Dan pays me well. It is my pleasure." He laughed and returned to the boat. In a few minutes, they heard it zip away.

"Let's see the other rooms," Rick suggested. He led Maddy by the hand to the kitchen. There he found an ice bucket with a chilled bottle of wine inside. A fruit bowl mounded with tropical fruits was next to the wine.

They found a basket of crackers on the table with a note that said *Bread and cheeses are in the refrigerator.* Rick looked in, "Maddy, look at this." The 'fridge was fully stocked, with breakfast foods and things to make sandwiches to mouthwatering steaks in a clear bowl, marinating in some luscious-looking sauce. "Danny always could eat better than the rest of us. He's a real friend."

"Did you know he had this set up?"

"Not exactly. I called to see if he'd suggest a place close by, so we could go on one of his charter boats. By the time he finished describing this place, I couldn't pass it up. And the price is right!"

"I probably don't want to know." She shivered.

"It's his wedding present to us. He's not letting me pay a dime." Rick's eyes sparkled. "He's that well off, and that good a friend."

"That's amazing!"

The couple moved from room to room with a glass of wine. They found six bedrooms and three bathrooms besides the master suite. Eventually, they returned to their bedroom. Rick closed the plantation shutters and dimmed the lights, then ran a bath in the Jacuzzi. Madison found a bottle of bubble bath and slipped some into the water when Rick went to find matches for the candles. The mood was set; the night was theirs, to finally feel free to love the way they'd wanted to for so long.

Maddy woke to the sounds of tropical birds, and aroma of coffee drew her to sit up in bed. On her nightstand sat a steaming cup and a variety of warm pastries. She stepped onto the rug with bare feet and pulled on a silk robe. The coffee and plate of pastries in hand, she went searching for Rick. He was fixing his coffee at the kitchen counter.

"Good morning, Mrs. Malone."

She leaned in for a kiss. "With me, Mr. Malone," she directed, then walked down the hall toward one of the many bedrooms. "You know that door we thought was a closet? It isn't. Come see what I discovered when I couldn't sleep last night."

She led Rick up the winding stairs to a widow's walk on the roof. "You can see the whole island from here." She sat in a lounge chair, and he settled into a rocker next to her. "I watched a meteor shower after the moon went down. Maybe we can see it tonight, too."

"This is really nice. Look how beautiful the grounds are with all the flowers. I could live here; how 'bout you?"

"Are you kidding? Maybe for a few months at a time, if Bud was with us. Oh, and we could have Holly, Henry, and the kids come stay with us."

"But the kids would be in school in winter."

"Then they can come for spring break." She sipped her coffee and popped a mini banana nut muffin into her mouth. "I'm sure it must be too hot in summer, and there are those awful hurricanes. Yeah, we should only spend January through April here. What do you think Danny would say about that?"

"He'd probably say come on down. And then, of course, we'd have to invite him up for the summer at the cottage."

"Sounds like a plan to me. Does he have a family?" Maddy looked over the remaining pastries and chose a lemon-filled ball. She bit into it cautiously, then popped the rest into her mouth.

Rick got up to retrieve the coffee pot. "I don't know where his wife is, but she doesn't spend any time here anymore—not since the divorce. His son is married and his daughter is in college in Texas, at some law school." He filled Maddy's cup, added two creamers, stirred, and licked the spoon.

"Look," Maddy pointed to a pod of dolphins skirting the east side of the island. "Let's go down there."

"OK, but let's finish eating first."

That afternoon, the couple knew every path and shady hideaway on the island. Madison went swimming while Rick took a nap on the dock. She wore a mask and snorkel and dove around the posts of the dock. Rick heard some splashing and Madison yelling. He jumped up to see her swimming toward him with a lobster in her hand.

"That's mine; where's yours?" He knelt down with a net and scooped it up. "You need these gloves. You get one of the spines in your hand you won't be able to cook."

She caught the gloves he threw one at a time and put them on. Back under the water she dove, and in a couple minutes she surfaced with an even bigger lobster. This time she walked up onto the beach on the shallow side of the dock. "I'm hungry, let's fix these for lunch."

"OK. Do you know how to cook them?"

"I'll check on Pinterest. You can get cooking instructions and recipes for anything on Pinterest." She ran up the path toward the house. Rick followed with the first lobster.

Maddy found the recipe while the lobsters lay on ice in the freezer. Rick prepared a pot of water outside on the bar-b-que grill. "Yell when the water's boiling."

After they dined on fresh lobster tail with melted garlic butter and a salad, the newlyweds walked around the island. Maddy found shells washing up in the surf and asked if she should collect them to take to the kids. Rick nodded, then stepped into the water to help her pick them up. She carried an armload of large abandoned conch shells, and some scallops. When they returned to the house, they lined them up on the railing of the deck. Rick went inside to check his phone. He had a message from Danny.

He listened and laughed at the message his friend had left. Maddy lay in the hammock in the shade of a cluster of palms. "You think we should check in with your folks?"

"Sure. I bet they're having a good time too. Will we get to see Key West?"

"Did you listen to my message from Danny?" And then he laughed. "That's what the message was about. He wants to pick up us up here one morning and cruse out to Key West to spend the day. I'll call Jess and see when they can meet us."

"Great! I want to do some shopping. I want to see the Mel Fisher Museum, Turtle Crawls, the southernmost point on US1, and..." She trailed off when she noticed the look on Rick's face. Jess had given Rick some news, and it wasn't good.

Within thirty minutes, Danny had picked them up in his boat and they set off toward Key West. Jess had told Rick they'd taken Shirley to the hospital, with a possible heart attack.

Madison asked why they hadn't gone by car, but Danny assured her the overwater route was much quicker and safer. They reached the Key West City Marina just at sunset. Chip was there to meet them in a rental car. He sped toward the hospital.

By the time they discovered where Shirley was, the panic was over. She'd eaten a bad oyster, and her symptoms were much like a heart attack. With her history, Chip didn't want to take any chances.

"I'm sorry for the scare, Maddy. I've never seen food poisoning hit someone like that," Chip said.

"Don't feel bad, Dr. McClellan; a bad oyster can kill you quicker than most heart attacks," Danny said. "Now that Ms. Shirley is down for the night, how about we take in the night life?"

Rick perked up. "Sounds good to me! What do you think, Honey?"

"Sure—and can we take Chip? I think he needs a boost."

Jess declined, choosing to stay with Shirley, just in case. Chip thought it was a good idea to get a beer, after a hot and nerve-wracking day. He insisted Dan drive the rental car.

They parked in Front Street Garage, just a six-minute walk from Jimmy Buffett's Margaritaville Café. As luck would have it, Jimmy was the live music this evening. Madison could not believe they just walked in, ordered drinks, and Jimmy Buffett came out on stage. She leaned over and whispered to Rick. "Did you know he would be here?"

"No, and I don't think Danny knew, either. He seemed as surprised as we were."

After a thirty-minute set of old Buffett gold, he came over to their table and pulled up an extra chair. "Danny Boy, how are you? I haven't seen you in months."

"Jimmy, we just lucked up, finding you here tonight. These are my friends from Tennessee, newlyweds Madison and Rick Malone, and their friend Chip, the hometown doctor."

"Rick Malone? TBI Agent Rick Malone? Man, have I heard some stories about you!" Buffett laughed and shook Rick's hand hard enough to remind him his burns were not completely healed.

"Oh, please don't believe anything Danny might have told you. I'm sure he exaggerated."

"Ah, I see; gotta keep the new bride from knowing about your younger character," Buffett said. "Noah, a pitcher of my best margaritas for my friends." Then Jimmy left the table, going behind the scenes.

"Well, that was nice," Madison said. "I'm a JB fan!"

"I've been here many times and not been lucky enough to land on his night," Danny marveled. "He's unpredictable, and I think it's deliberate!"

The special drinks, called the perfect margarita on the menu, were poured up and enjoyed by his guests. Madison eventually became concerned about the time.

"Isn't it dangerous to return to your property this late at night?"

"Yeah, it is. That's why we're are going to crash at my condo." Danny toasted with another drink. "To new friends!"

"To new friends," the three said together.

"And thank goodness the X allowed me to keep my property in the Keys." Danny upended his glass.

"You have a condo here in Key West?" Rick asked.

"Well, you don't expect me to leave a good party early, do you?" Danny laughed, pouring the last of the frosty pitcher, a little in every glass.

"Walking distance, right?" Chip said.

They said good bye to Jimmy and left the bar. The moon was high and bright in the clear sky over Key West. As they walked toward the parking garage, Maddy mentioned her concern about not having things to sleep in. Rick asked that she not stress over it. He'd protect her.

"Maybe it's you I'm worried about," she laughed.

The condo was less than a block from where they parked. Danny's unit was on the top floor: the *entire* top floor. Featuring an enormous master suite and three additional bedrooms, it was plenty large enough and had all the comforts of home. Danny instructed Rick and Maddy to make themselves at home in the master, where they'd find sleeping apparel. He and Chip chose smaller rooms, each having its own bathroom.

"See you at sunrise for breakfast, and then we'll stop by the hospital before we take our return boat ride." Danny disappeared into his room for the night.

The master suite opened onto a balcony facing south. Maddy ventured out to look for meteors. "Oh Rick, come look. I see some already."

Rick joined her, carrying a blanket. He sat in the lounge chair and pulled her down to his lap, wrapping her in the blanket. "How's this for a comfortable viewing?"

"Great! Thanks, I was a little chilled."

"Yeah, I could tell," he grinned. "I like that T-shirt on you!"

The cosmic display went strong until dawn began to lighten the sky in the east. The couple had napped in short stretches, but pretty much stayed awake all night. They snuggled into the king bed and fell asleep for what seemed like just minutes.

Madison heard a loud knock on the door, then Danny's voice boomed, "You two going to sleep the day away?"

Rick rolled over and looked at his wife out of just one eye. "You want me to tell him to leave without us?"

"No, we can sleep this afternoon, on our island. Come on, get up," she said, as she bounced out of the comfy bed.

They dressed and were out the door in fifteen minutes. After stopping by the hospital to say goodbye to Jess and Shirley, Chip elected to stay there. It was 8:30 a.m. when they loaded onto the boat. Danny advised them that he hoped to get breakfast at Latitudes on Sunset Key.

"Sounds good. You're our guide," Rick said.

"I'm really hungry," Maddy added.

After breakfast, the trio headed full speed back to Islamorada. When they docked at the marina, Danny suggested Rick and Maddy take one of his small boats back to Paradise Island, in case they wanted to come ashore on their own. They accepted, and set off to continue their amazing honeymoon. Maddy stripped to her underwear and dove off the dock. She quickly came up with another lobster. Rick stripped also and tried to catch one for his dinner. Maddy came to his rescue and chased one into his waiting hands. They carried them to the kitchen, placing them into a deep pot filled with salt water.

"While I shower and get a nap, they can rest before dinner," Rick said.

"You're cruel! You know that?"

"When it comes to fresh lobster, you better believe it!" He disappeared into the master bedroom, and Maddy soon heard the shower running. She stripped off her wet undies and picked Rick's up, then put them in the washer along with their swimsuits on gentle cycle, and joined Rick in the shower.

25

L ate that afternoon, the couple woke feeling more hungover than rested. But this was their honeymoon, after all; they figured they could catch up on sleep back home in the mountains. Madison thought of their home, and Bud, and she decided to call Holly. The two talked for a half hour before Rick interrupted them, saying that dinner was served.

Just hearing about Paradise Island, fresh lobster, and the lovely clear ocean water, she sighed. "I wish Henry and I could see it."

"Maybe you can. Start talking it up to Henry, and I'll see what I can do on this end," Maddy said, and hung up.

Rick opened a bottle of wine to serve with the salad and lobster. He'd also managed to grill a sea bass that she hadn't known he'd caught. Much to her surprise, it was very good, too.

"I'm glad to see you can cook. I'll take the rest of the week off."

"I've been thinking. This week has gone by so quickly; we only have two days left, and we didn't get to shop on Key West or see the museums." Rick stopped to gather his thoughts. "What would you say to us staying another week?"

Madison jumped up and hugged him. "How 'bout the rest of the month? I could live here!"

"Are you serious?"

"Of course I am! Wouldn't you like that?"

"Yeah, I would. Let me talk to Dan, to be sure none of his other friends are planning to stay here. Maybe we can go back to the condo for a couple of days and see all the sights in Key West, too."

"That is a grand idea!" She returned to her seat. They enjoyed the meal, then took a second bottle of wine up to the widow's walk just as the sun was sinking below the horizon.

For a long while, neither spoke. Finally, Rick said, "Thank you, my love."

"For what?" She leaned in close and kissed him.

"For loving me, believing in me, and marrying me," Rick's voice sounded soft and seductive.

"Thank you, my love, for all the above. And especially for being patient with me. I was so afraid for the longest time. I felt like you were too good to be true. Thanks for showing me you are as wonderful as I first thought," she said.

Some time later, Rick said, "Danny should be off the water by now; let me call him to see what I can find out. There is nothing I'd like more than to spend the rest of our lives here, but we'd have to have Bud flown in."

"Absolutely! Bud would love the water. I bet I can even get him to catch fish!"

Rick laughed and took out his phone. Before he could find Danny in his contacts, Danny called him.

"Hey, Rick. I'm not disturbing you two, am I?"

"As a matter of fact, I was just about to call you. What's up?"

"I have a guy here who says he knows you. Wants to ride out to meet Madison. Do you know a kid named Sean Martin?"

"Sean? Yeah, I know him! Sure, bring him out!"

In twenty minutes, they heard a boat pull in to the dock. Rick walked down to meet them. Madison was clearing away the last of the clutter from their dinner when they walked onto the deck. She went out to greet them.

"Sean, this is my lovely wife, Madison McKenzie—err, Malone. Gosh, I nearly forgot. We're married now." Everyone laughed.

Sean shook hands with Maddy. She invited them in so Sean could see the house, and they let Danny take him on the tour. As soon as they returned to the deck, Sean asked if Dan ever rented it out.

"No, but I let my friends enjoy it from time to time. What did you have in mind?"

Sean explained that he was hosting a fishing tournament over Labor Day weekend, and wondered if he and his team could stay there.

Danny agreed, but asked that he not spread the word to too many folks. He didn't want to have to tell anyone they couldn't come, but it might get out of hand quickly; Sean had a lot of friends.

"No, this is too good to mess up. I'm sworn to secrecy. You don't need to worry about me."

Sean started to get on the boat, then said, "Oh! Rick, I meant to tell you, I really appreciate you finding the truth about Monique's parents. I just knew in my gut that things were not right."

"No problem, Sean. That's my job, and I like to get my man." Rick smiled sadly, realizing how much he'd miss that job.

As Dan started to leave, Rick pulled him off to one side. "I was about to call you to ask if Madison and I might stay longer, here on Paradise."

"Why, sure!" Dan placed a strong hand on Rick's shoulder, "You're like a brother to me. I'd love to have you here, for as long as you'd like. And if you want to go back to Key West I'll arrange for a car, so you can drive out there, and you can stay in my condo again. I know Maddy didn't get to do any shopping or see the sights. You tell her I'd love to have you. The next plans for Paradise Island aren't until the end of July, when it's mini lobster season. My son and his family will be here for a week. It's yours for as long as you like, 'til then."

"Thanks, Dan. You are the closest I have to any family, aside from Maddy and her folks. I appreciate you so much. And the invitation is extended for you to come up to the mountains, whenever you want. We have the perfect place for you. Not as upscale as this, but you'd be in the mountains close to hunting and fishing."

"I'd like that, Rick. Thanks; I'll check my schedule and see what August offers. I just might take you up on it, to cool off a bit this summer," Dan shook hands and then the two men embraced. "Call you later."

Rick couldn't wait to tell Maddy what Dan had said. They returned to the widow's walk to finish their wine and talk. "How long do you want to stay?" Rick split the remaining wine between their glasses.

"You mean you asked him already?"

"It's ours all the way to the third week of July, if we want it. He also suggested we drive to Key West and stay a few days in his condo. He's going to arrange for a car for us, after your folks head back home," Rick said with a warm smile.

"Oh, that's so nice of Danny. Has he always been like that?"

"Yeah, he has. Even when he didn't have anything, he'd give you what he had. Always there when I needed help with chores, or anything I wanted to do. He's truly been the brother I never had."

Rick stared off into space, immersed in thought. "Wouldn't it be nice if Henry and Holly could drive down? They could bring my truck, and Bud."

"And we'd all drive back together?"

"No, I'll fly them back. We can keep Bud and drive home: take our time, see a few sights in Florida... You know, just play it by ear. I think Bud needs a vacation, too."

"Of course!" She laughed and stood up, wobbled a bit, and had to grab onto Rick's shoulder for balance.

"Easy, gal, let me help you down the stairs and into bed."

"I think that bottle had more alcohol in it! I can usually drink more than two glasses of wine."

"Um, that was more like *four* glasses!" He wrapped his arms around her and guided her down the spiral staircase.

The next morning, Jess called to say they had pulled out of the campground and would be in Islamorada by suppertime. Maddy suggested she fix supper, and for them to plan on staying on Paradise Island for the night—or two, if they weren't in a hurry to head for the mountains.

They agreed, and Rick met them with the little cabin cruiser to bring them out to the island while Maddy prepared lobster, sea bass, and scallops. She was thrilled to say she'd caught them all by herself.

Shirley, Jess, and Chip toured the island with Rick. Shirley took dozens of photos of the tropical blooms. She told Jess she expected him to paint some of them for her, to hang on their walls. Jess dabbled with oils but his best artwork was done with watercolors. Maddy loved the way he'd made special pictures for her cottage.

Maddy was putting all the steaming pots on the deck as they returned. "Grab a plate and fill 'er up," she said. Rick handed out beers or wine coolers, and Shirley asked for tea or lemonade.

Rick told Madison's parents of their plans to stay awhile, and maybe even get Holly and Henry to come down. Shirley volunteered to stay out at the farm so the kids could go to school— and she'd keep the twins and the baby as well, if Holly would allow it.

Jess said that he'd talked to Henry, who said his mother and brother were there. They'd come in at Christmas and planned to return during summer, but they were there ahead of schedule.

"I'll bet Mrs. Jacobs would love your company, and your help with the kids."

"Ah, but Henry might not want to leave just yet," Rick said.

"But we are staying a while; they might come in a few weeks."

"Somebody's missing Bud!" Jess said.

"Guilty as charged," Maddy raised her hand, and so did Rick.

Maddy looked through the bedrooms to pick one for Chip and another for Jess and Shirley. She showed Chip to his room while Rick and Jess cleaned up the dishes. Shirley was out on the deck, taking pictures of flowers at sunset. Maddy joined her.

"This was a wonderful place for you and Rick to honeymoon. Are you happy, my dear?"

"Oh yes," Madison said, and hugged her mom. "We are so happy, and we love it here. I think Rick and Danny are so glad to be back in touch that we'll be down here again sometime soon. And Danny is going to accept our hospitality at the cottage, maybe during hunting season this fall."

"That's good. Remember, Jess and I are gone a lot, especially now with this new motorhome. We're planning a trip out west sometime soon. Danny can always stay at our house, for more privacy."

"How sweet! I'll tell Rick you offered." They walked down to the water, and Maddy showed Shirley some trails they could walk in the morning, before it got too hot. "Dad and Chip can fish, if they want. I caught those sea bass right off shore here. And I dove by the dock for the lobsters. Weren't they wonderful?"

"I've never had lobster that fresh. And I loved the scallops! Where'd you get those?" Shirley asked. "I'd like some to freeze and take home...maybe a few lobsters, too."

"We'll do it tomorrow. The scallops are in a little shallow area, just out there. I took a raft and then walked the rest of the way. You can just scoop them up and pile them on the raft, then paddle back. Or Rick can take us in the boat, if you'd rather."

Chip gave up early and went to bed first. He asked that the first person up in the morning please wake him; he didn't want to miss a minute on the island. Shirley and Jess followed about a half hour later. Maddy and Rick visited the widow's walk to look for any remaining meteors. The sky was dark, with the moon rising later, but the show cosmic was not to be on that night. They retired to their room, vowing to get an early start the next day.

The sun hid behind a troublesome cloud, but Rick woke anyway. He was amazed by how well he'd slept, and felt ready to get up. Madison rolled over but didn't really wake up. He went into the kitchen and started a pot of coffee. Shirley joined him and asked if she could help with breakfast.

"I've put my famous breakfast casserole in the oven. Coffee's ready. Bring your cup and come with me." He walked onto the deck.

Shirley brought her coffee mug and followed Rick into the shade of the co-conut palms beside the wraparound deck. "I've heard of your famous breakfast casserole. You have to share the recipe with me sometime."

"I'd be happy to. It's really very easy. The hardest part is remembering to make it up the night before."

Rick recited his recipe: "Six slices of bread—I prefer it toasted—cut into bite-sized pieces. Half a stick of butter melted in a nine by eleven glass dish. One and a half cups shredded cheese—I like Longhorn Colby. Five or six eggs, beaten well; I use a mixer. Two cups of half and half, and one pound of sausage, browned and drained. Salt and pepper to taste. Sprinkle the bread over the butter, add the sausage, then the cheese. Lastly, I whip the half and half into the eggs and pour it over top. Cover with foil and let it rest overnight. The next morning, you bake it at three fifty for forty to fifty minutes, uncovered for the last fifteen minutes.

"Which reminds me; I didn't set a timer. Excuse me for a minute." When he returned, he advised her it would be at least another half hour.

"I love it here. Your friend Danny sure has been blessed to have such a lovely place. And how generous of him to share it with you, and us."

"Yeah, he's the closest to a relative that I have. We've been close for three decades. He's just like a brother."

"Where is he staying while we're all here?" Shirley asked.

"Oh, he has a place near the marina. He doesn't even live here. This is for his retirement. His son and family will be here in July, and I'd imagine Dan will come to stay some, but this place sits empty quite a bit. That's why Maddy and I decided to stay longer. We just can't pull ourselves away."

"I can't blame you. I hope Henry and Holly will come down, too. I'll do my best to persuade them. Besides, Nell offered to keep the baby whenever she can. She needs all the practice she can get."

"Nell? Are you saying she's expecting?" Rick sat forward in his chair.

"You mean Nell didn't tell Maddy?"

"Not that I'm aware of. Gee, Nell and Drew having a baby. That's great! I think that's just great!" Rick stood up. "Be right back."

He walked into the master bedroom. "Did Nell disclose a secret to you recently?"

"What are you talking about?" Maddy stepped out of the shower with a towel wrapped around her body.

"Did you know that Nell is expecting their first baby?" Rick stood with his arms folded.

"*What?!* No! She didn't tell me! How do you know?"

"Shirley told me, just now." Rick handed Maddy her phone off the vanity. "Call her."

"Let me get dressed." She scooted past him, dropping the towel. "Why don't you fix me a mug of coffee, and I'll meet you in the kitchen?"

"We're on the deck. I'll take your coffee out there."

When Maddy came out all dressed and her hair in a long smooth braid, Rick was already on the phone. She took her coffee from the table and perched on a stool at the railing, surrounded by red and white blooms.

"Oh, that's a lovely setting, let me snap a photo," Shirley said. "Smile, and put the coffee down."

"No, just take it. This is me, au naturel, at sunrise," she argued.

Shirley snapped the photo and texted it to Nell, along with a note: *Your secret is out. You better explain to Maddy why you told me and not her.*

Rick handed Maddy her phone, still ringing. She waited for a few seconds, and finally Nell answered.

"Hello, Mrs. Malone! How is Paradise?"

"It's wonderful! How are you, Momma?" Maddy gave Nell a chance to answer. But she didn't. "Nell?"

"I didn't tell you, because you didn't need to think about me—um, us—while you're on your honeymoon. But we're fine, all three of us."

"Oh, I'm so excited! When is he do?" Maddy asked.

"Why do you say he?"

"I don't know; just a feeling."

"Holly wants a girl, so she and Maddie can play together." Nell sighed. "Of course Drew wants a boy. I'm due in October, around the fourth."

Nell and Maddy talked for a while. When she told Nell where they were staying, Nell got quiet. Finally, she told Maddy, "We were thinking of flying to Key West. If you're still there on Paradise Island, maybe we can get together."

"Hmm. Would you consider driving instead?"

Rick turned his head looking sideways at his wife. "What are you doing?" he mouthed in a low whisper.

Maddy dismissed him with a wave of her hand. "Nell, let me talk to Rick and get back with you." She ended the call and turned to face Rick. "Well, think about it. Henry and Holly would come if we asked them to. Even with his mother and brother there, and the new baby, they'd do it for us." She stood up, placed her coffee mug on the table and sat on his lap. "Nell and Drew have been through so much, and they want to fly down. Why not invite them, and then fly them back? It makes sense to do it this way."

"And you haven't asked Holly?" Rick said.

"No, I was going to call her today. Shirley, have you said anything to her yet?"

"No, I thought it was your place to tell her."

"All right. What do you think, Mom? Should we invite Nell and Drew? They never really had a honeymoon, because of his injury. Maybe this would be a good idea.

"Let's take a vote," she said. Maddy got up and went back into the house. Jess was coming through the kitchen with his coffee. "Is Chip up?"

"I think he's in the shower." Jess stopped to look into the oven. "Smells good; how long 'til we eat?"

"Let me look at it." Maddy turned on the oven light. "Not quite done, just a few more minutes." She walked her dad out onto the deck. "We have a proposal. I'm thinking of changing our plan. What do you think of us asking Nell and Drew down here, instead of Holly and Henry?"

Jess settled onto the stool Madison had been sitting on. He sipped his coffee, thinking the suggestion over for a minute. He said, "Makes more sense to me that way. This is not a good time for Henry to leave the farm. He and Russell are setting up the saw mill, Holy has the new baby, and Mrs. Jacobs is there, trying to get settled into her new home. Yeah, Drew and Nell are your best bet, in my opinion."

"All right then. Honey, call Nell back. Between the four of us, we can get Holly and Henry and the kids all down here sometime, but for now, it's Drew and Nell." Rick settled it.

"Hey Nell, is Drew there?" Maddy asked.

"Yeah; want me to put my phone on speaker?"

"Yes, this definitely concerns Drew too."

Madison tapped the speaker button, then put her phone on the table. "Hey, Drew, can you hear us?"

"Congratulations, my friend! We're happy to hear your news." Rick leaned closer to the phone. "And we have a proposition for you and the Mrs."

"Thanks, Rick. Who else is there, and what is this proposition?"

"We're all here," Shirley and Jess both said.

"We have decided not to come home just yet, not for a few more weeks, at least. Our idea is, if you'll drive Rick's truck down and bring Bud, we will buy your tickets to fly back home after staying here with us for a honeymoon vacation." Rick explained.

"Aw, did Nell tell you we were so jealous that we've been discussing a trip down to Key West?"

"It fits our plan perfectly. We want our truck and our dog, and we have an entire island to ourselves. We think it's a great time for you two to come down. That is, if you don't mind driving. It is a lovely trip." Madison said.

"Nell is feeling all right, isn't she? I mean, I hope she's not having any morning sickness," Shirley added.

"Yes, I'm fine, Shirley. I think driving would be great fun. How long does it take?"

"Comfortably, two days. You'd want to stay the night somewhere around St. Augustine or Daytona," Jess suggested.

"We'll cover the hotel too," Rick said.

"Nope, you don't need to do that, or the ticket back. We aren't a charity case, you know."

"We can work out the details later. You two discuss it, and let us know when you want to come. Call us back soon, will you?"

"I don't think that's necessary," Drew said. "We can leave as early as day after tomorrow."

"Great, then it's all settled. I'll text you some information." Rick hung up, and sent Drew the promised text immediately.

The rest of the day was spent collecting scallops and lobsters. The evening, Jess and Chip went fishing. Rick saw they were not having much luck from the beach, so he loaded them into the boat and took them out a little deeper. They watched the sunset on the water, and brought in their limit of fish.

Chip and Jess cleaned and wrapped the fish, putting them into the freezer. Maddy and Shirley had put five pounds of scallops and 27 lobsters in as well. They would have been allowed 36, but ran out of legal-sized lobsters. Rick borrowed two coolers from Danny's supply, and the frozen seafood was packed away for transit.

Shirley and Jess hated to leave Paradise Island, but they knew Chip had been away from home long enough. He had patients in Cold Creek who missed him. Truth be known, Jess missed the mountains anyway. Now that they had this awesome motor home, they wanted to tour the Tennessee and North Carolina campgrounds before the onslaught set in when school was out for summer break.

The coolers were loaded into a lower storage compartment of the motor home. Jess pried Shirley away from Maddy, and they closed the door. Waving goodbye, they headed north on Route 1. Rick and Maddy returned to Paradise alone.

Madison thought about how they had been blessed to have this amazing place to stay, and how nice it was to share it with family and friends. She worried that Holly might feel left out, though. *But Rick did promise we'd return at a better time for the Jacobs. Wouldn't this be a grand place to spend Christmas?* She daydreamed about at the possibilities.

26

As Jess drove north on 95, he thought about where they'd spend the night. They had heard of a campground right on the water at Beverly Beach. He punched it into the GPS, getting the phone number to the Camp Town RV Resort.

"Chip, will you call this campground and see if they have an opening?"

"Sure," Chip replied. He took out his phone, somewhat surprised when his call was answered on the first ring—and that he immediately spoke to a person. "Would you have an available space for a thirty-six-foot class A this evening?" He listened for several seconds.

"Full hookups? Awesome!" He looked at Jess, giving him a thumbs up. "We should be there no later than what, five?" He raised his brow, and Jess nodded. "Oh yes, and we look forward to seeing you. The name is Jess McKenzie. That's correct, a thirty-six-foot motorhome. Yes, thank you."

"What is this all about?" Shirley walked from the back to the drivers' seat.

"Just thought we'd set up camp in an easy place for Drew and Nell to stay the night. What do you think? You want to call her?"

"OK, I'll see what they say about it." Shirley returned to the bed in the back. She was watching a movie when she heard Chip's voice.

"Hello, Nell. How's your packing coming along?"

"We're all packed. I'm going out to get Bud this evening."

"How do you feel about staying with us in the motorhome on the beach?

259

We're parking there for the night, and we'll stay tomorrow night, too. It seems to be the perfect halfway point."

"I had no idea there were camping spots on the beach. Where is it?"

"Just south of St. Augustine, near Flagler Beach."

"We were thinking of stopping in St. Augustine. But do you have room?"

"Sure; the bunks are double, and we sleep in the queen bed across the back. Chip sleeps on the table bed. That leaves both bunks for you and Drew. Oh, and the sofa makes a full bed. It's just a thought."

"Well, it's a good thought, I'd say. I'll let you know what Drew says when I call you back?"

"OK, but no hard feelings if you choose not to.?"

Nell drove out to the Jacobs farm. Bud, Bear, and the twins met her at the driveway. She was escorted into the house by all of them. Holly was expecting her, so she'd managed to give Bud a bath to prepare him for his trip.

"Congratulations, Nell. I'm so happy you're growing a playmate for Maddie." She hugged Nell immediately.

"Well, Madison is pulling for a boy. Maybe she wants a husband for your Maddie." They both laughed.

Nell and Bud returned to Cold Creek. Drew picked up Rick's truck, a new Ford F-150. He checked all the fluids and gas, making sure it was ready to go. They loaded their suitcases into the back under the tonneau cover that night; all they'd need to put in the next morning was themselves and Bud. He had a nice bed made up on the back seat. Nell had seen to that, so he'd be comfortable. She knew the dog was used to short drives, but wasn't sure how he'd handle all day in the truck. They'd stop several times for breaks, for him as well as themselves.

The alarm went off at 5:00. Nell was already awake, thinking of some last-minute items. She let Bud out to use the bathroom, and then they were ready to begin the trip. Bud loaded up as if he understood.

When Nell phoned Maddy a couple of hours down the road, she used FaceTime so Bud could see his momma. He was so excited he couldn't contain himself. He jumped up and down like he expected her to materialize from the phone screen. Madison was very anxious to see him.

Around 3:00 p.m. Drew exited I-95, as the GPS instructed, and they drove straight to the campground. Bud ran all over the motorhome looking for Madison. Shirley sat down and told him that he'd see her tomorrow. Bud laid his head on her lap and whined, not wanting to wait one more day.

Just after dark Madison called, to FaceTime with Shirley. Bud heard her voice and ran to the back of the camper. He pawed at the iPad, whining. "Tomorrow, Bud; we'll see you tomorrow."

Rick walked up the stairs to the deck and noticed Maddy's eyes were red. "You've been talking to Bud, haven't you?"

"Maybe this was a mistake, not bringing him in the first place."

"Aw, come on... Honey, he's fine. You'll have him here by this time tomorrow, and all will be forgiven. He's going to love this island!"

Madison nodded and blew her nose on a napkin from the table. "I hope nothing delays them."

The next morning, Rick told Maddy to get dressed for a boat ride, he was taking her someplace special. She put a couple of towels and a change of clothes in a beach bag, and wore a swim suit under shorts and a T-shirt.

Rick steered to the Moss Marina, where he docked the small cabin cruiser and tied it up. He held his hand out to Maddy. She picked up her beach bag and stepped onto the dock, then they walked to the section of the marina where the charter boats were docked. Several people had loaded onto one Maddy recognized as Danny's personal dive boat.

"Oh, so Captain Dan is taking us out?"

Rick just smiled as they took their place onboard the dive boat. A young woman sat down next to Maddy. She introduced herself as Glenda. "I'm Madison, and this is my husband, Rick."

"Nice meeting you both," she said with a distinct accent. "Have you been to Pennekamp Park before?"

"Um, no," Maddy said, looking at Rick. "This is our first trip. How about you?"

"No, but I've heard what fun it is. I came to the Keys just for the diving." Glenda wore a bright blue short-sleeved neoprene dive suit. "I'm from down under, you know?"

"I thought so." Maddy smiled. "I guess you dive a lot in your country."

"Yeah, the Great Barrier Reef is practically my home. But at least here, you don't have the danger of a lot of predators."

The boat began moving slowly, and everyone stopped talking to settle into a safe position. Madison noticed there were a dozen scuba tanks secured at the back of the boat. She'd always wanted to learn to dive, but now it gave her an uneasy feeling.

The ride was quick and loud, so no one talked much, except Rick. He whispered in Maddy's ear, "Don't look so solemn; we're going to snorkel."

Maddy let out a sigh of relief. She hadn't been aware he noticed her worry. She nodded her approval.

The boat slowed at the *No Wake* sign posted at the entrance to John Pennekamp State Park. Madison remembered reading about the shallow water dives. There were statues and tons of fish to see while shallow diving or snorkeling. She felt more at ease knowing they weren't actually in open water or very far off shore.

Danny instructed the scuba divers to gear up and hit the water first. Snorkelers took a position at the bow of the boat. Maddy watched as Glenda fell backwards into the water, holding her mask and regulator on her face. She signaled she was OK with her hand, that she was ready to dive. Her buddy hit the water close by and signaled too. They put their heads down and their fins in the air to launch themselves downward.

At this point, Maddy was envious that they were breathing under water and enjoying the world of the fish. In just a few minutes, Danny called the snorkelers to jump in or use the ladder. Madison and Rick held hands and jumped feet first. They had learned from diving off the dock on Paradise Island to hold the mask; this kept it from being shoved off as they hit the water.

Maddy cleared her mask and signaled to Rick to let him know she was good. Rick signaled back. They swam with the ease of fins, remaining close to the surface so they could breathe. When they spotted the statues, Rick signaled that he wanted to dive. Madison took a deep breath and nodded.

The water was clear and crisp as they dove to twelve feet. Rick righted himself to clear his ears, and Maddy did the same. Then they tried to reach the statues, but it was too deep for Maddy's breath capacity. She had to surface and Rick followed. She pulled the snorkel out of her mouth and said, "You go ahead. I don't think I can make it that deep, but I want to watch you."

"OK," he said, replacing the snorkel and diving again. This time, he went all the way down on one breath. She circled on the surface, longing to dive with him. He was a much stronger swimmer, however, and she recognized her limitations.

When he resurfaced, she said, "I'm sorry, I'm just not that a strong swimmer."

Danny overheard their conversation. "Rick, take her to that buoy. The dive is shallower there, and you'll see plenty of statues. This is nearly a full atmosphere. I'm surprised you got all the way down on one breath."

Rick waved and he and Maddy struck off for the red and white buoy, about twenty yards away. There was no problem with Maddy's swimming on the surface. She felt invigorated with the swim fins.

They dove and played in the shallow sections for a long while. Maddy said she was tired and wanted to return to the boat, so they turned back. Danny met them with a snorkel and mask on his face. "I was coming to let you know it's time to pick up the divers. You two must be worn out!"

During the trip back to Moss Marine, the ship's mate brought out a cooler of sandwiches and drinks. The guests could choose from ham & Swiss, chicken salad, or peanut butter. They were all given bottles of water to drink.

After everyone unloaded their gear from the charter boat, Danny walked over to Rick and Maddy, watching from the shade. "You two should take our diving class, since you'll be staying a while longer."

"I've always wanted to learn to dive. But there aren't that many places in the mountains to dive," Madison said.

"Sure there are," Rick said. "There's always the sunken towns."

"But visibility is nothing like here." Madison expressed her delight with wide eyes. "Today was amazing! I've been diving out at the island, but the park was so much fun!"

"Well, if you decide you want to, just give me a yell," Danny waved goodbye and moved toward his boat.

"Hey, Danny," Madison called out. "Can you come out for dinner one evening, while our friends are here?"

"I sure can, if you'll let me bring the wine. What are you serving?"

"Spaghetti?" She sounded as if that was a question.

"Homemade?" he asked.

"Yes," she replied, then laughed.

"Better make plenty! I'm a big eater!"

"I will, and thanks for the offer of the wine. We like what you chose for us so far."

"I'll get a variety. I own the liquor store!" He laughed as he disappeared below deck.

Rick and Madison returned to Paradise to wait for word from Drew and Nell. Maddy fixed a big salad, readied some fresh seafood to put on the grill, while Rick squeezed a dozen fresh lemons for lemonade. Maddy took four already baked potatoes from the refrigerator and scooped them out, reserving the skins. With a double boiler, she heated the potato chunks, mixed them by hand with a potato masher, and then heated them with half and half, butter, sour cream, and a little salt in a saucepan. She stuffed the shells with scoops of smashed potatoes, added a slice of cheese to each one, put the reassembled potatoes under the broiler to wait until time to reheat them.

It was nearly 5:00 p.m. when they got the call that their friends—and Bud— were at the marina. Maddy raced Rick down to the dock, beating him into the boat. Seven minutes later, they tied up at the dock of Moss Marine. Bud ran from the building and jumped into Maddy's arms, nearly knocking her off her feet. He wiggled free and ran to Rick, licking his face frantically, and then ran back to Maddy. Nell and Drew stood by and watched.

After the dog's effusive greeting, the humans were given hugs. Nell and Rick went to the truck to retrieve their bags and Bud's travel kit. The four humans and Bud loaded up and motored to Paradise Island.

Nell could not believe her eyes. "I saw Shirley's photos, but in person? This is *unreal!*" She accepted Rick's hand, stepping onto the dock.

"Careful, Momma," he said. "I'm so happy for you two!"

"Don't you mean surprised?" Drew stepped up next, holding out his hand. Suddenly he snatched it back. "Not sure I trust you, Rick." They both laughed.

"Aw, come on, Drew. You brought us our four-legged kid. Why would I throw you off the dock?"

Madison and Bud ran along the beach so Bud could unwind from the long two-day trip cooped up in the truck. She still had her bathing suit on, so she dove under the water. Bud acted very confused, but he jumped into the salt water to follow her. She hugged him and picked him up in her arms, then walked out of the surf before putting him down.

She led Bud to the bottom of the steps, wanting to use the outside shower. She picked him up again and held him under the warm water for a moment, then Rick dropped a couple of towels down to her. She wrapped Bud in one towel, and carried her furry baby up the steps. Rick took him from her so she could dry her own feet and legs. She wrapped the towel around herself, then carefully pulled the T-shirt off, leaving it on the railing to dry.

"Come in, Nell. I'll show you your room. Drew, you might want to snag the hammock before Rick gets it, or we'll never eat!"

Bud followed his favorite human; the sounds of his toenails tapping on the wood floor were very comforting for Madison.

"I've missed that sound, Buddy." She bent at the waist to rub his wet neck. "Thanks so much, Nell. You don't know what this means to me, to us."

"Yeah, I kind of do. He's a family member. I get it." She laughed.

Madison opened the door on the opposite side of the house from their room. "This is the only room with windows on both sides." She pointed to the south and east facing windows. "There's a nice breeze across the bed when they're both open. Dad and Shirley loved this room. This time of year, we can turn the AC off as soon as the sun sets. We usually spend our evenings up on the roof, in the widow's walk. I'll show you later."

She showed Nell the linen closet, their private bath, and the spiral stairs to the roof. "If you need anything, and I mean anything, Danny's got it here! Paradise Island is truly the perfect name for this place. I'm so glad you could come and spend time with us! We're going to make a trip to Key West in a couple of days. Dan also has a condo there we can stay in." Maddy put her hand on Nell's arm. "We have so much to talk about!"

Rick turned the oven on and warmed up the grill. He offered Drew a beer. They drank a couple before their meal was ready.

During dinner, Rick's phone rang. It was Jess, so he took the call. "Just wanted to let you know we made it home safely. Did your guests arrive?"

"Yeah, we're eating dinner right now. How was your trip?" Rick asked his father-in-law.

"It was good. Always nice to be home, though."

They talked for only a few minutes, and Jess let Rick return to his meal.

Bud stayed beside Maddy all evening, not letting her out of his sight. She fed him pieces of her fish. Rick set his plate down for Bud to eat what remained of his boneless fish as well.

"This is not wasteful, considering we love Bud, is it?" Maddy asked.

Drew laughed. "It's all right just this once. But if there's any more, I get it."

Rick stood up. He got another serving of the mahi-mahi from the grill. "You're right, this is too good to feed to a dog!" He slid the portion onto Drew's plate. "You get the last of it."

"Bud isn't a dog, Rick. He's a family member." Nell reminded them.

Bud walked away from the table as if to settle the argument. His belly was full, and he was looking for a place to nap. Maddy set a cushion on the deck, pulled from one of the lounge chairs. She laid a dry towel down over the cushion and snapped her fingers. Bud wiggled all over, then settled onto his special bed.

Rick cleared away the dishes, allowing the women to sit and sip lemonade. He brought Drew another beer and one for himself.

"Oh, we've missed the sunset," Maddy said. "Well, it's still lovely up there. Anyone up to sitting on the widow's walk?"

Drew said he was perfectly comfy in the hammock, but Nell stood up, "I want to see the sights." She and Maddy went into the house; Bud followed, but stayed at the bottom of the spiral stairs.

The next morning Nell and Drew slept late. Maddy and Bud went out at sunup to walk the trails. Rick puttered in the kitchen, making some sort of breakfast. His phone rang and again, it was Jess.

"Well, you're up early. What's going on?" Rick answered the call.

"Been up all night, Rick. Macy is missing. Ella and Bill went to dinner and when they returned, she was nowhere to be found," Jess said.

"What do you think happened?"

"Well, Watts escaped. He put a guard in the hospital, and the guy might not live. Watts has been out since the weekend. Bill fears he might have returned to Walkers' Mountain. Macy didn't know he was out. We're worried that he might have come and taken her. Don't tell Maddy—

"Oh, hold on! I *have* to tell Madison, because I'm coming home. He's just crazy enough to kill her. I'm needed there! Yes, I *will* tell Maddy."

"It's your call, Rick. Let me know when you'll be here." Jess ended the call.

"What's happened?" Drew said from the hallway.

"That was Jess. Watts escaped, and Macy is missing. Man, I gotta go home. Jess didn't want me to tell Madison and Nell, but I have to."

"Yeah, we can't keep it from them. Ah, this *sucks!*" Drew sat on one of the tall stools at the bar.

Rick slid him a mug of coffee and the sugar bowl. They were both nursing their second cup when Nell came in.

"I hope you saved me some of that. I waited, but you forgot to come back with it."

"Sorry, Nell; that was my fault. I've been talking to him," Rick said.

"What's wrong?" She took one of the stools next to her husband. "Where's Maddy?"

"Out running with Bud." Rick gave Nell a cup of the hot caffeinated brew. He got the milk from the refrigerator, asking, "You take it with milk, right?"

"Thanks, that's very observant of you." Nell took the carton of milk and stirred a small amount into her cup.

At that moment Maddy and Bud walked in. She went straight to Rick and kissed him. "We had a great run. Bud loves the trails. He even raced with me." She accepted the cup of coffee Rick had made for her. "What's wrong?"

"Jess called. Watts escaped, and now Macy is missing." Rick said.

"Oh, no! Did he take her?" Maddy dropped into a chair at the small kitchen table.

"They don't know yet. She was gone when Bill and Ella went home after having dinner out last night. Jess was up all night, he said; he and Shirley didn't want you to know. But I insisted; I couldn't keep this from you." Rick stood behind her and rubbed her shoulders. "Maddy, I've gotta go home. You understand that, don't you?"

"Yes, I do. We should all go back." Madison said.

"Now wait a minute. What can you and Nell do, or Drew for that matter? I can fly home and keep you posted as to what's happening. The three of you should stay and go on to Key West. When will you get a chance to do this again?" Rick argued.

"You know, Rick is right. Taking two days to drive back, they might find her today. She might have just wandered off. Let's do as Rick says." Drew looked at Nell. "What do you want to do?"

"Maddy, I'm pretty tired. Like Rick said, what can we do? I say we stay here."

"You're right. I just hate to be here and Ella needing us there. You agree that if something dreadful happens, you'll let us know so we can drive home, OK?"

"I'll text you every hour, if it makes you feel better. We'll find her. Don't think the worst; Macy is very resourceful. She can handle herself. Watts might not have had a thing to do with this. Let me make some calls. I'll talk to Bill Conway. He might know something that Jess doesn't know."

Rick walked onto the deck. Maddy looked in the oven. Rick had put some canned cinnamon rolls in and they were sure smelling good.

"How about some breakfast?" Maddy asked. "We can have eggs and pancakes—or waffles, or Rick's cinnamon rolls."

"I'm waiting for the rolls. I love pastries for breakfast. We'll need another pot of coffee, though" Drew stood up.

"Stay there, Drew. I'll make another pot and the rolls will be ready any minute." Maddy poured the remaining coffee from the pot into Drew's mug, then started a fresh pot brewing.

She used a hot pad to take the cinnamon rolls out, opened the tube of frosting, and squeezed it onto the hot rolls.

After a while Rick rejoined them and said he'd booked a flight out of Miami International Airport. Danny set him up with a helicopter ride to the airport from the marina. "Don't even ask," Rick laughed. "Danny has a girlfriend with a helicopter. Imagine that!" They all laughed.

"Is there anything this guy doesn't have?" Drew asked.

"One of you needs to run me over to the Marina. Who's the boater between the three of you?" Rick asked.

"I guess that would be me," Nell said. "I had a boat to play with when I lived in Knoxville. Of course, that was on the river. Can't be a lot of difference; water is water, isn't it?"

"The ocean is easier, really. The signs are the same, there's just less traffic," Rick said. "I'll be ready in thirty minutes." He walked into the bedroom, Maddy following.

In thirty minutes, Nell and Maddy took Rick over to the marina and watched the helicopter take off. From the island, Drew and Bud waved as the helicopter circled overhead. In another five minutes, the women returned to the island.

Nell rested the entire day, sleeping in the hammock or napping in her bed. Maddy recognized it was a side effect of pregnancy. Otherwise, Nell would have been out there diving for lobsters with her and Drew.

Drew had been reluctant to try swimming, but the swim fins made it easy for him. The exercise was really good for his muscles, but he was careful not to overdo it. Maddy insisted he take a hot Jacuzzi bath afterward in the master suite.

They ate scallops and fresh steamed vegetables for supper. Leaving the dishes in the sink, they climbed the stairway to the widow's walk just in time to see a magnificent sunset. The air felt a little too cool to Nell, so she and Drew went down to the living area.

Maddy and Bud stayed for a while, talking to Rick on the phone. He'd had Jess pick him up at Tri-Cities Airport. There was no news on Macy. Rick and Jess drove the motorhome to Jennings's store by Walkers' Mountain so that they could use it as headquarters. A volunteer search party made up of twenty Cold Creek residents and another half dozen of Mr. Sanders' neighbors were gathering at sunup in the morning to walk the dense underbrush of the mountain.

Shirley hadn't gone with Jess. She chose to go out and help Holly and Mrs. Jacobs move furniture around, so that Henry's mother could have the master bedroom downstairs. They needed to move the nursery and all the baby's things as well. Henry and Russell had moved the beds the day before, so the smaller furniture was not much of a problem for the women. Besides, they had the twins to give them a hand.

Madison hated that she was missing all the work Holly needed done, but Holly and Mrs. Jacobs needed the time to get reacquainted. Shirley had offered to help in Madison's absence.

When Madison and Bud returned to the kitchen, the dishes had been loaded into the dishwasher and all the pans were cleaned up and put away.

"Hey, thanks for cleaning up," Maddy said. "I'm going to bed. Good night you two."

"Good night, Maddy—and Bud."

27

Meanwhile in Tennessee, Rick and Jess were up before dawn to meet the folks gathering at Mr. Sanders' Store. Mrs. Sanders had made sausage biscuits and a giant pot of coffee for anyone who wanted to eat.

Rick studied a map of the area, drew some grids, and assigned team leaders to take it section by section. They would comb Walkers' Mountain until every inch was covered. Just as they were about to leave the store, Henry and Blu arrived.

"Am I glad to see you! You too, Henry!" He slapped Henry on the back.

"Thanks. It's nice to be needed, Rick."

Henry took Blu on up to the Walker's house at the top of the mountain. Ella gave him a scarf her sister had worn just days before to scent. Blu sniffed and sniffed until Ella became discouraged.

"It's OK, Ella. He sorts out the freshest scent, and then he'll be on his way," Henry explained.

Sure enough, Blu howled that he had the scent and headed toward the thickest part of the woods behind the house. Henry let him run, while he and two other volunteers followed Blu's baying. It was Henry's idea that if Macy took this path, it meant someone was chasing her. He found young underbrush broken down flat, and some small footprints in the mud at a creek crossing. Then he noticed larger boot prints pressed overtop the smaller ones.

"Rick, Blu is on her trail, and it's obvious she's been followed," Henry said over the walkie-talkie.

"Which way do the prints lead?" Rick asked.

"West from the Walker house."

"Keep me informed. I'll guide a team in your direction."

Henry and his accompaniment followed Blu up and down the mountainside in a zig-zag pattern. Macy knew these woods; Henry thought she was looking for some place to hide. About that time, Blu stopped baying. *He's lost the trail.* Henry saw his hound walking in circles. "Where'd she go, fella?"

The three men sat down and gave Blu a chance to search. A few minutes passed before he took off again, but he soon came back. *Blu doesn't get confused easily.* Henry watched his hound closely. He examined the patch of ground the dog kept returning to. It was rocky and no prints showed up. *From this position, she could have jumped to that rock and climbed up,* Henry thought. He picked up Blu and lifted the dog over his head onto a rocky ledge. Immediately, Blu was back on the scent.

Henry and the other two guys climbed up and followed. The rocks jutted out from the hillside like icebergs in an ocean. Between them were narrow passages the dog and a small woman could pass through, but not these three brawny men. They returned to the base of the outcroppings and searched for another way up to the top.

The team approaching from the south soon joined them. One of the group was a local man who admitted to hunting this area as a teen. He told then about rumors of a cave under the rocks, but he'd never located it.

Henry called Rick on the walkie-talkie again. He explained the problem and the theory of a hidden cave. The sun was setting, so Rick called them in, as well as the other teams of searchers. Some went home for the night; others pitched tents to sleep in, so they'd be able to get an early start in the morning.

Mrs. Sanders served beef stew and biscuits to the searchers. Mr. Sanders set out three cases of sodas and a couple cases of water. Ella and Bill came down from the mountain to talk with the volunteers, and thanked them for their efforts.

Henry pulled Ella off to the side to ask her about the cave. She told him she'd never heard anything about it. *She was so young when they were sent to FL, why would she know?*

Jennings overheard his question. "Henry, I haven't been to the cave in decades, but I used to know where it was. I'd be happy to go with you tomorrow and see if we can locate the entrance."

"That would be helpful, Mr. Sanders. I'd appreciate it. Blu lost her scent, and then the rocks were so dangerous that I pulled him off just before dark."

"I know someone else who might be able to help." Jennings walked away with purpose to his step. He called out to a tent set apart from the rest. "Buster, I need to speak with you. Come out here, will you?"

"That you, Jennings?"

"Yes," he replied.

Buster stepped outside the tent and stood up. "I ain't doing no drugs on your land."

"I don't even care about that right now. I just want to ask you some questions. I know you was raised up in these woods. Your old man trespassed every hunting season, but I don't care 'bout that either. What I want to know is, can you lead these fellers to the cave up in them rocks?"

"Maybe... Y'all thinking that's where she might be?"

"Dog followed her scent to the rocks, then he got all confused. They'll go back up there in the morning. Can you show Rick and Henry how to get to the cave?"

"Maybe." He scratched under his beard. "I ain't going in, if I can even find it again. Ain't been there in a couple decades. The trees are all grown up there now."

"Just show them where; you won't need to go inside," Jennings said.

"That cave has a lot of turns and dead ends. A feller can get lost in there real easy."

"They'll be fine. Be ready to go at sunup. I'd be indebted to you if you do this for me."

"How indebted?"

"Just be at the store before the sun is up." He turned and walked back down the hill.

Jennings knocked on the door of the motorhome. "Rick?"

Rick opened the door. "Jennings, come on in." He stepped back to allow the tall man to enter.

"I got that feller Buster Brown to say he'd take you in where the cave entrance is."

"Oh, that's great! Thanks," Rick said.

"Hey Jennings, come on up here and have a seat." Jess walked in from the back room. "Did I hear you say Buster? I thought you didn't have any use for that guy."

"Don't, usually. But he knows how to get into the cave. His dad hunted that property all the time. Raised that boy in the woods, if you could call it raising. His mom disappeared; can't blame her, but she should have taken that boy with her. He ain't much more than an animal. Never went to school, never was taught nothing but how to hunt and fish. He don't even know how to have a real conversation with folks." Jennings shook his head, "But if he can help find our Macy, I'll make it worth his while."

Rick's phone rang, so he excused himself and walked outside. "Hey, Honey. I was going to call you in just a few minutes. We just got everyone settled for the night."

They talked as Rick sat on a log watching a bonfire some of the volunteers had built in the field down from the store building. Maddy told him all about Drew enjoying swimming with the fins, and how much Bud loved the water.

"Be sure to rinse him well with fresh water every time after his swim. You might want to put some conditioner on his fur and leave it," Rick advised.

"I'm way ahead of you. I used Skin So Soft Oil, and it helps repel the salt water. We both shower by the stairs before we go onto the deck."

Rick promised to call her as soon as they had some news to report. Otherwise, he'd call again after dark the next night. They hung up, and he went back to the motorhome to get some sleep. Henry tied Blu in the back of his truck, then he stretched out on the sofa bed in the motorhome. Jennings left to sleep in the store, against his wife's wishes—but he was afraid the boys might get rambunctious and bother Rick and Jess.

The sun rose ay too early for most of them, but Rick was up and out before anyone else. Buster joined him, introduced himself, and asked could they get going. Rick stood up and said, "Let me tell Jess and Henry. I don't want to face this fellow alone, if you get my meaning."

Buster nodded and stuffed a plug of tobacco into his mouth. "I'll be across the road, just there." He walked off without waiting for a reply.

Rick called Jess on the walkie-talkie to let him know he and Henry would be out ahead of the others. Jess stepped up and promised Rick he'd organize the groups and send them to girds that were not checked yesterday. "I appreciate that, Jess," Rick said.

Henry and Blu met Rick and Buster, and they were off in single file. Buster was not a slow walker. He moved through the tall weeds with ease, and his sharp eye warned the men behind him of slippery rocks—and once, even a copperhead snake. "Little early for you, fella," Buster said. The poisonous snake was cold and lethargic, fresh out of his hole early in the morning. Buster lifted him with a stick and tossed him off the trail. Rick and Henry stepped more carefully from then on.

They came to a steep section and followed a switch-back deer trail leading around huge boulders. The sun could not penetrate the canopy of hemlock and blue spruce covering the hillside.

Henry was surprised by the size of their trunks. "This is a virgin forest. Do you know how many years it takes trees to grow to this size?" He glanced back at Rick.

"Centuries, not decades, I'm guessing," Rick answered.

"Definitely. I had no idea there were any this size in these parts." Henry lingered for a while, staring at the giant trees.

He and Blu caught up when they arrived at house-size boulders completely covering the hillside. Blu bellowed the way he had the evening before when he'd found Macy's scent.

"This just don't look right," Buster took his cap off and scratched under his mop of hair. He stared up the rocks and down again. "I was a lot littler then, though."

He studied the terrain for a long while, making Rick question his recollection. Then he did something puzzling: He lay on the ground and put his ear to the earth. Rick cut his eyes to Henry, indicating his distrust. Henry leaned down and disconnected the leash to let Blu sniff around.

The dog meandered for a while, then returned to sit next to Henry. Finally, Buster said, "I think we're in the right area, but it's changed a lot in nearly twenty years."

"What were you listening for?" Henry asked.

"Water," Buster answered.

"A creek runs behind the house, but there's nothing on this side. I mean, from what we covered yesterday, I didn't see one," Henry said.

"You wouldn't; it's underground." Buster walked around the edge of the protruding rocks. "It's this way, I'm sure."

Rick followed, but he was really skeptical. Henry's look of confidence in the young man gave Rick hope, though. He allowed Blu and Henry to go ahead, and he brought up the rear.

Jess called him over the walkie-talkie. "Rick, do you read me?"

"Yeah, go ahead Jess,"

"Got another fellow here that says he knows where the cave is. Says he can lead me right to it. What do you think?"

"If he leads you to where we are, then we'll have our answer. Up to you, Jess," Rick said.

"See you in a few."

Rick had to climb hard and fast to catch up with Henry and Buster. They were definitely on a trail of some sort, winding through the rocky outcroppings. Blu bayed as though he was on the scent again.

Henry stopped, looking back to see where Rick was. He motioned as though they'd found something. When Rick reached the top of the trail, he felt the cool air before he saw the opening.

"Looks like his memory was right," Henry said, pointing down into a crevasse.

Rick saw the top of Buster's head as he descended into the narrow opening. "I've got a penlight but it would really be great to have a pine knot torch," Henry said.

"Come on down, guys," Buster called out. "Got a match? I found a pine knot."

"Well, there you go," Henry laughed. He worked his way down to where Buster stood, then pulled out a lighter and the torch became a glowing flame. "Someone's been here recently, that's for certain. What would they come in this cave for?"

"Some say my old man made shine in here." Buster grinned. "But I wouldn't know; I was just a kid."

"Yeah, I understand. My old man made some shine in his day, too," Henry confirmed. "He wasn't likely to get caught here. But he'd have a hard time packing it out of here."

"That he would," Rick stated, when he finally joined them. "Buster, have you ever explored this cave?"

"Not since I was ten. Got lost in here for a couple of days once. Old man whupped me when he finally found me. I never strayed off no more. Once ya had one o' Dad's whuppins, you didn't do that again." He rubbed his backside as if he remembered how much it hurt so well he could feel it all over again.

"So, we'll need to use a string to get back. I brought some, just in case." Rick tied one end off around a heavy rock at the entrance, then he slid the spool onto a small stick he'd picked up along the walk. "There. Now we can at least find our way back out."

The three men walked single file, and all of them stepped very carefully along the jagged ledge. Rick brought up the rear so the twine got fed out smoothly and was not stumbled over. The thought of Macy climbing around these rocks and on this dark ledge put a dread in Rick's gut. He shined his pen light down into the drop-off. It was like there was no bottom, just blackness. Encouraging as it was to see nothing appeared to be disturbed, he realized if someone as small as Macy slipped over the edge, they'd leave no trace. They moved down a bit farther, then climbed up toward a high ceiling. Once they made the top, a large room opened up before them. It was dry, dusty, and cavernous. Stalactites and stalagmites had formed along the edges. It was no longer a cave; now it was a cavern. But there was no water, and Buster remembered water.

"Where is the water?" Henry asked.

"I ain't seen this room before," Buster removed his cap and scratched his head. "I didn't have nothing but a little flash light. Maybe I was here. I can't be sure, but there was water, I heard it, and I smelled it. That's when I turned and went back the way I come in."

"With only a flashlight, you couldn't see the size of this. There's for sure no water here; no sound, either, but maybe we haven't gone far enough." Rick pulled out the penlight again, shining it along the walls. "There, look; it's an opening."

Henry moved toward Rick's position, but he stumbled. He'd been looking up at the light, not where he was stepping, and had fallen in the darkness. Rick grabbed for his arm, but Henry fell over the edge. Buster dove, catching his hand, but Henry was heavy—Buster's grip slipped. Henry fell out of sight, landing with an echoing thud. Rick fell face down, shined his penlight over the edge, and saw Henry was face up, flat on his back. He lay about twenty feet below on a narrow ledge, his eyes closed, motionless.

"Henry!" Rick yelled. "Henry, can you hear me?" He swept his light from side to side, searching for a way down. But there was none; the ledge was too narrow to move around on. He had to get Henry's attention, so he'd lie still. "Henry!" he shouted again.

Buster crawled over to the edge with the pine knot torch. He dropped a small clod of dirt next to Henry's head, and Henry flinched.

"*Henry!*" Rick yelled, as loudly as he could.

Henry stirred just a bit, mumbling something. Buster dropped another clod on his arm. Henry slapped at it then opened his eyes, looking up at them. He coughed a few times and took in a deep breath.

"Knocked the wind out of me," he managed to gasp.

"Don't move, Henry!" Rick called. "You're on a narrow ledge. Don't roll over, or you're gone!"

"OK. I don't think I can move anyway," Henry said.

"And we can't get down. Stay right where you are. Just breathe, and don't try moving. We'll get a rappel team in here. You just hold on!" Rick turned to face Buster. "Go out and meet Jess, and tell him to get a rescue crew with ropes to rappel down to Henry, and a stretcher to pull him up. You got that?"

"Yeah, meet Jess, rappel rescue, stretcher. I got it!" Buster stood up, "I'll need the light or this torch to find the way out."

"Keep the torch, and hurry—but be careful, Buster!" Rick said.

Buster raced out of the cave like it was no big obstacle. He jammed the torch into a hole on the wall, leaving it to burn. Leaping from rock to rock to rock with the grace of a Dall's sheep, it only took him a few minutes to meet Jess and the team coming up the mountain. He gave Jess Rick's message, then turned to lead the team back to the cave entrance. Jess and his guide waited for the rescue crew. They had already staged with the volunteers at Jennings' store.

Jess and the remainder of the rescuers hurried up the rocks to the opening. Their spotlights lit up the cave as they made their way toward Rick's location.

Rick kept Henry talking to keep him conscious. Henry was trying to tell him a message for Holly, but Rick wouldn't listen. He kept telling Henry to hang on just a few more minutes and the crew would be there. In his heart, he felt sick even thinking of how to tell Holly and her boys that Henry was hurt. He'd been through so much, and so had Maddy, but Henry was a rock! He had the responsibility of the family resting heavily on his shoulders. He couldn't be hurt, or worse. Henry was needed in so many lives! Rick whispered a prayer. "Not for me, Lord, for them..."

Just then the entire room glowed. He rolled over to see ten men in single file, like an army of ants coming down the steep path into the cavern.

He jumped to his feet, "Henry! See, the cavalry is here! Hang on buddy; we'll have you out of there in a jiffy!" Rick let out a long sigh.

What a relief it was to see the Mountain Rescue Team go into action. They had head lamps on hard hats, and harnesses. Before he could say another word, one of the men repelled over the edge and was at Henry's side. A second man went over behind that one. He wore a white armband with a red cross on it. Large reflective letters glowed across his shoulders: *EMT*.

Rick stepped back, leaning against the solid rock wall. His knees felt weak and his head was dizzy. The rush of adrenalin overwhelmed him. *Thank God I didn't had to take the news to Holly.*

Out of the corner of his eye, he thought he saw a movement to his right. But when he looked straight at it, there appeared to be nothing more than a continuation of the rock wall. He looked back at Henry, as the EMT checked him over and they lowered a stretcher. Henry was in good hands, so Rick walked toward the spot on the wall. It turned out to be an optical illusion. There was no solid wall, it was a crevasse. On the ground, he could make out prints, maybe a small bare foot, but there was a large boot print over part of it.

He slipped through the opening, shining the penlight ahead on the ground and up the walls of what had widened into a passage. Smoke drifted into his nose. After moving slowly for a few more yards, he turned off the penlight and could see a glow at the end of the passage. It danced like the glow of a campfire, and the smell was that of wood burning. He moved carefully as the way widened into a big room and the sound of rushing water filtered to his ears.

There, on the other side of the open room sat Macy, barefooted and in a ragged dress. She'd obviously torn the fabric running through the forest. There appeared to be blood on her ankles. She was not tied; he could see her hands were free. She brushed her hair back off her face, exposing dirt and maybe some bruising. Had he beaten her, or did she injure herself while running from him?

Rick stood very still in the shadows. His eyes scanned the room for Watts. Just then, he came back up from the water level. He had a bucket of water, and placed it over the campfire. He approached Macy and she stood up, moving away from him. He stopped, turning back toward the fire.

"You'll come around, Hannah, I know you will."

Hannah? He thinks Macy is his dead daughter. This guy is really out of his mind!

Rick studied the situation of the room, looking for possible weapons—but he saw none. On one wall was a lantern hung from a rocky outcropping. Just below the light was a pick ax sunk into the side of the wall, as if someone had been digging with it. He looked toward the water; it was shallow, but flowing strong. At the opposite side it seemed to run under the wall, or maybe it swirled and made a curve. From where he stood he wasn't sure.

He stepped into the light and called out, "Snyder Watts! TBI, don't move."

Watts wheeled around, looking to see where the voice came from. He spotted Rick and barreled toward him. Rick stepped aside and allowed the man to crash into the wall head first. "Macy, are you alright?"

"Yes, " she replied. Macy stood, hugging her chest in sheer panic. "Be careful, Rick!"

The man recovered quickly from the sudden jolt of colliding with the wall. He started toward Rick, a bit less aggressively this time, more cautious. Rick pulled his gun and said, "We can do this the easy way or the hard way. Which do you want?" Rick clicked the slide on his Glock, readying one in the chamber. "I don't want to have to carry you out of here, so I'd rather not shoot you."

Watts let out a growl and lunged at Rick. Rick stepped aside again, allowing the mass of anger to plunge over the edge into the water.

"Just give me an answer, and I'll end this. Do you want to die?"

"No, you're gonna die!" He dripped from head to toe with cold water, and a trickle of blood ran down his face from contact with the wall. "You gonna' die today, G-Man!"

"Nope! Not me—but it *is* going to end today, you're right about that!" Rick walked closer to Macy. He handed her the pistol. "Use this if you have to. There's one in the chamber ready."

"Rick! What are you doing? Shoot the monster!" Macy screamed.

Rick held the gun closer. "Take it, Macy!"

She slipped both hands around the handle and backed up against the wall

"Now you're on my level, just you and me. Let's do this!" Watts laughed. "She won't shoot and I know it. She's going to watch you die."

Rick moved sideways one step at a time. He kept his eyes glued to Watts, waiting for the perfect time to strike. But Watts struck first. He lunged at Rick and caught him around the middle, knocking him off his feet. Watts tried to kick him, but Rick was too quick; he rolled out of the way of the large foot aiming at his head, catching it to flip Watts into a twist that sent the big man to the floor with a jolt. Rick was on him in a second. He clasped one hand behind his back and tried to cuff the man's arm. It was too large for his cuff. Watts rolled with the force of a mad gator, twisting Rick to the floor. He was on top and punching Rick's jaw before he could react.

"You think you're tough, G-Man? All I've had to do the last fifteen years is get in shape to fight. Your luck ran out when you gave up your weapon. I do hate to mess up that pretty face, seeing as how you just got married and all. You're making that Sheriff a widow already!"

Rick head-butted Watts straight in the nose, and blood shot out all over Rick's face. Watts' fists unclenched, and he tried to rub the blood from his eyes. Rick gave a mighty shove and the man stumbled backwards several feet. Rick got up before Watts could see and attack him again.

They moved slowly in a circle, fists in a defensive mode and ready to throw the first blow. Rick's jaw ached, feeling like it was out of socket. He shifted it back with one painful movement. Realizing he could not match the Watts' strength, Rick devised a plan. *If I can maneuver him into just the right spot...*

Down Rick went, falling backwards flat on his back. Watts let out a yell and lunged toward him, as if to smash the life out of him. Rick's knees came up to his chest and he kicked up and out with both feet, sending Watts flying back into the wall.

The big man stayed there. Macy pointed the pistol, poised to shoot when he lunged at Rick, but he didn't move at all. Blood poured from his mouth, *lots* of blood; he was stuck on the pickaxe, just as Rick had planned. Macy looked at Rick, still lying on the floor, then back to Watts.

Rick got to his feet slowly, as if watching for any movement from the monster. His aim had been true. The point of the pick jutted out of the man's sternum, along with the right side of his heart. Rick walked to Macy and slipped his hand over hers, taking the gun. He pulled her to his chest, hugging her tightly. "I'm so sorry you had to see that."

"Are you hurt? Rick, he hit you awful hard. I thought he'd kill you."

"So did he. But his mistake was to underestimate my brain. I had to out-smart him, because I for sure wasn't going to out fight him!"

"Are you sure he's dead?" Macy looked past Rick's battered face toward the man on the wall. "He's just stuck there."

Rick turned around and approached the form with great caution. "See this?" he said, pointing to the sharp pick. On the end of it, there was a piece of dark red muscle tissue. That's the right ventricle, if I'm not mistaken. He was dead the second he hit the wall."

Macy walked closer, "How did you know?"

"I try to never enter a situation without knowing all the variables, but I was taking a chance that the pick wouldn't fall out as his weight slammed against it. I got lucky." He wrapped his arm along her narrow shoulders, "Let's get out of here."

"Shouldn't we take him out with us?"

"No, we'll let the coroner handle that." Rick pulled the pen light from his pocket and aimed the light toward the opening leading out.

When they reached the place where Henry had fallen over the edge, he was being carried out on a stretcher by four men. Jess and the others turned when they heard Rick and Macy come out of the crevasse. "What happened to you, boy?" Jess asked.

"I ran into a bear!" Rick said, spitting blood.

"He rescued me." Macy rushed into Jess's arms. "You should have seen him, Jess! He's my hero!"

Rick instructed the rescue team to wait for the coroner. He said, "He isn't going anywhere this time."

28

On Paradise Island, Madison and Nell sat on the widow's walk drinking wine. They had been to Key West, and Drew was worn out. They hadn't walked a lot because the Conch Train runs all over the island, but going in and out of shops, museums, and restaurants had been a lot of effort for Drew. He was, after all, still recuperating from the fall that should have killed him. But as Nell said, "You can't keep a good man down." And everyone agreed, Sheriff Drew Perry was as good as they come.

Drew retired just after sunset on the day they returned to the island. They had spent two nights in Danny's condo, but were ready to return to the private Paradise Island. Eating in the wonderful waterfront seafood restaurants hadn't been difficult to get used to, but the three mountain people longed for some fried potatoes with onions, and corn bread with soup beans. Since Maddy grew up in Shirley's Restaurant, she was an excellent cook. Nell put together an apple cobbler, and she even found a half gallon of French vanilla ice cream as a topping.

Maddy's phone rang, and she saw that it was Rick. "It's about time you checked in. Are you alright?"

"I'm OK, and it's over. We found Macy, and she's OK. I'll tell you all about it when I see you," Rick said.

"When will that be?"

"Tomorrow, Honey. I'm going to bed soon because I have the early flight out of Tri-Cities. Dan's helicopter is picking me up in Fort Lauderdale just after nine thirty, so I'll see you in the morning." There was a pause, then Rick said, "How's everything in Paradise?"

"Lonely, without you. Bud has been sleeping on your side of the bed, but it's just not the same."

"You tell that mutt to stay out of my bed!" he laughed.

Madison was sure she heard him wince, with a noise in his breathing she recognized as Rick's pain sound. "Are you sure you're all right? You sound funny, like your jaw is stiff. Now tell me the truth."

"My jaw is a little sore. I got clobbered by a bear."

"I knew it! You let that Watts beat the crap out of you. I should have been there to shoot him."

"No, nothing like that. I assure you." Rick didn't consider his dislocated jaw getting the crap beat out of him. "See you in the morning. I love you, Maddy."

"I love you too, Rick." She tapped the red button on her phone. Her background had a photo of Rick's flawless, handsome face. It was from not long after they met, almost seven years before. She knew him well enough to suspect that he was not telling her the entire story, not even close.

The next day, she and Nell took the cabin cruiser over to the marina to meet the helicopter. They pulled up to the dock, where one of Danny's men tied off the boat for them. "Where's Bud? I thought he'd be here to meet Mr. Rick."

"Not a chance. I slipped away from him. Left him on the other side of the island with Drew," Maddy said.

"Let's go in; I want to pick out some T-shirts for Holy's kids," Nell said.

They shopped until they heard the helicopter pass over the building. Nell took seven shirts and a baby's bonnet to the counter. She told Maddy to go on out to see Rick while she paid for the merchandise.

"This is only seven; you get another one free, if you want it." The lady behind the register said. "Bosses orders, you all get two for the price of one."

"Oh, how sweet of Danny. Let me go back and look. Does it matter if it's adult or a child's?"

"No, whatever you want."

Nell returned with one for Drew. He hadn't let her get him a shirt at Margaretaville, so she'd give him one from Dan's Paradise Marina with a charter boat printed on the back. She took the bags and walked outside to locate Maddy and Rick. As she approached, she catalogued the damage to Rick's face: cut over the eye, a bruised chin, and most pronounced, swollen jaw with a couple of sutures.

"Oh, man. You look like heck!" Nell slid in for a gentle hug. "Does it hurt?"

"Only when I laugh," Rick said, his glorious sense of humor intact.

"Maddy, did you know that you and your guests get a two for the price of one sale in the marina shop?"

"No, I'd better get some things for Jess and Shirley when we're ready to leave."

They made their way to the boat and Rick sat down behind the driver's seat. He looked at Nell, "You checked out in this one yet?"

She laughed as she stashed her bags under the side bench, sat in the driver's seat, and started the engines. "I can drive the box it came in."

Back on the island, Rick sat on the deck in the shade, sipped the ice-cold beer Drew brought him, and told them the shortened version of Macy's rescue from the monster in the cavern.

Maddy sat quietly without interrupting her husband. But when he finished and tipped the beer up again, she said, "Guess I'll have to get the whole story from Macy. So how bad is Henry?"

"Oh, Henry went home from the hospital after a through exam; he's fine. Just had a couple of broken ribs from where he landed on a stalagmite and broke it. Lucky for him it hadn't been growing long. He brought it out with him as a souvenir. I'm sure the kids will enjoy playing with it."

"Amazing; we have another cavern in the county. Who knew?" Nell commented.

"What does Macy plan to do now? Did she and Ella go home?" Drew asked.

"Are you kidding? They said Walkers Mountain is a safer place now. You can't run those girls off. Especially Macy; she swears she's home to stay."

"What about Ella?" Maddy asked.

"She'll have to tell you her news herself. But I know she and Bill are clearing a site above the barn for a cabin." Rick downed his beer. "Drew, it's five o'clock somewhere, isn't it?"

"Yeah; want another?" Drew stood up to walk into the kitchen.

"I believe I do. And then I want to take a nap, right there in that hammock."

The old saying that all good things must come to an end never felt so sad as when they were leaving Paradise Island. When the two couples arrived at the marina with all their bags, Danny tried to get them to stay another week.

"At least give me a tentative date for your return trip. You too, Drew, Nell. In fact, bring the entire town of Cold Creek; we could find room."

They all laughed, but Captain Danny was not joking. He got a planner from behind the counter and handed it to Maddy. "I know I can count on you. You show me the dates you want to bring your friends with the children. Christmas week, I think you said? I have no plans, nor does anyone else, for spending Christmas on Paradise Island." He put the pin in her hand. "Go on, now. I fully expect to see Santa Clause come in on skis this December."

Maddy looked at Rick. He shrugged and smiled. She put her name on the Saturday before Christmas, then marked the 2nd of January to leave. "I guess that's about it, give or take a day or two."

Danny handed the pen to Nell, "And don't you two have an anniversary coming up soon?"

Nell looked to Drew. "What do you want me to put down?"

"Your decision; I'm game to move here, but Danny isn't going to go for that." Drew laughed.

"Don't forget, there's always the condo...less cooking," Danny said.

"That's what I want. OK! The condo it is!" Nell marked the week of their first anniversary. "Danny, you have to promise to come to Cold Creek. We want your word on that."

"I'll need to check some obligations for fishing tournaments, but I promise you, I'll be there this fall. I'll let you know."

With the truck loaded, Bud fastened into his seatbelt in the middle between the women in the back seat, and the guys in the front, they drove away from Islamorada, heading north on Hwy #1.

Bud had yawned and curled into a ball by the time they were rolling. Maddy loosened his seatbelt so he had room to move. She and Nell watched out the windows as they said goodbye to the beautiful aquamarine waters of the Keys, and thinking of that return trip later in the year. They would once again have

Paradise Island to themselves to enjoy; in Nell's case, all the shops of Key West awaited her return.

For now, they were returning to Cold Creek, to home and the beautiful, majestic Blue Ridge Mountains of East Tennessee. The temperature might reach the eighties or nineties on a hot summer day, but the cool of the evening, when the sun goes behind a mountain, always gives your body a recharge.

Madison and Rick had enjoyed a memorable honeymoon. Facing death was nothing new to either of them. They had survived one of the worst traffic accidents possible, and pulled through stronger for their experience. Their love only grew, through separation, pain, and anguish. With support of family and friends, once again the network of love held.

The tragedy of Walkers' Mountain will never be forgotten. The survivors rose in triumph by facing their fears. Macy discovered strength from beyond the grave and Ella found peace in protecting her sister.

Who are we to say ghosts don't exist? Angels walk among us, leading us on the right path—when we listen. Our hearts store memories we can draw from when we trust in the higher power. It's all a simple plan, just not always easy to recognize at the time. We must learn to trust our gut and our judgement. Learn from mistakes, and grow with the outcome.

The End

ABOUT THE AUTHOR

Bev Freeman was born in VA, living in the Appalachian Mountains until her teens. Her family relocated to Florida in 1963. Missing the mountains, the tumbling streams, and changing seasons birthed a love for writing, allowing her an escape, for at least short stays.

After high school, life and a career in the dental field got in the way of returning to the mountains when she married a Floridian and raised a son.

1993 brought shattered dreams, divorce, and she followed her family back to the Appalachian Region. In 1996, she married a local, God-fearing man, and life is beautiful in TN with two spirited grandsons living close bye. Bev and her husband, Bill, enjoy weekends touring the backroads of the beautiful Blue Ridge and Great Smoky Mountains on their Goldwing whenever possible.

www.ingramcontent.com/pod-product-compliance
Lightning Source LLC
Chambersburg PA
CBHW030648020726
47493CB00006B/1922